The Chimera Seed

Matthew Tully

Comfort PUBLISHING

The Chimera Seed

For information, address Comfort Publishing, 9450 Moss Plantation Avenue N.W., Suite 204, Concord, NC 28027. The views expressed in this book are not necessarily those of the publisher.

This book is a work of fiction. Any resemblence to anyone living or dead is purely coincidental.

First printing

Book cover design
by Colin L. Kernes

ISBN: 978-1-935361-32-9
Published by Comfort Publishing, LLC
www.comfortpublishing.com

Printed in the United States of America

Acknowledgements

I would like to thank Mary Stackpole of Mo' Juste Literary Services without whom this project would not have been possible.

Dedication

To my father, the greatest storyteller of all time.

Prologue

"Is that checkmate?" asked Richard Tiernan [DAD] as he carefully examined the marble chess pieces. "I believe it is. You're really getting good at this."

"You let me win, Dad," said his son, Michael [Inherited]. "You could've taken my queen. Didn't you see it?"

Richard smiled and tussled the boy's hair. "It's time for you to go to bed. You'll be like a feral kid in the morning if you don't get enough sleep. Go and say goodnight to your mother." The young boy ran into the kitchen where his mother was finishing the dishes. She dried her hands on her apron and stooped down to plant a half dozen kisses on his cheeks.

"Sweet dreams," said Sarah Tiernan [Mom]. "I'm making pancakes for breakfast."

"Yes!" said Michael with his characteristic fist pump. "With chocolate chips?"

"With blueberries. Chocolate makes you bounce off the walls in school."

"Okay, but will you make them for me this weekend?" bargained the precocious young man.

"We'll see. Don't forget to brush your teeth."

"Goodnight, Ma," said Michael as he jumped on his father's back, hitching a ride upstairs.

"Which story would you like to hear tonight?" asked Richard. The bookshelf was beginning to buckle under the voluminous books.

"You pick," said Michael.

"Alright, how about this one?" Richard removed an old hardcover from the rest and ran his hand over the tattered edges. "I loved this story when I was a boy."

"What's it about?" said the young Tiernan with the impatience of a typical seven-year-old.

"It's a legend that your ancestors used to tell, an ancient legend," said Richard as he opened to the first page.

The Legend of Tír na nÓg

Once upon a time, long ago, in a land of emerald green surrounded by a sea of deep blue, there lived a handsome young man named Oisín (Uh-Sheen). One day, Oisín was hunting in the forest with the Fianna, a group of strong and just warriors, when he saw an extraordinary sight. Out of the sea, on the back of a stately white mare, rode a stunning young woman, her long red hair streaming behind her. The mare's movements were so fluid that she seemed to float across the earth. The majestic horse and her beautiful rider came to a sudden halt before the group, golden sparks spraying from the fieldstones beneath them.

"I am Princess Niamh (Neev)," said the red-haired maiden. "I am from the land of Tír na nÓg." Her green eyes, bright as emeralds, emanated a profound peace.

Oisín stepped forward to greet the rider. "We are the Fianna and we bid you welcome to Ireland." He bowed gracefully.

A strange sensation seized Oisín; he was filled with a joy he had never experienced before, and yet he understood that Princess Niamh was his destiny.

"A home awaits you in Tír na nÓg," said Niamh, also smitten with Oisín. "Return with me and never die."

Oisín couldn't resist. He jumped on the mare's back and he and the princess rode across the sea to Tír na nÓg.

Having lived on the Emerald Isle his whole life, Oisín would never have believed that a more beautiful land existed, but as he gazed upon Tír na nÓg, he was stunned by the beauty around him.

"Welcome to Tír na nÓg," said Niamh, handing Oisín a golden chalice filled with a steaming purple liquid. "Drink and live forever."

Niamh and Oisín built a life together in the magical land where no one ever grew old or fell sick. There, all time existed in the ever-present now, and the people knew nothing of anxiety, jealousy, envy, anger or fear. Tír na nÓg was eternally blissful and innocent, and the couple lived in happiness. Soon their love had grown so deep that it was no longer possible to tell where she ended and where he began. They were two bodies, one soul.

Three-hundred seven years had passed as though it were but a single day.

Since time was reckoned differently in the enchanted land, Oisín thought that he had only been in Tír na nÓg for a very short time. In spite of the beauty of the land and the deep love that Niamh and Oisín shared, a part of Oisín's soul felt incomplete and he longed to see his family, the Fianna and his beloved Ireland. Because such feelings were unheard of in Tír na nÓg, and despite her efforts, Niamh was unable to ease Oisín's suffering. The seed of loneliness had taken root in Oisín's soul and each day it grew stronger. When he could no longer bear the pain, Oisín confided in Niamh and told her of his desire to visit his family and the land of his birth.

"Very well," said Niamh. "Return to Ireland on the back of the white mare. But, my love, your feet must never touch the ground. You must always remain on the horse's back. Go, and return to me whole."

Oisín rode the white horse across the sea to Ireland where he discovered the Fianna's grand castle overgrown with ivy. His family and friends were nowhere to be found. For several days, he searched for his loved ones, but it wasn't long before Oisín realized that this was not the same Ireland he had left. Everything had changed, and he soon came to understand that hundreds of years had passed. Oisín was so overcome with grief that he neglected to care for the mare. Finally, with a forlorn heart, Oisín decided to return to Tír na nÓg.

On the way to the sea, Oisín saw a little stone and decided to take it back to Tír na nÓg as a souvenir. He pulled the reins, commanding the white mare to stop. The saddle had become loose on the starving horse and, as Oisín reached down to pick up the stone, the saddle slid, causing him to lose his balance. The moment his flesh touched the earth, he aged 307 years. Frightened by her rider's demise, the white mare reared up, ran into the ocean and returned to Tír na nÓg.

When the mare returned without her beloved Oisín, Niamh knew sorrow for the first time. To this very day, Niamh still pines for her beloved Oisín. The soul that had loved so profoundly would never again be whole without its other half.

Occasionally, when the moon is full and the sea is restless, fishermen and lighthouse keepers claim to see a shimmering white horse dancing in the waves along the shores. Some say it is the red-haired maiden who rides the horse, still searching for Oisín, hoping that some miracle will reunite her with her lost love.

"Did she find him yet?" asked Michael.

"No," said Richard, "the princess is still searching to this very day. She will never give up hope."

"Not even in a million years?"

"Well, hope is a powerful force – strong enough to withstand eternity. So, I don't think Niamh will ever stop searching for him."

"Was that a true story?" asked Michael.

"All Irish tales are true, didn't you know that?" his father replied.

"When I grow up, I'm going to find Tír na nÓg and then you, me and Mommy can live there forever," he said, smiling a sparsely-toothed smile. "Do you think we'll need a magic horse to get there?"

"I'm not sure, but I'll do a little research and I'll let you know," said the doting father. "Goodnight." He bent over and kissed his son on the forehead.

"Dad, leave the door open a little," said Michael as his father exited. "Just a little."

"Oh, yes, I forgot." His father complied, leaving the door open just wide enough for a sliver of light to creep into the room.

The
Chimera
Seed

Comfort PUBLISHING

Marc = nightwatchman   Friend to SON

Michael Tiernan = inheritee   Jimmy = bald/fat hairy

Timothy Lynch   = lawyer

Richard Tiernan   = dad

Debra & Graham(John) = scientists for Oisin Pharm.
Lewis

Ivan Falters   = partner to dad/scientist —

Marn Mckenna = biracial beauty, Tighte's spy

Mark Reed = EPA guy

Vincent Tighte = administrator of EPA
       rapist

Scott Lehman   EPA deputy administrator

George Pendergast = coworker

Lori Adams = raped by Vincent Tighte

Ryan
Connor   = boss likes Lori

Francis = secretary to connor

Jimmy Galante = cute guy monkey supplier

Eileen   = secretary to inheritee

     Ryan Connor = Pres of Lionel Pharm

Lionel = Company
Pharm.   Lori Adams = senior executor
               = southern

Naomi Linden = White House Communications Director

Regenerol = grow body parts

Dionysinol = fountain of youth
         Resveretrol & Jellyfish

CHAPTER 1

TIMOTHY LYNCH BRACED himself for the encounter. Dr. Michael Tiernan, the new CEO of Oisín Pharmaceuticals, was unpredictable and often unpleasant. He straightened his tie one last time before he buzzed his secretary.

"Ellen, please show Dr. Tiernan in." Extending his hand, Lynch got up to greet him. "Dr. Tiernan, I'm so sorry for your loss. Your father was a remarkable man. Please, have a seat. Can I offer you something to drink?"

"No, thank you," said Tiernan. "So, why couldn't this have waited until the estate hearing?" He sat down in the comfortable leather chair, crossed his legs and waited for the explanation.

"Your father left very specific instructions and, as his attorney, I'm obligated to carry them out," said Lynch.

"Well," said Tiernan, "let's get on with it."

Lynch opened his safe, removed a silver key and handed it to Tiernan.

"What's this?"

"It's a key to a safety deposit box. Your father never told me which bank housed the box – said you would know where to go."

Tiernan searched his mind briefly. "Nothing's jumping out at me. Didn't leave a hint, did he?"

"I'm afraid not, but perhaps when you have time to think, you'll remember. When you do manage to find it, you'll need to present these documents to the manager," said Lynch, handing Tiernan a sealed envelope. "They'll need to see a death certificate and the papers proving that you're the executor of the will before they let you in."

"Alright," said Tiernan, taking the envelope. "So, until Wednesday?"

"Yes, sir. I'll be at the mansion immediately after the funeral, as you've requested."

"Very good," said Tiernan. "Thanks for the key."

The door closed behind Tiernan. Lynch sighed in relief.

ĆŠ

Tiernan was on his third bank before the manager at Global Commerce confirmed that Richard Tiernan had, indeed, procured a safety deposit box there. After the security check, the manager escorted Tiernan into a private room where he could examine the contents. Tiernan closed the door and waited a moment before proceeding. He didn't know what to expect and, despite the grim circumstances, was excited to see what his father had left him. He lifted the lid slowly. A sealed manila envelope sat squarely in the center; seven sealed vials of purple liquid lined the sides. He picked one up and held it against the light, tilting it slowly back and forth, examining the viscosity. A rubber stopper sealed with wax kept the liquid airtight. Putting the vial gently back into the box, he reached for the manila envelope and tore it open. A thick, ornate, leather portfolio slid into his hands. He untied the strings, opened to the first page and immediately recognized his father's handwriting.

I hope that you will never have to read this, and hope is a powerful force. My life's work is now yours.

I love you,

Dad.

Tiernan flipped through the first few of the handwritten pages. Equations of increasing complexity were scribbled helter-skelter around the margins. Tying the strings together tightly, he closed the portfolio, wiped his eyes with the back of his hand and left the empty box behind.

CB

Tiernan centered the Last Will and Testament on the meticulously organized desk and poured himself a glass of bourbon. His father's scent still lingered in the air and it filled him with an awful, empty feeling. He stood very still and looked around the room at objects he had seen countless times. His gaze fixed on the bronze statue standing unassumingly on the bookshelf. It was a plain statue of a gravely injured man propped up against a tree stump. He had made a mental note several times to ask his father about the strange piece, since it was peculiar and simply too morose to be decorative – he'd never gotten around to it. Seeing the statue again, he was acutely aware that his father was dead; he would never ask him anything again.

Tiernan poured himself another glass of the bourbon from his father's crystal decanter and slugged it down. He looked down at the Will and a wave of emotion washed away the warm feeling the bourbon had so kindly left, replacing it with an icy realization; he was alone in the world. He threw back the amber liquid and welcomed the burn.

"Michelino?" said Marinella. The diminutive but robust elderly woman didn't wait for an invitation to enter the den. Still vested in the traditional Italian black funeral garb, she walked in and placed a cup of tea on the coaster. "Tesoro," she said adoringly. "Povero ragazzo. Ti voglio bene amore." Tears streamed down her face as she clung to Tiernan. "Il mio cuore."

"Grazie, Mari," said Tiernan, fluent in Italian since he was a teen. She hugged him tightly, pressing his cheek to her bosom, the physics of which caused him to bend awkwardly from his standing position. Yet, he succumbed to her motherly embrace gratefully, heaving a sigh and momentarily relaxing his body despite the ungainly dynamics. There was no pretense with her. She was, after all, the woman who had raised him from the time he was a boy, and it was her firm hand and unconditional love that had carried him through the loss of his mother. Sarah Tiernan had only been ill for a few weeks when ovarian cancer had claimed her. Just a week after his 13th birthday, Michael had become a motherless child. At 36, he was an orphan.

The doorbell sounded throughout the mansion, which seemed much emptier now, and Marinella went to the door.

"Good afternoon, I'm Timothy Lynch. I have an appointment with Dr. Tiernan."

❧

As Tiernan signed his way through a mountain of documents, Lynch produced from his briefcase an addendum to the Last Will and Testament.

"Dr. Tiernan," said Lynch, "there is one more item we need to discuss."

"And what's that?" said Tiernan. Lynch handed him a two-page document.

"Your father had a few assets that were kept off Oisín's books," said Lynch. "I know very little about them – your father insisted on his privacy." Tiernan skimmed over the highlighted portions.

"A house and a vineyard in Sardinia? When did my father buy a vineyard? And for what?" He pictured the vials of purple liquid sitting snugly in the desk drawer just a few inches from him and wondered if they were samples of wine. "How much are these assets worth?"

"I'm not certain," said Lynch. "But I can get you some figures."

"Yes, do that, and then just sell the damn place! I'm too busy to deal with this. Isn't that what I pay you to do?"

Lynch felt the back of his neck heat up. He cleared his throat uncomfortably before continuing. "I'm afraid it's not that simple," he confessed. "Two weeks before your father passed away, he asked me to make a few small changes to the Will. From your reaction, I assume this is the first you're hearing of it."

"What exactly did he ask you to change?" said Tiernan, still reading.

"He wanted to leave half of the Sardinian assets to someone named Ivan Falters," said Lynch.

"Who?"

"Ivan Falters," repeated Lynch. "Apparently, Mr. Falters and your father had some business dealings over in Sardinia. As Oisín's financial situation worsened, your father couldn't pay Mr. Falters without raising a red flag with the accountants, so they compromised."

"Alright, whatever," said Tiernan. "I knew he was dipping into our capital. Anyway, this is what I want you to do. Sell my half of the property to Falters. Start by offering it for 5 percent below the market value and allow him to haggle you down to 10 percent. I have a company to run; I don't have time for this."

"I'm afraid you must make time, sir," said Lynch nervously. "I spoke with Falters and tried to negotiate another arrangement, but he made it clear that he will only deal directly with you, and it needs to be in Sardinia. He's expecting you as soon as your schedule permits."

"Expecting *me*?" said Tiernan. "I should be expecting *him*. Arrange a meeting at Oisín for sometime next week."

"Again, I'm sorry, sir," said Lynch, "but you're going to have to travel to him. As I've said, I tried to get him –"

Tiernan abruptly cut him off. "Goddamn it, Lynch! Now I have to clean up this mess too? Did my father leave any more surprises for me?"

"I can make the travel arrangements if you'd like," said Lynch.

"Yeah, yeah," said Tiernan. "Is there anything else?"

"Just the travel arrangements, sir," said Lynch. "When would you prefer to depart?"

"I'd prefer not to go at all," said Tiernan. "But, since that seems beyond your ability, book a ticket for Thursday and make it an evening flight."

"Very well," said Lynch. "I'll have the itinerary sent to your secretary. Have a good evening, sir."

Tiernan was reluctant to leave his father's den. He refilled his glass with bourbon, weakening it with some seltzer. *What the hell is in Sardinia?* he thought as he paced the room.

He sat back down at his father's desk and examined the leather portfolio. He held the rich brown leather up to his nose and inhaled its strong, distinctive scent. He ran his hand over the cover, touching the intricate stitching around the edges. The case was soft and well-worn, yet sturdy and elegant.

His life's work, he thought. He wanted to untie the strings and let the portfolio spill its secrets, but could not bring himself to do it – not just yet. He felt a mixture of shame, regret and anger, thinking back on all the wasted opportunities to spend time with his father, the petty arguments and the times he could have been a better son, a better friend. Would he ever manage to forgive himself for calling his father a coward?

He pulled open the heavy drawer and extracted a vial of the purple liquid. He sat it atop the portfolio and rolled it back and forth. He was about to break the wax seal and investigate the liquid when she called.

"Michelino, pronto al tavola!" yelled Marinella Santarelli. "Devi mangiare qualcosa."

"Eccomi," responded Tiernan. He wasn't hungry, but it wasn't worth the hassle that would ensue if he were to refuse dinner.

As he left the den, he whispered heavenward, "Please, just don't let me find a mountain of debt towering over those damn grapes."

CHAPTER 2

"GOOD MORNING, LITTLE guys," said Dr. Debra Lewis as she tapped the glass and waved her finger in greeting. The salamanders scurried under leaves and rocks, unaware of the futility. She had designed the tanks to minimize the animals' stress by simulating their natural habitats. *Ignorance of one's captivity and true freedom are equivalent,* she thought. She glanced quickly at the tanks to check for fatalities. The starfish rested peacefully among the rocks and the turtles basked under the heating lamp. The animals lived in blissful ignorance until they became unwilling sacrifices at the altar of science.

Debra's gaze shifted from the animals to her own reflection in the glass. She repositioned a strand that had strayed from the clips corralling the bangs of her short brown hair. Her bushy eyebrows overshadowed her deep brown eyes and her smile revealed that she had never been to an orthodontist. She was not unattractive, but plain; everything about her outward appearance was ordinary. She dressed for comfort, not style, and she devoted little attention to the cosmetic.

Growing up, Debra Lewis was a shy girl whose petite stature and soft-spoken voice had made her almost invisible to her peers. A traditional set of Greek grandparents, a cop for a father and an inclination toward introversion had contributed to the scarcity of friends. Her ordinary features and disregard for the art of beauty had garnered a paucity of suitors.

Debra lost herself in the written word. She would escape to faraway lands one day and plunge into the depths of mathematical truths on another. She read everything she got her hands on and didn't limit herself to any particular subject. Eventually, she began to favor the certainty and simplicity inherent in the sciences. She studied genetics in college and never wasted an elective. Knowledge was her companion, her lover and her comfort. It was never dull, always dynamic and, unlike love, it never disappointed.

As Lewis walked down the hall, she glanced into the employee lounge. John Graham had not arrived yet. She wanted to wait for him, but the suspense was too much. She put on her white lab coat and headed down the short corridor where she and Graham had stored the isolated samples 72 hours previously.

Her hands were shaking when she turned the key to unlock the door. Stepping inside the cold, dark room, silently closing the door behind her, she closed her eyes and took a deep breath. She flipped the switch and the fluorescent lights blinked a few times before waking up to illuminate the room. She wanted to run over to the table to verify what she thought she saw, but her legs would not cooperate. The talented Dr. Debra Lewis stood immobilized, mouth agape and eyes fixed on the Petri dish 20 feet in front of her.

"Oh my God," she gasped, "I can't believe it worked."

A perfectly formed eye stared up from the dish. The white of the sclera contrasted with a strange pink iris, but the shape was unmistakably human. She stood spellbound by the miracle wrought by her own hand, worshipping at the tabernacle of modern science until Dr. John Graham arrived 10 minutes later.

"Hello, my dear," said Graham. "I knew I'd find you in here – your impatience makes you highly predictable. What are we staring at? Or rather, what is staring at us?"

"We did it, John. It worked." She did not realize she was crying until Graham handed her his handkerchief.

"*You* sure have, haven't you?" said Graham. "Well, this changes things a bit, wouldn't you say?"

Dr. Lewis' discovery of the link between human stem cells and the regenerative properties of the simple salamander had turned the tide for Oisín's latest endeavor – Regenerol, a drug originally intended as a revolutionary fertility treatment designed to treat defective ovaries by regrowing new ones. The research and development of the new drug was under Michael Tiernan's direct supervision and was the first major project that Richard Tiernan had left completely in his son's hands. Michael knew that the company would rise or fall with Regenerol – it needed to succeed.

At first, Tiernan had intended to develop Regenerol at Oisín Pharmaceuticals and then sell the patent to either Merkel or McCaff when he had a viable substance. The two pharmaceutical giants were already marketing fertility drugs of their own, and the business-minded Tiernan wanted to start a bidding war between the two financially secure companies for the patent. He reasoned that both William Masterson of Merkel Pharmaceuticals and Gerard McCaff of McCaff Pharmaceuticals would be very anxious to prevent another drug from cutting into their profits, and might even buy Regenerol's patent for that reason alone.

However, with the successful creation of the generic stem cell – the *Mimic* cell – Regenerol was no longer limited to the ovary, making the drug much more valuable. Now that Tiernan would not have to contend with the politics surrounding the use of embryonic stem cells, it just might be financially feasible to manufacture Regenerol at Oisín, but it was a huge risk. Tiernan knew that he did not have the resources to absorb any additional costs should unexpected problems arise. A big enough mistake could prove fatal for Oisín Pharmaceuticals, but Tiernan was tired of running a second-rate company.

α

"John, I need another batch of Mimics for the next experiment. Have you finished yet?"

Graham looked up from his station. They never shouted in the lab. It wasn't against the rules – they just didn't do it. Refusing to shout his response, he walked over to Debra's station.

He smoothed back his thick gray hair and adjusted his glasses. His face seemed more drawn since the funeral, and his wrinkled skin was uncharacteristically decorated with white speckles from lack of shaving. Since Richard's sudden passing, Graham seemed older, more fragile.

He and Richard had been friends for decades, and Richard's death had deeply saddened him. It stood as an unwelcomed reminder of his own fleeting existence.

"My goodness, my dear, you are in rare form today," he said in his calm, grandfatherly manner. "One doesn't shout in the lab." Just looking at Debra made him feel better.

Debra ignored his mild reproach. "Oh, and I'd like to run a comparison between the Mimics and Lot 296."

"We've already used Lot 296," said Graham. He put his arm around Debra's shoulder. "I think you've earned your pay for today. Come now, let's have one of those gyros you keep telling me about."

Debra was also dealing with the impact of Richard's death. She felt alone since the funeral. Death – anyone's death – always reminded her of time's cruel and unstoppable progression towards *the end*. Somehow, just being with Graham comforted her. He took her arm, interlocked it with his own and walked to the elevator. "You ought to be so proud," he said as they strolled along.

"I just hope the human trials are successful this time," said Debra, lowering her voice to a whisper.

"We *must* succeed this time," said Graham. "It's our last chance."

CHAPTER 3

A SEA OF faces bobbed and gawked anxiously behind the arrival gate at Fiumicino Airport in Rome as they waited for their loved ones. As he headed toward the exit, Tiernan saw a towering, blonde-haired man holding a sign with his name scrawled across it. "I'm Michael Tiernan," he said.

"Good morning, Dr. Tiernan. I am Ivan Falters. The world suffered a great loss; your father was a brilliant man." Falters appeared to be in his 30s – much younger than Tiernan had imagined. Standing over six feet tall, the muscular Falters would have intimidated most, but not Tiernan.

"Thank you," said Tiernan. "But I have to say, I'm not happy about having to come all the way here to settle this. I hope you have a good reason for dragging me here."

"Everything will be very clear once we arrive in Sardinia, but we must leave now. A storm is gaining strength and I dislike flying in bad weather," said Falters as he hailed a cab.

"Tell me," said Tiernan, "how did you and my father end up working together? I don't remember him mentioning you."

"I imagine there are many things your father chose to keep to himself," said Falters. "That should be sufficiently clear soon enough."

ᘓ

Upon arriving at the little airstrip in Civitavecchia, Falters lifted a hatch on the side of the plane and motioned to Tiernan to stow his bags. "Now we'll fly to Sardinia," he said as he climbed into the cockpit. "Get in on the other side."

"We're flying in this thing?"

"Yes," said Falters, offering nothing more.

Tiernan had always assumed that his father's frequent trips abroad were the prelude to his official retirement. After the Chimera seed ordeal, Richard Tiernan distanced himself from the daily operations at Oisín Pharmaceuticals and delegated most of the responsibility to his son. *Maybe he had the right idea,* thought Tiernan, imagining his father standing barefoot in a barrel of grapes. "So, what type of wine did you two produce at the vineyards?" he asked.

Falters didn't answer, but merely shook his head slowly. Tiernan was about to repeat the question, assuming that Falters hadn't heard him, but his attempt was silenced as the propellers coughed to life. Falters motioned to the headphones suspended from the ceiling. Tiernan put them on, effectively dulling the noise, but only slightly. Conversation would have to wait.

Left alone with his thoughts and the vulnerable feeling of flying across the Mediterranean in a twin-engine plane, Tiernan allowed his mind to wander back over the Atlantic where Oisín Pharmaceuticals was dangerously close to bankruptcy. Tiernan reasoned that if he could manage to squeeze any equity out of the newly-found Sardinian property, the inconvenience of the trip would be justified.

"We're here," said Falters. "We'll land just over that ridge."

Tiernan sat up straight in his seat, trying to see the runway. Fields of green and gold extended as far as the eye could see. Clusters of homes appeared asymmetrically among acres of cultivated crops, and herds of wild goats scattered, frightened by the sound of the twin engines as the plane made its descent.

"Where's the runway?" said Tiernan. He wasn't naïve enough to expect anything resembling an international airport, but he recoiled in horror as the plane approached a short, unkempt road that looked more like an abandoned railway line than a landing strip. His heart pounded as he envisioned the journey ending in a fiery crash.

"The Germans used this runway during WWII," said Falters as he brought the plane to a stop. "They flew supplies of fresh fish, regional wines and cheeses back to their headquarters in Rome. Not even the barbarians could resist Sardinian formaggio con i vermi."

"Did you say *con i vermi?*" said Tiernan, still rattled, but determined not to let Falters see it.

"Yes, with maggots," said Falters. "Didn't your father ever tell you about it?"

"No, he didn't. I'm sure I'd remember something like that."

"Well, I must tell you the story about the time I tricked him into eating some," said Falters. His expression showed a flash of emotion, but it faded quickly. "Come," he said. "We have only a short walk from here."

"Walk? In this heat?" asked Tiernan. A stroll in the Sardinian countryside may have been pleasant under different circumstances, but Tiernan was dragging a suitcase, which had seemed much lighter at the airport. Its wheels were not meant to navigate the rough, gravel-strewn roads and they protested by refusing to cooperate. The freakishly powerful Sardinian sun was relentless. Sweat poured down Tiernan's face as he swatted at the gnats.

"It would be easier to carry the case," said Falters without looking back. "It sounds like the wheels are getting clogged with gravel. You should pick it up."

Tiernan continued to drag the case – more to make a point than anything. Falters' lack of hospitality was astounding and Tiernan disliked him already. The two had been walking wordlessly for about three kilometers when Falters broke the silence. Standing at the crest of a hill, he stopped and waited for Tiernan, who lagged behind.

"There they are." Millions of grapes hung from the vines, leaves rustling in the imperceptible breeze. "Your father's creation – the Niamh grapes."

"Yeah, they're great," said Tiernan unenthusiastically. As they continued to walk, however, the enormity of the property revealed itself and his attitude softened. The magnitude of the vineyards was astonishing and excitement began to swell within him as he guessed at the property's value. "My father owned all this?"

"Yes, and now it's yours. Welcome to Tír na nÓg Vineyards."

CHAPTER 4

DEBRA AND GRAHAM strolled arm-in-arm down the avenue toward Delphi's, exchanging small talk as they ambled along. Theirs was a somewhat formal relationship, but a great source of comfort to them both. Graham had never married and most of his friends were either dead or just about, and Debra was married to her work. They were glad to have each other.

"Here we are," said Debra. "Boy, are you in for a treat. I can't believe you've lived in New York City all this time and have never eaten a gyro!"

"I am not very adventurous when it comes to comestibles, my dear," said Graham. "Bland, ordinary foods suit me fine."

"Always the Englishman. You can take the man out of England but not the England out of the..." said Debra. "No, wait, that's not how it goes. You can take the English out of England but not...oh, forget it."

"I never get those clever sayings right either, my dear," said Graham.

"Well, I am glad that you are brave enough to accompany me on our little adventure," said Debra, smiling.

"I'd accompany you anywhere," he replied.

The hostess escorted Graham and Debra to a booth toward the back of the sparsely-filled restaurant and dropped two menus unceremoniously on the table.

"John, can I ask you something?" said Debra.

"Of course, my dear."

"Supposing Michael decides to manufacture Regenerol at Oisín, where is he going to find the money to fund the trials?" she said. "Everyone knows that we're a hair's breadth away from bankruptcy and legitimate trials aren't cheap. Don't you think it would be wiser to stick with the original plan and sell the patent outright? Merkel and McCaff will pay handsomely for it, especially now that we have the Mimics. What do you think?"

"As of this morning, my dear, I'm afraid that is simply out of the question, so it doesn't really matter what I think," said Graham. "The creation of a viable Mimic cell will make manufacturing Regenerol more economical. Young Master Tiernan will never sell now, so it's a moot point."

"What do you think Richard would have done?" said Debra.

Graham repositioned himself in the booth. The transition was instantaneous. "Well, my dear, all too often in this wretched business, virtue is vice. Richard Tiernan was a simple man with a genius IQ. His only crime was having integrity, and the competition tore him asunder. But, of course, you were hired after the Chimera corn seed fiasco, and never really knew the *old* Richard Tiernan."

Debra nodded.

"But I'll tell you this, if Richard had succeeded in seeing his Chimera seed through to the end, we wouldn't be having a conversation about money – of that I'm sure," said Graham.

"I'm not completely unfamiliar with the story, or at least a version of it. You can't work at Oisín without hearing the gossip," said Debra. "After he sold the patent, he essentially left Michael in charge and took off sightseeing. Where did he travel, again? Corsica, wasn't it?"

"Italy," said Graham. "He loved Italy. But, don't fool yourself, dear. Richard was always a scientist. I suspect that he was doing a bit more than sightseeing. And, in any event, I wouldn't say Richard burdened his son. In fact, Michael was quite eager to assume the role as CEO. Richard was always a scientist first and a CEO second – the opposite is true of Michael."

"Double major?" asked Debra. She did her best to pretend that she was asking for the sake of conversation and not because the handsome Michael Tiernan – his wavy black hair, emerald eyes and the ruddy cheeks that gave him the look of perpetual good health – had occupied her nightly fantasies for years.

"I'm not sure," said Graham, "but judging from the time he spent in college, he may very well have a triple major. I seem to recall Richard mentioning that Michael took a minor in the biological sciences, but his first love was always business."

"Mmm," said Debra. "The goal of business is to accumulate money. Maybe that's exactly what Oisín Pharmaceuticals needs, a genuine businessman. One cannot serve two masters."

"True, but there's quite a difference between *acting* and *de facto* CEO, wouldn't you agree? Richard may have made a few financial mistakes, but he nonetheless kept the company afloat."

"Well, yes, I suppose you have a point there," said Debra.

A short, stout waitress caught Graham's eye, bringing the conversation to a halt. She was carrying a tray of ice waters, distributing them to the patrons. Graham did not realize he was staring; his eyes fixed on her bulging belly. *Eighth, possibly ninth month,* he thought. When their eyes met, Graham began to tremble as her dark, Aztec features initiated another episode. Clearly alarmed by his horrified stare, the waitress miscalculated the table's edge and a glass of water smashed to the floor.

The flashbacks always started the same way – the hot and humid Mexican summer, the revolving fan distorting the sounds of the thunder and lashing rain, the dirty floors still slick with the blood of the martyrs of science. John Graham was a prisoner in his own mind as the vivid scenario began anew.

Surrounded by panicking people, blood and death, and little lumps of lifeless flesh lying in sterile metal trays, the doctors tried desperately but impotently to save at least one mother or one child. The screams of agony-elicited supplications roared in his mind.

Dios te salve Maria! Santa Maria, ayuda me! No quiero morir!

Graham! Get your ass out of here! There's nothing more you can do. They're worm food, man.

The image of Jimmy Galante hastily wrapping the corpses, fetuses and medical waste all in thick tarps before loading them into the van always preceded the final scene. As Jimmy hoisted the last body into

17

the van, an arm fell out from under the covering and a bloody Rosary fell to the ground before the van doors slammed shut.

The memories never faded, never dulled and never relented. They attacked his mind with unpredictable frequency, making the anticipation of their arrival as savage as the memories themselves.

"I'm sorry, Miss," said Graham, getting out of the booth. He avoided eye contact and started to pick up the pieces of broken glass.

"John," said Debra. "You'll cut yourself. Leave the glass there while they get a broom."

A boy came promptly and swept the shards into a dustpan while another one mopped the spill. Thirty seconds later, Debra and Graham were alone again. Only a damp, shiny section on the floor remained of the accident. She reached for his hand.

"John, are you alright? You're very pale."

"I'll be fine," said Graham, pulling his hand away.

Debra knew exactly what had happened, but she had learned not to push. It would eventually pass.

The human trials will work this time, Graham repeated to himself. *They did not die in vain.*

CHAPTER 5

Partner

FALTERS LED THE way down the cobblestone lane to a circular driveway in front of the house. A statue of Venus de Milo sat regally adorning a fountain, which stood in the grassy knoll in the center. The fountain sprayed a mist into the air and, when the conditions were just right, it created a rainbow, giving the statue an ethereal and eerily life-like appearance. Tiernan stopped to admire it, but became distracted by the two cars sitting idly in the driveway.

"Are these my father's cars?" asked Tiernan.

"Yes, they were."

"Didn't occur to you to drive one to the airstrip, huh? It would have saved us the walk," said Tiernan, making no effort to hide his irritation.

"I enjoy walking," answered Falters. "I didn't know if I would get the chance to walk today, since you were scheduled to arrive. Come, I would like you to meet someone."

Falters climbed the stairs to the porch and hunkered down next to a sleeping dog. The haggard setter barely stirred from its sleep as Falters stroked its mangy, muted red coat. "I bet that poor thing has seen better days," said Tiernan, slightly disgusted by the sight. "Yours?"

"I suppose it's mine now. And I would imagine it enjoyed its life more when it was younger – doesn't every sentient creature?" said Falters. "Perhaps you wouldn't mind coming closer; I need your assistance." Falters abruptly turned and went into the house, the screen door clapping behind him. When he returned a few moments later, he handed Tiernan a quill filled with India ink.

"Please, come closer. I would like you to write a word or phrase –

something you will recognize as yours – on the dog's bare skin."

"Why? What is this, a Sardinian welcome ritual?" said Tiernan. "I'm not even going near that thing – forget about autographing its flea-bitten hide."

"Please, I promise you will understand in time," Falters replied. Tiernan took the quill and scribbled *Crazy Bastard*. The dog barely stirred.

"There," said Tiernan.

"Now, just one moment more of your cooperation." Falters retrieved a vial of purple liquid from his pocket and handed it to Tiernan who instantly recognized it as identical to those he had found in the safety deposit box. He kept silent, not wanting to reveal more than necessary.

"When I received the news that you were coming, I thought I would expedite matters by arranging a demonstration," said Falters. "Break the wax seal and feed the vial's contents to the dog."

"For what?"

"Just do it, please," said Falters.

Tiernan hesitated, but complied, pouring the purple liquid into the dog's mouth, spilling a little onto the porch.

"Excellent," said Falters. "Let's go inside."

Tiernan followed Falters through the front door of the house, dragging his suitcase up the charcoal slate-stone steps.

"Would you like to rest before we begin?" asked Falters, standing in the foyer.

"Begin?" repeated Tiernan. "Begin what?"

"Your father's sudden death complicates matters exponentially," said Falters. "We should have prepared for such a contingency – an obvious oversight."

"Oh, I'm sorry. Allow me to apologize for the immense inconvenience my father's death caused," snapped Tiernan. "There's absolutely no excuse for that type of behavior."

Judging by his reaction, Falters discerned that the young Tiernan had no inkling as to his father's legacy and was greatly relieved. "There's no need for sarcasm. I only meant to emphasize that I urged your father to tell you about this place," said Falters, "but he always said you weren't ready for a responsibility of such magnitude. Let's hope that he was mistaken."

Tiernan realized he still had his carry-on bag draped over his shoulder and his suitcase in hand. He dropped the bag to the floor. "What responsibility?" he said. "Of caring for a vineyard? Well, I wouldn't worry about that, Falters; I have no intention of keeping the place."

"There are four bedrooms in this house," said Falters. "Your father slept in the room facing east. I recommend that you settle in there. Perhaps you should rest before we begin. Shall we say two hours?"

Tiernan briefly entertained the possibility that he was dreaming and still aboard the transatlantic flight. He wiped the sweat from his brow. "Where are the bathrooms? And, good Lord, why the hell is it so hot in here?"

"There are three," replied Falters, ignoring him. "One is upstairs connected to your father's room, another is here on the ground floor and another is in the laboratory. It's hot because it's summertime."

"I meant *inside* the house. You two ever consider installing an air conditioning system?" Tiernan made a mental note to investigate the cost. *Anything to boost the selling price.*

"We will meet here in a couple of hours. I recommend that you get some rest. We have much to discuss," said Falters as he walked out the front door, disappearing into the vineyards.

"Whoa, Falters, wait a minute. Did you say there was a lab? Hey!" But when the door closed, Tiernan was alone.

"What a jackass." Tiernan stood still for several minutes after the exchange. At least now he knew he wasn't dreaming; it was never this hot in dreams and people were seldom this rude. He surveyed his surroundings. The house was simple and sterile. The walls were all slightly off-white and clean but completely barren. The hardwood floors were immaculate and had been spared the dulling effects of traffic. He noticed an empty picture frame on a lone table at the base of the dual staircases leading to the second floor.

The upstairs was equally as Spartan. He walked down the hall and opened the last door on the left. *This must be my father's room,* he thought. When the familiar scent embraced him, he knew. Tiernan savored the faint odor as he closed the door behind him. He dropped his bag on the bed, walked to the opposite end of the room and gently pushed the heavy wooden door, which creaked open to reveal a spacious bathroom with a large antique tub. He washed his hands in the small porcelain sink adjacent to the tub and splashed a little water on his face. He instinctively reached to his right for a towel but found none. He dried his hands on his shirt and sat down on the bed. He kicked off his shoes and lay down, pushing his bag off the bed with his foot. *Maybe I should rest my eyes for a few minutes and gather myself.* But the memories, strengthened by the familiar scent, hijacked his mind and forced him to remember things he would have just as soon forgotten.

"You're scared, I understand," said Tiernan. The memory returned with a cruel, almost sadistic vivacity. *"Selling the Chimera seed to Lionel is just plain stupid. It's like you're admitting defeat before the battle even begins! We can win this. You're thinking like a cowardly scientist, not a businessman. Trust me, Dad, you're making a tragic mistake."*

"I know you think you have the world all figured out, Michael, and although I've never doubted your business sense, things are not as simple as you think," said Richard. "This situation needs to be handled delicately. I've been around a little longer than you have, so I guess you'll just have to have a little faith in your old man." Richard leaned in and put his arm around his son's shoulder. "We'll be okay, I promise. I'm not going to let the company go under."

Tiernan jumped out of the bed and walked to the window, effectively arresting the memory. He felt the pangs of regret welling up within him and tried in vain to escape, diverting his mind elsewhere. He tried to open the window, but, realizing it had been painted shut, he abandoned his quest for fresh air and stared out through the dirty glass and over the vast vineyards. Rows of grapes rolled across the land

and seemed to continue to the very horizon itself. *So this is where Oisín's capital went*, he thought. *You spent our operating budget on yet another useless endeavor – at least you were consistent.* The sight of the vineyards stirred the memories and Tiernan could not help but recall the event that separated his father's life into a before and after – *the origin of the Chimera Seed.*

The Chimera Seed had revealed itself to the late Richard Tiernan while he was recovering from a bacterial infection. A terrible fever had laid him up for weeks and he had spent most of that time in the intermediary place where dreams and reality are indistinguishable.

One afternoon while napping under the delirium that accompanied his fever, he dreamt that he was standing amidst fields of corn, abundant and flourishing, as far as the eye could see. Millions of stalks swayed in the breeze, creating the sound of a thousand whispers across the moonlit plain. Abandoned crop dusters lay in the adjacent field, rusting and obsolete. He continued to walk through the fields, marveling at the quantity, wondering how hunger could still exist with such abundance. Seas of rustling maize moved in unison across the vast expanse, leaving the impression that the individual stalks were part of a greater, self-aware whole. He plucked a few ears of corn to examine them. The corn stalks opened their hidden eyes, became animated and sang in an eerie, slightly dissonant harmony, until the entire crop joined the chorus, singing: "We are Chimera. We are Chimera."

The next morning, fever broken and enthusiasm renewed, he rose early and headed to the labs to begin working on what he hypothesized would be the answer to world hunger. When the staff arrived at Oisín later that morning, they found Richard already there. He didn't look up from his notepad. Instead, he continued to scribble furiously, enraptured.

"We are going to create a new species of insect-resistant corn, a hybrid plant that grows like bamboo!"

Richard created a hybrid of such magnificence that one could easily imagine God himself nodding in approval. The cost of creating the chimaeraic corn had all but exhausted Oisín's capital, but Richard was confident that his incredible seed would bring enough wealth to dwarf any debt by comparison. He was badly mistaken, having failed to factor human greed into the equation.

Ryan Connor, president of Lionel Pharmaceuticals, was much too savvy and had too many favors banked for Richard Tiernan to succeed. Numerous delays by the FDA caused Oisín to hemorrhage cash and the USDA's repeated requests for additional studies left Richard with two options: claim bankruptcy or sell the Chimera seed to Lionel Pharmaceuticals. He chose to sell.

Richard Tiernan's hybrid seed was a work of art and very expensive to manufacture. Connor was determined to do something about the cost. Why profit millions when one can profit billions, trillions? After the sale of the Chimera seed was complete, Lionel Pharmaceuticals destroyed all evidence of its existence. With the superior and costly version of the seed gone, Lionel was free to create its own hybrid species without the fear of competition. Connor knew that, although Lionel's transgenic corn was woefully inferior to Oisín's, Lionel would rake in record profits the way only a monopoly can. He was right.

Although the FDA and the USDA were initially suspicious of Lionel's transgenic corn, Connor bought enough politicians and funded enough scientific studies to appease those who mattered. Thus, a new species came into existence.

CG

"Dr. Tiernan, are you sleeping?" said Falters, simultaneously rapping the door.

"I'll be down in a few minutes," said Tiernan, startled by the sudden and powerful knocking. He looked at his wristwatch. He had been asleep for three hours.

Tiernan walked down the stairs and into the sitting area where Falters sat with the same stoic expression. He gestured to the couch and Tiernan sat down.

"What I am about to tell you will be difficult to hear all at once," said Falters. "But we do not have the luxury of time. You see, our work required a great deal of secrecy and –"

"Work? What work?" After the Chimera seed debacle, everyone had, including Tiernan himself, assumed that Richard had admitted defeat and sought to spend his few remaining years in relative peace.

"You see," continued Falters, "things are seldom as they appear. To the average observer, Richard sold the Chimera seed under duress and gradually delegated the responsibilities of running Oisín Pharmaceuticals to his next of kin. I'm referring to you, of course."

"I would hope so – I am an only child. Or are you going to tell me something different? Are you my long lost brother?" Tiernan laughed a little, but Falters wasn't amused.

"To these same observers," continued Falters, "the CEO of Oisín Pharmaceuticals had surrendered and begun traveling the beautiful Italian countryside while his son took over the doomed company. This was exactly the perception Richard had sought."

"Why would anybody want that?" said Tiernan.

"Because he needed the protection that insignificance provides. While creating his chimaeraic corn, he inadvertently stumbled upon something miraculous, something with the potential to change life as we know it." Falters lifted his finger in a pre-emptive request for silence. Tiernan complied with thinly veiled irritation.

"As I'm sure you can imagine, creating a viable hybrid organism is an arduous task. Mother Nature guards her secrets well, so successfully combining the genes of different organisms is challenging, to say the very least. However, the difficulty grows exponentially when one tries to create a hybrid with all the characteristics your father sought. His ambition was second only to his extraordinary discipline.

"In the beginning, he spent most of his time combining the genes of diverse plants, attempting to breed a strong hybrid. The results were mixed, but, 90 percent of the time, he produced seeds that failed to germinate. Of the 10 percent that did germinate, none inherited the traits his chimaeraic corn required. Despite all the disappointments, your father never wavered. Somehow, he knew success was forthcoming. He never gave up hope.

"Then it happened. A random experiment bore another kind of fruit, if you will. Richard created a hybrid grape seed by genetically modifying several species with the robust Muscatine variety, with the intention of exploiting certain traits. These hybrid seeds produced grapes with exceptionally high levels of resveratrol, the anti-aging, life-extending substance often credited for giving the Mediterranean people above average longevity and good health. The first few harvests failed and put additional strain on Oisín's already dwindling capital, but Richard was determined."

Yeah, thought Tiernan, *determined to use up all Oisín's assets pursuing his hobby.*

"The next few harvests produced similar disappointments, but his persistence was rewarded with a truly amazing hybrid, which he named the Niamh grape. For all its magnificence, though, the Niamh grape was truly a mystery and all attempts to combine its desirable traits with maize species failed. There was, however, something very special about this plant – it was *uniquely* unique. Your father decided to store the seeds for further study at another time and went back to work on the corn hybrid," said Falters.

"Eventually, Richard created a corn seed hybrid, which he named the Chimera seed, but the effort had exhausted most of Oisín's capital in the process. The president of Lionel Pharmaceuticals took advantage of your father's financial situation and manipulated him into selling his creation. But Richard was not defeated. He set out to find an isolated place where he could experiment with the hybrid Niamh grape. He chose this place."

"You can stop right there," said Tiernan, emotions raw with resentment. "My father got royally screwed by that jack-booted bastard, Ryan Connor, and nearly lost the company in the process. I'm still cleaning up that mess, but, trust me, that's never going to happen again." Tiernan stood up, then realizing he had nowhere to go, sat back down. "Well," he continued, "as much as I've enjoyed the trip down *bad* Memory Lane, I have a company to run back in the States. I'm selling this place – special grapes 'n' all."

"You won't sell," said Falters, "I'm sure of it." He got up and walked into the kitchen. "Come, you should see the results of your father's work."

Tiernan got up and followed Falters into the kitchen. *I wonder if Lynch has those figures I asked for,* thought Tiernan, as he calculated the profit he stood to make from the sale.

Meet Everyone

CHAPTER 6

MARY MCKENNA WALKED down the corridor, looking professional yet wickedly attractive in the business suit she hated. She never failed to accentuate her desirable features with just the right amount of cosmetics, applied with the precision of Donatello.

Mary had silky, mocha skin, blessedly free from any blemish or imperfection – the product of a biracial union. Her jet-black hair was all one length and it spilled over her shoulders and cascaded down her back. Her bespectacled brown eyes were intense and captivating and complemented her shapely nose and full lips. She was quite something to behold and she knew it.

Mary had learned that her brains and strong personality were always going to be a liability in a world where men dominated the workforce and, to a disappointing degree, reserved key positions for fellow members of the immortal boys' club. At a critical juncture in her career, a superior had told her that men did not like women who could *outsmart* them and advised her to *dumb it down a little*. That day, she achieved enlightenment and implemented a drastic career change. In her new profession, she would justify the lies and deceptions that would ruin many lives and careers by a simple yet flawless logic: *only the fittest were meant to survive.*

RAPIST

Vincent Tighte, the administrator of the Environmental Protection Agency, had recently commissioned her to handle an extremely delicate situation. Posing as a doctoral candidate writing her thesis on the practices of the EPA, Tighte *hired* her as special advisor to the Office of the Administrator and Deputy Administrator. No one except Vincent Tighte and Scott Lehman knew her true role.

"Ah, Miss McKenna," said Tighte, as Mary entered the conference room. "How nice of you to grace us with your presence."

Mary navigated the narrow space between the wall and the long table, taking the only remaining seat next to the deputy administrator, Scott Lehman. He handed her a portfolio and whispered *page seven,* pointing to his identical copy.

"If I may call attention to the elephant in the room," said Mark Reed of the FDA, Office of Biological Oncology Products. "The studies we're addressing were funded by independent sources and they all say the same thing." His faced flushed as it always did when he spoke in front of large groups, but, this time, anger darkened his crimson visage.

"We're on the brink of a crisis! Our actions will determine the quality of life for millions here and abroad!"

Mark Reed had been opposed to the approval of the transgenic corn seed for human consumption from the beginning. Although no one could have predicted the impact a new species of plant would have on the ecosystem, it seemed obvious to him that it would have some effect. How could millions of acres of a new species of corn that exudes a toxic bacterium not affect *something?*

"Slow down, Chicken Little," said Mary. "Those studies do not explicitly blame the transgenic corn and you know that."

"Some of those studies claim that this new mutant corn is also linked to the decline in the number of Monarch butterflies," said Nathan Hanraty of the USDA.

"True, but that could just as easily be a result of global warming, according to those studies," said Naomi Linden, the White House communications director.

"Lionel's transgenic seed was subjected to unparalleled scrutiny from all of your agencies," said Lori Adams, a senior executive at Lionel Pharmaceuticals. "Each of you sitting here right now gave it the green light, or is our corn causing memory loss too?"

Lori stood up and walked to the front of the room where Tighte looked a little concerned. "Our labs have confirmed the safety of the seed, *ad nauseam.* We conducted every little test y'all asked for and the conclusions were always the same: the seed is completely innocuous except to the intended insects."

Tighte turned his chair to face her, clearly uncomfortable with her hijacking of the meeting and the efficiency with which she usurped his authority. He wanted to object, but thought better of it.

"We've created a quality product and we stand proudly behind our work," said Lori. She began pacing a little while she spoke. All eyes followed her. "These studies shamelessly blame the transgenic corn crops for the disappearance of bees, ladybugs, butterflies, Jimmy Hoffa, but we all know they're pure speculation. I say we issue a collective statement confirming the safety of the seed and put this thing to bed," she said with a smile.

Lori lifted Tighte's glass of water and sipped a little without as much as a glance in his direction. Tighte noticed the huge smudge of red lipstick left on the glass, purposely done, no doubt. "Even as we speak, our scientists are working on another derivative of the seed, one that requires only a fraction of the water traditional corn plants need. We are dedicated to the continuous improvement of our products, except those that are already perfect," Lori smiled impishly.

"Does this *new* seed use harmful bacteria, too?" asked Mark Reed, assuming his usual argumentative role. "I've always admired Lionel's ingenuity, but I've made my objections clear from the very beginning on this one. Genetically-modified organisms are dangerous at best, and, at worst, can cause potentially catastrophic events."

"Aw, now, Marky, I don't remember you being so bitter," said Lori, flashing her disarming smile. "You're too young and handsome to be carrying all that anger around."

"Four-hundred million pounds," he replied. "That's how much honey we Americans consume annually."

"Wow," said Lori. "No wonder we're a little chubby." She patted her stomach.

"It takes billions upon billions of bees to satisfy our demand for that amount, and we're losing millions of bees at a time because of that damn corn. You do the math."

"Not to mention the $14 billion worth of free pollination they provide annually," said Naomi Linden. "The farmers are reporting major decreases in crop yields of clover and almonds, and some say this is just the beginning."

Lori was skilled at spinning issues. Her Southern charm was spellbinding. She could get away with saying the most sexist, outrageous things with her mesmerizing twang, and no one would get offended or, at least, no one ever complained.

Lionel spent millions in advertisements and endorsements creating the impression that its transgenic corn seed was the greatest blessing science had ever bestowed upon humanity – the eco-friendly answer to hunger, pesticide control and farmer subsidies. Recently, however, as Lionel sang the praises of its new corn seed, it poured obscene amounts of cash into finding an alternative seed, racing against a clock that moved at merciless speed.

"Let them go after the cell phone companies," Lori continued. "Who knows what all those radio waves are doing."

Gratuitous laughter erupted.

Einstein was erroneously credited as saying that the disappearance of the bees would precede the end of the human race by, at most, four years. And the bees were disappearing. The fact that Einstein did not utter the prophetic statement did not alter its validity. Something was killing them, and their murder was kept from the public with all the efficiency that only money could buy. The public was lulled back into its apathetic slumber with lowered commodity costs and feel-good advertisements.

Before adjourning, the group scheduled a meeting for later that month. Lori Adams gathered her things and gave Tighte a passing glance as she left. Most of the people were too occupied to notice, but Mary McKenna caught it. She admired the way Lori handled the room.

"Miss McKenna, I need to see you and Mr. Lehman in my office in 15 minutes," said Tighte.

Lehman looked up at Mary from his seat and she looked back at him. "This will not be good," said Lehman. "Not good at all."

Mary went into the restroom to compose herself. She looked in the mirror and noticed a set of dark circles forming beneath her eyes. She retrieved a powder compact from her bag and gently patted her face. A toilet flushed and out stepped Lori Adams. She joined Mary at an adjacent sink and smiled as she washed her hands. Mary noticed the beautifully ornate, jeweled nails that adorned Lori's hands that were beginning to show the first signs of aging. Lori looked at Mary in the mirror when she could have just as easily turned her head a few inches.

"See y'all soon," said Lori.

"Take care."

Lori adjusted a few strands of her blond hair and walked out of the bathroom. Mary stood by the mirror and felt envy, admiration, fear and exhilaration all clamor to be her primary emotion. She settled on fear-infused admiration.

Scott Lehman was already there when Mary walked into Tighte's office.

"Oh, hey, Mary, Vince will be here in a few minutes," said Lehman. "Here, sit down. You look especially nice today."

"Thanks, Scott, you too," replied Mary, scanning Tighte's desk.

"Really?" said Scott. "I wear this all the time."

"It must be your hair."

"Well, I did try this new shampoo that my sister..."

Tighte entered and slammed the office door, rattling the pictures on the wall. "That bitch got Oisín's original seed!" he said, veins popping out of his neck, straining to keep his voice at an intensified whisper. "I swear to God, McKenna, if you don't fix this, I swear to God, I'll –"

"Vince, relax, buddy," said Lehman, putting his hand on Tighte's shoulder. "They can't touch us. We covered all –"

"Get off me, you moron!" Tighte shoved Lehman hard against the chest, knocking him back into his seat. "She was baiting us! Couldn't you morons see that?"

"Yes, she was baiting us, and it demonstrates one thing," said Mary, as confidently as she could manage.

"And what's that?" snapped Tighte.

"She's scared, Vincent, real scared," Mary continued. "Because she hasn't managed to obtain the Chimera seed. Trust me!"

Tighte seemed to gain a little composure and walked to the other side of his desk. He took out a stained handkerchief and ran it across the sweat beads that had begun to multiply on his forehead. The circumferences of the permanent sweat rings widened around his armpits, saturating the office with his offensive odor. Mary fought to hide her revulsion.

"Hey, Scott, didn't mean to push you so hard," said Tighte, reaching for the half-eaten muffin sitting on his desk.

"Don't worry about it." Lehman felt emasculated and didn't want anymore attention called to his humiliation. He changed the topic. "Lionel owns the patent on the Chimera seed, right?"

"Yes, they do," said Mary. "Pride goeth before the fall. They discarded it when they created the cheaper version in case someone from the inside leaked Oisín's original and much safer version."

"Wouldn't want the public to perceive Lionel as a greedy, self-serving enterprise, now would we?" said Lehman. "Altering a perfectly good seed with a dangerous poison just to make money; how disgusting. Serves them right."

Tighte opened his desk, took out a bottle of rye and poured a helping into his cup of three-hour-old coffee. He returned the bottle without as much as an offer. "If we don't get a hold of that seed, our plan is shot in the ass," he said. "We'll be stuck with the pittance we had in the beginning. After everyone gets paid, we'll be left with scraps."

Vincent Tighte had used his position as administrator of the EPA to green-light Lionel's derivative seed. He had expedited the process by cashing in every favor he had banked during his tenure in government, and was now feeling the pressure. In Washington, D.C., favors cost money and his creditors were demanding payment. Opting for Lionel stock as compensation for his illegal activities, Tighte had become an overnight millionaire when the FDA announced the approval of Lionel's seed. Although Lionel's stock had skyrocketed, Tighte couldn't touch a cent of his money. If he were to cash out too soon, he would be hand-delivering a caseload of evidence against himself to the attorney general. On the other hand, if Tighte adhered to the original plan and waited until he adequately covered all tracks, Lionel's corn seed scandal might explode and force the company into bankruptcy, rendering the stock worthless.

In the midst of the approaching storm, Tighte saw an opportunity. If he were able to secure the original Chimera seed, he could use it to blackmail the president of Lionel Pharmaceuticals into issuing more stock. If Connor refused, he would threaten to sell it to a competitor. Tighte knew that, although Lionel owned the rights to the Chimera seed, they would lose more if the public learned that they had buried it in the interest of profits. Vincent Tighte was playing a dangerous game, but the desire for wealth inebriated him and clouded his judgment. He underestimated the difficulty he would have getting Richard Tiernan to cooperate. After several attempts to secure the seed directly from Tiernan, he resorted to less traditional methods and hired Mary McKenna.

"Get to Richard Tiernan," said Tighte. "Use that pumpin' body, shake your tail and run into the bushes; he'll follow. Wouldn't mind chasing you in there myself. Do whatever it takes to get me that damn seed."

Mary boiled inside as she felt his eyes slither over her body. She imagined picking up the paperweight on his desk and hopping it off his skull. "That's not going to happen," she said. "Richard Tiernan died of a massive heart attack and his son, Michael Tiernan, is the new CEO."

"Then shake your tail for the younger Tiernan."

Tighte revolted her. She wanted to vomit all over him, but, instead, stifled the dry-heave as she fought to suppress the images of his fat, greasy hands reaching for her – the smell of the rancid Brylcreem-laden hair. She shook it off and continued.

"Michael Tiernan is gallivanting in Italy somewhere. I haven't been able to contact anyone who can help me locate him."

"That's great, just wonderful," said Tighte.

"I can't believe those stupid idiots over at Lionel didn't keep at least a copy of Tiernan's original," said Lehman. "What were they thinking?"

"I've told you already. It was too expensive and time-consuming to reproduce the original. Richard Tiernan and Lionel Pharmaceuticals had very different motives for creating the seed," answered Mary. "Richard Tiernan's version cost more to produce. Lionel looked for a cheaper, more efficient means and then buried the superior version."

"Get to Michael Tiernan, Mary," said Tighte. "Convince him to give you the Chimera prototype. I don't care what you have to do, just get me that goddamn prototype. Do it and I'll dump another $700,000 in escrow. Then we can go our separate ways."

"I'll get it," said Mary. "I always do."

"Get to Tiernan before Lori Adams does. You know what it means if she gets to him first."

CHAPTER 7

TIERNAN FOLLOWED FALTERS into the kitchen. In the corner stood an inconspicuous trapezoidal-shaped door, which looked like the entrance to a storage closet. Falters opened the door to reveal a downward winding staircase.

"Be attentive. The stairs are narrow," said Falters, as he struggled to crouch low enough to enter. Tiernan followed him and wondered how his aging father hadn't broken his neck while trying to walk down the stairs. At the bottom, a dim, uncovered incandescent bulb lit the dank, moldy basement. Bottles of wine lined the damp walls. It was a small space, enough for a couple hundred bottles.

"So he did make wine with the Niamh grapes," said Tiernan.

"No," said Falters, as he groped along the wall. An audible click preceded a grinding sound and, within seconds, the wall opened outward to reveal a long, dark tunnel.

"Follow me." Falters navigated the path easily, having made the journey thousands of times, but Tiernan needed to use the cold stone walls to steady himself as he tried to keep pace. After walking for a few minutes with considerable effort, Tiernan caught up to Falters, who had come to a stop.

"We're here. This is the lab," said Falters.

"Are you serious?" said Tiernan. "What kind of a lab —"

As Falters flipped a switch, a burst of light silenced Tiernan. Two glass doors at the top of a couple of stony steps slowly opened, granting them entrance to a pristine lab. Tiernan quickly took a mental inventory, recognizing the modern pieces of equipment. It was obvious that his father was doing more than squashing grapes. Upon further inspection, he determined that the lab was as equally advanced as Oisín's lab in the States. As he surveyed his surroundings, Tiernan could hear the false rock wall sliding back into place beyond the glass doors. On the adjacent wall stood a large aquarium hosting several species of fish in compartmentalized tanks. A chorus of muffled barking erupted from one of the adjoining rooms.

"What the hell is this place?" asked Tiernan. "What were you two doing down here?"

Falters walked around the lab flipping switches, adjusting knobs and checking computer screens before pulling out a wheeled stool from under a stainless steel table. The black leather seat hissed under his weight and glided easily as his powerful legs pushed against the floor. The stool slowed to a stop next to Tiernan. "Take a seat," he said as he gestured to a matching stool. Tiernan pulled it out and sat down, never taking his eyes off Falters.

"Are you going to tell me or do I have to guess?" said Tiernan. "Answer me, please. What is this place?"

"As I was saying before, when your father first set out to create the Chimera corn, there were thousands of failures. He crossbred hundreds of species until he found one that worked," said Falters, "but, in the process, he stumbled upon the Niamh grape. Like all great discoveries, the Niamh grape was an accident, of sorts."

"Yeah, so?" said Tiernan.

"It happens all the time in your business," said Falters. "Take Finasteride, for instance. Scientists set out to engineer a drug to treat enlarged prostates and ended up creating a drug that treats male pattern baldness instead."

"This shouldn't surprise anyone with an education," said Tiernan. "The human body functions synergistically. Altering one system necessarily affects others. This is a fundamental problem in drug development and, incidentally, in life – causality. We don't always get the effect we were hoping for, but we always get *some* effect."

"But my favorite one," said Falters, ignoring Tiernan's pseudo-deep insight, "is a drug for the treatment of frigidity in women that ended up as a best-selling anti-obsessional drug. The irony amuses me."

"Like I was saying," said Tiernan, "anybody in the pharmaceutical industry could tell you that the most successful drugs were mistakes – accidental finds – drugs originally intended for something else, but let's get back to the question at hand: What makes the Niamh grapes so special and, more importantly, why should I give a damn?"

"In the beginning, your father hoped to engineer a grape seed that would produce exceptionally high levels of resveratrol, and hypothesized that any insect feeding upon it would die," said Falters. "He combined the grape and the corn plant and hoped for the best."

"But?" said Tiernan motioning with his hand.

"But instead of killing the insects, the corn-grape hybrid extended their lifespan up to 35 percent and increased the number of their offspring by nearly 50 percent. To make matters worse, the corn-grape hybrid plant proved to be useless for our purpose. But it wasn't a complete failure," said Falters. "The findings inspired us to investigate alternate uses for the Niamh grape."

"That is a wonderful story," said Tiernan, enunciating each word. "And I'm sure it must be especially exciting for the bugs, but I'm afraid I didn't hear anything that would even remotely persuade me not to sell. Sorry, but it's time to pack it in. I'm going for a fast sale – listing it under market value – so I wouldn't waste any time packing up if I were you."

Falters sighed. "Perhaps Mr. Lynch failed to make this point clear: you cannot sell Tír na nÓg without my consent. But that's irrelevant, considering the reality."

"And what's the reality?" said Tiernan. The frustration and anger had reached critical limit. "What's this reality that only you're privy to? Years of *research,* a constant drain on Oisín's capital and all my father managed to produce is a damn plant that extends the lifespan of bugs? And now, for added fun, I have to negotiate with a stranger to sell my own property?"

"I suppose that one could reduce our accomplishments to that, if one chose," said Falters. "However, I would choose to express it differently since it fails to explain the reality."

"Okay, and how would you say it, huh?" shouted Tiernan. "How would you sum up the fact that my father chose to spend his last remaining years in a goddamn underground tunnel? He spent my inheritance screwing around with grapes and bugs!"

Falters merely looked at Tiernan as if he were studying his behavior, which infuriated Tiernan even more. Tiernan gave a forced laugh of exasperation. "Maybe I'm being a bit too harsh. I mean, he did manage to create a special plant that seems to help the bug community, so it wasn't a total waste, right? Tell me, is that how you would sum it up? I'd really like to know."

Falters seemed unaffected by Tiernan's outburst. "No. Actually, if I were pressed to sum it up, I would say that your father found the cure for aging."

Tiernan assumed he must have misunderstood. "What did you say?"

"It's true. We found a way to stop the aging process. We named the drug Dionysinol, for obvious reasons," said Falters.

"Cured aging?" snickered Tiernan. "I must admit, I wasn't expecting you to say that – especially since my father is dead. You must think I'm a real dope, buddy."

"Your incredulity is understandable, but I assure you, it's true. Come with me," said Falters.

"This I gotta see," said Tiernan as he followed Falters into the adjacent room. A series of spacious cages lined the walls and the inhabitants jumped with excitement upon seeing Falters. The barking ceased when he raised his hand and let out a slow, steady *shhhh*. Tiernan counted nine dogs, all sitting attentively, waiting for Falters' next command.

"They're well trained, I'll give you that. If your cure for aging doesn't pan out, you can always open a kennel," said Tiernan sarcastically.

Falters didn't respond, but opened one of the cages. The dog jumped out excitedly, wagging her tail furiously. Falters petted the dog affectionately. "Do you recognize her?"

"Should I?"

"That depends," said Falters. "What would you say if I were to tell you that this is the same dog you saw when you first arrived?"

"I'd say, get the hell outta here." Tiernan carefully examined the dog that had migrated from Falters to him. It lifted its paw in greeting. A shining red coat covered its muscular chest and solid body frame. Tiernan searched for any signs of aging around the dog's eyes, graying of the hair, cataracts forming in the irises, but there was nothing. "There's no way."

Falters handed Tiernan a pair of electric shears. "Start cutting the area where you marked her with the India ink."

Tiernan took the shears and switched them on. He laughed at the preposterous situation in which he found himself as clumps of red hair fell to the floor. The laughter stopped abruptly when he made out the first few letters of *Crazy Bastard*.

"Under different circumstances, I might have enjoyed that trick," said Tiernan, "but now I'm just pissed off. How the hell did you pull that off?"

"It's not an illusion. All of these animals were at least 15 years old when they were treated with Dionysinol," said Falters, pointing to the cages. "I would estimate this particular dog's age before treatment at approximately 20 years. Your father thought of the idea to get the animals from the pound; the volunteers gladly accommodated his requests by providing us animals with advanced years. No one else would've adopted them and it saved the shelter the cost of having to euthanize." Falters walked over to a file cabinet and removed a file.

Tiernan looked more carefully at the dog, examining the writing on its back. "I gotta hand it to you," he said, "the writing is very close, but playtime's over. Tell me how you did it."

Falters was almost smiling when he handed him the thick file. A photograph of Richard with his arm around an elderly dog was fastened to the jacket with three paper clips. Tiernan examined the file, skimming through the contents before returning to the photo of his deceased father.

"What's this?"

"It's a file on the first test subject. We gave each dog varying doses of the Dionysinol. Of course, I need to run more tests, but I suspect that the onset of the effects varies directly with the dosage," said Falters.

"You're serious, aren't you? You actually want me to believe that this is the same animal?" said Tiernan, holding the dog's paw, alternating his attention between the file and the dog.

"Again, that depends on how you define *same*. I would say that the essence, or personality, of the original animal remains intact, but, as you can see, it's not the same dog."

Tiernan concentrated his attention on the file. He recognized his father's handwriting, the same beautiful penmanship that graced the leather portfolio. Tiernan regretted having only skimmed it. *If he had discovered something this big, he would have told me. Wouldn't he have?* The writing, the sentence structure undoubtedly belonged to Richard Tiernan and, evidently, he believed in the project – at least enough to have gone to the trouble of hiding samples of the Dionysinol in a bank vault.

"We've tested the Dionysinol on several species, all with consistent results, but, unfortunately, there were also some paradoxical occurrences that I still do not fully understand."

"Paradoxical?" said Tiernan, still reeling.

"Yes, while inadequate, it's the best word to describe the phenomena with regard to the Turritopsis nutricula."

Tiernan put the folder down on the metal table. "The what?"

"The Turritopsis nutricula is a jellyfish. This amazing creature, along with the Niamh grape, is what makes Dionysinol possible."

"Wait. Jellyfish?" said Tiernan.

"Yes. The Turritopsis nutricula reverts to the polyp stage after reaching sexual maturity and then begins the cycle all over again," said Falters. "It continues this indefinitely, so, essentially, it is immortal. Apparently, nature has produced several species that are impervious to the effects of aging."

"So you're saying that they're immortal? That jellyfish is immortal?" said Tiernan, pointing to the tanks where the translucent miracles of nature floated aimlessly.

"Potentially immortal," said Falters. "If I stab it with this pen or pour bleach into its tank, it will die. However, if left alone, it will live indefinitely. We used its DNA as a blueprint for the new species of plant. The Niamh grapes resulted from our mixing the Turritopsis nutricula's DNA with the Niamh grape. From the resulting hybrid, we produced the drug."

"You hoped to exploit the age-defying powers of the jellyfish and extend it to other species, am I right?" asked Tiernan.

"Precisely. Surely you recall the monumental discovery on cell division by Leonard Hayflick," said Falters. "In 1961, he discovered that cells divide about 50 times before they lose steam and die out. This crudely accounts for the effects of aging. He coined the phenomena the Hayflick Limit. Your father joked about coining his discovery *Tiernan's solution to the Hayflick Limit.*"

Something about the way Falters spoke, reacted, interacted caused a dissonance in Tiernan's mind. It was almost mechanical, systematic, as if Falters was acting out a predetermined plot to which only he knew the ending.

"Your father and I conducted tests on several species of mammals, fish and amphibians," said Falters, "all with similar results. But, when we tested the substance on the very species that makes the drug possible, we had to revise our assumptions."

"And what were those assumptions?" said Tiernan.

"It's easier if I show you," said Falters. He walked over to the other side of the room, where he opened a drawer and retrieved a small vial with a dropper top. He unscrewed the dropper and filled it with a purple liquid. "You've witnessed the power of Dionysinol to breathe life into something. Now watch it suffocate it out."

Tiernan sat back down on the stool. His weight caused the stool to shift and roll a little toward the fish tanks where the jellyfish swam obliviously, gracefully, like apparitions.

"Pardon me," said Falters, leaning over Tiernan. "Pay attention. It happens fast."

He squeezed the dropper top and a stream of purple liquid squirted into the clear water. The jellyfish continued floating undisturbed for a minute before it tensed. Tiernan's eyes widened as he witnessed the demise of the hydrozoa. At first, the jellyfish squirmed, attempting to escape the invisible assailant. Within minutes, it became a shriveled, gelatinous glob. Falters stood silently watching the tank.

"We have theories, but, in truth, we don't know exactly why it kills them," he admitted. "We have successfully tested dozens of species, but the jellyfish is the only one that reacts like this consistently."

"What the hell just happened?" said Tiernan. "What is that stuff?" He stared at the little bottle in Falters' hand. Still, despite the impressive theatrics and the theoretically-feasible explanation, Tiernan couldn't bring himself to seriously entertain the possibility that Falters was telling the truth. His head instantaneously filled with conflicting thoughts as his gaze bounced from the vibrant canine to the newly-dead jellyfish, repeatedly. Life and death.

"I don't know what angle you're playing," said Tiernan, still alternating his attention from the dog to the tank, "but I congratulate you on putting on a damn good show."

"Dr. Tiernan," said Falters, "your world is about to change. I present to you your father's greatest accomplishment. Behold Dionysinol."

CHAPTER 8

VINCENT TIGHTE HAD met Lori Adams 10 years earlier at a convention in Iowa, where representatives from the EPA, USDA and the Farmers' Union, along with the vice-president of Lionel Pharmaceuticals, George Prendergast, had gathered for a weeklong retreat to discuss Lionel's new insect-resistant hybrid corn seed and its astonishing yields. Lionel Pharmaceuticals had funded the retreat, hoping to entice the Farmers' Union to endorse large-scale adoption of the miraculous seed.

Depending on one's perspective, 10 years can be a very short time or an agonizingly long time. For Lori, the event that had happened a decade ago was in the ever-present now – the perpetual now that was never far from her conscious mind. For Tighte, it was an event like many others, unworthy of long-term recollection and easily forgotten.

Upon checking in at the hotel, Lori learned that she and George Prendergast had been booked in the same room – one room, one king bed, one reason. George Prendergast had invited Lori Adams to the convention. He had exploited her dreams of one day having a career and enticed her with the networking opportunities at the convention. Lori had just completed her associate's degree at the local community college and was beginning to believe that she might make something of herself.

"Oh no, darlin', there must be some kinda mistake," said Lori. The clerk typed nervously as he searched for a vacancy.

"I'm sorry, Mrs. Prendergast," said the clerk, "but we're all booked up on account of the convention. There aren't any rooms available."

"My name is Miss Adams and, please, look again."

"Don't make a scene, sweetcakes," said Prendergast. "We'll make do." He pulled Lori by the arm to an area where he could speak freely. "Look, let's just make the best of it. There's no reason to get your knickers in a twist."

Lori was speechless, a rarity for the North Carolinian, and she be-rated herself for being so gullible. *How could I have been so stupid*, she thought. *He must think I'm just some kinda whore.*

"And, who knows," continued Prendergast, "you might like it. I haven't had any complaints from the other secretaries." He put his arm around the small of her back and pulled her in close as he whispered into her ear. "You play your cards right and I'll take you to Texas next month. There's a big conference there." He winked.

"You can take your conference and stick it up your narrow li'l ass, Mr. Prendergast," said Lori. Her voice echoed throughout the lobby. "Of all the sleazy, double-crossin' things I've heard about you, this has got to be the worst. And to think I defended you the other day in the break room."

"Shut your stupid mouth," Prendergast said. "We're representatives of Lionel Pharmaceuticals. Stop acting like a dumb hick."

Lori was devastated. She had truly thought that the vice-president had chosen her because he saw potential in her. Although Prendergast did see a form of potential, it wasn't her clerical skills. Lori pulled away from him and left the lobby. Standing among the other participants of the conference, she felt completely alone. With $19.13 in her fake leather purse, she had very few options. And then Vincent Tighte came along.

Tighte had approached the naïve country girl who had not yet per-fected the art of dressing sexy, yet modestly. Lori was self-conscious and spent most of the evening by the open bar where several whiskey sours with those *darlin' li'l uhm-brellas* helped her deal with the realization that she was nothing more than corporate chattel; George Prendergast hadn't really been impressed by her associate's degree.

Tighte, whose misogynistic tendencies exacerbated his sociopathic pathology, took advantage of the situation. He courted Lori with serpent-like stealth and, as those *darlin' li'l uhm-brellas* increased in number, her inhibitions disappeared.

Tighte was understanding, caring, reassuring and kind. He was appalled at the horrendous story, displaying all the right emotions at all the right times. Lori suspected nothing when Tighte offered to *pull some strings* and get her a room. She suspected nothing when he returned without having secured the room. But she swooned when Tighte offered to sleep in his car and abdicate his own room so that the lovely Miss Lori Adams could preserve her honor.

"Well," said the intoxicated Adams, slurring her words, "I must say, you have restored my faith in mankind. My momma used to say that God looks out for His children."

Alcohol permits one to overlook inconsistencies that sobriety would render suspicious and, if Lori had any doubts about Tighte's motives, a combination of the whiskey sours and Tighte's skillful performance banished them. Of course, being a hospitable, decent and Christian Southern woman, Lori insisted that they share the room. She would take the bed, and he, the couch.

That night, after social hour had ended, Lori and Tighte retired to their room. But, instead of preserving her honor, he introduced her to new and brutal forms of depravity, the likes of which had never entered the mind of the naïve Southern girl. She tried to resist, but, when it was obvious that she could not physically escape, she started to scream.

"Get your paws off a'me," said Lori. "Help me! Somebody, hel –"

A straight fist to the mouth followed by a vice-like grip silenced all except the gurgling desperation for air; only her eyes continued to scream and the surge of adrenaline sobered her instantly. Terror seized her when she locked eyes with him and saw an emptiness so profound that it changed her idea of Hell.

"Scream and I will cut your throat from ear to ear like the Southern pig-whore you are," hissed Tighte.

He raped her, but standard violation no longer satisfied him. He brutalized her with his fists, releasing all the repressed evil civilized society would not tolerate, the evil that lies dormant in all sociopaths. After the ordeal, she lay there bleeding, praying that her mother's sage wisdom was true and that God would smite the rapist down. But He didn't. That night, something in her broke, snapped and never recoiled.

"Go ahead, tell someone," said Tighte. "Who's going to believe a white trash whore like you, anyway?" Lori was careful not to make eye contact with him. "Shit, what do you think you were brought here for? Only difference is who got you, that's all. If you know what's good for you, you'll keep your stupid mouth shut. Now, get the hell out, you pig."

ॐ

Lorraine Adams arrived at Holy Name Hospital and walked into the emergency room. Blood and yesterday's makeup were caked around Lori's mouth and her left eye was swollen shut. She retained her composure until the desk nurse looked at her in horror, and then the previous evening's fear and rage burst forth. She began screaming and thrashing about, fighting off an assailant that only she could see. The hospital staff restrained her and the attending physician injected her with a hefty dose of Lorazepam.

Several hours later, when the police came to interview her, Lori claimed to have amnesia. The on-call psychiatrist explained that the amnesia was normal. It was the mind's way of protecting her, and he predicted that the memories would return gradually, in quantities she could handle. The results of the doctors' examinations revealed a half-dozen fractured ribs, two broken teeth and internal bleeding. They managed to retrieve biological samples and the police logged all materials into evidence. But they would never link the samples to Vincent Tighte.

George Prendergast arrived at the hospital under the direct orders of the president of Lionel Pharmaceuticals. Lori had no one else to call, so she dialed the company's president, Mr. Ryan Connor, who, in turn, called Prendergast. When Prendergast arrived, the two officers looked at him with suspicion.

"Did this man hurt you, Miss Adams?" asked the younger of the two officers. "Take a good look and take your time." She shook her head. Tears rolled down her bruised face and soaked the gauze that covered her freshly-stitched lip.

"No, that's Mr. Prendergast. He's the vice-president at my job," she said.

"We're gonna find whoever did this to you, Miss Adams. We gonna find 'em and fix 'em good, I promise."

Lori rose from her seat with great difficulty. Both officers assisted her and guided her out the door and into the car. The ride home was very uncomfortable for Prendergast, but Lori seemed only marginally conscious of external stimuli. She stared out the window of the limo, occasionally tracing letters on the fogged up glass. *Why?*

∞

When Prendergast returned to Lionel, Connor punched him in the mouth. "You think our assistants are here for your pleasure?" said Connor. "You sick, perverted imbecile!"

"I didn't do anything," said Prendergast through swollen lips. "I didn't mean —"

"You let this happen. Your stupid actions put the company in jeopardy. You're fired. Get out of my sight."

Lori and Connor grew close. Although the circumstances under which their friendship began were awful, Lori considered herself fortunate to have him. Connor insisted that Lori remain working at Lionel Pharmaceuticals and provided her with an education at the company's expense. Lori blossomed into one of the best investments Ryan Connor had ever made. She advanced quickly and, within a few years, became a senior executive. After that infamous night, though, Lori Adams was no longer looking for a career.

Vincent Tighte would never face the justice system for his crimes. According to Lori, the justice system was too civilized. Tighte's crimes merited a much more severe punishment, and his time was almost up.

49

CHAPTER 9

"BEHOLD DIONYSINOL, HUH? Looks like this guy isn't as excited about the product as you are," said Tiernan, knocking on the glass. "In fact, I think you killed it."

"Yes, it's definitely dead," said Falters. "I'm sure you must be hungry. We can continue this conversation over dinner."

Tiernan found himself following Falters again. They headed back through the rock tunnel and up the winding stone steps into the kitchen. As they made their way back, Tiernan wanted to interrogate Falters – to catch him in a lie – but reconsidered. Given enough time, Falters would slip up – Tiernan was sure of it.

As the two emerged from the subterranean caverns, a three-course meal was sitting on the table as if by magic. The hunger, bolstered by the smells, temporarily distracted Tiernan.

"Where did all this come from?"

"One of the locals has a son who has aspirations of becoming a chef in Rome. I pay him to provide me with two meals a day, except for Sundays," Falters replied. "The Italians, especially the Sardinians, consider food to be one of life's greatest pleasures. They take great measures to make each meal a delight."

Tiernan inhaled deeply as he placed the linen napkin on his lap and swallowed the deluge of saliva in his mouth. Falters sat across from him and reached for the pasta dish, serving himself first. After he scooped two generous helpings onto his plate, he spun the dish around. Tiernan picked up the spoon and landed a single, but hearty, spoonful onto his own plate. Falters had already ripped off a large piece of the unsliced bread and placed it on a napkin to the left of the pasta plate.

The meal was simple, but exquisite. Tiernan was no longer hungry, but continued to eat simply because it was impossible not to. Conversation was limited to comments about the region, food and wine during dinner, but the air was heavy with the unspoken. Tiernan pushed his plate toward the center of the table and refilled his wine. He lifted the glass to his nose. "Is this from the vineyards?"

"No," answered Falters. "The grapes at Tír na nÓg would make disgusting wine. They have a fishy flavor. I do not recommend tasting the Niamh grape."

"Yeah, well, can't expect them to do everything, now," Tiernan said.

"The high content of resveratrol and the jellyfish DNA pervert the natural taste of the grape," said Falters.

"What do the locals think we're doing with all these grapes?" Tiernan asked. "Surely, they must get curious."

"We told them that the grapes are used in a skin product sold in the United States," answered Falters. "It's a feasible story. Would you like a digestivi?"

"Sure. Whatcha got?"

"Several kinds of grappa," said Falters. "What do you say we sit on the porch and continue the discussion we were having in the lab?"

"Great," said Tiernan, "and while we're there, how about discussing the real reason I came all this way?"

"Dr. Tiernan, Dionysinol is the real reason you're here. Trust me."

"You see," smirked Tiernan, "that's just it. I don't trust you."

"You will."

The sun was low in the sky. Bronze rays poured forth, gently dappling the vines. The heat subsided a little and a cooling breeze made the evening pleasant. Falters handed Tiernan a generous serving of limoncello. They sipped the cool, strong drinks on the front porch where Venus de Milo stood ever-vigilant in the charge to beautify the entrance. The fountain was no longer spraying mist and the statue stood lifelessly in the center. A couple of birds splashed about in the base of the icon where a few inches of water escaped the evaporating power of the sun.

A thin, grey stream emanated from Falters' pipe and the red-hot embers glowed as he pulled another drag. A sweet, spicy scent filled the air as wisps of smoke lingered around the porch.

"I have another pipe if you wish to try this tobacco," said Falters. "It is from my hometown in Russia."

"No, thanks," said Tiernan. He stood up and put his hands on the wooden railing. The sun had now disappeared behind the hills, leaving a fiery summit of gold that seemed too perfect to be real. The vineyards, no longer myriads of distinct rows of genetically engineered fruit, became one dark mass covering the countryside. He was finding it difficult to resist the charms of the Sardinian landscape.

"Tell me," said Tiernan, slugging back the grappa, "and please don't take this as a sign that I believe a word you've said, but have you tested the drug on humans?"

"Before we had observed the violent effects it had on the hydrozoa, we had sufficient reason to infer that it was safe for humans," said Falters.

"And?" said Tiernan.

"And I was hasty, but lucky," said Falters. "The next person might end up like that jellyfish." The decomposing, gelatinous glob flashed into his mind.

"You? Oh, come on."

Falters nodded his head slowly. "It's true. I am the first. I am the newest version of our species."

"New species? That's rich," said Tiernan, holding the empty glass. "Human 2.0, huh? Tell me, are the original models obsolete now?" Tiernan laughed, expecting Falters to react in kind, but he wore the same stoic expression. Seeing that Falters wasn't amused, Tiernan redirected his approach. "You're full of fantastic claims, none of which, I might add, carry with it a shred of verifiable evidence. That's rather convenient, wouldn't you say?"

Falters didn't address the accusation and continued his thought. "I was intoxicated by the drug's potential. I was in my twilight years then, and anybody who had cared about me was long dead; I had nothing to lose. In retrospect, it was a stupid thing to do."

"Okay, I'll play along. How old were you? Or should I say, how old are you?" said Tiernan.

"I will have endured 90 years of life before you can boast 40," said Falters. "Wait here while I get a few things that may help you."

Falters got up and went into the house. When he returned a few minutes later, he presented Tiernan with a pile of photographs, a marriage certificate, newspaper clippings – anything he thought would help Tiernan wrap his head around the impossible. The pictures of Falters and Richard were especially convincing. "Keep in mind," said Falters, "that we didn't intend for you to find out about Dionysinol under such circumstances."

"Are you telling me that this is you?" asked Tiernan. He held a picture of the two men, one who he instantly recognized as his father.

"Yes," said Falters. "That was taken six days after I had taken the dose. We didn't know what to expect."

"This old guy is you?" asked Tiernan. "The resemblance is uncanny. But, how do I know that this guy isn't a relative of yours? Or, more likely, you altered the photo?"

"You don't have any reason to believe – not yet, anyway," answered Falters. "But, enjoy this time. It won't be long before doubt is no longer an option for you. Then, our real work will begin." He knew Tiernan's mind would rage against even the most convincing evidence, but whether Tiernan believed it or not, Falters was the first human successfully treated with Dionysinol. He had taken a moderate dose of the drug five years ago and had been growing younger since.

During the early stages of their research, Richard Tiernan and Ivan Falters had been sure that the Dionysinol would merely slow the aging process with the same efficacy that had been observed with caloric restriction, but without the agony inherent in eating the meager rations of food required in such diets. Despite their draconian requirements, these under-nourishing diets boasted a 30 percent increase in lifespan for virtually every species tested.

However, when Falters began to show signs of increased vitality, increased immune function and renewed elasticity of the skin around his face, they knew that they were witnessing something much more potent. Soon, Falters' appetite had increased and he developed an insatiable desire for sweets. He ate more, lost fat and gained muscle. He seemed to have boundless energy available for both mental and physical activities. Richard and Falters then theorized that the age reversal would follow the same pattern they observed in the jellyfish. It seemed logical that, after Falters' cells had reverted to the age of sexual maturity, they would begin aging again and repeat the cycle indefinitely. Up to that point, they had been wrong about everything.

After seeing the effects, Richard had considered taking a dose of the Dionysinol. However, prudence dictated that he should wait lest they both succumb to some unforeseen side effect that would put the project in jeopardy. He waited too long.

Tiernan began thinking about the implications if Falters' fantastic story were true. It would be the most profoundly tragic tale ever told. The creator of the miraculous elixir, Tiernan's own father, lay cold in the grave and would never benefit from the miraculous discovery. Yet, despite his doubts, all Tiernan could think about was the money he would earn if the drug were legitimate.

"I have this horrendous feeling that I am going to regret even entertaining this, but I'm willing to give you the benefit of the *extreme* doubt," said Tiernan. "I'd like to see another demonstration, only, this time, I'll pick the test subject."

"Certainly," said Falters. "I assume you would like to do it sooner rather than later, yes?"

"The sooner, the better," said Tiernan.

Falters emptied his pipe into a large flowerpot refashioned into an ashtray. "I'm getting tired. Perhaps I should retire for the evening," said Falters.

"Already? Really? I thought you were going to suggest that we go out and cruise the local hotties," said Tiernan. "This town's gotta have its share of fine ladies. We are in Italy, right?"

"Boroneddu is an ancient town with sensibilities you wouldn't understand," said Falters as he rose from his chair and stretched out his arms. "You would need to drive to Cagliari to find the sort of establishment you seek."

"Hey, maybe we should put Dionysinol into their water supply," said Tiernan jokingly. "What do you think?"

Falters didn't respond.

"The place is beautiful, don't get me wrong, but I would die of boredom here," said Tiernan.

"Self-denial builds character," said Falters. "Besides, you should rest. We have much to accomplish tomorrow."

"Yeah, you're probably right. Knock on my door when you wake up, okay?"

The door closed behind Falters and, seconds later, the porch light went out, leaving Tiernan in the dark.

Ignoramus, thought Tiernan. He knew that sleep would not come easily.

CHAPTER 10

THE PAGER BUZZED in the oversized pocket of Debra's lab coat and she knew another supply of Mimic cells were ready. Knowing that time was always against them, the two scientists had streamlined the procedure to make it as efficient as possible.

"The new batch is ready, John," said Debra, holding her pager. "That is the fastest time yet."

"Very good," said Graham, "but let's not rest on our laurels. We need to push ahead if we want to complete the tests before young Master Tiernan returns."

Debra stared pensively at her hands, marveling at the simplicity, the complexity of life. The life that science had afforded her was very gratifying, yet, at times, it stood in stark contrast to the conservative religious values that had been burned indelibly into her very being. Was it really in her purview to create life or was she destined to share the same fate as Icarus? Was she not defying the natural law? Wasn't the creation of life the exclusive domain of the *Causa Sui?* Was she reopening Pandora's box?

"Are you wrestling with God again?" said Graham who seemed to have unfettered access to her private thoughts, no matter how she tried to conceal them. "Surely, you can't believe that He would have endowed you with such an intellect if He hadn't intended you to use it."

"I don't know what I believe anymore," said Debra, "but I'm relatively certain that a breakthrough of this magnitude comes along once in an epoch. Regenerol will forever change the way medicine is practiced." She stared back down at her hands, opening and closing them, watching the fluid motions of the amazing design structure. "Imagine the possibilities," she continued. "We have a responsibility to the human race."

"Then why the hesitancy? It's only your DNA, and whatever we grow will have to be destroyed immediately afterwards," countered Graham. "I don't think God will miss a few drops of blood, do you?"

She smiled.

"You'll go down in history, my dear, as the first human to have an organ *mimicked*."

"You already have that distinction, John. The eye, remember?" she said.

"Oh, well, no one need ever know about that, my dear," he said, "and, besides, it was a dreadful-looking thing, wasn't it? We want to make our debut with a beautiful, healthy ovary, not some decrepit, cataract-ridden eye. Wouldn't you agree?"

Within the first few weeks of the Mimic cell's creation, Graham and Debra had successfully created several functioning organs. The eye was the only human tissue they managed to produce, but each successive win spurred them on to more ambitious endeavors. The most important test was yet to be conducted, and Debra Lewis was getting cold feet. If the Mimic cells couldn't faithfully grow a functional ovary, the Regenerol project would be set back two years. She was terrified that it wouldn't work and that she would have to see the disappointment on Michael Tiernan's face.

"Okay," said Debra, holding out her pointer finger. "Stick me."

"Now, this might sting a little, my dear, but if you're a good patient, I'll give you a lollipop. Hold still." Graham smiled as he swabbed her finger with the alcohol pad. Debra cringed in anticipation. "Hurry up, John."

"I have never seen a scientist so deathly afraid of needles," remarked Graham as he squeezed a sample of her blood onto the slide. "All done. Now that wasn't so bad, was it?"

"Where's my lollipop?"

"I'll tell you what," said Graham, "if we return to find a viable ovary, I'll buy you as many lollies as you want."

Debra grabbed his hand and held it tight. "It's going to work, I just know it."

"Of course it will, dear. Let's grow a human ovary, shall we?"

ରଃ

The next morning, Tiernan awoke at sunrise. Weak rays of light crept through unshaded windows and slowly reclaimed the room from night. He felt surprisingly refreshed, which was unusual for him, typically suffering from jet lag for days after traveling. He decided to go for a quick jog around the hamlet before the sun unleashed her full fury. Sardinia had brutal summers, and Tiernan happened to be in the middle of one of her hottest.

The Sardinian countryside was waking up, preparing for a long, hot day. The morning fog in the surrounding fields was burning off as the sun gained strength. Tiernan hadn't been running long before he noticed the strange stone structure in the adjacent field. The sturdy construction stood majestically, like a visitor from an earlier time. Tiernan climbed over the fence to get a better look at it. He jogged across the field toward the mysterious edifice.

The circular structure was built from laying thick square stones on top of one another, decreasing in size as they ascended, forming a cone-like truncated tower. From what Tiernan could observe, it didn't seem to have a foundation. *What the hell is this thing?* he thought. *Looks almost like an igloo made out of rocks.* To enter the structure, one would have to crawl through a small archway standing at about three feet. Tiernan was curious to see the inside, but decided that he couldn't afford to waste time sightseeing. He chose to head back. Falters was sitting on the porch when he arrived at the house.

"Good morning," said Falters.

Tiernan rested his hands on his knees as he bent over and gasped for air. "Morning," he managed between inhalations. "Gets hot pretty early."

"Would you like some coffee?" asked Falters.

"Yeah," said Tiernan, straightening up. "Is it espresso or American coffee?"

"Whichever you prefer," said Falters, who remained seated while gesturing to the house.

Tiernan walked past him and into the house, reemerging a half an hour later with a cup of coffee and a head of wet hair.

"Not a fan of the shower attachment, I see," remarked Tiernan as he took a seat. "Nothing like sitting in a lukewarm bath of your own sweat."

"Perhaps we should find a dog for our experiment," said Falters.

Tiernan blew into the cup. "Okay, but I'm picking the shelter. I don't want to leave any doubt as to the impartiality of the test subject, you know what I mean?"

"Yes," said Falters, "you want to reduce the chances of possibly choosing an animal I planted."

"Bingo," said Tiernan as he took a sip of the coffee before immediately spitting it out. "Ugh, that's disgusting. It tastes like it was filtered through a dead animal or something."

"Apparently," said Falters, "you chose the American coffee. That can has been here since I arrived six years ago."

◌

Graham and Debra arrived simultaneously at Oisín Pharmaceuticals that morning. As they rode the elevator, Debra concentrated on her breathing, slowing it down as much as possible. She appeared calm, effectively quelling the raging storm of emotions she held inside, but Graham knew how anxious she was. When they entered the lab, would they find a human ovary or a decomposing mass of undifferentiated cells?

"You go in," said Debra standing at the lab's locked door. "I can't."

"Oh, come now, dear," said Graham. "Can't you grace science with a modicum of the faith you lavish so generously on religion?"

"No, I don't think I can. And the day I do is the day that I become useless to science."

"Very well," said Graham, not wanting to upset her. "I'll go in alone."

Debra Lewis stood outside the door, biting what was left of her fingernails, for five minutes. Graham knew that her curiosity would overpower her fear. When she couldn't stand the suspense any longer, she opened the door. He was sitting down at the stainless steel table, gingerly cupping the beautiful sight in the palms of his hands.

"Dr. Lewis," said Graham, "I believe this belongs to you." The off-white, smooth tissue seemed to glisten in his hands. Even from where she stood, Debra could tell that they had succeeded.

"Come to Momma." She was smiling so intensely, her jaws began to hurt, but she couldn't stop.

After they had run a series of tests, Debra and Graham were satisfied that they had a viable ovary. The next logical step would have been to test the results against a human specimen, replacing a defective organ with a Mimicked version to see if the host body would accept the transplant. However, since they hadn't petitioned the FDA for permission to begin testing the drug on humans, they would have to settle for the next best thing. With Tiernan out of the country, the responsibility of obtaining an alternate specimen fell on Graham and Debra. Under normal conditions, this wouldn't have been a big deal, but Oisín rarely had any circumstances that could be considered normal.

"We do not have the time to go through the proper procedures," said Graham. "You know the ridiculous amount of bureaucratic nonsense we'll be up against – Galante will bypass all the red tape."

Debra was reluctant, but knew Graham was right. They couldn't afford to waste a moment. "Okay," she said. "I'll call him, but you have to stay right here while we speak. I get nervous even thinking about that guy."

Graham dialed the number and handed her the phone. "Hello? May I speak with Mr. Galante? This is Debra Lewis calling."

"Who?" said Jimmy Galante.

"Debra Lewis. I work for Oisín Pharmaceuticals and was asked to call you."

"Yeah, and what might you be looking for, angel cakes?" said Galante.

Debra blushed and felt her tongue stiffen. She had never had the experience of meeting Jimmy Galante in the flesh, but had heard enough about him to know that he should be avoided. She was extremely uncomfortable with the scenario, but would endure much worse if Michael Tiernan needed her to.

"I'm calling on behalf of Dr. Tiernan," said Debra. "He tells me that you're the best man for the job."

"Oh, yeah?" he answered suspiciously, "Well, that kinda depends on the job. Who's askin', anyway, Richard or Mikey boy?"

"Um, Mikey boy." She felt ridiculous referring to Tiernan with such a diminutive. "And, in case you hadn't heard, Richard Tiernan had a heart attack and died." *Oh, my God, I am such an idiot,* she thought.

"Nope, can't say I did. What can I do for you, toots?"

"Yes, um, thank you," said Debra, stumbling over her words. "I'm looking for a monkey."

On the other end of the phone, Galante enjoyed a laugh. He was no stranger to uncommon, even bizarre requests, but this was a first. "A monkey?"

"Yes, please," said Debra before she could stop herself. "I mean, I need a female capuchin, no older than six and no younger than four. Can I tell Dr. Tiernan that you will be able to fill his order?"

"You can tell Mikey boy that if he wants a cappuccino monkey, he'll get a cappuccino monkey." Galante laughed again. "I'll be in touch soon, sweetheart." The line went dead and Debra was left holding the receiver, talking to herself.

"A *capuchin,* not a cappuccino. Mr. Galante? I need a female capuchin."

John Graham took the receiver out of her hand and replaced it on the base. "Don't worry, he'll get it, dear, and thank you. I haven't seen nor heard from Jimmy Galante since the affair in Mexico, and I still can't quite bring myself to do it. I do hope you understand."

Debra gently put her arms around his troubled head, resting it on her shoulder. Although she didn't know the more graphic details surrounding the botched, and highly illegal, experiments in Mexico, it was obvious that they had profoundly affected Graham. She could never be certain what would trigger an episode, but she assumed that talking with Galante would be as likely to do so as anything else.

"I understand," she said, caressing his thick grey hair. "We will get through this, I promise." She didn't know whether her use of the collective 'we' offered any consolation to Graham, but she reasoned that if she were in his situation, just knowing that she was not alone would make all the difference in the world.

CS

Tiernan was well fed up with the heat as they approached the 150-kilometer mark in the base model Fiat. Falters sat in the passenger's seat, reading the map. "According to this," he said, "we should have seen the landmark by now. Perhaps we should turn around."

Even though he knew that Falters could have planted several dogs in any number of kennels throughout the island, it gave Tiernan a sense of control – he was going to choose the test subject even if it meant driving all day.

"Nah," said Tiernan, "we're not going back without a dog. Maybe you're not reading the map correctly. Let me see it."

"That won't be necessary. I see it coming up in the distance," said Falters, pointing. "Turn left at that farmhouse. The kennel should be about a kilometer and a half down that road."

"Thank God," said Tiernan. "They better have a bathroom and a soda machine or something."

"Of course they have a bathroom," said Falters.

The volunteers at the shelter were surprised when the strange men asked to see the oldest dogs they had. Luck seemed to be on their side; four dogs were to be destroyed the next morning and three of them were riddled with arthritis.

"That one," said Tiernan, pointing to a listless black and white dog sleeping in his cage. Flies buzzed unmolested around the mongrel's cloudy eyes and grizzled muzzle; it looked like a carcass. Only the rhythmic movement of its abdomen assured Tiernan that the dog was still alive.

"Are you sure, signore?" said the volunteer. "He won't last a week, I'm sure of it."

"I'm sure," said Tiernan. "And I'd like to buy the cage as well." He

63

removed a wad of American dollars to facilitate the transaction.

Both Falters and Tiernan carried the cage and placed it in the back seat. The volunteer stood waving as they drove off, two crisp $100 bills in his hand. "Come again," he shouted, smiling from ear to ear.

After driving a short distance from the shelter, Falters retrieved a vial of Dionysinol from his pocket. "Judging from its condition, we should give the drug to it immediately. It may not even survive the journey home."

Tiernan adjusted the rearview mirror. "Shit, is it dead already? Sure smells like it."

Falters examined the dog. "No, but let's not tempt fate. Pull over and feed this to it." He handed him the vial.

Breaking the wax seal, Tiernan popped the top off and carefully lifted the dog's head. "Don't bite me, dog," he said as he slowly poured the contents into its mouth.

"Go slower," said Falters, "you don't want to spill it."

"Relax, he's drinking it." After finishing the Dionysinol, the old dog laid its head back down and returned to sleep. "Nothing happened," remarked Tiernan.

"Give it time. Patience is a virtue," said Falters, handing Tiernan the map. "Take this in case you forget how to get back to Boroneddu." Following the dog's example, he slept for the remainder of the trip.

CB

When the little capuchin arrived at Oisín, it was unconscious, sprawled out spread-eagle at the bottom of a dirty cat carrier. Galante, nursing a bite wound, explained that the primate had fought so violently that they'd had to sedate it for transportation.

"Yeah," said Galante, "when he wakes up, you guys might wanna check the little bastard's arm – think I broke it getting him into the cage. He'll think twice before biting someone again."

"It's a female," said Debra who managed to conceal her horror. "And animals attack when they feel threatened."

"Tell Mikey boy I'll be in touch, okay, toots?"

Debra felt the room brighten as the door closed behind him. She turned her attention to the capuchin and hoped that the trauma wouldn't affect the outcome of the operation.

Hold on, Nala, she thought as she placed her hand over the monkey's abdomen. *You'll be good as new in a few hours.* She examined its arm. It was definitely fractured – probably the result of Galante hyperextending it. She knew that they should have postponed the surgery until they had treated the fracture, but Graham would never agree to it. She felt responsible for inadvertently contributing to the abuse of the innocent creature and hated herself for it, but couldn't allow her emotions to compromise the experiment. She proceeded to carefully mix the sterile shaving lotion in a stainless steel bowl and ran a straight razor under scalding water.

It wasn't the kind of guilt one associates with culpability – she understood the value inherent in animal testing – but, each time Debra Lewis cut into an otherwise healthy creature, she felt her soul wither. Conflicted by diametrically-opposed value systems, Debra vacillated between feelings of excitement and remorse as she tried to avoid looking down at the anesthetized capuchin strapped to the cold, steel table. She respectfully shaved the region of its stomach where a 15 blade would soon slice the animal open. When she finished, she dried the monkey and marked the spot with an X.

"Is it prepped?" Graham asked as he entered the room, sterilized hands held out in front of him. He glanced at the checklist before proceeding.

"*She* is ready," answered Debra. "The Mimicked ovary is viable. Let's just hope Nala survives the surgery. She had quite the experience getting here."

"Nala? You gave the monkey a name? You know that you should always maintain a healthy detachment from the test subjects."

"I do," said Debra.

"Then let's begin," said Graham.

She looked down at the little creature one last time before handing Graham the scalpel.

ः

"Nope, that's not happening," said Tiernan. "The dog stays with me – end of discussion. Now, help me carry this damn thing up to my room, would ya?" As they carried the cheap wire prison up the staircase, the dog whimpered in pain, still lying parallel to the cage's floor.

They put the cage down in the corner of Tiernan's room. "Hey, do you have a bowl so I can give him some water? He's probably dying of thirst."

"It's not dying, I assure you. But I can give you a bowl of water for it anyway."

Tiernan hunched down and peered into the dog's cage. Although it remained in a lying position, the dog lifted his head and met Tiernan's gaze before reclosing its eyes. Falters returned with a bowl of water and put it in the cage next to the sleeping dog.

"How long before we see something?"

"Not long, probably tomorrow or the next day," said Falters.

"Should we give it some more? Will that speed things up a bit? I really gotta get back to Oisín. We have some major things in the works and I need to be there."

"We've given it enough," he responded. "Have some patience." Falters walked out and closed the door behind him.

Tiernan decided to join the dog and take a short nap. He kicked off his shoes, stretched out on the bed and didn't wake up until Falters pounded on the door, announcing the arrival of the evening's meal.

"Man," said Tiernan, sitting down at the table, "I was in a coma. The heat really knocked the hell outta me."

"How's the dog?" asked Falters, pouring a generous helping of wine into a mug. "We should start seeing a few subtle changes anytime now. We've never been able to predict, with any consistency, when the de-aging process begins, but it won't be long."

"Good, I'm looking forward to it." Tiernan yawned unabashedly, offering no apology for the breach of etiquette. "After I eat, I'd like to read through some of the data from the earlier experiments. Can you get me the files?"

"Yes, I'll bring them to your room. I assume you'd like to read them in your room."

Tiernan smiled and continued eating. "I need to keep one of you in my sight at all times."

೮೪

After a few hours of reading through volumes of data, Tiernan was beginning to believe that his father may have discovered something monumental, but when he looked over at the sleeping dog, still old and decrepit, he reverted back to skepticism. He washed up and went to bed.

A few hours later, the smell woke him from a deep, jet lag-induced sleep. His head spun from the disorienting power of the odor, and he stumbled out of bed and over to the window. After a few violent tugs, he remembered that it was painted shut and couldn't be opened. He quickly opened the bedroom door and ran into the hallway, attempting to escape the foul smell that was so putrid, it was physically painful to inhale. It was only after taking a few breaths of fresh air that Tiernan learned of the smell's origin – the dog had soiled the cage. Peering into the room as he held his breath, he beheld the power of Dionysinol once again. A young and energetic dog looked back at him and began to whimper.

"Holy shit!" he said aloud. "I don't believe it." But he did believe it; he had no choice. He closed the door to his room, walked down the hallway and rapped on Falters' door with considerable force. "Hey, Falters," he shouted. "Get up. We need to talk."

"Is it the dog?" said Falters. "Dead?"

"Nope, but you can't tell from the smell. Meet me downstairs. I'll brew some coffee – it's gonna be a long night."

A few moments later, Falters walked downstairs and into the kitchen where Tiernan was pacing the floor. "Start from the beginning and tell me everything," said Tiernan. "And if you wouldn't mind repeating yourself, I'd appreciate it. Earlier, I wasn't giving the subject the attention it deserved."

67

CB

Tiernan listened intently as Falters once more related the sequence of events that had led to the discovery. "And that's how we learned about the aphrodisiac-like properties," said Falters, finishing an espresso. "Once a treated subject releases its scent in the air, other members of its species are powerless to resist." The two had been talking for hours. Falters recounted his experiences after he had first taken the Dionysinol.

"Powerless, really? Why?" Tiernan was intrigued.

"Without the benefit of a cerebral cortex, the animals have no choice. They are unable to reason and can only focus on one thing: the satisfaction of the appetites. This seems to be another consistent feature of Dionysinol. All animals treated with it are irresistible to other members of their species."

"And in humans?" said Tiernan.

"The effect is the same," said Falters, "but most homo sapiens have the ability to reason and, therefore, can resist. By the time I had started to experience the effects of Dionysinol, local women found excuses to come to Tír na nÓg, aggressively seeking me out. Although they didn't know why, they were attracted to me on a primal level. Richard had theorized that these women were somehow subconsciously aware that my genes were unique, desirable, better. I withdrew with great difficulty, putting the safety of the project before my carnal desires."

"Oh my God," Tiernan laughed. "This stuff just keeps getting better and better. So, tell me, why isn't there a line of fine young Italian women fighting for you? I'll take a few off your hands. It's been months since I had..."

"Because I have discipline," snapped Falters.

"Alright," he said, "we can get to that later and, trust me, we are definitely coming back to it. But, tell me, what would be the best way to transport samples of the Dionysinol back to our labs at Oisín? I'm going to need to take some of the drug back with me and have it analyzed in a real lab."

Falters immediately looked anxious. "I'm afraid that I cannot allow that. The Dionysinol must stay here, but feel free to use our lab to conduct any test you wish."

"Whoa, slow down, buddy," said Tiernan. "I don't think you understand. The Dionysinol is mine – I'll take it where I damn well please."

"Your father and I had a different arrangement. We agreed to never compromise on certain principles."

"I understand," said Tiernan, "but he's gone now and I'm in charge. You don't want to mistake me for my father. I'm not as patient as he was."

"You needn't worry about that, Dr. Tiernan," said Falters. "But I'm going to assume that you have some of his decency. I have more to fear of you than you do of me."

"I'm not gonna screw you out of your due, Falters. You'll get what you deserve. I'm not a scumbag. You don't understand, you see, I –"

"It's you who doesn't understand," said Falters, cutting him off abruptly. "I will not allow you to leave with the Dionysinol until we can control it."

Tiernan paused before responding. Pieces of seemingly unrelated information swirled around in his mind and organized themselves into a coherent, linear pattern. *No need to argue with this idiot,* he thought. *I already have samples of the Dionysinol back in the States. Keep him in the dark until he's expendable.*

"You're probably right," said Tiernan with the effectiveness of a seasoned manipulator. "I have a tendency toward mania." Then, looking down at his notepad, he asked his next question. "What's the dosing schedule? How often do you have to take it to maintain?"

"This is an area of concern," answered Falters. "The subject need only take one dose and the effects last a lifetime."

Tiernan didn't like the financial implications. "Definitely gotta fix that," he said as he jotted additional notes into his pad. "It'll be much more advantageous for us to manufacture a drug that one has to take forever. That's going to be one of our priorities. We'll put our best people on it. I'll get the money." But, from where, he didn't know.

CS

Tiernan walked away from the check-in counter, boarding pass in hand and sat down next to Falters who graciously offered to wait with him until he boarded.

"I was just thinking," said Tiernan. "Maybe we can find additional uses for it. I mean, think about it, a drug that affects the sex appeal of its users...I'm talking trillions!"

"Dr. Tiernan," interrupted Falters, "there is much to learn about Dionysinol. We have an obligation to fully understand the substance before we consider unleashing it onto a desperate humanity."

"Yeah, and we will! We will test the hell out of it. I am not looking to wind up in the middle of a class-action lawsuit. Don't worry, I know what I'm doing."

"Dionysinol has a property that, if discovered, might be the end of us."

"Well, we'll just have to make sure no one ever discovers it," said Tiernan, slapping Falters on the shoulder. "What is it, anyway?"

"As you now understand, Dionysinol extends the life of everything we tested, with the exception of the Turritopsis jellyfish," said Falters.

"Ah, don't worry about that," quipped Tiernan. "Jellyfish don't buy pharmaceuticals anyway."

"If Dionysinol were to fall into the wrong hands, the results could prove catastrophic. Dionysinol can easily be turned into a very effective and devastating weapon. Your father and I tested it once. When you return, I will show you the Brimstone file."

"Let's not get ahead of ourselves," said Tiernan, straining to hear the announcement over the antiquated system. "Let's perfect the anti-aging problems first, and then we can discuss other applications."

"They are calling your flight," said Falters. "I will run the tests we discussed. I'll have the results by the time you return."

"Okay, then," said Tiernan. "Thanks for everything. I'll be in touch." He shook Falters' hand and walked through the gate.

CHAPTER 11

HIGH ON THE promise of eternal youth and unlimited wealth and power, Tiernan glided through the airport. He boarded a direct flight from Rome to New York and settled into the plush, first-class seat. For the first half of the flight, he stared out the window, the cumulous and cerulean a canvas for his fantasies. He noticed a pleasant feeling emanating from his chest, and radiating down his arms and legs. He was unsure about the cause of the feeling until it dawned on him: he was feeling the sensation of true satisfaction.

After dinner, Tiernan took out the large binder that Falters had put together for him. Photocopies of his father's handwritten notes were organized chronologically. *The originals must be in that leather portfolio,* he thought. He made a commitment to himself to read the complete contents of the portfolio when he returned. He ordered another drink, flipped through the notes and started reading.

Although I'm faced with the data, I still can't believe it. The Niamh grape. What were the odds? A million to one? Our conservative estimates put it at more like a quadrillion to one, but it happened. Sarah used to buy those lottery tickets at the grocers and I remember teasing her about it. I would say, 'the odds of winning are a billion to one,' to which she would reply, 'yet, someone wins every week.' A game that gives a billion to one odds of winning has a winner every week. She taught me to ignore the dissuading power of odds. Probabilities – chance events – are, by their very nature, incomprehensible. The Niamh grape seed won the genetic lottery. We won the lottery.

Tiernan closed the heavy binder and reclined in the seat. *Why didn't he share this with me sooner?* he thought. *Not ready for the responsibility? I was responsible enough to run Oisín and provide him with the financial*

71

resources that made his discovery possible.

Tiernan's emotions assailed him, but the alcohol mitigated the pain. When he had managed to gain a foothold over his emotions, suspicion took over. *Falters could easily return to Russia and take the Dionysinol with him. I should never have left him there with everything.* By the time the plane touched down, Tiernan's head was teeming with incertitude. He retrieved his bags and walked through customs.

"Dr. Tiernan," a voice called out from the crowd. Tiernan looked around and kept going, but Lori caught up to him. "Well, aren't you the most adorable thing?" said the lady with a Southern accent. She offered Tiernan her hand. The bejeweled nails caught his eye.

"I'm Lori Adams and I've got the opportunity of a lifetime for you."

"Another opportunity of a lifetime? Wow, this must be my lucky week. I'm sorry, who are you?" asked Tiernan.

"I just told you, darlin', I'm Ms. Lori Adams," replied Lori in her drawl. "And you are Michael Tiernan.

"I'm sorry, but I don't remember you, Miss Adams," said Tiernan, smiling broadly as he remembered the real reason he crawled under the secretaries' desks. "Did you work for my father?"

"No, I can't say I did, but I knew of the great Richard Tiernan. I did my graduate thesis on his invention, the Sporacap technology. Your father was very helpful – let me interview him a bunch a'times. I'm so sorry for your loss."

"Thank you," said Tiernan. "What can I do for you?"

"I would like to talk to you about the Chimera corn your father created."

Tiernan figured that Lori Adams was either a reporter or connected to Lionel Pharmaceuticals. Very few people knew the name *Chimera corn*. When Lionel had purchased the patent, Lionel changed the name and buried all traces of the original. In either case, Tiernan wanted nothing to do with her.

"Miss Adams," said Tiernan, "I'm not interested."

"Please, sugar, call me Lori." She locked her arm around his. "And you haven't even heard what I have in mind."

"You're either a reporter, or worse, you work for Lionel Pharmaceuticals," said Tiernan. "Where's my driver? I have a feeling you might know." *southern*

Lori feigned shock at the accusation. "Who, me? Would I do such a thing?"

"I think you may have," said Tiernan, tapping his temple. "How long did it take you to convince him to leave me stranded?" He was impressed with her resourcefulness and imagined her charming his driver.

"I was sitting at the bar over there, mindin' my own business when an elderly gentleman bought me a drink. I was so surprised to learn that he was your driver that I just took it as a sign." Tiernan shook his head, but couldn't prevent the smile.

"You know he's in big trouble, don't you," said Tiernan. *son* "Drinking, womanizing and abandoning his boss at the airport, all in one day?"

"Aw, you ain't gonna do a thing to that sweet li'l man," said Lori. "Come on, I can give you a lift home."

Arriving at the limo, she smoothed her white skirt behind her before she slid onto the leather seats. Tiernan handed his bags to the driver and got in.

"You have about one hour before we arrive at my house," said Tiernan. "If I'm not interested by the time we get there, I'm not going to be interested. Understand?"

"Yes sir," said Lori as she removed a bottle of bourbon from the bar. "Would you like a li'l taste?" Tiernan nodded. Lori poured him a healthy portion and gestured toward an ice bucket.

"No ice. Ruins it."

"I agree. Cheers."

"Cheers."

Lori talked for most of the hour. She talked about her position at Lionel and her humble beginnings, and he found himself liking her. The limo arrived at the mansion and Tiernan was surprised the time had gone so fast.

"Alright, time's up." Tiernan was feeling the effects of jet lag and the bourbon. "And I still don't know what you're after."

"Now, why would you say it like that? Why do people always assume the worst?"

"Maybe because most people are rotten to the core. People are necessarily selfish and will invariably act in their own best interest." Stepping out of the limo, he noticed that the driveway was remarkably similar to the one in Sardinia – the same circular driveway with the same grassy nook in the center, minus the statue of Venus and the transgenic grapes. Excitement welled up in his chest again as he remembered the Dionysinol. Was he dreaming or did it really happen? Lori's voice brought him back.

"I agree with you, honey. People usually act in their own best interests, but can't a situation render mutually beneficial results?" she asked.

"Not usually and, if it does happen, it is most likely accidental. The vast majority of the time, someone gets screwed."

"Well, if anyone is going to get the better deal in our case, it'll be you, darlin'. Can you at least hear me out?"

"I listened to you for an hour already. I'm tired and jet-lagged. I just want to sleep." At this, the driver pulled away from the mansion, leaving Tiernan and Lori standing there. Tiernan knew it was a ploy, a prearranged contingency orchestrated by this very clever lady.

"Oh my," said Lori, putting her hand to her mouth. "He left me stranded here. Serves me right for renting by the hour, huh?"

"Yeah, right," said Tiernan. "You probably own the limo. You're a slick one, Mrs. Adams."

"It's *Ms.* Adams." Lori locked arms again as he dragged the suitcase with the abused wheels into the house.

"Whatever. I'm calling you a cab, lady."

"Okay, right after I get a li'l somethin' to quench my thirst. You wouldn't let me ride all the way back to the city without a li'l nightcap, would ya?"

Tiernan walked into the house and disarmed the alarm.

"Where's the ladies' room?" she asked, leaning over Tiernan's shoulder.

Tiernan pointed.

In the bathroom, Lori opened her purse and retrieved her .22-caliber. The Saturday night special was always fully loaded. She checked the barrel and spun the chamber before placing it back in her bag. She retrieved the small canister of chemical mace, concealed it with a band around her forearm and pulled her sleeves over it. She didn't think she would have to use either of them. Tiernan seemed like a gentleman, but she had made the mistake once before and would never make it again.

"I called you a cab, Ms. Adams," said Tiernan, handing her a nightcap. "It'll be here in about 10 minutes."

"Thank you. Mind if we sit until it arrives?"

The two sat at the dining room table. Tiernan wanted her out; he was understandably suspicious. Lori put her drink on the table and ran her hand over the finished wood. "This is beautiful," she commented. "Was it in the family long? It looks antique."

"My mother," said Tiernan, taking a sip of the bourbon before continuing. "It was in her family for generations. Came from the old country aboard the Queen Mary."

"Well, it is just an amazing piece," said Lori who lifted her glass off the wood and placed it on a coaster.

"Okay, let's get down to it. Why are you here?" asked Tiernan.

She pushed the untouched glass of bourbon to the side and placed her hands on the table. Her nails were reflected in the sheen of wood and triggered a moment of déjà vu in Tiernan. He had seen those hands before. Those unique nails were in his memory, but attached themselves to no specific event. It made him slightly uneasy.

"I need the prototype of the Chimera seed," she admitted. "Lionel screwed up royally when they messed with your father's idea, and now we are in a big mess."

"Delighted for them," chortled Tiernan. "You bastards deserve what you get." He felt a moment's regret for including Lori in that category, but continued without apology. "My father offered you people the prototype years ago and was blown off, ignorantly, I might add," he added. "And don't they have the original seeds anyway?"

"Unfortunately, the originals were lost," said Lori, "but, even if we did manage to find them, we couldn't reproduce them without his notes – really complicated stuff." Lori ran her nail around the edge of the glass, still untouched. "Legally, we are entitled to the prototype," she continued, "but we can't afford to get mixed up in a high-profile legal battle. I think we both know that it's only a matter of time before someone proves that Lionel's version of the transgenic corn seed is causing the various *eco-screw-ups* we're experiencing. I don't even want to think about what we'll do if that happens."

Lori looked over Tiernan's shoulder at the headlights that pulled into the driveway. "We are willing to *buy* the prototype – the prototype that we are legally entitled to – for $10 million. Be reasonable, Dr. Tiernan, we will get it in the end."

"Yeah, you probably will, but not without a lot of negative press, and that'll cost you way more." He opened the door and Lori walked past him. "The publicity will ruin you; you won't risk a lawsuit."

"Does that mean you won't sell?"

"No. That means your offer is too low."

"One-hundred million dollars. Ryan Connor has authorized me to offer you $100 million for a damn disk containing the procedure that we own anyway. You gotta be crazy not to take it!"

Tiernan smiled at her as she got into the cab. He respected her cutting right to the upper limit of Lionel's willingness to avoid the hassle. She rolled down the window and blew a kiss as the car pulled away. Tiernan wasn't back in the United States three hours before the money presented itself. He took it as a sign. *This is only the beginning. I am going to be the richest man on Earth.*

☙

"You asked to see me, sir?" said Graham as he stood at the threshold of the door to Tiernan's office.

"Yes, John. Come in. Have a seat. I just finished reading the reports. Looks like you guys really made a lot of progress."

"Yes, but all the credit goes to Dr. Lewis, I'm afraid," said Graham with the usual modesty. "The ovary transplant was a success; the monkey is recovering well."

"That's good to hear. Tell me, how long before we can impregnate it?"

"Well," said Graham, "I would like to wait until the fracture heals, but we could possibly do it sooner if you wish."

"No, we can wait," said Tiernan, "but, in the meantime, I'd like to ask you a favor."

"How may I be of service?"

Tiernan reached into the inside pocket of his Armani suit and retrieved a vial of Dionysinol. "I want to know everything there is to know about this stuff," said Tiernan. "And let's keep this between us."

"Very well, sir," said Graham. "I assume you'd like a full chemical analysis?"

"The works."

"It would help tremendously if there were any background information available."

"Make do without it," said Tiernan. "This is a priority, so put a temporary hold on everything else – the things that can't wait, kick down to Debra."

"As you wish. Is there anything else?"

"No. Thank you, John. My father was lucky to have such a good friend. He trusted and respected you."

"Those feelings were mutual. I miss him a great deal; the world's a cold and lonely place without friends."

"I'm sure it is." Tiernan was a little apprehensive handing over the vial. John Graham had been with Oisín Pharmaceuticals from the beginning, and he and Richard Tiernan had been very good friends. Surely, Michael Tiernan could trust him. But the nagging anxiety resurfaced. *Why didn't my father tell him? If Graham was so trustworthy, why didn't my father bring him in on his discovery?* He shook it off and handed Graham the vial. "That's all, John. Thanks."

"Eileen," said Tiernan, pressing the intercom.

"Yes?"

"Get Timothy Lynch on the phone."

Lawyer

CR

Tiernan informed Lynch that he had decided to keep the property. Since he wasn't certain how he was going to fund both the Regenerol and the Dionysinol projects, Lori Adams' proposal was looking very attractive. Nevertheless, the Regenerol project was still Oisín's first priority and he couldn't allow himself the luxury of distraction.

Tiernan reorganized the research and development staff into two groups, creating a new laboratory for the new team. Dr. John Graham headed up the old team and Dr. Debra Lewis was promoted to head up the new one. He didn't try to hide his motive for splitting the team. He was very forthright with Graham and Debra, advising them about the need to compartmentalize the information, limiting those with access to the entire enterprise. Only Tiernan, Graham and Debra knew how all the pieces of the puzzle fit together.

Regenerol was in perpetual danger of sabotage and nobody was above suspicion; Tiernan needed to create new security measures and cultivate a cautious, if not paranoid, disposition. Oisín was attempting to smash the thick glass ceiling strewn with the corpses of those who had tried and failed. Dionysinol would have to wait, but not for long. Regenerol was in its final stages, and soon Oisín would file the IND application with the FDA so the human trials could begin – legally, this time.

CHAPTER 12

HER MORNING ROUTINE took the better part of two hours. She had brewed the coffee extra strong this morning. Last night's bourbon had hit her harder than usual. Adhering to her doctor's advice, she decided to cut down on the amount of unhealthy choices comprising her usual breakfast and fried only three pieces of bacon with two eggs. She skipped the butter and ate the toast dry.

Sacrifices, life is all about sacrifices, she thought as she washed the toast down with cream- and sugar-laden coffee. Despite eating a diet consisting primarily of foods that kill, Lori wasn't in bad shape. Age was beginning to mark its territory and gravity pulled at various undesirable places, but it had not been overly cruel. She was in her late-30s and didn't try to hide it. The makeup and stylish clothing weren't attempts to conceal a battered self-esteem; they were rewards for surviving.

Lori greeted her driver in her usual way – a kiss on the cheek – and handed him a cup of her famous coffee. "I made it a little stronger this morning, Edward, so watch out," she said as she stepped into the car. Edward closed the door behind her and took a sip.

"Whoa, that'd keep you awake for three days after you died!" he joked. "I don't taste the chicory. Did you put any in?"

"No more chicory for us, darlin'," said Lori. "Mr. Connor told me that it's toxic. Damages the retina or somethin'."

"Really," said the driver. "Oh, that's too bad."

The ride from Lori's apartment to Lionel's headquarters took about 15 minutes if traffic was merciful; otherwise, it could take upwards of an hour.

"How's the traffic?" asked Lori from the back seat. "Do I have time to get into my stories?" Lori loved her soap operas but was never free while they aired. Edward recorded the shows for her and left them in the DVD player in the limo. DRIVER

"No," Edward said. "The traffic is light, so we'll be there in a jiffy. Save 'em for the ride home."

"All right, darlin'," she said. "I'll just catch up on the news."

Lori arrived at Lionel and walked straight into Ryan Connor's office. She greeted everyone as she passed, with *G'mornin' sweetness* or *Well, don't you look pretty today?* or the more common *Mornin', sunshine.* Connor sat at his desk typing an e-mail. Promising to be with her in a second, he greeted Lori without looking away from the screen. If anyone else barged into Mr. Connor's office without an appointment, there would be some rather unpleasant consequences. Lori Adams had immunity, but no one knew why. It became common knowledge that Lori Adams was untouchable and enjoyed a privileged relationship with the president of Lionel Pharmaceuticals. Oddly, her esteemed status evoked no ill will from the underlings. Instead, people sought Lori's intercession, intervention or advice, knowing that her influence at Lionel Pharmaceuticals was unparalleled. Whatever Lori asked of Ryan Connor, it was granted.

"So," Connor said as he turned off the computer monitor. "Did he go for it?"

"He didn't say no, but I don't think this boy is motivated by money," responded Lori. "Richard Tiernan won't be dead so long as that boy lives."

Connor's secretary knocked before rolling in a cart on which sat a silver coffee pot next to three varieties of biscuits.

"Well, g'mornin', Frances," said Lori. "You smell nice. What's that you're wearing?"

"Oh, isn't it great? It's called Autumn's Breeze. My friend and I –"

"That's all, Frances. Close the door on your way out," interrupted Connor.

"I'll get the details on your break, honey. I'll stop by and see you," said Lori, winking. She got up and started fixing the coffee.

"Like I said, I think he's looking to vindicate his father's memory," said Lori. "I told you about being kind to people. You never know when you'll need a favor." Lori handed him a cup of coffee and sat down. Connor took the coffee and nodded a thank-you.

"Whenever someone acts like it's not about the money, you can assume that money is the most important component. My guess is that he's bluffing. I doubt he's that much of an idiot to pass this up."

"I don't know, honey," said Lori. "But I think you may be getting ahead of yourself."

"What do you have in mind?"

"Do you see me concerned?" asked Lori as she sipped her coffee. "No, you don't, and do you know why?"

"Enlighten me," said Connor.

"Because I'm gonna steal it back from him," she chuckled. "Heck, it's ours anyways!"

"How do you propose to do that?" he asked, careful not to sound doubtful of her convictions.

"1, 24, 43, 12," she said. "Or 1244312, that's how." She took another sip and put the coffee down. The doctor had also admonished her for her junkie-like addiction to the bean.

"And what, may I ask, is that?" said Connor removing his glasses.

"The alarm code for his house, of course," she said. "There's bound to be somethin' in that mansion more valuable to him than that li'l ol' seed formula."

"Have I ever told you how priceless you are?" said Connor as he rounded the desk to sit next to Lori. He took her hands in his and kissed them.

"I know, darlin', I know," she said. "Now, let me get to work. I just have to know where Frances got that perfume."

Connor scribbled an additional note on his calendar: *Send Frances out to buy Lori a case of that perfume.*

CHAPTER 13

Son / Secretary / scientist

"DR. TIERNAN," SHOUTED Eileen. "Dr. Graham is here to see you."

"Show him in," answered a startled Tiernan, "and, please, stop screaming into the intercom. I can hear you fine."

Graham entered the office and closed the door behind him. "Might I have a moment?"

"Sure, what's on your mind?"

"Well, I'm not quite sure," admitted Graham. "I ran some preliminary tests on that substance."

"And?"

Graham sat down without an invitation – a first for him. "I don't quite know how to put this," he said, "but I guess I'll start with something I suspect you already know."

"Which is?"

"It's unlike any substance I've ever seen. Where did you get it?"

"I'm not at liberty to say," said Tiernan, averting Graham's eyes. "What have you discovered?"

"I'm almost embarrassed to say this," confessed Graham. "If I hadn't run the tests multiple times, I wouldn't believe it."

"John, I'm getting impatient and I have an unbelievably busy day. Give me the report."

Graham reluctantly handed him the folder, which Tiernan promptly opened.

"The substance is alive," said Graham.

"Alive? Explain to me how a liquid can be alive."

"I can't, but that is an exceptionally intriguing question, one to which I would love to know the answer myself."

"Is that it?"

"Eh, no, sir. Before I began the tests, I separated the liquid into three containers. After the tests were concluded, I returned the liquid to a single vial."

"So?"

"Here is where it gets interesting," said Graham. "The separated liquid became, how shall I say this –"

"Just say it."

"When I poured the individual vials into a common container, it attacked itself."

"What the hell are you talking about?"

"To answer that question honestly, I don't know. But it seems to me that when the liquid is separated and then combined again, it is rendered inert."

Tiernan opened his desk drawer, took out a sealed manila folder and threw it on the desk in front of Graham. "Run these tests, too, but keep the liquid in one container this time," said Tiernan. "Get the animal specimens from our usual sources and, remember, proceed with utmost discretion." Tiernan looked very serious.

Graham nodded in understanding as Tiernan handed him another vial.

"Eileen," said Tiernan into the intercom, "get me Debra Lewis. I want an update on the monkey's arm." Before he could remind her about her excessive volume, a thundering reply bellowed from the speaker.

"Right away!"

I gotta get rid of one of them, the new intercom system or the secretary, thought Tiernan as he massaged his ear.

CHAPTER 14

Tighte's Spy

MARY MCKENNA TOOK the commuter train home. She turned the laptop slightly to skew a fellow passenger's view of her screen. The man realized he must have been staring and compensated by turning his body away, hoping the attractive lady understood that he was apologizing in *subway* and didn't think he was ignorant. Her beauty had that effect on men.

Mary searched for a folder labeled *Résumés*. It had been quite a while since she needed it and hoped that she hadn't transferred the large file to an external hard drive for safekeeping. After a few minutes, she found it. She perused the contents, cutting and pasting a preliminary document from several résumés to create the perfect one. She needed to submit the right résumé with the right credentials without looking suspicious. If she were too qualified, she wouldn't be seeking employment at Oisín. If she were under-qualified, she wouldn't get the job. It was a fragile balance.

France, she thought, *the University of Paris, earned a degree in pharmacology and emigrated to the U.S.A. to fulfill my lifelong dream of working in New York City.* Mary began practicing her accent in her mind. The French accent was very easy for her to imitate and it always carried with it a certain erotic undertone.

She flipped open her cell phone and hit a series of three keys. *Calling Vincent Tighte* appeared across the screen. She held the phone to her ear and turned her body toward the window. The train had emerged from underground, indicating to Mary that she was halfway home. She looked out at the city as it flashed by and marveled at her species' ingenuity. She was about to entertain a philosophical thought about existence and the cessation thereof when Vincent Tighte's voice sounded in her ear.

"Yeah, you got something?" he asked. Mary despised him with every fiber of her being. Often before interacting with Tighte, Mary found it necessary to prepare herself mentally. She had forgotten to do it this time and she probably should have.

"No, I don't got something," said Mary before she could stop herself. "I need a French passport and transcripts from the University of Paris."

"Tall order. By when?" Tighte asked.

"ASAP, of course," she said. "I'm interviewing at Oisín tomorrow with someone named Debra Lewis. She sounds like a real tight-ass, so I need my ducks in order."

"I'll make a few calls," said Tighte before hanging up.

"Good-bye to you, too," said Mary to a dead line. "I hope you die in your sleep."

☃

Scientist
Debra Lewis arrived at work earlier than usual. She had never felt more alive in her entire life – heading up her own team felt good. Along with the pay increase and title came longer hours and more responsibilities. She missed working with Graham but knew that this was a great opportunity to make a major contribution to the field. The increased interaction with Michael Tiernan didn't hurt either. She was hopelessly attracted to him, every interaction deepening an abyss of infatuation that already seemed infinite. *There must be a scientific explanation for this phenomenon,* she thought. *Perhaps it has to do with breeding.*

Her thoughts would wander from the realm of science and she would imagine herself the mother of Tiernan's children. *Mostly Irish, with the hint of Greek. They would be so beautiful,* she would think before forcing herself to return to her work.

Debra Lewis' mother, Irena Liulakis, came to America from the Island of Hydra when she was 16 years old. Her family left their homeland when Greek relatives who had immigrated to the new land years before enjoyed enormous success in the restaurant business and offered

86

them the opportunity to invest in another diner. Irena's father loved his homeland but wanted more than his beloved Greece could offer his children, so to America he went with hopes and dreams of a better future for his kids.

Irena Liulakis met Damien Lewis, a mixed-breed Bronx boy whose good looks and city charm were more than she could resist. They were married despite objections from Irena's family whose xenophobia was overt and unapologetic. Inebriated by the potency of teen love, the star-struck couple believed love would see them through anything the world could throw their way; they were in love and unafraid.

Damien put himself through college and studied criminal justice while working full-time at the family restaurant. He joined the police force and climbed the ranks quickly and easily. Years passed before Irena's father was forced to admit that he had harshly judged Damien, and gave the marriage his full and unconditional blessing.

"Good morning, Marc," Debra said as she greeted the newly-hired night watchman. "Uneventful night, I assume."

"Yes, Dr. Lewis," he responded. "Everything is as you left it seven hours ago." Debra didn't appreciate the reminder of her tendency toward workaholism but responded pleasantly. "Okay then, off you go."

"Have a great day, Dr. Lewis, and don't work too hard," he said more out of habit than in reference to Debra's particular situation.

"Oh, don't worry, I'm hardly working," responded Debra who forgot how the played-out retort went. She always messed up the punch lines. She headed to her office and rearranged it several times before settling things back to their original order. She would interview her eighth candidate for the open position on her team today, and felt oddly self-conscious about the whole thing. She could not find anyone who filled all of Tiernan's requirements. Tiernan was looking for someone who appeared confident yet approachable; strong yet understanding; intelligent yet open to learn from anyone. When she realized that rearranging her furniture would probably have no effect on the candidate's qualifications, she stopped trying and decided to get some coffee instead.

 CB

SPY

Mary McKenna walked into the building and straight to the reception desk. "On which floor might I find Dr. Debra Lewis of Oisín Pharmaceuticals?" Her French accent was flawless.

The underpaid desk jockey pointed to the cabinet hanging on the wall that contained floor numbers followed by incomprehensible codes. Mary was glad she was not really seeking information from the man at the reception desk, such was his level of concern.

"Merci," she said as she summoned the elevator. Mary stepped in and pressed 17 on the control panel.

CB

"Yes, hello, I have an appointment with Dr. Lewis," said Mary. "I am a little early." Before the secretary could answer, Debra Lewis, who was waiting anxiously for her arrival, leaned out of her office. "Marie Delacroix, I presume."

"Yes, I am Marie Delacroix, but I prefer to be called Mary, if you don't mind."

"Of course," said Debra. "Please come in. Did you find us alright?"

Mary was amazing – her accent, her demeanor, everything about her screamed foreigner. "It is a difficult city to traverse. I am still getting habituated to your subway system. I find it very complicated."

"We are all getting used to it," said Debra. "Please have a seat. May I offer you some coffee, tea or water?"

The interview lasted about 45 minutes and Debra was so excited that she asked if Mary Delacroix would mind interviewing with Dr. Tiernan that morning. Had Debra not been so preoccupied with pleasing Tiernan, she would have dismissed this candidate the instant she saw her. Mary Delacroix was the type of woman Tiernan dated, but, unlike the usual bimbos that were graced with her beauty, Mary also had intelligence.

"Dr. Tiernan, I mean, Michael," said Debra after lightly knocking on the door to his office. "I have someone I think you'd like to meet." She escorted Mary Delacroix into Tiernan's office. Only after Dr. Debra Lewis had walked out did she consider that she may have made a mistake – but it was too late. An hour later, Mary Delacroix was in the Human Resource department setting up a health plan. She would start Monday.

03

Mary took a cab home from Oisín, compliments of Dr. Tiernan. The interview went more smoothly than she had anticipated. She walked into her apartment, hung the keys by the door and headed into the kitchen. She filled an old-fashioned black kettle with tap water and put it on the stove to boil. Her kitchen was a small but quaint design, large by New York City standards. She walked into her living room while she waited for the water to boil. She dialed Tighte's cell number and removed her earring.

"How'd it go?" asked Tighte. "Everything work out?"

"Perfectly," Mary said. "I start on Monday." Mary put the earring on the coffee table and sat down.

"They didn't ask for my transcripts, but I'm sure they will. Do you have an ETA on the documents?"

"Marie Bernadette Delacroix. <u>DOB:</u> 1975 Sceaux, France. <u>Citizenship</u>: French National. <u>Status</u>: Legal Resident," answered Tighte, sounding very proud of his accomplishment. "I can have the college transcripts by Friday of next week, so you'll have to stall them if they ask. Tell them that you were waiting to see if they wanted them sent directly from the university or if a sealed copy would do."

"No problem," said Mary. "I didn't expect to get hired so quickly, so I'll need to study this weekend. It's been quite a while since I've gone undercover as a scientist."

"Well, get on it. That's what you get paid for," answered Tighte. "Call you on Sunday night with a meeting time. I want to deliver the documents myself."

"Fine. See you then," said Mary before snapping the flip-top cell phone closed. The kettle was boiling in the kitchen. She took a cup out of the cupboard, dropped two tea bags into it and poured the steaming liquid over them.

God, I hate that filthy animal, she thought. Mary dunked the tea bags to strengthen the brew. *I deserve a little treat for my brilliant performance.* She retrieved a box of sugar cubes from the cupboard and dropped two little lumps into her large cup. *Two lumps,* she thought, *I earned two lumps.* She removed the tea bags and threw them in the sink.

Mary retired to the living room where she would spend the better part of the weekend studying the policy and procedure manuals for Oisín's Research and Development staff. She took the large three-ringed binder labeled *P and P* and a small black folder labeled *Regenerol* and placed it on the couch next to her.

Regenerol, she thought, *sounds like a shampoo or something.* She skimmed through the black folder. It gave general information about Regenerol – its history and Oisín's projected timeline for its debut. The second section of the folder outlined her job description. From what she gathered, none of the team members had complete access to the files on Regenerol. *Clever boy,* she thought as she noticed that Tiernan had split the staff into teams, allowing no one-person access to every-thing. She sipped her tea and smiled when the sugary brew passed her lips. *Don't get friendly with the sugar, McKenna,* she thought. *You don't want to end up looking like your father did.*

Declan McKenna and Charlene Washington were married two weeks after meeting at the Blarney Stone, a bar in New York City. Their story gives pause to even the most skeptical when debating if there is such a thing as *fate.* Full-blooded Irish, brogue and all, Declan was stocky and short and not the most attractive specimen Ireland sent to the new land. Charlene Washington was tall, dark and slender. Her friends would describe her as *not unattractive,* but that is seldom a sell-ing point for blind date candidates. It is the description reserved for those who conform less to the traditional idea of beauty. Her unwilling-ness to straighten her hair, to apply makeup, to dress sexier, kept her single for most of her adult life.

Declan had never seen a woman more beautiful and Charlene had never laughed as hard with anyone else. Their attraction was strong enough to withstand the objections they faced from family and friends.

The Irish side was more incredulous than anything; Irish people just did not marry blacks, plain and simple. It wasn't prejudicial; the Irish weren't exposed to many blacks in Ireland. Many were genuinely curious to see what type of children resulted from such a union.

The black side was suspicious of the immigrant's possible motives. Green card or citizenship were the most likely incentives – anything but true love. Declan was a bartender and a high school dropout, facts that only made their suspicion worse.

Charlene was never happier and Declan was enamored of her. Their first and only child, Mary, was born nine months after their wedding, which also provided fodder for the rumor mills. Nevertheless, their marriage stood the test of time, lasting longer than those of most of their critics. Declan eventually bought his own bar, but still needed to work 12-hour days to make ends meet. Charlene worked as a secretary for a law firm and never seemed to find the right time to go back to school and finish her degree. Mary was the apple of her father's eye and the delight of her mother.

At a very early age, Mary demonstrated the characteristics of an intellectually-gifted child, characteristics that went into remission for lack of a proper school. She would often get into trouble in school for her mischievous deeds and practical jokes, which were dealt with harshly in Catholic school. Contrary to what most of the nuns thought, she was not a bad child. She was just bored and earned Cs in most of her classes because she just did not care. Mary continued this pattern in high school where most of her classes were geared toward those who would provide blue-collar services for society. The boys were crazy for her and many a fight broke out among those vying for her attention. She used her striking appearance to her advantage and learned that she had a built-in weapon that worked on both men and women.

The week before she graduated from St. Raymond High School in Yonkers, NY, the principal called Mary down to her office. Sister Claire sat at her desk in full habit, determined to remain a living sign of fidelity for those sisters who had *kicked the habit* and wore lay clothes. The traditional garb made her look angry and Sister Claire didn't need any help in that department.

"Sit down, Mary," said Sister Claire.

Mary learned not to speak before hearing what they *had on her* first. She mentally reviewed the week's events and noted three possibilities for the summons. If she remained calm, she would get away with whatever the nun had on her; after years of trial and error, she was quite an accomplished liar. Sister Claire pushed a box of tissues toward Mary as she took a seat.

"I'm afraid I am the bearer of bad news," she continued. "The police called a few minutes ago." Mary's stomach churned a bucket's worth of acid, but she remained calm. The criminal mischief she was recently involved with replayed in her head. The nun spoke and, with her next sentence, changed Mary's life forever.

"Your mother and father were in a car accident on the Cross Bronx Expressway. Jesus has taken them home, Mary. Father Oxley is at the morgue now."

Mary McKenna sipped the last of her tea and savored the sweeter portion at the bottom of the cup. She swallowed hard to combat the lump in her throat that formed every time she remembered her parents.

Mary Delacroix, she thought, *I am Mary Delacroix until I secure the files on the prototype corn.* She picked up the three-ringed binder containing the policy and procedure for Oisín and began her long weekend.

Friday night bled into Saturday morning, and Mary awoke to find she had nodded off to sleep under an avalanche of paper. After a quick shower and a breakfast of plain wheat toast and black tea, she dove back onto the couch and immersed herself in all that was Oisín.

When Sunday rolled around, she almost welcomed the break until she remembered the purpose: to obtain documents from Tighte. She put her disheveled hair under a baseball cap, pulled a light sweatshirt over her T-shirt and headed out to meet him. Even in exercise attire, she looked like a model. She tightened the string of the sweatpants and made a mental note to eat soon. The dry toast and black tea had long been metabolized.

After a quick bus ride and a few blocks' jog, Mary walked a leisurely cool-down walk to their rendezvous point. Tighte was sitting down in the outside cafe in Little Italy, sipping a cappuccino. He lifted his hand when he saw Mary. She didn't need any help; she'd had a lock on him long before he'd noticed her.

"Over here," he said. "Sit. Have a coffee."

"Tea," she said. "I never drink coffee, remember?"

He didn't remember, nor did he care. A waiter came to the table and Mary asked for a cup of hot tea.

"I got you everything except for the transcripts. We need a little more time on those, so stall 'em," Tighte said. "I'm heading back to D.C. tonight."

Mary took the envelope from Tighte and placed it on the table. "That was fast," she said more out of concern about the quality than the expedience of Tighte's work. "Have you inspected the workmanship?"

Tighte slugged back the cold and frothless remains of the cappuccino and wiped his mouth with the back of his hand. "McKenna," he said. "You're not undercover in a mob ring or anything. Relax!"

"I know the assignment, Vincent," she said. "But underestimating your rival is an amateur mistake; I don't leave room for error."

"Don't worry, I checked the documents. They're fine."

"Okay," said Mary, realizing that she didn't want to engage in any more conversation than necessary. "Did you deposit the fee into my account?" She knew he had not because she had checked before leaving her house.

"Not yet, but don't worry. Have I ever stiffed you?" he said.

The very fact that he was sitting upright and still possessed the ability to eat solid foods was evidence enough that he hadn't, but that didn't imply that he wouldn't.

"No, Vincent, you haven't," she said and removed the tea bag from the cup and lifted her hand to summon the waiter. The waiter came promptly and Mary asked for two biscotti, recalling her mental note to eat something before she passed out.

"But, speaking of money, that reminds me," he said. "The EPA auditing department flagged your 'internship' and sent me a request for clarification. Do you remember how we justified your job?"

"Yes," said Mary. "I don't have a job, so I don't draw a salary; I'm a special assistant doing an internship to gather research for my doctorate."

Tighte blushed, cleared his throat and looked very guilty. The average observer would not have noticed, but there was nothing average about Mary. "Oh, okay," he said. "They must've screwed up again."

But they hadn't screwed up. He put in for a salary for Mary and used her information to set up a joint account where he siphoned the cash into a numbered account and deposited all his ill-got booty. Mary was no fool but didn't care. This was just an example of the greed that consumed Tighte – greed that Mary was certain would be the end of him eventually.

"Vincent, don't forget about the 700k bonus," Mary said.

"Was it 700k?" he asked. Mary didn't dignify the question with a direct response, knowing that he remembered the amount perfectly well.

"I want that bonus wired in the same transaction as my fee," Mary said in a tone that commanded attention. "I'm done after this. I'm out forever."

"Yeah, okay, sure you are," Tighte said, sniggering rudely. "You'll leave this life when you're dead, McKenna."

"I'm serious. I'm out," she said. "This is the last job for me, so believe it. I want that cash wired before you get anything."

Tighte looked at her, considering the effects of all possible responses to her ultimatum. He thought it best to placate her and nodded quickly. "Fine," he said. "But if you try to screw me, McKenna, you'll pray for death by the time I'm finished with you. Once I verify that you've secured the prototype, I'll wire the entire amount." He pushed his chair back from the table and stood up. "But if that bitch Lori Adams gets it first, I wouldn't want to be in your shoes."

Tighte walked away from Mary McKenna, leaving her stuck with the unpaid bill. A smile crept onto her face. It wasn't the visible sign of happiness that one associates with such an expression. The smile appeared because Tighte had tipped his hand. She looked down at the unpaid bill and somehow knew Tighte did not intend to pay her. When he secured the prototype, she would be expendable. She needed to put an insurance plan into action.

Scientist loves Debra
Debra loves boss
loves tiernan
son

CHAPTER 15

JOHN GRAHAM HAD a very predictable routine. He would arrive at work at 8:00 a.m. sharp, head to the lab, sit down in a small break room and read his morning paper. At 8:30 a.m., he would fold the paper neatly and leave it sitting on the table for others to read, should they wish, then go to his station where a typewritten list of the day's tasks sat atop a notebook.

After reviewing the list, he would set out to accomplish the tasks. When the tasks were complete, he would ready a list for the next day and, after printing it out and laying it on his desk, he would go home. Graham would end his workday when the list was complete. If he happened to accomplish his tasks early, a stroll in Central Park would reward his efficiency. On the other hand, if 10:00 p.m. snuck up and he hadn't completed all the items on the list, he paid no mind to the clock.

The clock, he would say, *is not our master, but two lines pointing to arbitrary symbols denoting numbers, which incidentally, are pure abstractions.* Richard Tiernan had never questioned Graham's unconventional attendance. He had known that Graham was the type of employee that a company is lucky to have on staff.

Since Michael Tiernan had split the research and development staff into two teams – located on different floors – Graham and Debra no longer saw each other as frequently. It bothered Debra, but the change greatly affected Graham. He looked forward to seeing Debra every day. Before the teams were separated, the two would venture out of the lab and have lunch in the city at least once a week. It was always an impulsive decision and Graham would adjust his list by jotting in the margin: *lunch with a brilliant scientist.*

Graham changed his routine to compensate for the separation. Instead of reading his morning paper in the break room, he now situated himself in Debra Lewis' office and read. They didn't often chat during this time but enjoyed a mutual silence that only friends can. Their lunch dates were temporarily suspended, but they were working on that too.

"John, can I ask you something?" said Debra, who looked a little out of place sitting behind a desk. "Were you ever in love?"

Graham was a very private man. Colleagues who had worked with him for years knew nothing about his private life, and his workspace was as silent as he was. Neither pictures nor any indication of social connections outside Oisín adorned his desk, and it looked none the barer for it. He looked up from his morning paper and sat upright, a sign that Debra had come to recognize; it meant Graham was serious and believed the subject matter to be the same.

"Well, my dear," he started, "I believe that I have been graced with that pleasure, yes." Graham had never married and he had never given any indication that he had a lover of either sex. Not that it would have mattered to Debra; she loved him unconditionally and was more liberal than one might suppose her Orthodox Greek upbringing might have allowed.

"I have been a lover of life," he continued. "And yes, I, too, have felt the burning sensation of lust like everyone else, but was too cerebral to allow the messengers of urgency to dictate action." Graham folded the paper into quarters and placed it neatly on Debra's desk.

"What do you mean, John? I'm not sure I understand."

"I want you to think about that one, dear," he answered a little bashfully. "I am not sure I am comfortable getting into such a conversation without the benefit of a little brandy to loosen the lips."

Graham knew that the purpose of the question was not a probe into his personal life, but a segue into a concern that Debra needed to discuss with him. He felt so honored that this little Greek goddess deigned him worthy. He allowed the appropriate time to pass and then asked, "My dear, were you struck by Cupid's arrow?"

"Oh, John, I think that Cupid sent an army of archers and used me as a pincushion," answered Debra, coming around the desk and sitting in a chair next to him.

"I've always admired him from afar," she said, "and the rarity of our interactions made it easier." Debra clasped Graham's elderly hands. The wrinkles reminded her that he, too, would be gone soon and that life was a brutal joke if it only offered what appeared prime facie. "I see him every day now. I can actually smell when he comes into the office and it's starting to get to me."

Graham knew exactly whom she meant. He was a scientist, an observer of phenomena – very little slipped past him. He knew that Debra had been in love with the heir of Oisín since the moment she had set eyes on him.

"Dear," said Graham, "I cannot say that the years that have been bestowed upon me were squandered, even if I were to die today." He released her hands and gently lifted her chin with his finger. "But I think if I were given the chance to do it again, I would share my joys and fears with someone."

"I love him," she said. "I love Michael Tiernan and he will never love me."

"Oh, my dear," said Graham as he smoothed her hair away from the tears, "you don't know that. Young Michael is an intelligent man and, after the fires of youth have died down a little, he may realize that he has been looking for a girl like you all his life."

Debra Lewis appreciated the thought even though she knew it probably wasn't true. What she did not know was that Graham had been looking for a girl like Debra all *his* life and his heart was breaking right there in front of her.

"I have to get a grip on myself," she said. "We have a new employee starting today – Marie Delacroix, from France."

"From France?" asked Graham, raising his eyebrows. "That's quite a commute."

Debra smiled and wiped the residual moisture the tears had left on her face. She handed Graham a file labeled Marie (Mary) Delacroix:

EID: 26192. He opened the file and immediately understood why Tiernan had hired this woman without a thorough background check. Mary Delacroix stared back from the employee identification tag that hung snugly to the inside of her file. It looked more like a glamour shot than the usual mug shots the other employees wore. Even from the small square-inch image, it was apparent that she was a beautiful woman.

"So, tell me," Graham said, "what are Miss Marie Delacroix's credentials?"

"We're waiting for a few more documents to arrive from France, but she is highly qualified, a real find," Debra concluded. "I was getting worried that I would never fill that vacant position and Michael would be disappointed."

Graham knew that Debra must have realized that Tiernan would find Mary Delacroix attractive – who wouldn't? But Debra's desire to please Tiernan dominated all other desires.

"You should stay and meet her, John," suggested Debra. "I want her to feel welcome here. She must be homesick and New York City can be pretty intimidating."

"I'd be happy to," said Graham as he reopened his paper. "I'm sure she'll find a warm welcome here."

CHAPTER 16

spy

MARY DELACROIX ARRIVED at Oisín at 8:30 a.m. Monday morning.

"Good morning, Dr. Delacroix," said Debra. "I'm so glad you're here. I want you to meet my very good friend, Dr. John Graham."

Graham stepped forward with an outstretched hand. "Bonjour, Madam. I'm afraid that exhausts my command of the French language. Welcome to Oisín." Graham shook her hand and excused himself. "I must get going. I have many things to accomplish today and, if I don't get started now, I'll be here until midnight. I'll see you two around."

Debra gave Mary a tour and introduced her around the office. She pointed out the bathrooms and break rooms and gave her insider tips on where to get the freshest coffee. Mary followed Debra around, taking mental pictures of everything.

"Where does the other team work?" asked Mary. "Are they on the same floor?"

"No, they are three floors down," replied Debra. "But we meet three times a week, so you'll have the opportunity to get to know everyone. We're like a family here."

"That's wonderful," said Mary. "I was hoping that there would be friendly people here. I haven't had the best experience in New York so far."

spy   *Scientist*

"Don't worry, Mary," said Debra. "You'll be one of the gang in no time."

Debra gave Mary an employee I.D. card and informed her that it served as a key card. Debra swiped the key across the sensor outside her office. A simultaneous *ding* and the flash of green preceded a gentle click and the door opened.

"We are given different levels of clearance. Your key is entry-level, so you can open bathrooms, supply closets and such, but it won't open any offices." Debra closed the door to her office. It clicked shut and the little green light turned red. "I'm still getting used to them myself. Dr. Tiernan had them installed very recently."

Debra reattached the I.D. tag to her white coat.

"And speaking of Dr. Tiernan," she said, "here he comes right now."

Mary watched Debra very closely. Within five seconds, Mary had acquired a very useful nugget of information. As Michael Tiernan approached, Debra Lewis adjusted her posture, her respiration increased, the pulse in her neck beat more rapidly, her eyes dilated and her face underwent a slight, almost imperceptible change of hue. *Ah*, thought Mary McKenna, *little Debra Lewis is in love. Perfect.*

"Good morning, Dr. Tiernan," said Debra rapidly. "I would like to introduce you to Marie Delacroix." Before she could retract her statement or at least adjust it to lessen her embarrassment, Tiernan responded, "I interviewed her. I hired her, remember?" Now the previously imperceptible hue changed to a loud crimson.

"Yes, I know. I mean I want to welcome her...or, no, I want you to welcome her to Oisín."

Mary McKenna quickly extended her hand and interrupted.

"I am Mary Mic..." She stopped herself and, without missing a beat, turned to Debra and said, "Did you introduce me as Marie?" She gave a staged frown. "I am trying to assimilate, so you two must call me Mary."

Tiernan smiled and declared, "Mary it is! Welcome to Oisín, Dr. *Mary* Delacroix. I hope you have a long and rewarding career with us."

Debra's face transitioned back to its normal color. She experienced a flash of emotion. A mixture of desire, embarrassment and fear produced a new and very uncomfortable sensation in her gut. Tiernan looked at Mary Delacroix for just a second too long. His eyes lingered on her body for an instant more than a casual glance would take.

"Debra," said Tiernan. "After you get Mary situated, can I meet with you?"

"Certainly," she replied. "I was going to bring her down to Lab One and introduce her to the other team, but I can give her some of the research to review."

"No," said Tiernan. "We don't want to bore her to death on the first day. Have John Graham show her around Lab One and introduce her to his team. Mary can shadow him until we finish."

"Alright," said Debra.

After a second round of welcomes, well wishes and thank-yous, they went their separate ways.

Debra knocked lightly on the door before pushing it open.

"Ah," said Tiernan. "Come in. Close the door." He didn't notice that she had dabbed a little perfume on her wrist and smoothed a little lip-gloss on her thin lips.

"Is anything wrong?" Debra was a competent scientist and she knew it. Ever since the promotion, however, she'd become a little paranoid. Was she really as talented as she had previously thought? Recently, she had begun to second-guess many of her decisions and it disconcerted her. She wondered if she was really a fraud and was only now discovering it. Love plays cruel tricks on the mind. It can make one believe the most ridiculous things and doubt the most certain. Tiernan responded to Debra's tone more than the question. He sensed that she needed reassurance. The last thing he needed was his most innovative scientist to devolve into some neurotic mess.

"Yes, something is very wrong," he continued. "You're underpaid." He hadn't planned on giving her a raise, but went with his instincts.

"You've really come through for us. Without those Mimic cells, I don't know where we'd be. I want you to know that I appreciate it. I'm adding another $10,000 to your base salary and throwing in an additional week's vacation time."

Debra was speechless. She didn't care about the money and rarely used her vacation time, but the affirmation from Tiernan was more valuable. "My goodness, Michael," she said blushing again. "I don't know what to say." *son boss*

"You don't have to say anything," he said. "Just keep up the fine work." *Son* Tiernan needed to transition the conversation to where he had previously intended it to go, but gave her a moment to revel. When she didn't say anything other than *thank you* rephrased in different ways to conceal redundancy, he continued.

"Debra," he said. "I need to travel to Sardinia again. I would like to leave you in charge while I'm gone." She was speechless a second time. "I want you to take over the day-to-day operations at Oisín while I'm away. I shouldn't be long."

Debra Lewis was trembling inside. Whether it was the prospect of assuming the role of CEO in Tiernan's absence or the awesome feeling of knowing that he clearly had confidence in her, she couldn't be certain.

"So," she said mustering up the strength to speak over the roar of her heartbeat. "Are you sure you want to leave the fate of the company in my hands?"

"You'll do fine," he responded. "Are you up for the challenge?"

"Whatever you need me to do, Michael," she said. "I'm a team player." Debra had a fleeting thought about how John Graham might react to Tiernan's decision, but his strong jaw line and intoxicating smile mesmerized her and erased all other considerations.

"Great," he said. "I'll update your keycard." Tiernan held his hand out and she placed the card squarely in his palm.

ભ

Southern Lori Adams applied another coating of fire engine red lipstick as she entered the elevator. Her blond hair was styled in an outdated fashion, but it suited her. A large quantity of Aqua Net hair spray was required to cement the style in place and periodic reapplications were, unfortunately, a necessity. The dark roots that were just noticeable revealed that her hair wasn't the result of Nordic genes, but a bottle of dye and a busy schedule.

"Oisín Labs, please," she said to a well-dressed gentleman who obliged by pressing the appropriate button. She returned her lipstick to its place in the little Prada bag that Connor had bought her for no reason whatsoever and took out a compact mirror. When satisfied that the reflection was fine, she spritzed a generous portion of Autumn's Breeze on her neck. The fellow behind her also got a generous helping of the somewhat strong scent, but didn't comment except for a cough reflex – an attempt to expel the spray from his lungs.

"Oh, darlin', I'm sorry," said Lori. "That was just awful a' me." Lori looked for a tissue for the man, but stopped when he retrieved a handkerchief from his pocket.

"That's quite alright, ma'am," he said. "It will keep my wife on her toes."

Lori chuckled and handed him the bottle of perfume.

"Give this to your honey tonight," she said. "There is no reason to make a lady jealous." Before he could refuse, the elevator door opened and she stepped out.

"T'care now."

ଔ

"No, I don't have an appointment, but I just have to see him," Lori explained to Tiernan's secretary. "There was a misunderstanding and I just feel terrible about the whole thing."

Lori's charm had a powerful effect on women, too. The combination of innocence and power exuded from her in quantities that overwhelmed the majority. She had a disarming demeanor that held people temporarily spellbound, leaving many wondering how she persuaded them to do this or that.

"I'm sorry, Miss Adams," the secretary apologized quite sincerely. "But Dr. Tiernan is very busy today and can't be disturbed."

Lori smiled at her and persisted.

"My Lord," she lilted. "Is this what our lives have become? You mean, you can't even tell him that I am here?" Lori held her hand to her breast to convey disbelief. "Is he a mean ol' boss who'll take your head off for just asking?"

"Of course not," the secretary said. "But he just requested five minutes ago that I hold his calls and not disturb him. He's in a meeting right now."

"Well, I'll just wait a few," said Lori. "Maybe he'll take a bathroom break." Lori pulled a chair over, sat down across from the secretary and lifted a magazine from a small coffee table.

"If he doesn't come out soon, I'll pull the fire alarm or something. He can't blame you for that," Lori whispered, leaning toward the secretary and giggling in her childlike manner. "What's your name, honey?" asked Lori. "You have the most beautiful eyelashes. Do you use mascara?"

"I'm Eileen. I only use a little bit to bring out my eyes. Do you think it's too much?"

"Not at all, darlin'," she said as she thumbed through the magazine. "They look professionally done."

Eileen looked around and whispered. "He has a lunch meeting at 12 noon in Gypsy's Tavern, but you didn't hear it from me."

Lori mimed a locking motion across her lips, crossed her legs and winked before returning to her magazine.

The door to Tiernan's office opened and Debra Lewis emerged. She closed the door behind her as requested. Lori smiled at Debra, who headed back to her office. Debra smiled back as she remembered that she had given Tiernan her keycard and needed it to access her office. She returned to his office and, out of courtesy, stopped at Eileen's desk.

"Eileen, I left my keycard with him," she admitted. "Do you have an access card I can borrow?" Eileen looked over at Lori Adams and winked.

"No, Dr. Lewis, I don't. I'll have to interrupt him."

"Well, maybe you shouldn't –"

Eileen had already knocked twice and opened the door before Debra could finish her thought.

"Sorry, Dr. Tiernan," she said. "But Dr. Lewis needs her card for a minute. I'll bring it right back." Tiernan was on the phone. He lifted Debra's keycard and tossed it to Eileen. She caught it and turned on her heel, leaving the door slightly opened.

"I need to use the ladies' room, Dr. Lewis, so I'll walk with you," said Eileen as she winked again at Lori, letting her know that the desk would be unmanned for a few minutes. Lori folded the magazine and threw it on the coffee table. Eileen was a respectable distance when Lori stood up and walked into Tiernan's office, closing the door behind her.

"Okay, so I'll be there in the late afternoon your time," said Tiernan, still on the phone. He looked up at Lori and shook his head.

"Eileen!" shouted Tiernan.

"Now, don't you even try it, mister tough guy!" said Lori. "That sweet little thing is not to blame. I took advantage of her leaving to help out that petite lady in the lab coat."

"What do you want?" Tiernan said. "I'm really busy."

"Have you considered our offer?"

Tiernan stood up and walked to the other side of the desk. He sat down on the corner of the desk, next to Lori's chair, and shook his head again. "This prototype must be very important to Lionel if you are pursuing it so vehemently," he said.

"I think our generous offer let that cat outta the bag, don't you?" said Lori. "I didn't make you believe otherwise, did I?"

"No, you didn't," said Tiernan. "I'm giving serious consideration to your offer." He got up and opened the door. "I will let you know as soon as I've had time to really consider it. Can you give me some time to think about it without following me to Italy?"

"Italy again?" Lori observed. "There must be a little Signorina over there or something."

"Or something," Tiernan said. "Now, go, before I change my mind."

"Okay, but don't wait too long," said Lori, smiling a thankful smile as she passed Eileen. As she stood waiting for the elevator, she casually glanced at a group of people walking past her. Mary McKenna was the last person she expected to see at Oisín. Their eyes met for an instant, an immeasurably short time. Mary couldn't be sure if Lori realized who she was and, if she did, Lori didn't give any indication of it. The elevator doors opened and she stepped in. Mary did her best to prevent

Lori from catching another identifying glance, successfully camouflaging herself in the herd of white coats. She initially considered an abort mission, but it was a millisecond's glance, she rationalized. She allowed herself to believe that the glasses, white coat and different hairstyle were enough to conceal her true identity and decided not to inform Tighte of the possible breach.

Before the elevator reached the ground floor, Lori had dialed Connor's direct line. "You'll never guess who is working undercover at Oisín."

CHAPTER 17

THE FLIGHT SEEMED shorter this time and the dual propellers less frightening. Even if Falters failed to bring a car, Tiernan was prepared. "I packed light," he said as they approached the landing strip. "Did you happen to bring a vehicle?"

"Yes, I did," Falters answered.

Tiernan looked out the window and felt a strange feeling of familiarity overcome him. He stepped out of the little plane and inhaled deeply. He closed his eyes and took another inhalation of the sweet scent of the Sardinian flora.

"Would you like to drive?" Falters asked.

"Why not?" said Tiernan, catching the keys.

✿

After resting for an hour, Tiernan headed down into the lab. He now understood the need for secrecy and appreciated the effort his father put into concealing the lab, although he thought that building a lab under 20 feet of solid rock was going a little overboard.

"The Nazis used these tunnels during WWII," said Falters.

"They went to a lot of trouble to build them, considering Sardinia wasn't integral to the war effort," Tiernan commented. "Thank God for stupidity."

Falters was fiddling with a printer but was still actively engaged in the conversation.

"Those Nazi pigs didn't build these; I said they *used* them," said Falters indignantly. "Do you think I would work down here if my workspace was a result of Nazi masonry?"

"Calm down, buddy," Tiernan said as he sipped his cup of fresh insomnia. "If not them, then who built them?"

Falters stacked the printed pages neatly and laid them down next to similar piles of previously arranged folio. "During your runs around the hamlet, did you notice those huge rock structures?" he asked.

Tiernan blew into the cup after having burned his lip and tongue for being overzealous with the brew. "Yeah," he responded. "They're pretty hard to miss. What the heck are those things, anyway?"

"They are called Nuraghi and no one knows for sure what they were used for," answered Falters. "The structures were built by an ancient people called the Nuragics. The Nuraghi are the largest stone structures in the Mediterranean after the Egyptian pyramids. About 7,000 of them exist."

"So, you're saying that the Nuragics built the tunnels too?"

"Yes," said Falters, ending the topic of conversation. "Come, there is much to read."

Tiernan walked over and sat on the stool. Falters handed him a stack of papers.

"I'll leave you in peace to read the data from the recent experiments; we'll reconvene for dinner."

Tiernan gave him a salute and rolled the stool toward the couch, coffee cup in hand and a stack of papers under his arm. He placed the coffee on the table, removed his shoes, stretched out on the couch and began reading.

αβ

Falters was apprehensive about Michael Tiernan. Out of respect for Richard, Falters felt an obligation to tell his partner's son about the miraculous drug. He had always assumed that there would be many similarities between the great Richard Tiernan and his only child, but he was mistaken; Michael Tiernan was nothing like his father.

αβ

The data was hypnotizing and confusing. Tiernan wasn't certain what all the data meant, since Falters found it necessary to add new words to the considerable, but lacking, lexicon currently used by the scientific community.

A few hours later, Falters, deciding against using the intercom, came down to the lab to call Tiernan to cena. He found Tiernan in the same spot where he had left him.

"You read like your father did." Falters pointed to the scattered array of folders opened on the table. "Richard read data the same way."

Tiernan didn't quite understand what Falters meant, but smiled and stood up to stretch his bones. "A chip off the ol' block, I guess," Tiernan said.

"No, this is the only similarity I've seen so far," said Falters. "You must take after your mother. Dinner will be here shortly."

"Good, I'm starving." Quickly transitioning, Tiernan asked the first of a series of questions he had jotted down while reading the files. "Do I understand these results correctly?"

"That depends on your understanding. If you mean to ask if all of my recent attempts to engineer a multiple dose version of Dionysinol failed, then yes, you've understood correctly."

"We're going to have to bring in some help," said Tiernan. "I realize you're not crazy about the idea, but, financially, the drug is worthless if it only requires a single dose."

"I've exhausted all avenues of recourse; bringing additional people in on this will not help us. There is simply no way to alter the drug to suit your purposes. Dionysinol was not meant for the masses."

"My purposes? I was under the impression that this was a team effort. Was I wrong?"

"Forgive me, but I think you are blinded by the promise of the wealth that Dionysinol could bring you. This has the potential to end very badly."

"Would you like to give the stuff away for free? I know, maybe we should include samples of the drug with government handouts," said Tiernan. "I can see the public service announcement now: *Government cheese and Dionysinol. Now you can live long enough to suck the system completely dry.* How 'bout it?"

"I just noticed another similarity," said Falters. "Your father would get very irritable when his blood sugar dropped; I see you've inherited the same disposition."

"Yeah. Sorry about that – it's been stressful lately. Let's talk about this after I've eaten something." With that, the two walked through the ancient rock tunnels to the entrance of the house.

Tiernan knew that he had only understood about half of the data he read regarding the subtle properties of the drug. However, he did understand the financial burden the current form of Dionysinol would inflict on his already-diminishing capital. Dionysinol was going to be more costly than he had originally anticipated – much more costly – and his new partner seemed to have a different philosophy. However, that didn't concern Tiernan. If all went according to plan, money would never be an issue again, even if that meant eliminating Falters from the project.

CHAPTER 18 *Tighte*

Raped by Driver

"RIGHT HERE, DARLIN'," said Lori. She and Edward had scoped out the area before and had decided that this was the best spot. Edward opened the truck and carefully removed the black tarp.

"I'd help you, darlin', but I'd bust a nail for sure," said Lori. Edward didn't think the tarp was necessary. It was the dead of night, the nearest neighbor was miles away and they had not seen a car for almost an hour, but Lori didn't want to take any chances. Edward covered the car with the camouflaged tarp and walked with Lori through the woods. After walking a couple hundred yards, Lori suggested they look back to see if they could see the car. He was impressed with the result. Neither of them could pick it out.

"Let's just hope we are able to find it when we come back." Edward smiled and extended his hand to Lori. She thanked him and took his hand.

He was used to going beyond the conventional job description of *driver*. Lori Adams had hired him when no one else would. Edward O'Malley had a less than desirable résumé to begin with, but the DWI conviction was the kiss of death for him. No one would hire a driver with both a DWI and vehicular manslaughter conviction. He did some time in prison and, after his release, the only employment he could find was bagging groceries at a local supermarket. When he met Lori Adams in that very supermarket, his luck changed.

His was the fiercest loyalty, a loyalty born from true gratitude and the understanding that he would never be able to repay Lori for her kindness. He would die before betraying her and she knew it.

"Darlin,' I need to stop for a second," said Lori. "I think I have a rock in my shoe." Holding on to Edward's shoulder for balance, Lori removed her shoe and emptied the phantom contents. Edward smiled at her.

"Remind me why we're breaking in here."

"We're taking back somethin' that belongs to us. We ain't stealing, honey. Little Michael Tiernan is all grown up now and he is being a little difficult – making me go out in the dead of night like this."

Edward didn't worry about being arrested for breaking and entering or for any other crime Lori Adams had him assist her with. Chances were, even if they were caught in the act, Lori would find a way to get them both out of it. Besides, all those years that he worked for her were gravy. Before Lori, his life had been rapidly spiraling downward.

"Do you have a description of the thing we're stealing?"

"I told you, honey, we ain't stealing," answered Lori, a little out of breath from the brisk pace. "Besides, I need to go in myself." Lori laughed a little and confessed that she didn't know exactly what she was looking for. "But I'll know it when I see it."

Tiernan had housekeepers – Lori knew that. She wasn't sure if they lived in the mansion or in the guest quarters. As she and Edward approached the mansion, they squatted out of sight to survey the house. She had remembered he had automatic lights in the driveway and had planned accordingly.

"We need to get to the side of the mansion without tripping the lights," Lori said. She looked like a child getting ready to play a joke on her friends, not a middle-aged woman about to commit a felony. "Isn't this exciting?" she giggled.

They crept around the side of the mansion where the question of the housekeepers' accommodations was answered. Separate quarters were obvious by the little cottage adorned by a statue of Padre Pio.

Edward wielded the glasscutter, removing a section large enough for his hand to unlock the window from the inside. His efficiency betrayed something about his younger days. "When I slide the window open, you have about 30 seconds to enter the code by the door," he warned for the eighth time.

"I know, I know," Lori said. "Get down on all fours and give me a boost, would ya?"

Edward complied and Lori climbed on his back. He heard the window open and felt Lori's weight double as she used his spine as a springboard. She climbed in easily enough and Edward moved his fingertips to reassure himself that the crackling sound was not his spine snapping. He counted. When 30 seconds had passed and no alarm had sounded, he knew she had successfully entered the code. He waited patiently for her to return.

Lori clicked on her little flashlight and a surprisingly luminous beam burst forth. She didn't know exactly what she was looking for, but started searching the upstairs rooms anyway. After the fruitless rummaging through bedrooms and linen closets became monotonous, she walked back downstairs and tried the door to the den. Locked.

Ah, thought Lori. *What do we have here? We only lock up the special things we want to keep safe. What's so special to you in here, Doctor Tiernan?* She walked back to the window. "Edward, Edward?"

Rustling leaves announced his approach. "What's wrong?"

"Nothing's wrong, honey. I just need your help. Climb up and pick this lock for me, would ya?"

Edward climbed in through the window and held his back. He didn't mention that her bouncing on it had caused a significant amount of pain, something akin to a broken spine, he imagined. Within minutes, he picked the lock and they entered the den.

Edward sat at the desk, reclined in the chair and lifted a cigar out of a box. "Cubans," he said as he ran the cigar under his nose.

"Take one, honey. I'm sure he won't miss just one."

"I think I will."

As Edward relaxed, holding the unlit cigar, Lori searched the office. Opening the desk drawers, she came across the leather portfolio and removed it. Under the ornate folio, vials of Dionysinol sat securely in a foam box. *Hmmmm, what's this?* she thought. She picked one up and shook it hard before losing interest. She placed it on the desk and opened the portfolio.

"Hey, Ed, I think I found something. Listen to this. It says, *I hope that you will never have to read this, and hope is a powerful force. My life's work is now yours. I love you, Dad.* I think these might be Richard Tiernan's notes."

"That's what we're looking for?"

"I don't know. Hush, and let me examine it."

Lori flicked through the pages in the leather portfolio, skipping the sections dedicated entirely to equations and diagrams, but Richard Tiernan spoke eloquently enough from beyond the grave for her to understand that she had found something important. She could hear the excitement with which Richard Tiernan wrote, the admixture of disbelief and faith in this amazing substance – the substance from which the deceased scientist evidently derived no benefit.

Lori felt a strange maternal instinct for an instant, thinking of Michael Tiernan. She imagined him reading the details of his father's life's work, missing him and feeling the loss that never quite fades to black. In that brief instant, she wanted to protect him. *How could this boy be so stupid?* she thought, referring not to a boy at all, but to a man who possibly possessed the secrets of eternal youth. *Why would he leave this so unprotected?*

Fate's mode of instruction seems to favor the ironic, the asymmetrical. With so many changes happening so quickly, it was an understandable mistake, but one for which Tiernan would pay dearly.

CHAPTER 19

MARY MCKENNA READIED herself for another day of being Dr. Mary Delacroix. Her French accent was impeccable and she had managed to fool her new colleagues with her recently-obtained scientific knowledge, but time was pressing. She had completed the orientation training and was now expected to perform the duties of a real scientist; it wouldn't be long before she was discovered. She needed to expedite the process and took a shot at what seemed to be her best option: befriending Dr. Debra Lewis.

"Debra," said Mary. "Can I ask something?" Debra was putting the final additions on the IND application for human trials of Regenerol. She resented these constant interruptions, but since she had agreed to step in for Tiernan as CEO for a few days, she couldn't complain. *How does he get any work done?* she thought. Determined not to let her new employee see her irritation, Debra responded with a smile. "Of course, what is it?"

"It is of a personal nature," warned Mary. "I hope this is okay."

Debra always shied away from personal questions, allowing only John Graham into her personal life. Bravely, she nodded in affirmation.

"How long have you and Dr. Tiernan been a couple?" The question resonated in Debra's being. *You, Couple, Dr. Tiernan.* Was this woman, this French floozy, asking so she could gauge her own chances with Michael Tiernan? Was she testing the waters before diving in and stealing away the only man that Debra Lewis had ever loved – albeit in secret? Debra's heart pounded in her ears. "No, we're not a couple." The sentence saddened her.

"Oh, mon Dieu," apologized Mary. "I just thought by the way he looked at you that, uh, how do you say?" Mary pretended to fumble with words as she let the full impact knock all caution and inhibition out of Debra. After the appropriate pause, Mary continued her assault on Debra's natural defenses and acquired distrust for outsiders. She applied just the right amount of sensitivity seasoned with the hint that she may have witnessed something that would set Debra's world on another trajectory.

"I am engaged, myself," said Mary. With this loaded sentence, Mary Delacroix was transformed from potential dream-wrecker to new friend. "Plus, I was born and raised just outside of Paris; I am a Parisian. We know love when we see it, even if the lovers don't see it themselves," Mary said, landing the final blow.

Debra Lewis' love of the scientific method, mathematics and philosophy had estranged her from other girls who were more receptive to society's unspoken messages: there are jobs for boys and jobs for girls. These disciplines, not quite verboten for the fairer sex but not encouraged either, offered comfort and solace to Debra during her somewhat lonely high school existence. Debra related better to men; her career choice made that a necessity. But Mary Delacroix was different, and Debra was discovering that she liked her.

"Pardon my intrusion into your private affairs, Dr. Lewis," said Mary. "In France, friendships formed at work are often the most rewarding and I keep forgetting that I am no longer there."

Debra was at a loss for words, so she just looked at Mary and nodded slightly. Mary went in for the kill. She embraced Debra and kissed both of her cheeks.

"I hope you will forgive my blunder," Mary said with convincing sincerity. "My homesickness is getting the better of me."

"There is nothing to forgive, Mary," said Debra. "Michael Tiernan and I are just friends. I have great respect for the man."

"Oui, oui, I mean, of course you do," answered Mary, sensing that Debra wanted to hear more about the manufactured observations. "I too often speak my mind, and when I saw love in the doctor's eyes as he spoke to you, I assumed such love could only be sustained by, how do you say, reciprocity?"

"Reciprocity?" asked Debra.

"Oui, but there is a better word for this." She pretended to search her mind. "Mutual love, maybe?"

Debra's heart threatened to begin pounding again. Did Mary Delacroix see love in Tiernan's eyes? And, if she did see love, was it for Debra? Mary Delacroix sealed the deal with her next comment. "I can understand why you choose not to have a relationship with your superior," said Mary, giving the impression that she assumed Debra *chose* not to date Tiernan. "In America, there are always lawsuits for this kind of thing, yes?"

Graham's sudden appearance rescued Debra before she had to respond to Mary's erroneous assumption.

"Debra," he said. "Do you have the IND report? I'm going to the post office and thought I would mail it for you."

Debra had not finished the IND report that should have been completed two days ago. "I'll mail it, John," she said, not wanting to admit to Graham that she hadn't finished her only real assignment that day. "I just want to put the finishing touches on it."

It was the first lie Debra Lewis had ever told John Graham.

"Okay, dear," said Graham. "Then, can I interest you in some lunch?"

"Not today, John," said Debra in a tone dangerously close to sounding like exasperation. "There are just too many things to do before Michael gets back. But why don't you two go?"

Although Graham felt slighted, he smiled and extended his elbow to Mary. "Shall we?"

"This is fine, Dr. Lewis?" said Mary.

"Yes, please, enjoy yourselves," answered Debra.

Graham didn't want to go to lunch with Mary; he wanted to spend time with Debra. He was acutely aware of her absence and he missed her more than he wanted to admit.

When Graham and Mary left the floor to have a lunch that neither of them wanted, Debra Lewis headed for Tiernan's office. She gestured a greeting to Eileen, who always seemed to be busy yet available. Debra closed the door behind her. Tiernan's office smelled like him – not quite an artificial scent that one associates with a cologne or aftershave, but a subtler odor.

Debra sat in Tiernan's chair, folded her arms on the desk and cradled her troubled head. *How can another human being elicit such emotional turmoil in another by simply existing?* she thought. Michael Tiernan was wreaking havoc in Debra's mind. His mere presence was enough to delight or destroy her. Debra logged in to her Oisín account from Tiernan's office, deciding that the IND application would have a better chance of getting done there.

CB

Graham and Mary had hardly reached the ground floor of Oisín when he slapped his forehead and looked apologetically at Mary. "Oh, dear," he said. "I'm afraid I'm having a senior moment."

"Senior moment?" repeated Mary, pretending not to understand.

"Yes," Graham said without clarifying the meaning. "I have completely forgotten about a previous commitment." The elevator doors opened and the stale air of the lobby rushed in. Without exiting, Graham pressed buttons 14 and 17. "I'm afraid I have to cancel. Do forgive me."

Mary was relieved. She had the distinct impression that Graham may have been suspicious of her and she wasn't looking forward to a one-on-one Q&A over lunch.

"This is no problem," said Mary. "We all get senior minutes."

The doors opened on floor 14 and Graham stepped out. Mary breathed a sigh of relief when the elevator resumed its ascent to floor 17 where she could continue her, up to now, fruitless mission. The doors opened and Mary headed back to Dr. Lewis' office. She knocked on the partially-open door before walking in. Debra was not in her office and no one noticed when Mary Delacroix closed the door behind her. The green light blinked twice and turned red – clicked, locked.

Sitting at the desk, Mary shook the mouse, tapped the keyboard and Debra's computer arose from its power-saving slumber. As the screen brightened and the text became clear, Mary smiled.

Bingo! Control, File, Print...

Mary read from the screen as the printer hummed out a hard copy.

Chemistry and Manufacturing Introduction:

"At the beginning of this section, the sponsor should state whether it believes: 1) the chemistry of either the drug substance or the drug product, or 2) the manufacturing of either the drug substance or the drug product, presents any signals of potential human risk... *stemcell*

Regenerol is a unique drug. Its chemical structure is similar to...

2. Drug Substance [312.23 (a)(7)(iv)(a)]:

Sponsors are reminded that, under present regulations, references to the current edition of the USP-NF may be used to satisfy some of the requirements, when applicable.

Information on the drug substance should be submitted in a summary report containing the following items:

a. A description of the drug substance, including its physical, chemical, or biological characteristics;

b. A brief description of the drug substance and some evidence to support its proposed chemical structure should be submitted...

c. The general method of preparation of the drug substance:

A brief description of the manufacturing process, including a list of the reagents, solvents, and catalysts used, should be submitted. A detailed flow diagram...proposed clinical study(ies):"

Mexico?

*Note to self: No reference to Mexican data can appear in any data. Fine tooth comb...

Mexican data? she thought. *This isn't the file on the Chimera seed.* Mary reached into her bra and removed a flash drive. She placed it in the USB port and made a digital copy of the Regenerol file while performing a general search for files containing MEXICAN STUDIES – eight files found. She added them to the transfer queue. She had almost forgotten her main objective.

Mary searched Debra's computer for any reference to the Chimera seed. Nothing. She dried her sweaty palms on her lab coat and wiped her brow with the lapel. She was nervous. She filled the flash drive with all of Debra Lewis' files, including her saved e-mails folders, before returning it to its inconspicuous hiding place.

The door handle jiggled and Mary heard a muffled version of Debra's voice. On the other side of the door, Debra stood patting her pockets in the futile attempt to locate her keycard, which she had a habit of losing. Mary quickly removed the printed copy of the IND application, which contained all the blood, sweat and tears of years of research, and attempted to find a way to conceal it before Debra opened the door.

CHAPTER 20

LORI ADAMS DIDN'T find a single document that mentioned the Chimera seed and began to doubt that it had survived the years. After hours of searching, she granted a temporary suspension on her previously-held rule of no drinking on the job and poured herself one. She handed Edward a glass, which he gladly took without having the slightest intention of imbibing; he had learned his lesson.

"To us," she said as she lifted her glass. Edward bumped glasses with her, although he didn't know what they were celebrating. He didn't care. As long as she was happy, that was all that mattered.

"So we've succeeded?" he asked.

"Yes, we did, darlin'," said Lori as she drained the glass.

"We were successful without getting what we came for," she giggled. "Imagine that!"

Lori tucked the leather portfolio and the vials of Dionysinol into her booty-bag while pointing to a shelf behind Edward. "Hand me that statue of the dead man, would ya?" Edward complied and lifted the bronze statue from where it had stood unmolested for years. "It's heavy," he remarked. "Why do you want it?"

Lori looked at the statue and blew a thin layer of dust from it. *Housekeeper must be short or lazy,* she thought. She read the Gaelic words written on the base of the statue, butchering the pronunciation in the process. "Fionn mac Cumhaill?" she read in question form. "D'you know who that is?"

"Not a clue," said Edward.

Lori put the statue in her bag. "I'll look it up later," she promised. "Now, help me get this place back in order."

Edward didn't remind her that she was technically stealing. He was just glad that she was happy.

⊳

Lori's Boss

Connor's cell vibrated on the nightstand, rattling and dancing across the polished wood. He picked it up quickly before his light-sleeping wife could use it as an excuse to complain.

"Hello," he whispered. "You okay?" Connor knew it was Lori.

"Well, aren't you a night owl?" twanged the familiar voice. "I am so happy I didn't have to wake you up. Are you up for good?"

Connor looked at the clock by his bed and squinted tighter and tighter until the numbers revealed a coherent pattern: 3:37 a.m. "Up for good if you need me to be," he responded. "Is everything alright?"

"Everything's fine, but I am plumb tuckered," Lori replied, using a more Southern vernacular, an occurrence by which familiars could gauge her level of exhaustion. "I need to straighten a few things out tomorrow, but I'll be in touch. I think we're in a position to cut a deal with Tiernan."

"Excellent. Be careful."

"Always, honey."

Connor knew Lori would never betray him if she were caught. In truth, he really wasn't guilty of anything except, perhaps, failing to report someone's *intention* to commit a crime, hardly worth the hassle of a busy prosecutor. But it wasn't the law he was concerned about – it was Lori Adams herself. Ryan Connor and Lori Adams were friends, and no matter how much money Connor had, he knew that no one was wealthy enough to afford to throw away a friend.

After her tragic ordeal, Connor had done everything he could to ensure Lori would live comfortably. Admittedly, he had been surprised by how quickly she had absorbed the knowledge gleaned from the college courses he had provided her. He had never thought that Lori Adams would prove to be one of the best investments Lionel had ever made.

Lori had seemed to him, a diamond in the rough, an unfortunate victim of genealogy and geography who had been guaranteed to per-

124

petuate the vicious cycle of mediocrity begetting mediocrity. She had wanted a better life – better for the kids that she hoped to someday have and adore. She had worked hard and taught herself to love the written word. She had educated herself as best she could and, when she had read all of the outdated volumes the business section of her local library shelved, she applied for a position – any position – at Lionel Pharmaceuticals.

Connor blamed himself for her rape, although Lori would balk at the thought. George Prendergast had been hand-selected by Connor to be the V.P. of Lionel. Connor had had no idea that the power-intoxicated Prendergast had intended to take the new secretary, the naïve but ambitious Lori Adams, to the Corn Convention and use her body as a playground.

CHAPTER 21

spy

MARY MCKENNA REMOVED the document from the printer's tray, a redundancy in light of what the flash drive nestled close to her breast contained, but she might not get an opportunity like this again and she couldn't be sure the contents had transferred without corruption. She tried to fold the document but stopped after realizing it was too thick. She opted for rolling it and placing it between her shirt and skirt, hoping her well-muscled abdomen would hold it in place until she could conceal it better.

The door clicked open and Eileen let out a startled gasp.

"Oh my God, you scared me half to death," she quantified, holding her hand to her breast. "Dr. Lewis is searching all over the place for you. What are you doing in here with the door locked?"

Mary McKenna snapped into character and burst into tears, emitting a sobbing sound that eclipsed all previous concerns Eileen had and replaced them with a single one.

"Oh my God, what's wrong?"

Mary felt the document slipping. Any sudden movement and 150 pages of stolen information would spill onto the floor. Panic began to set in when John Graham and Debra Lewis joined Eileen at the door. Mary needed to prevent the document from cascading out of her skirt while giving a plausible explanation as to why she was in Debra's office alone with the door locked. Mary let out a shriek and doubled over, effectively securing the document.

"I think I'm having a miscarriage," she cried and let out another howl of pain. Graham told Eileen to call an ambulance.

"Dr. Lewis," Mary pleaded, "Please get my bag. I thought I left it in here, but I can't find it. My medicine is in that bag."

Debra Lewis ran into the locker room where she assumed Mary had stowed her bag. Graham tried to comfort the agony-stricken foreigner who was most likely miscarrying right in front of him. He put his hand lightly on her shoulder and asked if she would like to try to sit.

"No," Mary shrieked while remaining doubled over. "Lead me to the bathroom, please." Graham complied and walked Mary out of Debra's office and past a herd of frightened onlookers. Mary managed to hold her stomach and the document long enough to enter the women's bathroom where she left Graham standing at the door.

Less than 10 seconds after Mary locked the stall door, Debra Lewis flew into the bathroom and called out to her. "Mary?" she said. "I have your bag and the ambulance is on the way."

Mary let out a series of groans and cries before shouting, "Slide the bag under the stall!"

Debra complied and asked helplessly, "Is there anything I can do?"

Mary removed the document and quickly placed it in her bag. She removed a pocketknife from her bag and hid the sound of it clicking open by another shriek of false pain. She cut small incisions on both of her inner thighs and let the blood stream down her legs. When a substantial amount had accumulated on the floor and her legs, she unlocked the stall door and walked out. Debra gasped at the sight of the blood, assuming the obvious.

"I lost my baby," Mary cried. "I lost my baby." She fell to the floor in an embrace with Debra Lewis and sobbed. When the ambulance arrived, Mary McKenna demanded to go alone; she wanted to grieve and asked that no one from the office accompany her in the ambulance.

CŚ

Mary McKenna slipped out of the hospital unnoticed and took a cab home where she applied a layer of triple antibiotic ointment and bandages on her self-inflicted cuts. She booted up her computer and inserted the flash drive into the port. It was going to be a long night of mining the jewels of valuable information from the worthless junk an office computer accumulates.

She walked over to her answering machine and pressed play. She made another mental note, the fourth of its kind that month, to call the phone company and have them add voice mail to her package. She listened to the messages while she rummaged through her fridge and kitchen cabinets, removing items that seemed to go well together, things that would comprise her dinner that evening. She was listening to the messages with the attention one gives a familiar movie happened upon while surfing channels. The last message on the machine caused Mary's spine to stiffen and her blood to run cold. The combination of the voice and the contents of the message caused her to lose what was left of her appetite.

"Well, hello, darlin'! Long time no see, or should I say talk, since I did get a little glimpse of you recently?" There was a short pause before Lori Adams continued speaking. "How's the job at Oisín going? I hear that you are now a French scientist! My, how things change!"

Mary smiled and bit into a raw carrot. *She's good,* she thought, *really good.* The message ended with Lori Adams asking the courtesy of a return call and well wishes. Mary rewound the message, wrote down Lori's number and erased the tape. She took another bite of her carrot and began dialing the number. *Better to rip off the bandage in one swift motion,* she thought. Lori Adams answered the phone by addressing Mary and greeting her kindly.

"I think we need to meet soon, woman to woman. You interested?"

"Do I have a choice?" asked Mary.

"Not really," said Lori. "Meet me in French Charlie's Park in two hours, and come alone."

CHAPTER 22

MOUTHWATERING AROMAS FILLED the air as Tiernan and Falters sat down to eat. Steam rose from the large white bowl containing the spaghetti. The tomato sauce clung to the pasta and the fresh basil added color and a flavor against which all future dishes would be measured. The pork chops were seasoned with something Tiernan couldn't identify but were nonetheless delicious. Tiernan lifted his glass and offered a toast.

"To the power of the grape," he exclaimed. "Il potere degli uva." Falters hesitated, but obliged. "Salute."

"So," said Tiernan, "tell me about the fatalities I read about in the report. What caused them? Is this the first time you've observed this phenomenon?"

"The *Second Dose Phenomenon?*"

"Yeah. A second dose is lethal? Are you sure?"

Falters lifted the wine glass and drank deeply. He refilled it completely before answering. "There is very little I can say about Dionysinol with certainty, but this seems to be the case. Once a subject has been treated with Dionysinol, it cannot ever be exposed to it internally. We've tested the theory on every species treated with the substance. Even the smallest second dose has this effect."

"Even for humans? I mean, you can't be sure, right? You couldn't have tested this effect on humans," interjected Tiernan, "considering you're the only one to have ever taken it. Or did you test that theory on yourself as well?"

"Of course not," said Falters. "And I don't intend to, either. But you're welcome to try, if you please."

"Nah," said a smiling Tiernan. "I think I'll wait for the results of the clinical trials before I take even the first dose." *Was that my father's intention — to wait to ensure the drug's safety before telling me? Probably didn't think I had the discipline not to imbibe.* The thought, which made him flush with anger and shame, was yet another confirmation that his father, though he may have loved Michael, had regarded his son's judgment as questionable.

"Have you read the Brimstone file?" asked Falters. "I noticed that it was unopened."

"On my to-do list," said Tiernan. "You said it's a weapon or something, right?"

"Correct," said Falters.

"We can explore that option later, but first thing's first," said Tiernan. "We still have to work out all the bugs on the longevity application before we tackle other ventures."

Falters remained silent. He had made a mistake — it was undeniable and he would have to correct it. He had thought Michael Tiernan would come to the same conclusion that he and Richard had. It was now obvious that Michael had a different perspective. Falters knew what he had to do.

After they had eaten the delicious bounty Sardinia's rich soil and hardworking people offered, Falters rose from the table and retrieved another Sardinian treat. He brought a plain glass bottle from the kitchen and placed it on the table next to Tiernan.

"What's this?" Tiernan asked as he picked up the bottle, uncorked it and took a whiff. "Smells like grappa."

"It's a very special type," answered Falters, "made from the berries of the Mirto plant. Very tasty." Falters poured Tiernan a glass and slid it over to him.

Tiernan picked it up and slugged it down. The burning sensation was unlike other digestivi. They all burned, but this burn radiated throughout his entire chest cavity and down his arms to the tips of his fingers.

"Wow," he exclaimed. "Now, that's what I call a drink. Pour me another." Tiernan grinned. His teeth and tongue glistened with a purplish coating left by the drink. Falters smiled and obliged.

"You're not indulging?"

"No," answered Falters. "I don't mix wine with liqueur."

Tiernan lifted the glass to his nose. "Smells like those little plants outside," he said. "Are those plants in the front of the house Mirto plants?"

Falters stood up from the table with his pipe in one hand, wine glass in the other. "Yes, they are everywhere in Sardinia. Tourists always ask what causes the island to be so fragrant; it's the Mirto plants," answered Falters as he packed tobacco into the bowl of his pipe. "Come, let's continue our conversation outside."

With that, the two headed out to the porch. Tiernan breathed deeply. The distinctive smell of the Sardinian countryside greeted him and he understood why his father chose it to be the birthplace of his greatest accomplishment. At that moment he imagined that, if Heaven existed, it would be like this. He sipped the purple liquid slowly this time, holding it in his mouth, savoring the sensation more than the taste before swallowing it and closing his eyes as his chest radiated, spilling the sensation down his arms again.

Tiernan, a Catholic by upbringing, had abandoned all belief in God when the Deity decided to take the little boy's mother from him. If God did exist, Tiernan didn't like him very much. As a child, he had attended religious education classes as mandated by the Church for those wishing to receive the Sacrament of Confirmation. During one of the lessons, he had argued that God is not perfect.

"I mean, look at the situation," young Tiernan had announced. "Everything that He creates eventually dies. Either He allows it or He can't do anything about it. Either way, He isn't perfect." After that, he received his catechism lessons from Marinella at home.

The sound of a match striking the tinderbox caused him to open his eyes again. Falters was sitting comfortably. Tiernan felt a strange happiness, a childlike excitement. Although he was jet-lagged and the past few months had been almost completely devoid of any leisure time, he felt energized, almost giddy.

The burning embers lit Falters' face as he took another pull of the pipe. "Do you remember when I told you about the formaggio con i vermi?" he asked. He didn't wait for Tiernan to respond, but continued his thought. "Your father was the type of man who needed to think about things excessively, sometimes at the risk of losing opportunities. He was cautious, too cautious sometimes."

Falters took another pull of the pipe. Tiernan didn't respond; he just listened to the sounds of the nocturnal inhabitants chirp and scurry under the cover of the impenetrable darkness.

"The villagers celebrate the Feast of San Lorenzo each year with a gathering on the hill," Falters continued, pointing to the hill in question. "As a landowner, your father had an obligation to contribute to the festival the fruits of the Sardinian soil." Tiernan listened as he finished the remainder of his new favorite drink.

"This was in the beginning, when the grapes were still not producing the levels of resveratrol we needed for Dionysinol," Falters continued. "We could have brought grapes to the festival, but your father insisted that I bring something else."

"I'm sure that there were plenty of grapes there anyway," suggested Tiernan.

Falters didn't respond and continued, "I brought formaggio con i vermi. Bought it locally, of course. It was dark at the festival, as was the tradition. Most of the villagers believe that the Feast of San Lorenzo is marked by an increase in shooting stars. They spend much of the evening gazing into the night sky, marveling at the shooting stars, which, incidentally, are no more plentiful on that evening than on any other. Anyway, I took advantage of the limited visibility and served your father a helping of the maggot cheese on a piece of bread."

"What did he do when he found out what he was eating?" asked Tiernan, disgusted.

"I can't remember. It doesn't matter," said Falters. "The important thing was that the cheese became Richard's favorite treat and he thanked me for making him eat it. There was always formaggio con i vermi at the table."

Tiernan was a little disappointed with the story that had so much potential but fizzled out and ended abruptly.

"That's it?" he asked.

Falters wasn't looking at him when he spoke again. He peered into the night sky. "Sometimes, you have to impose your will for the betterment of a situation."

Tiernan didn't ask for clarification. "Are you very tired? Because, oddly enough, I am wide awake."

Falters restocked the pipe with tobacco, indicating that he was in no hurry to retire. Tiernan had many questions about the data he had read earlier and attributed his lack of fatigue to the excitement he felt.

"Tell me more about you," said Tiernan. "You must have some great stories."

For hours, the two sat on the porch. Falters smoked his pipe like an elderly man. It looked terribly ill-placed in his young hand. His stories were almost too fantastic, yet something in his demeanor compelled belief. He recounted stories of the harsh existence that Communist Russia offered her children. His descriptions of the cold, uncaring elements assaulting the hungry citizens as they stood in line for bread were too vivid, seemed too alive to have been the imagination of one attempting to deceive. Yet, he retold these stories without the emotion that one would expect to accompany such memories. That changed when he spoke about the war.

"I was terrified," said Falters, eyes widening as if the memory itself could inflict harm. "I had seen battle before, witnessed my friends die in my arms and, still, never did I realize my own mortality until the bullet struck." He reached into the pouch again and retrieved another pinch of tobacco. Pausing to refill his pipe granted him an excuse to compose himself. "I thought I would bleed to death right there on the field. It seemed so unjust, and one does not experience injustice until one has lived under Communism." Again, he paused to draw from his pipe. "The fear of death has remained with me ever since," he said. "Perhaps that is why I took the Dionysinol."

Tiernan was getting uncomfortable with the conversation. He

135

took advantage of the pause to regain control of its direction. "So," he said. "What do you need from me in order to get Dionysinol ready for the market?" Unlike Falters, Tiernan didn't pause for long between thoughts. "I think we should move the entire operation back to the United States as soon as possible. You would have Oisín's research and development team at your disposal. We can develop both Regenerol and Dionysinol simultaneously. You'll be handsomely compensated for providing us with consultation, in addition to receiving a percentage of the profits from the sales, of course."

"I had hoped you would come to this conclusion on your own," said Falters. "Dionysinol will never be ready for human consumption. We must destroy the vineyards and all evidence of the Niamh grapes' existence. Your father and I had been considering that possibility for some time now. You will, too."

The declaration was abrupt and unexpected.

"Destroy it? The hell I will," said Tiernan. "Are you out of your mind?" He sat looking at Falters in disbelief. "What do you mean, destroy the vineyards?" Tiernan wanted to hear him say it again; he *must* have misheard him.

"It is the only way," said Falters.

"The only way to what?"

"To survive," said Falters.

"Why would I want to destroy the most important component of the most ground-breaking discovery the world has ever seen?" asked Tiernan.

"Because, if the human race were to find out about Dionysinol, it would destroy itself within a few generations." Falters paused for a moment to let the sentence register.

Tiernan wasn't sure how Falters had reached his conclusion, nor did he care. He was sure, however, that he'd destroy Falters before he allowed him to eradicate the Niamh grapes.

"As you are slowly coming to accept, Dionysinol doesn't simply slow the aging process. It halts it completely and forces it to retreat," said Falters. "Subjects exposed to Dionysinol are rendered as immortal as the Turritopsis nutricula. Humans would effectively live forever."

"So?" said Tiernan, missing the implication. "That's why everyone will want to buy it. We can charge anything we want and people will pay gratefully. We have a few glitches to work out, but we will get it right!"

Falters got up abruptly, walked back into the house and refilled his wine glass before returning. Tiernan was getting used to his socially-ignorant behaviors.

Falters took a drink before continuing. "Humans shouldn't be immortal; the planet cannot sustain much more than the numbers we have now. Imagine what would happen to our resources if we doubled, tripled, quadrupled in number. If anything, there should be fewer humans with shorter life spans, not more with indefinite longevity."

"If that's your only concern, you're worrying about nothing. People will continue to die. Stupidity is always going to be the leading cause of death and the most efficient way to thin out the herd," said Tiernan.

"Even if we assume you are correct, other considerations exist," said Falters.

"Let me guess," said Tiernan. "Fair distribution? How do we decide who gets the drug? What about the poor, disenfranchised majority that would never be able to afford Dionysinol? These are the weakest elements of our race, a burden on the rest of us. Screw them – the planet would be better off without them."

Tiernan had had a tendency toward greed ever since he was a little boy. Richard Tiernan had been a frugal man, not because of an innate character trait, but because of an acquired discipline. Money and power can be extremely corrosive to kindness and decency in susceptible people. Richard had tried to impress his views upon his teen son with little success. Michael Tiernan enjoyed money and became drunk with even the slightest power – a constant source of worry for his father. The power that Dionysinol possessed and, by proxy, that Tiernan now possessed, was an absolute power and he wasn't going to let a subordinate ruin it.

"Be that as it may," said Falters, "and although I disagree with your assessment of the situation, I was referring to a concern that reaches beyond the scope of the present generation. Once a subject has been treated with Dionysinol, it passes the mutated genetic code to its offspring."

"You mentioned that," said Tiernan, "but I'm sure we can fix that. Can't we?"

"I don't see how," said Falters. "We had our suspicions ever since the first control group, but I recently repeated those experiments and can say unequivocally that the progeny of treated individuals will inherit immortality. It would take years to understand how to circumvent that."

"Maybe we could engineer it so that it only worked on certain blood types or only on specific DNA markers present in the subject," suggested Tiernan. "Breed out the dummies, the morons."

Falters remained stoic.

"And, remember, we also have to engineer it so that people will have to take it continually to sustain the effects; otherwise, we won't profit as much. One dose? I mean, come on."

"You're not seeing the whole picture," said Falters.

Tiernan didn't address the accusation. "How difficult will it be to engineer the drug so that it cannot be passed down to offspring? That's our new first priority, even before the single dose dilemma. I need a list of what you have tried so far," Tiernan said.

"We haven't tried to circumvent the proliferation effect, so I don't know," responded Falters. "But I don't care, either."

"You don't care? Why not?" asked Tiernan.

"Because someone else will find a way to undo it and we will be in a worse situation," answered Falters.

Tiernan wasn't listening to Falters; he was merely acting out scenarios in his mind. He didn't understand the mechanism by which the drug worked, but that had never stopped anyone before. The same sentence appeared in the literature for every drug: *The mechanism is not understood, but it is assumed that the drug works by...*

"We can find a way! We must. This is my destiny, I can feel it," said Tiernan. "We can't stop until we find a way to control Dionysinol's power, a way to harness it. Can't you see? We will be like gods!"

"Gods reigning in Hell," said Falters. "Money would be useless in an overpopulated planet leeched of all natural resources, the inhabitants murdering each other over food and water."

"That's your past speaking," said Tiernan. "We're not in Communist Russia anymore."

"Perhaps we should retire for the night," said Falters, choosing not to address the offensive comment. "You may have a different perspective when you've had time to reflect."

Falters blew out a puff of smoke and reached over to pull the flowerpot closer to his chair. He placed the pipe on the ground and sat back. He started to speak and stopped.

"You gotta be kidding me," said Tiernan, laughing in spite of himself. "You can't be serious. You drag my ass all the way to *East Roast-your-ass-off-nowhereville,* tell me about the most amazing substance ever conceived and then say we have to destroy it. You're a piece of work."

"You can't see clearly yet," said Falters, "but you will come to understand, I'm sure of it."

"Don't bet on it," said Tiernan.

"I am going to sleep," said Falters as he stood up to leave. "I'm sure you have much to consider."

Not really, thought Tiernan. "I'm gonna stay out here a little while longer. Leave the light on this time."

The sun peered over the hillside and massaged the earth with her rays, gently awakening the diurnal flora and fauna. Tiernan sat alone on the porch for hours, replaying the evening's events over in his mind. It was as if Falters had reduced everything to first principles, beyond the reach of doubt, beyond the need for further clarification, and this unnerved Tiernan greatly. He was relieved that Falters hadn't taken it upon himself to destroy the project without consulting him. *I gotta make sure he never gets that opportunity again,* Tiernan thought. *Time to call in the big guns.*

附

Until the evening before, Ivan Falters had been the only human being with the distinction of being immortal — until that evening. The purple liquid that Tiernan had enjoyed so much had contained an added ingredient, one that accounted for his lack of fatigue. Falters had planned for Tiernan's resistance. Perhaps Tiernan would reconsider the fate of Dionysinol and the judicious rationing of the earth's resources now that he was going to need them for a long, long time.

WOW!!!

CHAPTER 23

THE SCREEN DOOR whined closed behind Falters as he walked out onto the porch. A haze hung over the vineyards, giving a mystical, almost foreboding impression as the sun started its ascent.

"You're awake early," said Falters, drinking from a little espresso cup. "I didn't hear you get up."

"That's because I dozed off out here," responded Tiernan, covered in mosquito bites. "Not that I got any real sleep with the crap you pulled on me yesterday."

"Dr. Tiernan, surely you can appreciate my position. I, too, am devastated by the turn of events, but I simply cannot take part in what would herald the destruction of the entire race."

"Stop being so goddamn dramatic, Falters," said Tiernan, as he stretched and yawned. "I think you're being an alarmist, but, if that's the way you feel, then I guess there's only one thing to do."

"There is never only one thing to do," responded Falters, "only one right thing to do."

"Yeah? And who gets to decide what's right? You?"

Falters remained silent.

"Huh? Tell me. You? I don't think so. In fact, I don't even know who you are. Is Ivan Falters even your real name? Doesn't sound too Russian to me. How did you and my father even meet?"

"Irrelevant." Falters stared out across the vineyards. "What matters is that your father and I trusted each other and this is what he would have wanted. The change to the Will wouldn't hold up in court; I think you know that."

Tiernan tilted his head and closed his eyes. "I knew it. Was Lynch in on this?"

"No. Your father's choice of legal counsel left much to be desired. Lynch is an idiot."

"So you and my father arranged this *joint ownership* scam so that I wouldn't sell the place immediately? It gave you a little time to handle me – is that it?"

"We were in the midst of putting contingency plans in place for the worst-case scenarios," said Falters. "He didn't want to tell you about Dionysinol until we were sure that we could contain it; that day never came."

"And *Lynch* is the idiot?"

"It is disrespectful to speak ill of the dead, but it shows an extreme lack of character for a son to speak of his father that way."

"Don't judge me, you arrogant prick," snarled Tiernan. "You don't know shit about me. Who the hell do you think you are?"

"I know very well who I am. Can you say the same about yourself?"

Tiernan got up and looked Falters in the eye. Falters didn't move, but returned his stare without any indication of fear. If Tiernan was considering an aggressive move, he reconsidered when he stood next to the towering Russian.

"As a matter of fact," said Tiernan, "I do know who I am. Allow me to introduce myself. I'm the guy who's going to be known as the man who cured aging, who defeated death, and you?"

"You will never have that distinction. Your birthright entitles you to Tír na nÓg, but you had no part in the Niamh plant's creation. You are nothing like your father and never will be."

His words stabbed Tiernan, but he didn't show any sign of it. "Well, that's too bad for you, isn't it? I bet you were hoping for someone just as easy to fool, right? Shame the way it turned out."

"Enough!" shouted Falters. His sudden bellow echoed in the hills. Tiernan jumped back and was instantly angry with himself for doing so. "Compensate me for my work and I will disappear. But remember this day – you will come to regret it like no other."

"I'll add it to my calendar, in case I do," said Tiernan. He brushed past Falters and walked into the house.

෪

Tiernan easily identified the keys to the Fiat parked in the drive-way and lifted them from the hook. Dust fell from the keychain as he pocketed them and walked outside. He got into the jalopy and hoped it would start. Falters sat on the porch watching him.

"Come on, baby, please just one more trip and then you can die," said Tiernan, addressing the dilapidated car. The car reluctantly obeyed. "Yes!" He put the car in gear, grinding it a little, before driving down the cobblestone path.

There's gotta be a phone around here somewhere, thought Tiernan as he drove into the neighboring town of Ghilarza. Finally, after consider-able difficulty, he found a public phone and placed a call.

"Jimmy? Hey, it's Tiernan. How've you been?"

"Tiernan, my man, how the heck are ya?"

"Good, good. Listen, I have a little situation. You interested in mak-ing a few bucks? You get to travel to Italy if you are." Tiernan wiped the stream of sweat from his forehead in disgust.

"Sure, why not? What the hell," said Jimmy. "A condition of my parole is that I can't leave the country, but you'll handle that, right?"

"Yeah, yeah, I'll take care of everything. Get a pen; this isn't the easi-est place to get to."

CHAPTER 24

southern

LORI ADAMS SAT on the park bench feeding the pigeons with day-old breadcrumbs. An army of birds surrounded her, eager to benefit from her generosity. Mary McKenna _spy_ didn't know what to expect from the meeting but assumed Lori's discretion would have a price tag attached. Twice during the walk to their rendezvous point, Mary had considered calling Vincent _rapist_ Tighte to tell him about the recent breach, but didn't. Tighte would be out for his own best interest and would certainly sacrifice Mary without a moment's hesitation.

Mary saw Lori feeding the birds and smiled despite herself. _She's a character,_ she thought, _no denying it._ The cooing of the elated birds seemed to harmonize with Lori's melodious greeting.

"Good evening, darlin'," Lori sang. "I hope I didn't take you away from something fun."

Mary joined Lori on the bench. She turned sideways to face her. She rested her forearms and chin on her elevated knee. Her posture spoke louder than her actual words. Mary McKenna was resolved to take any deal that Lori Adams proposed; she didn't have much of a choice.

"Are you going to turn me in?" Mary asked, tilting her head slightly, resting it on the crook of her arm. "Or is there something I can do to persuade you to not have me arrested?"

Lori scattered the rest of the crumbs on the ground. The cooing intensified as the birds pecked and bobbed up their _last call._ Lori crumpled up the brown paper bag with two hands and tossed the bag to Mary.

"Throw that in the trash behind you, would ya?"

Mary caught the bag and lobbed it into the can.

"Two points," Lori giggled. "Or is that three points? I don't know."

"What do you want, Miss Adams?" said Mary, getting right to the point. "Why am I here?"

A spandex-clad man jogged past them, frightening the birds. The flapping wings sounded like applause and a sudden gust of wind caused the remnants of the crumbs to take flight.

"Oh my," said Lori shielding her eyes from the debris. "It's like a wedding or somethin'."

Mary wanted to yell at the jogger, but the white wires swaying back and forth told her that he wouldn't have heard it anyway. Wiping a bread-crumb from her lip, she turned to Lori. "What are you going to do?"

Lori inspected herself for any debris after flicking a few crumbs from her shirt. "Well, that is up to you, Miss Delacroix," she said as she handed her a photocopy of the fake passport.

"Goddammit," Mary said as she inspected the page. "How did you get this?"

"A little birdie gave it to me," Lori quipped, having absolutely no intention of revealing her new source at Oisín – Eileen. "Now, let's see if we can find something to help each other out. I need that Chimera seed more than you do, honey."

Mary considered stalling Lori with promises of delivering the pro-totype, but, instead, she came clean. "I haven't been able to locate it and I can't risk going back there after today's stunt," said Mary.

Lori raised her eyebrows in interest.

"It's a long story," said Mary. "Suffice to say, I can't go back."

"That's a shame," said Lori, rising from the bench. "Then I guess we have nothing left to say to each other. Have a good night."

"Wait!" said Mary, grabbing Lori's arm. Lori instantly recoiled against the unsolicited touch. Mary apologized. "I think I might have something you want."

Lori sat down again and listened to Mary for the better part of an hour. As evening's light dimmed to dusk, the two women walked back to Mary's apartment. Lori dialed Connor and told him where she was going.

"Can't be too careful," Lori said as she snapped her phone closed. "If you try anything stupid," she continued, "Mr. Connor will be very angry and, boy, does he have an Irish temper."

Mary nodded in understanding.

∞

Lori Adams followed Mary McKenna into the apartment. Lori had her hand in her pocketbook where she kept her .22-caliber handy. She wasn't afraid and believed that she and Mary would work something out, but she was cautious all the same.

"Now, isn't this just the cutest li'l place?" remarked Lori. "What do you call it, *simple chic* or somethin' like that?"

Mary hadn't intended to decorate in any modern fashion. If she had achieved *simple chic,* it was by accident and not by design. "I don't know what it's called," she said. "I call it too busy to buy more furniture and decorations."

Mary looked around her own apartment, suddenly aware of how barren it looked. The white-washed walls were completely unadorned. The cream-colored curtains were heavy, chosen more to perform two functions than to beautify. They effectively blocked sunlight and kept the drafts to a minimum. Mary only then realized that the curtains were not white, as she had previously thought.

The TV sat on a plain stand that may have been designed for a different purpose, and the standard couch was beige. Everything in the apartment was ordinary – everything except Mary and Lori.

"I need to take a page outta your book, sweetie. I'm a pack rat and my poor li'l apartment is covered wall-to-wall with things," Lori said as if she were speaking to a friend. "You gotta stop by and help me minimize, simplify."

Mary McKenna didn't quite know how to respond. *Stop by?* she thought. *Is this broad for real?*

"Miss Adams," said Mary, "let's cut to the chase. What is it going to take for you to forget what you know?"

Lori looked around the apartment one last time before settling down on the couch. "Well, darlin'," she said, "I know quite a bit about you and it'll be hard forgetting some of the more, let's say, juicy things."

Mary sat on the other side of the couch. Both women leaned against the arms of the couch, looking like mirror images of each other. In many ways, they were. Lori spoke about Mary McKenna in the third person, giving a history of the girl's troubled past and highlighting the more indictable offenses for which Mary could still face charges.

At this point, Mary understood that she was completely at Lori's mercy and had no other choice but to comply.

"You work for Vincent Tighte, so I can assume that you know him pretty well, right?" asked Lori.

"What do you mean?" said Mary.

"You know his schedule, his routine, things about him, like security details 'n' stuff," said Lori.

Mary didn't know where Lori was headed and was almost too afraid to ask. "I hate that man," she said.

Lori took out an envelope and tossed it on the couch, halfway between them. Mary opened it, looked in and tossed it back to Lori.

"Those are some of the most gruesome crime scene photos I have ever seen. They never found out who killed that grotesque waste of a human life, did they?" Lori asked.

"They never will, either," said Mary. "The world's a better place without him. Anyone who deliberately harms a child should never see the light of day again."

Lori had enough evidence to believe that Mary McKenna was involved in the murder of a child rapist who had walked on a technicality. The mother of the child had been seen with Mary McKenna; the details were sketchy after that, but Lori had all the proof she needed when she saw Mary's face as she glanced at the crime scene photos. Lori couldn't be sure whether she saw pride, satisfaction or disgust in Mary's face as she looked briefly at the brutal photos. Any of the three was fine with Lori.

"I'm not going to kill Vincent Tighte," said Mary. "I don't do that."

"You don't do that *anymore*, but I'm not asking you to, honey," said Lori. "I've earned that pleasure. I need you to help me get away with it."

CB

Mary and Lori negotiated through the evening. The doorbell rang, announcing the arrival of the pizza – *extra everything 'cept the li'l fishys.*

Mary walked back with pie in hand, shaking her head, smiling in disbelief. A couple of hours ago, Lori Adams was her number one enemy, and now they were eating pizza and drinking flat diet soda like schoolgirls at a sleepover.

By the end of the evening, Lori had given Mary a vial of the purple liquid that was, at the very least, attached to a very interesting story. In exchange, she received the stolen files Mary had faked a miscarriage to get. Both women vowed to keep their respective mouths shut. Having compromised, they both walked away with more than either had anticipated. Mary ended up with a copy of Richard Tiernan's leather portfolio, an evening filled with incredible stories about eternal youth, a vial of purple liquid called Dionysinol, all the incriminating evidence that Lori had against her, and a promise of $10 million originally earmarked for Tiernan had he coughed up the Chimera seed prototype.

Lori ended up with the data on Oisín's new drug – Regenerol – including poorly-encrypted data on the illegal testing on Mexican women. Most importantly, Lori was going to get something she had been waiting for. Mary was going to deliver Vincent Tighte: he would be alone, drugged and helpless.

Before Lori left Mary's apartment, she handed her a Tracfone™. "There's about 300 minutes left on this one," she said as she handed her the disposable phone. "I entered all my numbers on this cell."

Mary had even more respect for Lori Adams after hearing about her ordeal, her horrifying experience, the life-changing event that set her on a path of revenge that would undoubtedly end with the death of Vincent Tighte. Mary did not feel guilty about the role that she intended to play. The expression that Lori wore on her face when she skimmed the reports of the illegal testing of Regenerol on infertile women in Mexico was enough to persuade Mary that this woman – Lori Adams – was unable to have children. She couldn't be sure if Lori's infertility was a result of the brutal rape she suffered at the hands of Vincent Tighte, but she assumed it probably was. At any rate, erasing Tighte from the face of the earth was a public service, as far as Mary was concerned, and, although she had reservations about killing him herself, she wouldn't begrudge Lori the pleasure.

"Were you able to get any samples of the Regenerol?" asked Lori as Mary walked her to the door.

"No," Mary answered. "It wasn't a mission objective. Tighte just wanted me to secure the prototype before Lionel, or I mean, you, got it."

Lori turned and added one more thing before she left the apartment. "Oh, I don't know if this affects you, but I thought I should tell you," she said. "Tighte sold all of his Lionel stock this afternoon. He seems to be fixin' to leave."

Mary smiled and nodded her head. *Bastard,* she thought. *I knew it.*

CB

Lori got into the car a few blocks from Mary's apartment. "My stories ready, hon?" she asked, settling into the comfortable, spacious limo. "I gotta catch up 'n' see if Barbara comes outta her coma."

"They're ready to go. Just press play," said Edward. "It's ready where you left off."

"Thank you, honey." She raised the privacy window and turned the volume of the TV way up. Edward was unable to hear the primal wailing, the heart-wrenching sobbing emanating from the back seat as Lori put both of her aging hands over her barren womb, knees drawn up in the fetal position. She had dreamt that one day her womb would be the warm abode of many children – the children that could never be, now. The unborn souls of the children she never conceived called out for justice. They shouted in unison. *"Avenge us, Mommy. Avenge us."*

CHAPTER 25

TIERNAN RETURNED TO Tír na nÓg, parked the Fiat and entered the house. He threw the keys down on the dining room table. "Falters!"

"I'm here," said Falters, looking down from the upstairs landing.

"Look," said Tiernan, "we need to talk. Can you come down here?" He gestured to the table. Falters came down and pulled out a chair, but, before sitting, picked up the Fiat keys and returned them to their rightful place in the kitchen.

"I don't want to throw you out on the street, but it's clear that we have to find a different arrangement. I can't leave you here unsupervised," said Tiernan.

Falters smiled. "Unsupervised, you say? I'm afraid you're the one in need of supervision."

"Let's not get into this again," said Tiernan. "I'm willing to settle up with you; give me a reasonable sum and I'll call Lynch to arrange payment."

"Money will not compensate me for my work," said Falters. "Your father and I had a different arrangement."

"Well, he's gone now and I'm in charge. Consider the arrangement you had with my father officially null and void."

"Very well," said Falters, "then our paths diverge at this junction. I will leave Tír na nÓg. Do you require my immediate departure?"

A surge of guilt assaulted Tiernan with fierce strength. He imagined his father's face and how it would have looked had he been part of the discourse. He would've been ashamed.

"No, of course not," said Tiernan. "This was your home for years, but I can't risk leaving you here alone. I've sent for someone to look after my interests in my absence."

Falters smiled briefly. "A sentinel to watch over your newly-found treasure, I understand."

"Yeah, something like that," said Tiernan. "It doesn't have to be this way." The guilt gained strength from Falters' submission to Tiernan's authority. "What are you going to do? Do you have somewhere to go?"

"You needn't concern yourself with me. You will have more than you will be able to handle soon – much sooner than you think."

"My friend should be here tomorrow. Jimmy isn't the brightest man on the planet. In fact, he could very well be one of the dumbest, but he's loyal. I wouldn't try anything if I were you."

Falters stood up from the table and headed upstairs. In the distance, the sound of the door closing told Tiernan the conversation was over.

That was easier than I thought.

⚃

Lori Adams retrieved her dark sunglasses and put them on to conceal the raccoon-like appearance the tears had produced. She wasn't ashamed of showing emotion – quite the contrary – but she was loath to have Edward worry, which she knew he would. The limo slowed to a stop and, a few seconds later, the door opened. Edward offered his hand to assist Lori out of the car. She draped the messenger bag containing the fruits of her negotiations with Mary McKenna over her shoulder. Edward knew the signs. The dark sunglasses meant something was wrong.

"Lori?" he said and stopped at that. That was enough. If Lori wanted to share, she would. She understood what he meant; he was offering himself to her for whatever she needed.

"I'm fine, darlin'," she said. "I had a bad headache earlier and I'm afraid it might be coming back."

Edward knew she was lying, but didn't pry. "This is for you," he said, handing her a poorly-wrapped gift. "I spent the whole night and

152

most of today getting it ready for you, so I skimped on the wrapping paper."

Lori smiled in spite of herself. She loved random gifts, especially when they were given out of love and not as a way to win favor.

"What's this?" she smiled, tearing the paper. "A book, huh?"

Edward smiled bashfully and turned the book in her hand to reveal the cover. *To the Most Amazing Woman on Earth.* The gold lettering contrasted well with the royal blue cover. *I Love You and I Always Will.*

"Well," Lori sang as she removed her dark glasses. "That is quite a title."

Edward smiled and explained that he'd gathered all the information available on Fionn Mac Cumhaill and had it all bound together in a neat little book. Lori kissed him on both cheeks.

"You changed my life too, darlin', and I will always love you."

Edward didn't expect to be invited up that evening. He knew she wasn't in the mood when she got into the limo earlier that evening. He was always in the mood. Although they never talked about their relationship, and he knew that they weren't exclusive, he never took another woman. Lori Adams was everything that he wanted and, if they never became more than what they were, he would still consider himself lucky.

As Lori headed toward the door of her building, Edward called after her. "It's pronounced, Finn McCool."

Lori smiled, nodded and walked into the building where the doorman greeted her with a genuine smile and a tip of his hat.

Lori sat on her couch and placed the file on Regenerol on one leg and Edward's gift on the other. *Finn McCool,* she thought, *now that's way better than the way I was pronouncing it.* She heard her cell buzzing in her purse and remembered that she hadn't called Connor back as she had promised.

"Oh, hell's bells," she said aloud, a phrase used in the most dire of circumstances. "Ryan? I am so sorry, darlin'. I lost my mind for a spell. I got it back now."

Connor was silent on the other end for a few seconds, then responded with a sigh. "I was worried, Loraine," he said. Lori knew that he was very serious when he addressed her as *Loraine*, so she refrained from her usual reaction to being called by her Christian name. Making light of it would only exacerbate his anger.

"If you hadn't answered, Mary McKenna would have had a very unpleasant night. Do you realize that?"

Lori realized it very well – all too well. "Ryan," she said, "I had some bad flashbacks and I miss my babies somethin' awful tonight."

Connor knew the babies existed exclusively in Lori's imagination but were no less real to her, no less dead. She mourned not a physical death, but something much more savage: a death of opportunity.

"Do you want me to come over?" Connor asked, forgetting everything else for that instant. "We can just sit and talk all night if you want."

"Aw, you're sweet," she said. "I'm okay, but thank you."

Connor told her to call him if she needed him, regardless of the hour.

"Oh, my Lord," Lori said. "I almost forgot. I tell ya, my mind is goin'. It's really goin'."

Connor didn't speak. He waited for her to continue.

"Lord, have I got somethin' for you, darlin'," she continued. "What would you say if I told you that I saved us about $90 million tonight? Huh?"

"I'd say *great!*" Connor responded, "and then ask how."

"I'm not getting into it tonight because then you'll keep me up all night asking questions and I won't get to read my book on Finn McCool," Lori said. "Just trust me, darlin'," she continued, "things are 'bout to get really interesting."

They agreed that they would meet for breakfast before work at the same diner they often frequented. After hanging up, Lori removed everything from the messenger bag that Mary had provided. She took a leather alternative from her closet and removed the tags.

"I knew I'd get some use outta you," she said, addressing the bag. "I refuse to carry that ol' beat-up thing around town." She put the stolen files in the beautiful leather bag and snapped the buttons shut. She reached for her book, opened the first page and read until she reached the last.

"Well, I'll be," she said as she sat alone in her living room. "This purple stuff is better than I thought."

CHAPTER 26

"TIERNAN! OVER HERE!" shouted Jimmy. "Now, that's a big boat, ain't it?" A balding, overweight man dragging a suitcase exited the ferry. His stained T-shirt didn't quite cover his hairy abdomen, and the sweat rings under his arms grew exponentially as he left the relative cool of the open sea.

Tiernan looked at the ship. "Yeah, she's a big one, alright. You made it, huh?"

"Barely, man," said Jimmy. "What the hell are you doing here? This place is in the middle of nowhere."

"Yeah, you think so? Just wait until you see Boroneddu. Come on, the car's this way."

⑅

"So, this Russian guy, he into you for some money? What are we talking about here?" said Jimmy as he admired the countryside from the passenger seat of the Fiat. "You want him worked over, threatened, what's the story here?"

"Nah, nothing like that," said Tiernan. "This is an easy one. His name is Ivan Falters, harmless really. I just need you to keep an eye on him until he leaves; make sure he doesn't rob me blind. I'd do it myself, but I gotta get back to the States."

"What's his story?"

"Doesn't have one," said Tiernan. "My father hired him years ago and his services are no longer needed. You know how it is."

"I sure do. Like those Mexy women, right?" Jimmy laughed and Tiernan hated himself. "Those broads got the shitty end of the stick,

157

wouldn't you say? Hey, did that drug ever come out? What was it called, Rebornatrol or something?"

"It's still under development," said Tiernan, "and no one has to die this time."

"No prob, Mikey boy," said Jimmy. "I came prepared anyway." He tapped his suitcase. "They didn't even check it."

"That was pretty risky, Jimmy," Tiernan laughed. "You really don't give a shit, do you?"

"Not really, bro. Hey, did you call my probation officer?"

"All taken care of," said Tiernan. "Look, I don't want any problems. Just make sure Falters leaves peacefully. He's not a bad guy. He just has a different philosophy, that's all."

"Whatever, man," said Jimmy. "My fee is still the same, capice?"

Tiernan nodded in acknowledgement.

CB

Falters stood on the porch and watched the Fiat make its way down the cobblestone driveway until it came to a stop in front of Venus de Milo.

"Holy!" said Jimmy as he looked out at the acres. "These all yours?"

"Yup, and I'd like them to be here when I get back, so watch this guy."

"Is that him?" Jimmy pointed rudely.

"Yeah, that's him. Remember, peaceful departure, okay? My plane leaves in four hours. We're cutting it close. Come on inside."

Tiernan introduced Jimmy and Falters, reiterated his instructions and felt satisfied that the situation would go smoothly. Falters, although highly offended, agreed to vacate the premises within the week, and Jimmy agreed to stay until told otherwise.

"As soon as I get back, I'll make arrangements for your replacement," said Tiernan. "I think I might have John Graham take a trip over here until I figure out what I'm doing."

"Hey, how's old Johnny?" said Jimmy. "I haven't seen that old stiff since Mexico."

158

"He's the same." Tiernan looked around to see if Falters was in earshot of the conversation. "Shhh. Jimmy, keep the small talk to a minimum, would ya? This guy doesn't need to know anything about Mexico, okay?"

"Yeah, sure. Sorry, Mikey, I didn't realize this guy wasn't involved." He made a locking motion across his lips.

"Alright, man," said Tiernan. "I'm heading out. Call me if there are any problems."

"Take care, man, but, don't leave me here too long. It's frickin' hot."

જ

Tiernan flew back to the United States. His decision to take Jimmy Galante out of mothballs weighed heavily on his mind. He'd placed the call impulsively and wondered if he had made the right decision. Jimmy had proved himself a very useful resource in Mexico and, despite his astonishing disrespect for the sanctity of life, Tiernan was indebted to him. The bodies of the Mexican women and the violently-aborted fetuses, buried collectively, deep in the sands of the Chihuahuan Desert, were never found. John Graham and Michael Tiernan had never discussed it. It was better that way – less real and surprisingly easy – although each of them fought very hard to keep the images locked in the dungeon of their respective subconscious – a feat that John Graham found more difficult than the others did.

જ

Debra Lewis was waiting for him at the Arrivals gate. She had rehearsed her lines a hundred times. *Better to get it out all at once,* she thought. *This way, the anticipation cannot add to the shock.* She saw Tiernan instantly as he walked through the doors.

"You look really refreshed," she exclaimed, but then wanted to slap herself across the face. *Idiot,* she thought. *How am I going to follow that up with the news that we lost our newest employee after she miscarried on the bathroom floor?*

159

"Well, thank you. I feel pretty good, too. Funny thing is," he added, "I got almost no sleep."

"Yeah, that is funny," Debra said, and then proceeded to blurt out the bad news. "Mary Delacroix had a miscarriage in the ladies' room at Oisín and hasn't been back to work since."

Tiernan gawked at her in disbelief. "Wow," he managed, "that left little to the imagination."

Twice in the five minutes since she had been in Tiernan's presence, Lewis wanted to melt into the ground and disappear. "We didn't lose anyone else, though." *Oh my God,* she thought, *I am such a moron!*

On the ride back to the mansion, Debra briefed Tiernan on the events of the week. He was disconcerted by the news that they had been unable to contact Mary Delacroix since the tragedy.

"Did you ask around at the hospitals?" asked Tiernan.

"Yes, but it seems Dr. Delacroix chose a different hospital than the one the ambulance took her to; St. Lucy's has no record of any Mary Delacroix or any bill charged to Oisín, either."

"Terrible, terrible thing," Tiernan said. "Did you try her apartment?"

"Yes, several times," said Debra. "No answer there, either. I know she's engaged to be married, so she is probably with her fiancé."

"Oh, that's where she probably is," said Tiernan. "Do we have an address?"

"No, unfortunately we don't even have a name," Debra answered.

Tiernan reached over and retrieved a bottle from the bar in the poorly-stocked limo. He poured himself a glass and drank it down. "Did you send the IND application to the FDA?"

Debra Lewis had spent every waking moment preparing the application to petition the FDA to allow Regenerol to advance to the next stage – human trials. She went over the lengthy process with a fine-tooth comb, double-checked every requirement, crossed every "t," dotted every "i," until exhaustion had gotten the better of her and she collapsed at her desk. Graham was sitting in her office when she awoke the next morning. He had been reading the paper as if there was nothing out of the ordinary, nothing odd about someone fully clothed, asleep at a desk, snoring and drooling on a stack of papers.

"Uh, Debra?" said Tiernan. "The IND?"

"Oh, yes," she smiled. "I'm sorry, I was ignoring you – NO, I wasn't – I mean, I was thinking of someone else – no, something else!" She prayed for a head-on collision, not enough to kill them, but enough to cause amnesia. "It's done. I sent it in. All's well."

She reached for the bottle of whatever it was and took Tiernan's used glass. She filled it to the rim and drank it like it was iced tea. Expelling the majority of the spirit in a projectile fashion onto Tiernan was the final humiliation of the evening. She handed him a napkin to sop up the regurgitated liquor.

"Strong stuff," she said before sitting back in unparalleled humiliation.

 CB

"I don't know why, John," Debra explained. She had just dropped Tiernan at the mansion and was headed back into the city. "I was like the nerdy girl with a crush on a date with the quarterback of the football team."

Graham gave the audible equivalent of nodding. "Mmm," he said, allowing Debra to continue confiding her humiliation to the man who had become her best friend.

"Oh, I'm so inconsiderate," she observed. "I didn't realize how late it is. Were you sleeping?"

He was – had been for hours. "No, dear," he lied, "I was still awake."

"Oh, good," Debra said and continued confessing her blunders. "He looked especially handsome, rested maybe," she said. "I was spellbound, lost myself, thinking thoughts I..." She stopped, realizing that she was dangerously close to mortifying herself all over again.

Graham understood her dilemma completely, for he felt the same way every time he set eyes on her. "Absence makes the heart grow fonder," he said. "You were just happy to see him, dear, and probably very relieved that you no longer had those enormous responsibilities he put on you in his absence."

161

Debra considered Graham's explanation and thanked him for being, for just being. "Oh, I hope so, John," she whined. "I can't have that happen every time I'm around him. You should've seen me; I was ridiculous."

"Get some rest, dear," Graham said, wishing things were different, wishing he was younger or she was older, wishing he didn't die a little each time he saw her or when she mentioned Tiernan. "Tomorrow you'll be right as rain. You'll see."

"Good night, John, and thank you. You're a real friend," Debra said, comforted.

"Good night, dear, and sleep well."

Graham got out of his warm bed and went into his antiquated kitchen. He opened the fridge and took out a container of milk, poured it into a saucepan and put it over the flames. *Warm milk,* he thought, *I'll just have some warm milk to help me sleep.* He sat in the dark, waiting for the milk of another species to warm and offer him a little comfort. Love never learned to consider age differences when enrapturing people, and this ignorance caused many a heart to break into a million pieces. *Love never fails to collect its debts,* he thought. *It's an expensive habit and I don't know how much longer I can afford to pay.*

Graham sipped the creamy warm milk, but wasn't able to convince his mind that his body needed sleep. After a few valiant attempts to summon slumber, he conceded and began writing a revised list of things to do.

CHAPTER 27

FALTERS SAT AT the dining room table, watching the pendulum of the old wooden clock keep time. *Time,* he thought, *what we wouldn't do to have more of it.* He hadn't seen Jimmy since he disappeared into the guestroom, but he knew he wasn't far. The smell of the evening's meal beckoned Jimmy like a muse and, within minutes of the food's arrival, he poked his head over the upstairs landing.

"Hmmmm, what smells so good?"

"Cena," said Falters, looking at the clock again. "There is more food than we can possibly finish."

Jimmy cultivated suspicion like a farmer cultivates produce. It kept him alive, although it wasn't conducive to attracting many friends. He cautiously approached the dining room. When he saw the table spread, his appetite buried his anxiety.

"This all for you?" asked Jimmy.

"Of course not. I wasn't expecting Dr. Tiernan to depart so hastily, so I arranged greater quantities of food for the next week."

"Shame," said Jimmy. "Looks good."

"The chef is a young man in the village. Please, sit," Falters gestured to the chair opposite him. "There is no reason to behave like enemies. I respect your responsibilities." He poured Jimmy a glass of wine.

"Damn, I'm hungry," said Jimmy, still wearing the stained T-shirt, although the sweat rings were receding. His sparse hair was disheveled and the crease on his face indicated that he had recently awoken from a nap. He pulled out a chair opposite Falters and sat. "Don't think that this means we're friends or nothing, understand?"

"Friendship is not something you acquire by offering a mere meal," said Falters. "This is simply an act of civility." Falters turned the pasta dish and allowed Jimmy to take the first scoop.

"Alright. Mikey said you were a decent guy, just had a difference of opinion. It happens."

"Yes, unfortunately it does."

"This wine from those grapes out there?" Jimmy slugged the wine as if he were drinking beer. "Good shit. Fill me up again, if you don't mind."

"Not at all," said Falters, pouring a second generous portion. "And, yes, the wine is from Tír na nÓg Vineyards; do you like it?"

"Do I like it? Hell, yeah!" Another slug followed two heaping fork-fuls of pasta; his T-shirt acquired some new stains as strands of spa-ghetti slithered free. "You mind?" Jimmy gestured to the steaks.

"No, please, eat as much as you wish."

"So, uh, you and Tiernan did business together?"

"Richard Tiernan and I were colleagues, yes."

"Found it hard to work for Mikey boy, huh? Yeah, he can be a real prick sometimes, but he's like a brother to me. We go way back."

"Yes, you strike me as the sort of character with whom Dr. Tiernan would associate."

Jimmy chewed with his mouth open, nodded his head in faux un-derstanding and dipped a piece of bread in the sauce. "What kind of business you guys running here?"

"Tír na nÓg is a vineyard; we sell wine."

"Yeah, I figured that. So what happened with you and Mikey?"

"We had a difference of opinion regarding the distribution of our product."

"Oh." Jimmy helped himself to another glass. "This stuff's great. I gotta bring some of this stuff back."

"I wouldn't plan on it. The product never leaves the vineyards. Like Oisín and Niamh in the old Irish legend, leaving Tír na nÓg is not an option."

"Huh?"

After enduring several minutes of innane conversation, Falters looked at the clock, got up from the table and walked outside.

"Hey, where ya going? You finished already? You're a lightweight."

Falters didn't answer. He stood halfway between the door and the porch and lit his pipe, blowing the smoke out into the night.

"Hey, how 'bout a little ice cream. You got any?" asked Galante.

He's even less intelligent than I had anticipated, thought Falters, who continued to smoke his pipe. "James, your name is James, isn't it?"

"Nah, it's Jimmy."

"When you stand up, I'm not so sure you will desire any ice cream, but, then again, we never tested that quantity on a human before. I'm very interested in seeing the result."

"What are you talking about? There's always room for ice cream."

"I suppose you're right," said Falters. "There's ice cream in the kitchen. Help yourself."

"Don't think I will? When I was growing up, you hadda eat fast and furious to get full. Eight brothers and two sisters – shit didn't go to waste in my house."

"The demons," said Falters, "Waste, Gluttony and Greed, are the most destructive powers in all of Hell. How much suffering and pain would be eliminated if these realities weren't so pervasive, so alluring."

"Yeah," said Jimmy. "So, I'm getting some ice cream. Want some?" He stood up and his head immediately spun. "Whoa, man, that wine was strong." He collapsed unconscious onto the hardwood floor with a thud, pulling the tablecloth and all the contents onto the floor with him.

Falters tapped the pipe against the flowerpot and exhaled a final plume of smoke. He walked back into the house, stepped over Jimmy's unconscious body and continued on to the kitchen. "Actually," he said, "I think I would like some vanilla ice cream."

❧

A few hours later, Jimmy woke with a start. "What the fuck just happened? You poison me or something?" He surveyed his surroundings and sat up. Falters had placed him on the couch, where he had remained.

165

"No," said Falters. "I gave you a dose of Dionysinol, a rather large dose, since you continued to drink more wine than I had anticipated."

"You gave me what?"

"You have received a rather unexpected gift, James. I had hoped that quantity would kill you, but I was mistaken. It seems that the rapidity of the onset of the effects is a function of the dose."

"You drugged me up?" Jimmy jumped to his feet. "Yeah? You think you can get away with screwing with Jimmy Galante? Well, I gotta little somethin' for you!" His anger clouded his perception. Had he noticed the ill-fitting clothes, the feel of a full head of hair, the inexplicable absence of his large, paunchy stomach, he wouldn't have run up the stairs to get his gun. Falters remained motionless as Jimmy ran swiftly up to the room.

"Holy shit! Oh my God, what the hell?"

Jimmy ran down the stairs and back into the room – one hand running through his new, thick head of hair, the other caressing the new washboard abdominal muscles previously hidden by layers of greed and gluttony.

"You are understandably confused," said Falters, "but, please, try to remain calm."

"Calm?! What the fuck is going on! What the hell kinda wine is that?" Jimmy pulled off the stained T-shirt and admired his new muscles in awe. Falters sat very still, like a large cat stalking its prey.

"I'm a chick magnet, that's what I am," said Jimmy. "Look at me! Am I hallucinating or something?"

"I don't think so; I'm seeing the same things."

"Oh, man! Ol' Richie Tiernan did it this time. That man was a genius, a real freakin' Einstein."

"An appropriate analogy, actually," said Falters. "Einstein helped create the atom bomb – and Richard Tiernan, the Brimstones."

"Yeah, cool. He made bombs, too?"

"Here, come sit down," said Falters, ignoring the question. "May I examine you?"

"Don't get frisky. I don't get down like that."

"The effects were rapid, more rapid than with any of the other species. I would be very interested in learning more from you, but I simply don't have the time." Falters checked Jimmy's eyes, heartbeat and respiration. With the exception of his accelerated heart rate and his substantially-elevated blood pressure, he seemed normal. "How do you feel?"

"I feel great! I feel like a teenager, like I could run the Olympics or something."

"You mean a marathon."

"Yeah, yeah, I feel like I could run a marathon."

Falters scribbled notes and continued to interview Jimmy, who looked down at the notebook.

"Is that Italian?"

"No."

"What language is it?"

"Russian," said Falters. "I truly regret not having the time to study you. I could learn a great deal from you, but, as I said before, time is of the essence." Resveretrol

Jimmy was oblivious to the outside world as the Dionysinol coursed through his veins, renewing each cell, perfecting each function. "Do you hear that? It's the bugs outside; they're loud as hell."

"The volume is the same. Your senses are heightened. I found it rather disconcerting when I first took Dionysinol, but I became habituated, learned to control them. You won't have to worry about that."

"Cool," said Jimmy. "Uh, does this last? How long will I stay like this?"

"Not long," said Falters. "Unfortunately, you would have to take more of the Dionysinol to make it a permanent change, but I'm afraid it's cost-prohibitive. Dr. Tiernan will be infuriated with me for even introducing it to you."

"Hey, man," said Jimmy, "why should you give a damn? Tiernan's cutting you out, ain't he? Well, you can give him a real *screw you* by, you know, giving me some more."

"I'm sorry, James. I'm afraid my ethical standards forbid me."

"Come on, man. Think about it, he was ready to throw your ass on the street. Screw him."

So much for your loyalty, thought Falters.

"I'll pay you, man," said Jimmy. "Tiernan's giving me $10,000 for this gig. It's yours. Whaddya say?"

"Ten-thousand dollars," said Falters.

"Yeah, $10,000 cash and, I swear, it's yours if you just, ya know, slip me a little more of the Diona stuff."

"Dionysinol. How do I know you will keep your word?"

"Come on, man, I'm good for it. I swear to God. I swear on my mother's grave."

"Ten-thousand dollars and Dr. Tiernan will never know of this, correct?"

"Nah, I won't say a damn word. Neither of you will ever see me again. Look at me, I got a chance to start all over. Come on, you gotta help me out."

"Very well," said Falters, placing a vial of the precious liquid on the coffee table.

Jimmy picked it up and shook it. "This it?"

"That is a normal dose. You took approximately four times as much, hence the rapid change." Falters looked at the clock. "You may take it whenever you're ready."

"Cheers, brother. You won't regret it." He popped the rubber stopper and drank it down. "Damn, that's nasty. Tastes kinda fishy."

Falters glanced at the clock again. "I have good news and bad news," he said. "The good news is that I don't expect you to pay me."

"You callin' me a liar?"

"I'm not calling you a liar, although you are very much a deceitful degenerate. You didn't let me finish. I haven't told you the bad news," continued Falters. "I don't expect you to pay me because, in a few minutes, you'll be dead."

"Yeah? And who's gonna kill me? You?"

"I already have. Goodbye, James."

Jimmy jumped up from the couch and into a fighting stance. "Come

168

on, Commie boy. You wanna try the new improved Jimmy Galante?" Jimmy lifted his fists and tucked in his chin. Falters sighed as he stood up, lifted his left leg and delivered a powerful blow to Jimmy's chest, sending him flying across the room. He glanced at the clock. Any time now.

"You son of a bitch. Oh, man, now you're gonna get it." Jimmy stood up again. "Now you're gonna taste a little blood, swallow a few teeth." He moved again toward Falters, who remained seated. Falters saw the wobbly gate, the glassy stare and he knew: decomposition was beginning.

Jimmy valiantly tried to remain standing, but his knees buckled from under him. Gasping for breath, he fell to the floor.

"You are a victim of your own greed," said Falters, standing over him. "You are decomposing, so forgive the dreadful etiquette, but I cannot allow you to rot in the house." Jimmy couldn't speak, but his eyes, full of hate and fear, spoke nonetheless. "Up we go," said Falters, grabbing Jimmy under the arms, dragging him into the kitchen and out the back door.

He dragged the semiconscious man out into the dark vineyards, a substantial distance from the house. He knew the smell of the decomposing body would be horrific to the average person, but, with his heightened senses, it would be unbearable.

"Here we are," said Falters, dropping Jimmy to the ground. "I would try to die soon, if I were you." Falters turned and walked back to the house.

As Jimmy lay decomposing, it occurred to him that his 15 minutes as a chick magnet were not quite what he had envisioned.

☙

Ivan Falters calculated the time in America – Tiernan was probably at home by now. Falters wasn't an emotional man. More than 80 years had left him somewhat blunted to life's inevitable pain. *Only the unintelligent get angry when confronted with the inevitable.* He had euthanized the last animal and felt an unfamiliar emotion sneak up on him as he put the lifeless dog in the bag with the other carcasses. *I liked this one,* he thought. *Kwala had a nice disposition; I wish I could have let her run free.*

Falters incinerated the animals, collected the ashes and mixed them with lye. He was methodical, robot-like in his adherence to procedure; it made difficult tasks easier. *It must be done, Richard,* he thought. *Your son has forced my hand.*

Falters had seen enough war in his life, fought against enemies who were once friends and alongside friends who were once enemies. Dionysinol would ignite the fuse that would set the world ablaze if it became known. War would be the necessary consequence; no one would ever be satisfied with a single lifespan if immortality were possible. War, death, cruelty, pain and suffering are the harbingers of progress, but the world had never experienced such a gargantuan leap forward – the potential to live forever would be the prelude to the end of human existence. *Not at my hand,* he thought. *If we perish, it will not be at my hand.*

Falters had wanted to emerge from his Italian exile and rejoin the human experience one day. He had fantasized about having another wife, a wife like Nadja before the Germans killed her. Perhaps he would learn to love again; perhaps time would erode the stony barnacles that clung to his heart and suffocated all emotion. He remembered his daughter and two sons, but banished the memory immediately. After seeing their ravaged corpses, the mutilated bodies laying alongside his beloved Nadja, he was unable to remember them in any other setting. At first, he tried to remember happy times with them – birthdays, holidays, rite of passage celebrations – but their young, beautiful Russian faces were replaced with the horrific scene that had scorched away the memory of how they'd looked before. It was easier to try to forget them.

War was an inevitability. As long as humans existed, wars would be fought. Humans *needed* war; they needed war like they needed food and water. If war is part of the human condition, the only logical, rational thing to do is to embrace it, to accept the inevitable, but manipulate the outcome. Falters had this in mind when he and Richard began to consider alternate uses for Dionysinol many years ago.

The drug was intended to extend life, thought Falters, *but it will be more effective at extinguishing it. It's time for the many to make sacrifices for the few.*

CHAPTER 28

LORI ARRIVED AT the diner first. She was always prompt for meals.

"Good morning, Jenny," she said as the waitress dropped four creamers on the table before pouring the coffee that Lori had not ordered yet. "Breakfast shift or all-nighter?" Lori asked, carefully tearing open the first of the four creamers.

"Breakfast shift," Jenny responded. "You want the usual?"

"Mmmm hmmm," Lori hummed as she shook her head. "My doctor told me I need to cut back a smidge, so easy on the bacon and just a little butter on the toast, 'k?"

Jenny didn't write down Lori's order; she knew it by heart, and this new development merely required a smaller portion of the biweekly ritual. Jenny was depressed, never smiled and looked years older than her tender age. When life gives lemons, only the delusional attempt to make lemonade. Jenny was realistic about her future, so what was there to be happy about?

Lori liked Jenny and, contrary to all appearances, Jenny liked Lori, too. "You do somethin' to your hair, Jenny?"

Jenny was busy wiping down the counter before the breakfast rush. "My sister tried to color it for me and mixed the ingredients all wrong," she answered, moving on to topping off the sugar bowls and ketchup bottles. "I know, it looks funny."

"Oh, no, honey," said Lori. "You have a face that can get away with any ol' hair color, pretty little thing." A seedling smile germinated on Jenny's face, but never blossomed as the bells jingled, alerting everyone that another person wanted to break his nightly fast. This one was Ryan Connor.

Jenny grabbed the decaf pot and headed over to the table where she knew the man would join Lori.

"Decaf, please," Connor said as he walked past Jenny, "and a western omelet with egg whites, and a small order of home fries." Jenny didn't have to put in his order, either. When she saw Lori, she knew the man would come shortly afterward. And his order was always the same too. Jenny signaled to the short-order cook who peered out the rectangular hole in the wall that separated the kitchen from the customers: thumbs up meant put both orders in now.

Lori was scribbling on a piece of paper as Connor slid into the booth. She folded the paper and put it under her coffee cup.

"Good morning, handsome," she sang. "You look rested. Sleep well?"

"Yes, I did," Connor said. "What's the news?"

"Oh, my Lord, I don't know where to start. I really don't," Lori said and took his hands and squeezed them with excitement. "I should be sloth tired right now, but I'm as giddy as a kid on Christmas mornin'."

Connor tasted his coffee and lifted his hand to summon the waitress. Pushing the cup to the edge of the table, he requested a fresh cup by shaking his head and pointing to the rejected beverage. Again, no words were exchanged; Jenny took the cup without remark. Connor looked beyond her – the orange-handled coffee urn sat under a clear stream of golden liquid. This ritual happened with predictable frequency and required no communication.

"You want more, too?"

"Not yet, honey," she shouted back without taking her eyes off Connor. These exchanges annoyed him, but he tolerated them and many other breaches of etiquette to be near her. Lori's company was addicting, and Connor tended to overlook anything that didn't interfere or dilute it. Decaf arrived.

"What's made you so giddy?" he asked. "And don't forget to tell me how you saved me $90 million."

"Oisín is pronounced Uh-Sheen, did you know that?" Lori said. "And this fella here is Finn McCool." She put the heavy statue on the table between them. Connor didn't comment; he waited.

"Now, you're probably wonderin' why on earth am I tellin' you this, right?" she said.

"Right."

"Well, you just enjoy your breakfast and listen while I tell a few stories," Lori said. "You should like 'em, too. They're Celtic."

Plates of steaming food arrived. Connor's omelet clanked down, a few home fries bouncing off the plate, while Lori's made a gentler landing. Jenny mumbled something that may have been *enjoy* or *oh joy*. A diffused ray of morning sunlight fought its way through the obstructions of city buildings and fell on the torso of the bronze statue on the table.

Connor ate his breakfast, listened to the entertaining tales and enjoyed them thoroughly. When Lori finished recounting, she sat wide-eyed in anticipation. She crunched the cold bacon she had neglected in spite of its olfactory allure. "Well?"

"Well, what?" He lifted his hand and pointed to his cup. The orange-handled carafe spilled its brew into it and Jenny dropped a handful of creamers.

"Oh, Lord," Lori said, "Do I have to spell it out for ya?"

"Yeah, I guess you do," Connor said.

"Tír na nÓg," she said. "Weren't you listening?"

"I was, but I'm still not getting it. Why don't you just tell me?"

"Uh-Sheen is the name of Finn McCumhail's son, okay?" she said, checking for basic understanding. "And he fell in love with this beautiful girl named Niamh. Princess Niamh was royalty in a place called Tír na nÓg where people never grew old."

"I'm still not getting it."

"Richard Tiernan was a genius, we all know that," she continued. "He just may have been warming up when he thought up the first Chimera seed."

Connor perked up instantly. Now she was getting somewhere. Was she going to say it? Would he hear, *which brings me to my point. I have the prototype?*

"Richard Tiernan created a Chimera plant and called the fruit it bears the *Niamh* grapes, and he's been growing acres of them in a little place in Sardinia," she continued. "Ya ever hear of resveratrol?"

"Go on," Connor said.

"Well, this little beauty is chock fulla that stuff, and if Richard Tiernan's portfolio has any truth to it at all, he'd been working on a longevity drug using resveratrol and some kinda fish or somethin'.'"

Connor put his elbows on the table and rested his chin on his thumbs. "Richard Tiernan's portfolio?" he said. "Now I'm really lost."

Lori retrieved the leather portfolio from her bag and placed it on the table. "I took it from the mansion, along with a few items that his son is gonna want back. I guarantee it," said Lori. "I think we'll find him a little more likely to trade the prototype in exchange for our silence and the return of his precious *Dionysinol*."

Connor mentally outlined his understanding of the morning's brief. Although he was still sketchy as to why Lori prefaced the meeting with stories of Irish lore, he seemed to have a better handle on their plan.

"Let me get this straight," he said. "You didn't get the Chimera prototype, but you stole, uh, *Dionysinol* and this leather portfolio that once belonged to Richard Tiernan?"

"Mm, hmmm," said Lori, applying a second coat of lipstick. The first was mostly on her coffee cup.

"What exactly is Dionysinol?"

"Don't know for sure," said Lori. "I couldn't understand most of it – all squiggly lines and numbers galore, but, from what I did manage to grasp, it seems to be connected to a drug to slow down aging. Ain't that excitin'?"

"Well, if anyone could do it, it'd be Richard Tiernan. Do you have any of it with you? I'll have it analyzed back at Lionel."

"I didn't bring any with me – thought it best not to walk around with it, but I'll try and swing by with a sample later."

"Okay," he said, "I'll take the portfolio with me. But, do you know what I'd really like to talk about right now?"

"What's that, sugar cakes?"

"I'd like to discuss how Mary McKenna convinced you to give her

$10 million. Ten-million dollars of *my* money."

"Mary's a really sweet girl. Didn't have it easy, either," said Lori.

"Ten-million, Loraine?"

Lori reached into her stylish leather bag, retrieved the folder and threw it on the table. It read, *Regenerol*. Connor opened the cover and saw a familiar sight: an IND application, petitioning the FDA for permission to begin human trials.

"Oh my, what do we have here?"

"I knew you'd like it, but that's not all. Look at the next section. Now you're really gonna flip." Lori clapped her hands rapidly and grinned.

Connor lifted the blue tab, read for two minutes and, after looking suspiciously around the diner, closed the folder. "Wow," he said. "It would be very unfortunate indeed if Dr. Bennett over at FDA headquarters were to learn of this, huh? Illegal testing in Mexico? Those poor women. Testing it out on the lower-class first. What a scumbag."

"Oh Lord, Ryan!" exclaimed Lori. "You know I hate that word."

"Sorry, I forgot," said Connor as he signaled for the check. "So, you're stopping by later?"

"I'll see what I can do; I have a few things to do today."

Jenny came and placed the check on the table.

"Oh wait, Jenny, honey," said Lori, "come back here a second."

She handed the waitress a business card and folded piece of paper. Jenny opened the note. *Raven, give this girl the works and put it on my tab. She is my friend. Love, Lori.* Jenny recognized the name of the upscale hair salon and almost smiled. Lori departed the diner with her usual well wishes to all, strangers and regulars alike. Twenty dollars sat under the lipstick-stained cup. The diner seemed a little darker, a little colder when the door closed behind Lori.

☃

Connor returned to his office.

"Frances," he said as he walked past her desk, "hold all calls."

"Yes, sir," she responded to the slammed door. The door quickly

177

reopened, allowing the bark of the second order to reach her.

"Clear my schedule for the rest of the day too."

This time, Frances didn't bother to respond to the door that again slammed shut and sent a gust of wind over her desk.

Connor sat at his desk and opened the classic Rolodex he hadn't upgraded as a form of protest. The wheel stopped at William Masterson: President and CEO: Merkel Pharmaceuticals.

"Hey, Will," Connor said after waiting several minutes to be connected through the layers of secretaries. "How is that fertility drug of yours doing?" It was public knowledge that the drugs were sputtering out meager profits. Connor leaned back in his chair and savored each word of the next sentence. "You stand to lose a lot more, buddy," he said. "I have something you need, Will, but it's gonna cost you."

The conversation was brief; there wasn't much love lost between the two. Connor reminded William Masterson to inform Gerard McCaff of McCaff Pharmaceuticals of the meeting. "Better if you call him," said Connor. "Old Gerard might have a stroke if I call and break the news."

With that, Connor hung up the phone and relished his long-awaited victory. Gerard McCaff and Ryan Connor had done battle before, and Connor's financial empire had retained a few deep lacerations from the encounter. Connor smiled broadly, imagining the conversation between McCaff and Masterson, and the befuddled look on McCaff's face as Masterson told him that Oisín Pharmaceuticals was about to get FDA approval on Regenerol and their vastly inferior drugs would be exposed for the ineffective placebos they were.

Billions, Connor thought to himself, *they'd lose billions.* The smile broadened and a warm feeling came over him. *Oh my, how sweet it is,* he thought. *God, please let it hurt really bad.*

CHAPTER 29

FALTERS WALKED DOWN into the lab, unlocked the old steamer trunk and slowly lifted the lid. The use of an old padlock to provide security was comical, in light of what it was asked to protect, but Richard and Falters had kept it on the trunk anyway. Five-hundred viable doses were all that were ever stockpiled at Tír na nÓg; the rest was kept in the flask and used for experimentation. But every drop was accounted for, including the tiny dose he had given Tiernan and the substantially larger portion he had given Jimmy.

Falters picked up the flask and poured the remaining purple liquid into a sink of bleach. When it was adequately mixed, he pulled the stopper up and allowed the inert liquid to drain into the earth. *Now for the vials*, he thought.

His meticulous adherence to detail compelled him to count the vials, the need for closure playing a significant role in the exercise. It was almost like a death ritual, a ceremony to bid farewell to a broken dream of a better future. Suddenly, he froze in terror. *Four hundred ninety-three*. He counted again – *493*. A third count confirmed seven missing vials, but how? When? Who?

One of Richard Tiernan's final acts had epitomized the adage: *blood is thicker than water.*

"Richard," shouted Falters. "Why?" He left the trunk and returned upstairs. He wasn't ready to admit defeat – not after all he had endured. Not yet.

ଔ

Ivan Falters presented the counterfeit American passport to the agent at the Alitalia Airlines gate. Ivan Velikovic: DOB: 1976. Citizenship: USA. "Va bene," said the agent. "Buon Viaggio."

Since his experimentation with Dionysinol and the subsequent transformations, his Russian passport was useless. The quasi-centenarian presented a passport alleging he was 32 years old and no one questioned it. If anything, he looked younger than the picture revealed.

He boarded the plane and sat uncomfortably in the coach seat that barely accommodated his large frame. He closed his eyes and prepared himself for a long and unpleasant flight across the Atlantic, mostly because people were staring at him with lust and then confusion and then more lust. The scent released by *Homo sapiens immortalis* was inebriating, and it affected those in the closest proximity the worst. One woman asked for another seat, preferably as far from this mysterious man as possible, but a younger female was not so prudent.

"So," said the attractive brunette, "business or pleasure?"

Falters kept his eyes closed, feigning sleep, but that couldn't deter young lust. "Because," she whispered in his ear, "I can make it quite pleasurable if you'd like. Care to join the mile high club?"

With his eyes remaining closed, Falters responded. "You couldn't handle me."

"Oooh," she said playfully, "you naughty boy." She giggled.

Falters opened his eyes. His icy blue eyes mesmerized her. She sat trancelike and submissive. He brushed away her hair, putting his strong hand on her neck, positioning his thumb over her carotid artery. He moved toward her, eyes closed, lips ready. She moaned in anticipation of the pleasure that never came. Falters squeezed hard and placed his lips over her mouth to stifle the scream. She slumped against the window, unconscious.

"Excuse me." The flight attendant came immediately. "May I have a sleep mask for my sister? Her doctor gave her something for nerves and I'm afraid it worked a little too well."

"Sure, right away, sir. Is there anything else I can do for you? Anything?"

"It's Father, and no, thank you. The mask will be fine."

Falters reached into his bag and retrieved a Roman collar and a powerful sublingual sedative. Like a priest giving Holy Communion, he placed the pill under the unconscious girl's tongue. When the flight attendant returned with the mask, she avoided eye contact with him and wondered how she had missed the Roman collar, a clear sign that this man was unavailable. He closed his eyes again and didn't open them until he arrived in the United States of America.

Falters landed in New Jersey's Newark Liberty International Airport and disembarked. *I could've put her down better,* he thought as he retrieved his bag from the jumbled mess in the overhead bin. The sleeping girl awoke and yelped in pain.

"Ah, Jesus, my neck!" she cried. "What the hell happened to my neck? I can't move my neck!" She pulled off the sleeping mask.

"You must have slept on it wrong," said Falters. "It should pass soon. It was nice to meet you."

෧෪

The airport was like most airports, where efforts valiant and vain to keep the floors clean are made, despite consistent failure. Falters felt uneasy here and tried to recall the last time he was in the United States. He followed the white rectangles with glowing red letters that promised to lead one to the outside. EXIT – the lettering became crisp as he approached. Beneath the sign, two automatic doors opened and closed with such frequency that one wonders why they just don't leave them open and save the electricity. With each opening, the sounds and smells of the dwindling petroleum supplies filled the room. The angry and prolonged blasting horns harmonized with the hissing of the busses that carried hundreds more energy consumers to long-term parking where SUVs and other inefficient modes of transportation awaited.

Disgusting, he thought. *The Americans are especially vile.* He looked at the populous – overweight and wasteful; privileged, yet undeserving; mediocre yet arrogant – with scorn and contempt. *Seven vials,* he thought, *and it will be contained. I must succeed.*

Falters walked up to the first taxi in line and handed the cabby a piece of paper with Tiernan's address neatly typed in bold print. "Can you take me here?" he asked.

"Yeah, sure, but it's gonna be expensive, buddy," the taxi driver answered. "You got enough cash?"

Falters opened the taxi door and got in without answering. The driver asked again about the cash and Falters nodded slowly, his blue eyes burning in his head. The bulletproof glass was a new addition, one for which he understood the need. He pulled the little glass door open, placed $300 in the tray and sent it forward with a thud.

"This is more than sufficient," Falters said. "The excess is yours, provided you make haste."

"No problem, buddy," said the cabby. "First time in the States?" The driver felt obligated to make small talk now that the tip was more than the fare.

"I do not wish to converse," said Falters. "Just bring me to that address expeditiously."

The driver punched the address into the GPS. "You got it, buddy."

CHAPTER 30

MARY MCKENNA WAITED in the car for a half-hour before Tighte arrived. "Get in," he said, leaning his head out the window.

"Let's take my car," Mary said. "He's expecting me and I don't want to spook him."

Tighte sighed with irritation at having to endure the inconvenience of parking and getting out of his car.

Mary was nervous. Her heart thumped in her ears and she struggled to gain composure. *He has no idea,* she assured herself. *He's blinded by greed.*

Tighte slammed his car door and brushed away the crumbs of cookies that had gathered on his shirt. His slovenly frame and repulsive personality were now even more repellent to Mary after hearing of Lori's rape and battery. Mary had always found him repulsive and despised being that close to him, but this new level of loathing was frightening. She wondered if he would be able to sense it – the danger he faced – and she experienced an instant of intense hesitation. It passed quickly when she heard the door slam and felt the car adjust equilibrium under his weight.

"Goddamn it, woman," he greeted, "why the hell are we catering to this prick?"

Mary was glad he was his usual repellent self; otherwise, she may have reconsidered.

"Michael Tiernan is unpredictable," she said. "He's been known to change his mind over the slightest deviation."

Tighte looked at Mary with disgust and adjusted his crotch unabashedly. Mary's blood ran cold thinking about what that organ had done, and she forced herself to close her eyes and breathe.

"This prick better not waste my time," Tighte said. "For his and your sake, he better not waste my goddamn time."

"Tiernan will bring the prototype, I guarantee it," said Mary. She put the car in gear and drove off.

As part of their deal, Mary and Lori had agreed that Mary would deliver Vincent Tighte to Lori under the guise of Mary having brokered a deal with Tiernan for the prototype. Tighte was a government official and, as the administrator of the EPA, he enjoyed a security detail that rivaled the president's; however, when Tighte was engaged in activities such as extortion or blackmail, he tended to give his security guards the night off.

"Are you sure you weren't followed?" said Mary.

"I'm sure. My security detail still thinks I'm in the house with Barbara. Scott Lehman helped me pull it off."

Mary McKenna considered asking Tighte how much he had told Scott, but thought better of it. She didn't want to give Tighte any reason for suspicion. *Scott Lehman wouldn't shed a single, bitter tear for this animal anyway,* she thought.

"Just so we're straight," said Tighte, "we're offering an exchange and nothing more?" Greed was brewing in his gut. "We'll return the file on the Mexican chicks tested with Regenerol and promise to keep our mouths shut, and he'll hand over the prototype?"

"That's the deal," said Mary.

"I think we can get more," he said. "It's gotta be worth more to him."

A verbal beating of gargantuan proportions rose like vomit in Mary's throat, but she stifled it with an "okay, let's play it out." She knew that there was no deal – no Tiernan and no prototype – so why argue the virtues of keeping one's word when the entire night was one big deception?

"Let's start high," Mary added. "Regenerol will make trillions before the patent expires, and who knows what other drugs they have up their sleeves."

Tighte was perspiring from the thought of the money. "I can help get it approved, streamline the application process for Oisín. I'll throw that in during our negotiations. I still got some pull in Washington," he said.

Not for much longer, Mary thought.

The house was dark when they arrived. A single light shone on the front door, leaving the rest of the place black.

"What the hell's going on?" Tighte said. "Whose place is this?"

"It's one of Tiernan's," Mary said, turning the ignition off. She got out of the car and began walking to the door. She wanted to turn around to see if Tighte was following, but continued walking. As agreed, the door was unlocked and she walked straight in.

"Where is he?" Tighte said.

"He'll be here. We're early and, besides, he told me he might be delayed."

Tighte shut the door behind him. Mary wanted to put him at ease, to lower his defenses. "He wanted to reschedule because of prior commitments, but I told him that Vincent Tighte would be unhappy if we didn't stick to the original arrangement." Mary waited for Tighte's ego to blind him to any inconsistency he may have caught.

"Damn right," Tighte said. "Screw him and the woman he rode in on." His laugher was nauseating. "Where's the bar?"

Mary McKenna had never been in this house before, so she didn't know, but she wasn't going to have to venture a guess. Lori Adams' voice answered him.

"Whatcha drinkin'?"

The sound of her stiletto heels echoed on the tile floor. The ripped, blood-stained outfit that a younger, more naïve Lori Adams wore that infamous day still fit her. Mary wasn't sure if Tighte realized that this was the same outfit he had torn from Lori's body as he had raped her, when he had ruptured her insides, damaging them so badly that she was rendered barren.

Lori lifted the gun slowly and pulled the trigger. The dart hit him in the chest. A second dart hit him in the throat, right before he fell unconscious to the floor. Mary and Lori stood silently over his body. There was nothing to say. Lori clearly had plans for Tighte. Why else would she shoot him with tranquilizer darts?

"You ought to go now, Mary."

Mary wanted to touch her, wanted to offer something to ease the pain, but knew she couldn't. Instead, she walked out the front door and hoped Lori's pain would dissipate with Vincent Tighte's final breath.

CHAPTER 31

"**HERE WE ARE**, buddy," the cab driver said. "Fast enough for ya?" Falters didn't respond. He exited the cab and walked toward the door. It wasn't quite dark; dusk still cast silhouettes, but they were fading fast. He rang the doorbell and, when no one answered, walked around back. Marinella was in the garden, selecting a few tomatoes for the salad. Diego was in the house, watching the evening news. The sight of Falters startled Marinella.

"Madonna," Marinella said, putting her hand on her heart. Falters put her at ease with the sound of her native tongue.

"Ah, perdone me, Signora," he said. "Sono Signore Falters, un amico di Richard e Michael Tiernan. Ho apena arrivato e mi sembra que Michael mi ha scordato."

"Ah," said Marinella, satisfied with Falters' introduction and tale of Tiernan forgetting him at the airport. "Viene i accomodatavi," she said, inviting him into the house. "Ma Lei ha mangiato?" she asked.

"Yes, I ate already, but thank you," said Falters. "Can we call Michael?"

"Subito," she said. "Right away."

Falters followed her into the house where Diego sat watching the Italian station RAI. Marinella introduced Falters to her husband and returned to the kitchen to get the list of numbers that hung suspended from a magnet of Italy on the refrigerator. She tried each number until she located Tiernan. She scolded Tiernan for his inexcusable breach of hospitality and ordered him to return home immediately.

"Certo, Mari," said Tiernan. "I'm coming home now. My secretary gave me the wrong date." He hung up. "Goddamn it," he shouted, "this is not good." He placed an international call. Where was Jimmy? The phone in Sardinia rang and rang until the operator returned with the helpful insight, "There's no answer, sir."

Tiernan parked his car in the driveway instead of the garage and went directly to the guesthouse where he found the three engaged in conversation, as if they had known each other for years. Diego and Marinella insisted that the four of them dine together the next evening and, afterwards, bid their new friend *buona notte*. Tiernan played along until they were out of sight.

03

Tiernan closed the door to the mansion and armed the alarm. "What the hell are you doing here and where's Jimmy," he asked.

"Where are they?" said Falters.

"Who?" said Tiernan.

"The stolen vials. I know you have them. Where are they?"

"Whoa, wait a second. I think you're forgetting something. I own Tír na nÓg and everything it produces. The Dionysinol is mine, and mine alone. I guess my father didn't trust you as much as you thought."

"It appears so," said Falters. "Not everyone enjoys the level of trust that you and your colleague, Jimmy, share. Wouldn't you agree?"

"Where is he?"

"He's in Sardinia, guarding the vineyards as you had commanded, I'm sure," said Falters. "Now I must insist you return the vials, Dr. Tiernan. Please don't make this anymore unpleasant than it has to be."

"What? What will you do if I refuse, huh?" said Tiernan.

"I will do what I must, nothing more."

"Here, you want the goddamn vials?" said Tiernan, walking into his father's den. "Here, fucking take them." He opened the desk drawer, but instead of presenting Falters with the Dionysinol, he opted for the .357 Magnum instead. "Or maybe I'll give you something else instead. Hmm?" He pointed the gun at Falters.

Falters took a step toward the gun-toting Tiernan.

"Don't be stupid, man," said Tiernan. "The Dionysinol won't protect you from lead poisoning, will it?" He cocked the gun and aimed it at Falters' head. "You can't believe the month I'm having, so make no mistake, I will blow your brains out and not think twice about it."

"I'm sure you would," said Falters. "That seems to be your modus operandi, doesn't it? Not thinking twice about anything. You're a fool, a mere shadow of your father."

"Yeah? Well, I'll have to learn to live with your disappointment, won't I? But, remember this, my father gave me the drug. Clearly, he knew that I would be the only one thinking rationally should something happen to him. Now sit down before I blow your goddamn brains out."

"Tell me," said Falters, keeping his eyes fixed on Tiernan. He pulled out a chair. "Have you noticed a change in the manner in which women respond to you, behave around you?"

"What does that have to do with anything?" said Tiernan.

"Didn't you notice the subtle changes? You sleep more soundly, you eat more ravenously and gain no weight?" asked Falters. "Have you noticed that you are different today than you were yesterday? Different this evening than you were this morning? Dionysinol seems to be consistent in that regard."

Realizing the implication, Tiernan froze. Acid poured into his stomach. A dry heave stifled him mid-sentence. "You didn't give me –"

"I had to," said Falters. "In time, you will thank me despite whatever you feel at present."

Sometimes, you have to impose your will for the betterment of a situation...

Falters sat calmly and gestured to Tiernan to sit also. Tiernan continued to stand, gun aimed and ready. "Holy shit," he managed. "Holy Mary, Mother of God."

"Since we are now on the same level, logical conversation is possible, whereas before it wasn't," said Falters. "You are going to be alive for a very long time; hence, all of your decisions will now be made from that vantage point."

The room spun. Tiernan sat, but kept the gun pointed in Falters' direction. "We don't know shit about Dionysinol, you arrogant bastard," Tiernan said. "We have no goddamn clue what side effects may develop. I could get cancer or, or –"

"We have nothing to warrant that assumption," said Falters. "The Turritopsis nutricula is immortal and –"

"Are you retarded? Did you live near Chernobyl in the '80s? Do I look like a fucking jellyfish?" He jumped up from the chair, and rattled off a series of threats. Falters sat, waiting for the adrenaline to burn itself out.

"Can it be reversed?" Tiernan asked frantically. "Can we ever go back to normal?"

"I don't think so, but, if you could, would you want to?" Falters asked. "We are not immortal in the true definition of the word. If you were to cut your own throat, you would bleed to death. If you were to jump from the Eiffel Tower, you would certainly splatter on the cement like anyone else."

Tiernan wasn't at all comforted.

"You are not a prisoner of life. If you want to end your existence, you retain that option. On the other hand, if you want to live indefinitely, you have the potential."

Self-preservation ruled supreme and knowing how scarce the natural resources were, Tiernan's perspective underwent an instantaneous change. It was as if the man who wanted to make Dionysinol the most sought-after substance on Earth had never existed. They had to contain it, had to prevent anyone from ever finding out. He couldn't imagine ever thinking otherwise, yet, still, he was ambivalent. The desire for life and the desire for a good life were indistinguishable to him. He could never understand how people retained their desire to live when they endured a hideous existence – a quality of life no one could envy. Yet they did. Despite all logic and reasoning, most humans hungered for life no matter how abysmal the conditions, and clung to existence with fortitude and defiance.

"We can't let the drug continue to exist," said Falters. "I think you can deduce from the current condition of the world that humanity is ill-equipped to exist in such large numbers."

"We can alter the effects," said Tiernan. "We can engineer it to stop working after a certain time, can't we?"

"We have already discussed this. How long do you think it would take someone to figure out how to manipulate the drug? We would be in a worse position since we would have no control over the distribution."

Tiernan asked Falters more questions about the effects of Diony-sinol on humans that evening than he had in all the time he had known him. He was, indeed, seeing it from a different perspective.

"Dr. Tiernan," said Falters, "would you mind not pointing the gun at my head? I will not harm you." Tiernan put the gun down, but kept it nearby.

"Can I get sick?" Tiernan asked.

"At first," said Falters. "But your immune system will revert to that of a teenager's, strong and resilient, but not invincible. As your exposure to bacteria and viruses increases, you will build more resistance. The antibodies your body creates are also affected by the Dionysinol and are, therefore, immortal. Theoretically, and contingent upon other variables, of course, you will get sick with decreasing frequency as time goes on."

"If Dionysinol were to become widely available," Tiernan said, "then one of two things could happen." He paused for emphasis. "One, illness would be a thing of the past as bacteria and viruses learned to form symbiotic relationships with their human hosts as millions have already done. The other possibility is that some bacteria or virus would mutate until a deadly strain wiped out our species."

"The *majority* of the species," said Falters. "If the past is a reliable indicator of the future, we are justified in the assumption that there will always be a few humans immune to any given pathogen. These unlucky few would survive."

"It can't end this way," said Tiernan. "It doesn't end this way."

"The vials, Dr. Tiernan, please return them. If not for the faceless billions, then at least for yourself."

Tiernan pulled open the desk drawer and froze. The vials were gone. "What would you say if I were to tell you that I seem to have misplaced them," he asked.

"I would assume you were lying, again."

"Not a bad assumption," said Tiernan, standing up to retrieve his father's crystal decanter. When he realized there were no clean glasses, he slugged right out of the bottle. "Not a bad assumption at all," he said, wiping his mouth with his sleeve, "but ultimately incorrect."

"Where are they?"

"Good question." He slugged another swig.

Falters stood up and took the decanter out of Tiernan's hands. He lifted the crystal to his own mouth and gulped. "You imbecile. How could you have been so irresponsible?"

...but your father didn't think you were ready for such a responsibility...

"Tomorrow, we find them. Then I would very much like it if I were never to set eyes on you again."

"Likewise. I'll show you your room," said Tiernan.

That night, both men locked their doors.

CHAPTER 32

TIGHTE STIRRED WITH the groggy awareness that his arms were bound. He jerked forward and tried in vain to make sense of the situation. Duct tape bound his torso and calves to the sturdy mahogany legs of an uncomfortable chair. White rope squeezed off the circulation to his hands, which were now an interesting shade of purple. He tried to shout, but only produced more drool as the ball gag muffled the intensity of his effort. His naked chest was drenched from saliva that had been flowing in a steady stream for the better part of two hours.

Where am I? he thought. *These bitches are gonna get it.* He fought against the ligatures with all his might, but the anger that fueled the struggle turned to fear when Lori Adams appeared.

"Oh, you're awake," she said. "Do you remember this outfit? I wore it just for you since you were so fond of it when we first met."

Obscenities and threats were incoherently issued through the ball gag, projectile saliva rocketing out of Tighte's mouth with each vocalization. His face was a shade of rage and his beady eyes glared a vicious litany of evil.

"Now, don't you go givin' yourself a heart attack or nothin'," said Lori. "That would ruin all the fun we're gonna have. Yes, sir, it sure would."

After Tighte had exhausted himself with futile attempts at communication and escape, he sat still.

"Would you like me to remove that ol' ball gag?" asked Lori. "I will, if you promise not to yell."

Scream and I will gut you like the pig-whore you are. Who's gonna believe you anyway?

Tighte's body was still, but his eyes couldn't lie; if he got free, he would kill her without hesitation. Lori unbuckled the tightly-bound gag. She had to yank it several times before the latch came undone. With a pop, the ball shot out of his mouth and was closely followed by a series of obscenities and vicious threats.

"It's my own fault," said Lori, "I should've known you wouldn't keep your promise."

Lori walked out of sight as Tighte roared vile promises of what awaited her when he got free. He couldn't identify the sound, but it became clear when Lori reentered the room holding a blowtorch. The competence with which she adjusted the flame revealed that she knew exactly what she was doing. The long, blue flame's hissing sound was quickly drowned out by shrieks of unimaginable pain. The flame wrapped around Tighte's naked genitals and charred the offending organ to a crispy, black cinder of burning flesh.

"Now, let's try to avoid using bad language," said Lori as she doused the smoldering remains of his organ with white wine vinegar. Tighte passed out from the pain.

After Lori injected the unconscious Tighte with a massive dose of a broad-spectrum antibiotic, she readied an adrenaline shot. Vincent Tighte was going to experience every second of his punishment with the help of modern chemistry.

"Wakie, wakie," Lori said and plunged the syringe into his thigh.

CHAPTER 33

MARY MCKENNA DROVE on autopilot, her mind still back with Lori Adams and Vincent Tighte. Several times, she almost exited the expressway, determined to return to the house whose ownership was still a mystery. Darkness fell hard and the night sky, obstructed by a heavy blanket of clouds, threatened rain, perhaps even a thunderstorm.

Just like a horror movie, Mary thought.

She arrested the smile before it made any progress and replaced it with a more appropriate expression. Was justice being served? Were even the vilest people not entitled to a fair trial, a jury of peers?

Tighte was going to die – of that Mary was certain – but how and by what means? A cruel and unusual death was a safe bet. Mary's conscience tugged with all its might using fear, reason, self-preservation and the elusive abstraction that transcends definition: justice. She turned on the radio and cranked the volume. As she passed over the bridge, she opened the window and sent the disposable phone to a watery grave. Music soothes the soul, even the guilty soul.

☙

Tiernan knocked loudly on the door three times. "Falters, you up?"

"I will be down in a moment."

Falters walked into the dining area where Marinella had prepared an Italian breakfast of strong coffee and a selection of small pastries. She smiled at him as he entered the room. "Buon Giorno. Lei ha dormito bene?"

"Yes, very well," Falters said. She poured him a cup of coffee and left the room.

"How young am I going to look?" asked Tiernan. "I mean, you're almost 90 and you look, well, you look younger than I do."

"I can't be certain," said Falters. "Do you have any suspects as to who may have stolen the vials? Did you tell anyone about the Dionysinol?"

"Look, you brain-dead idiot," said Tiernan as the anger returned. "I have a goddamn company to run. What do you think people will say when their CEO looks like a teenage kid? I'm going to have to disappear, withdraw from my friends, be alone," he said. "You've ruined my life. You've ruined my career!"

"I see you have a security system," said Falters. "That suggests that someone must have had the code. Give me a list of all the people who knew the code, along with any deliveries you may have had."

"I will never be able to marry, to have children, to have friendships. All this is verboten now because you played God with my future. What gave you the goddamn right?" said Tiernan, the volume increasing with each exchange.

"This discussion is counterproductive. I suggest that you try to gain some control over yourself. Do Marinella and Diego know anything about the project?"

"You infected me," said Tiernan.

"Infected you? You were already infected. A dose of Dionysinol was the only hope you had. Your desire for power and fame is the source of your infection," said Falters. "It blinded you to the real dangers of exposing the human race to something it isn't ready to handle. You weren't listening to reason, so the situation had to affect you directly. I had no choice."

Tiernan sat across from Falters, listening to things he didn't want to hear, but suspected they contained a sliver of truth.

"I was acting on behalf of our species," continued Falters. "Dionysinol would destroy us all."

"Michelino," called Marinella from the kitchen. "Telefono."

Tiernan rose from the table and answered the phone. It was odd to receive a call at this hour, especially on the mansion line.

"This is Tiernan."

"Michael Tiernan?"

"Yes, speaking."

"My name is Ryan Connor; I think we should meet."

Tiernan recognized the name, but couldn't understand why the president of Lionel Pharmaceuticals was calling until he remembered his promise to call Lori Adams back with his decision about selling the prototype. "I told Lori Adams that I'd get back to her," he said. "I'm still considering your offer."

A few seconds of silence passed before Connor spoke. "I'm afraid that offer is off the table. However, I have another offer that I think you will find more difficult to refuse. You certainly don't have the luxury of time, either."

"Yeah, and what's that?" Tiernan asked.

"I have a very special little leather folder that someone dropped off at my office anonymously – very interesting read. It must have belonged to your father. Would you like it back?"

Tiernan felt the back of his neck getting hotter and his stomach fill with anxiety. For a few seconds, everything felt surreal, as if he was witnessing these events from another's perspective. He heard Connor take a breath as if he was going to speak, but Tiernan cut him off.

"You're gonna pay for this."

"Three hours. My office."

Tiernan hung up the phone and rejoined Falters. "Hey, I know where the vials are. Let's go."

Connor leaned back in his custom-made, leather chair and smiled, holding the phone in his hand until the obnoxious off-the-hook sound emanated from the receiver. He sat up and gently hung up the phone, reached for the portfolio and ran his fingers over the smooth leather. His smile remained long after the conversation had ended.

CB

Tiernan called the lab from the car; he knew there was a good chance John Graham was already there. Graham answered the phone with his antiquated greeting.

197

"Good morning. Oisín Pharmaceuticals, this is Dr. Graham speaking. How may I assist you?"

"John, it's me," said Tiernan. "Cancel everything you had planned for today. When your staff arrives, gather them in the conference room with all their notes and recent orders – bring the call logs too."

"Eh, yes sir. May I inquire as to the reason?"

"We need to initiate the Cerberus Contingency, right now." Tiernan answered.

"Yes, sir," Graham answered and rested the phone gently on the receiver. He picked it back up and dialed Debra Lewis' number. After four rings, he disconnected and dialed her cell.

"Hello?" said Debra.

"Good morning, dear," said Graham. "What is your expected time of arrival this morning?"

"Why? Is something wrong?" asked Debra, who always thought something was wrong. "Is everything okay?"

"I'm afraid not, dear," said Graham with the calmness that acceptance brings. "Young Michael called and asked us to initiate the Cerberus plan."

"Oh my God," said Debra. "Why? Was there a leak?"

"Just hurry, dear," said Graham.

CHAPTER 34

TIGHTE HAD BEEN awake all night; the series of adrenaline shots made sleep impossible. Lori Adams slept upstairs. As she left the basement and the door closed with a thud, Tighte knew that she did not intend to release him, ever. He heard her footsteps above him, screamed with fury and raged in vain against the ligatures that bound him. Then the room went black – pitch black – without even the slightest evidence of light: it disoriented him and made him dizzy.

"You're dead!" he screamed. "Do you hear me? You're dead!"

But she didn't hear him – no one could. Lori had planned this for a very long time and a soundproof prison was only part of what awaited Tighte, the rapist and murderer.

The next morning, the door opened and light rushed into the foul-smelling room. The distinctive smell of human excrement coupled with a barrage of hate assaulted her senses. Tighte had finished a big dinner an hour before he set out with Mary McKenna on his fated journey. The dinner was now putrefying the air.

"Oh my Lord," Lori exclaimed, waving her hand in a fan-like motion. "You stink to high heaven."

"You pig. Eat shit, you Southern hick."

Lori walked back up the stairs and the door closed behind her.

"No, no! I'm sorry! I won't! I didn't! Please don't!" cried Tighte as he remembered the consequence for his use of offensive language and aggressive tones. Lori reappeared dragging a hose downstairs.

"I shoulda untangled this first, I guess – my own fault." She dropped the hose six feet from Tighte and returned upstairs. The squeaking sound of a faucet somewhere above him, the movement of the hose as it slowly slithered snakelike to life, informed him of what Lori had planned next. She came back down the stairs with a bucket in her hand.

"Now, this might sting a little. Oh, hell, it'll sting a lot," she said.

"What are —?"

Lori threw the contents of the bucket into Tighte's face and the screaming resumed. "It's mold and mildew stain remover. Smells just awful, don't it?" she said. "The container said that if you get some in your eye, you need to wash it out thoroughly, and, if you swallowed a tad, DO NOT induce vomiting." She had almost finished her sentence when Tighte's screaming was reduced to coughing and finally to vomiting. "See, now, you just don't listen," she said. "I just got finished sayin' that you should NOT induce vomiting."

The final dry heave was followed by a resumption of screaming, although the effects on Tighte's burnt esophagus altered the volume and timbre. Lori bent down and picked up the hose. She twisted the nozzle and a rapid burst of water ejected from it.

"Whoa," she said as she steadied herself again. "It's got quite a kick." The force of the water toppled the chair over and Tighte hit the floor.

"Gotta be clean now," she said inaudibly over the rushing water, and the gurgling and choking. The water streamed into a drain in the center of the room. After the hosing, Lori dragged the waterlogged hose back upstairs, this time with considerably more effort.

"Whew," she said. "All this luggin' and haulin' makes me hungry. You hungry, Mr. Tighte?" No answer. "Well, okay then," she said. "I'll just leave you be for now — leave you with your thoughts." She walked back upstairs and left the door slightly ajar.

Tighte waited for the lights to shut off before sobbing uncontrollably in the darkness. She was going to torture him for as long as she could. Then he found that the water had loosened the duct tape that bound his left leg to the chair and a ray of hope illuminated the basement far more brightly than any light could have. "I swear, God," he said. "If you help me now, I'll never do anything wrong again, ever."

The muffled sounds of Lori Adams' singing while preparing her breakfast leaked into the basement. The sweet and melodious sound produced in him a dissonance. The past invaded the present so thoroughly that he found it difficult to distinguish which sounds emanated from his mind. A sound from the past – of her ribs cracking under the blows of his fist – kept time with her singing, and her high-pitched arias of pain and fear harmonized. He still felt no remorse, no guilt, only fear. But he was incapable of feeling those emotions, those limiting emotions that prevent so many from achieving greatness, success and a comfortable life. It wasn't his fault that he was born free of the limiting faculty of conscience, but what good would assigning blame do him now?

– sociopathic

CHAPTER 35

DEBRA LEWIS ARRIVED at Oisín and headed directly to her office. John Graham wasn't there reading his newspaper as she had almost expected. *Must be down in the conference room already,* she thought and turned her computer on. As it booted up, Debra collected her notes on the recent data. Regenerol produced an exorbitant quantity of data; the teams were discovering new applications for it on a weekly basis. The rapidity of the new discoveries and the diverse nature of the experiments must have raised a red flag somewhere with someone. Someone must have smelled money and started digging – that was Debra Lewis' theory, anyway.

The computer sang its jingle to announce that it was ready to do her bidding and Debra responded to its call. She sat in the chair and pulled up the IND file for their cash cow, their Nobel Prize, their collective daughter – Regenerol. The very name called to mind a rebirth, a regeneration of the decayed into the pristine, and it warmed her to think that she was an integral part of its birth and upbringing. Soon she would send the drug into the world so that many could marvel at its beauty and elegance.

The warm feeling turned cold when she hit the print button and realized that the document had already been printed from her terminal. Her mind raced, attempting to reconcile the impossible with the evidence that the impartial monitor gave: *Job Complete: Collect IND-REGENEROL.doc in printer tray 216.* Her eyes darted over to her printer – tray empty, model no. 216.

Did I print a copy from this terminal? she asked herself. *No, I printed it from Michael's office on the laser printer. Who could have printed a copy?*

Mary Delacroix's face flashed into her mind. The miscarriage had happened almost a week ago and they still hadn't managed to locate her. In truth, they had been so busy and Mary Delacroix had only been there a few days, so the effort to find her lacked conviction. Hers was a tragic story and most people banished unpleasant thoughts whenever possible. She was all too easy to forget, which, ironically, was to her benefit. She waltzed in and was carried out, and that was that. Unfortunately, Debra was finding out that the story did not end there.

"John Graham to Dr. Lewis' office. Calling John Graham to Dr. Lewis' office." The intercom was a blessing at that moment. It allowed Debra to sit down and compose herself while Graham came to her. She was shaking, her knees too weak to stand. She stared at the monitor, hoping that she was mistaken, all the while knowing she wasn't.

"What is it, dear?" said Graham. His lungs and heart showed their age today, much more than usual. He breathed heavily, having run up three flights of stairs when he heard her voice beckon him. They both silently cursed his advanced years and the signs that his death was closer today than yesterday, last week, last year. "Didn't I tell you that we don't shout at work, dear? Are you so dissatisfied with the power of your own voice that you've resorted to using the intercom to bellow?" His breathing was returning to normal.

"Mary Delacroix must have been a plant. She stole a copy of the IND report, probably more, too," said Debra, looking like a child confessing to a grandparent. *Don't tell Daddy or Mommy, okay?* she thought.

"Oh, Jesus," said Graham. He closed the door behind him. "Are you sure?"

"Yes, positive."

"How sensitive is the information that she stole?"

"You know how sensitive it is, John," said Debra. She was pale and sick to her stomach. "The Mexican files, remember? They're encrypted, but let's not fool ourselves. She probably cracked it within minutes."

"Who else knows about this?" said Graham. The tone was loaded with suggestion.

"No one, of course," said Debra.

Graham felt his chest swell inside with love for her. He was the first person she ran to when she was in crisis and, although the situation was bleak, he couldn't help but feel an inappropriate contentment.

"I'll be fired. He's going to fire me today. You'll see," she said.

The contentment was now gone. Graham couldn't imagine spending the few short years he had left without her. Life would hold no fascination without her. If she were to go, life would carry her far from him and her youth would provide the stamina. She would forget him. Every human action can be traced back to a selfish desire, no matter how immaculate the intention or convincing the self-delusion. Graham wasn't immune.

"Don't say anything, dear," he said. "Not yet."

"What?" said Debra. "I can't conceal this!"

"Listen to me," said Graham. "If Delacroix, or whatever her name really is, has the data..."

"She HAS it," interrupted Debra. Graham held her hands gently to calm her. The pale skin on his hands, mottled with age, was thin and loose like a pair of surgical gloves. His hands looked decrepit next to hers.

"Yes, she probably does," Graham continued. "But let's see how this plays out. In most situations like these, money is the answer. She probably wants money."

"But, what if she sells the information to someone? What if she has a different agenda? What if she was working for Merkel or McCaff and their main objective was to bury Regenerol? What then?"

Graham smoothed back his gray mane. Age had repossessed the color but not the quantity of his hair. "Well, dear," he said, "if that were their intention, and it very well might be, there would be very little that could be done anyway. What good would your confession be?"

"Confession?" she snapped. "It wasn't my fault."

Graham regretted his choice of words, not because they were inappropriate but because they evoked a negative response.

"Sorry, dear. You're right," said Graham. "If anything is to blame, it's the human condition. Very unfortunate, indeed."

"John," she said. "He'll hate me. He'll associate me with this whole debacle and he'll hate me."

The message stung Graham, almost causing physical pain. Her motivation was love, just like his. She could not bear the thought of no longer seeing Tiernan, of being disillusioned of the dream of being with him. Everything was reducible to a very basic principle, the strength of which was unparalleled.

Graham suppressed the pain and conjured the strength to continue. "That is all the more reason not to say anything," he said. "I will remove this terminal and replace it with one in the lab after wiping the hard drive."

"You can't wipe the drives completely," she said. She was surprised that she was considering Graham's plan. "You can retrieve almost anything on a computer with enough determination."

"Yes, I know," he said. Neither of them said it, but the implication hung in the air like a storm cloud: *someone else would get the blame.*

CB

Falters and Tiernan arrived at Oisín. Graham had the staff convene in the conference room as Tiernan had asked.

"Good morning, everyone," said Tiernan. "We called this meeting to inform you that the Cerberus Contingency is now in effect."

CHAPTER 36

WITH THE FINAL violent pull, the duct tape snapped. The raw skin under the broken ligature throbbed in victorious anger as it wept tears of blood and water. The pain was secondary to that which emanated from Tighte's charred organ. Using pain as the medium, the remaining nerve cells sent urgent and continuous messages to his brain, alerting it to the damage. Looking at his disfigurement seemed to intensify the pain, so he tried to resist. The black mass of scorched skin and hair was all he could smell. He wondered if he would ever smell anything else again, or if the smell of his own burnt testicles would ever fade.

He strained with all his might against the leg of the chair. His anger and rage fueled his effort and helped him to ignore the excruciating pain as the duct tape fought to hold him captive. Blood seeped from under the remaining ligature. *If I get both legs free, I'll be able to stand,* he thought. *Then I can break the chair and free my arms.* The thought of grabbing Lori Adams by the throat and squeezing the life out of her sustained him. *I'm gonna have fun with you, bitch,* he thought, forgetting his promise to God. *I'm gonna kill you slowly, burn pieces of you one at a time.*

The ligature fought a good fight but was no match for Tighte's determination. His legs were free – bleeding and raw – but free. He stood awkwardly and looked around to determine the best way to break the chair. He wondered if Lori could hear him. He could hear her, so why not the other way around? Satisfied that it was a one-way soundproofing, he ran backwards with all his might and smashed the chair against the wall. The seat of the chair slammed into his kidneys, dropping him to his knees. It didn't break, but it wouldn't be able to withstand repeated attempts. Would *he*?

Tighte tried jumping up and falling to the ground several times, each successive attempt weakening the chair and his resolve. A final run at the wall and the chair relented. The fight was over, but it had been very close. He groaned, each movement causing more pain, but he was free. Now she was going to regret it.

He walked slowly up the stairs with a chair leg in hand. The concrete stairs didn't creak; soundless was his ascent. He reached the door and stopped. Should he wait there for her to open it and bash her over the skull, or attempt to open it himself? It wasn't locked, but opening it might alert her. He depressed the handle as silently as he could manage. The handle squeaked a little. Sweat dripped from his forehead and his heart raced. The latch yielded and the door opened. Music poured in from the living room.

"And kick and one and two and kick," said a commanding voice over the music.

The bitch is sweatin' to the oldies, huh? he thought.

He opened the door. In the distance, he could see Lori's frame. Her back was to him as she danced and kicked along with the DVD workout. The door from the basement opened into the kitchen, beyond which Lori kicked carefree, unaware of the wolf in her midst. Tighte looked for a knife. A glistening gun sitting on the table brought tears to his eyes. He reached for the gun, picked it up and kissed the barrel.

"I am going to make this last!" said Tighte. "You are going to beg me to kill you before this is over."

Lori shrieked in horror and stepped backwards, falling over her workout steps. "Don't! Please, don't!" she pleaded from the ground, holding her hands up.

"Don't what?" he said as he limped towards the horrified mass of spandex and makeup. "Don't do this?" he said as he pointed the gun to her kneecap and pulled the trigger.

Click, click, click, click. The barrel was empty.

Tighte's eyes widened and Lori smiled. He never heard Edward behind him. At first, he thought that the stinging in his back was the many splinters he had acquired from his battle with the chair. When the room began to spin, he recalled the darts. He passed out and slammed to the floor.

"One dart, right?" she said as she got up from the floor. "You only shot him once?"

"Yup, once, just like you said," Edward answered, trying to avert his eyes from the cinder that hung between Tighte's legs.

"Now, isn't this better than lugging his fat behind up the stairs?" she said. "Okay, let's get Phase Two into action."

Edward retrieved the tarp and covered the couch. He lifted with enormous difficulty the unconscious mass of rapist onto the plastic-covered couch and then went to retrieve the chains.

CHAPTER 37

STUNNED LOOKS AND the buzz of a dozen comments bounced around the room. "Cerberus is just a precaution – perhaps even an overzealous one – so don't be alarmed," said Tiernan.

He had installed the Cerberus Protocol Contingency – the CPC – on the mainframe in case of an emergency. Once activated, all data, all incriminating evidence would be wiped, without a hope of retrieval – all except for the backups that were routed to an undisclosed location. Only a few understood what the CPC actually did. Most staff thought it was a lockout program in case of insider leakage and that the present action was a trial run. Most of the work had been completed on Regenerol and there were many idle hours in the labs recently. The human trials could not proceed until Oisín was given permission from the FDA, which everyone believed to be forthcoming. Oisín was going to test their greatest endeavor yet – Regenerol – on a randomly-selected list compiled by a consortium of gynecologists and obstetricians. Only Debra Lewis, John Graham and Michael Tiernan knew the truth – until recently.

The initiation of the Cerberus Contingency meant that Oisín needed only a skeleton crew. Most of the staff was given a three-day vacation bonus, which was gladly accepted. Any concerns about breaches of security or newly discovered side effects disappeared as the staff readied themselves for a five-day weekend. And, just like that, the four were alone.

ം

"Close the door," said Tiernan.

Debra Lewis was the last in line to enter Tiernan's office, and complied.

"Please sit," Tiernan said. "John Graham, Debra Lewis, this is Ivan Falters," he said and offered nothing else.

"Mr. Falters," said Graham, "I heard an accent. What nationality are you?"

"I don't know. I was adopted," answered Falters.

"You look very familiar, but I can't place you. Have we met? Perhaps I know someone in your family?" asked Graham.

"Unlikely," said Falters.

"Michael," said Debra, riddled with guilt. "I think we have another problem."

Graham jumped into action. He couldn't allow Debra to admit fault. She would leave even if she weren't fired, and he couldn't bear the thought. He grabbed her hand and squeezed it tightly, the grip so powerful it startled her.

"We can fill him in on this later, Debra," said Graham. "We've got much more pressing issues, judging from this morning's actions. Michael, why have we released the Cerberus?"

John Graham had named the protocol Cerberus after the hound in the Greek myth. Cerberus, a monstrous three-headed dog with snakes for his tail and mane, prevented anyone from leaving Hades, and Graham had hoped that he could do the same for the sensitive information housed in Oisín.

Tiernan diverted his attention from Debra's statement to Graham's question, forgetting her completely.

"I got a disturbing call this morning from Ryan Connor over at Lionel. He may have something on us," said Tiernan. "I have a meeting with him today. I'll let you know how it goes, but we should get ready for the worst."

"Bribery?" asked Graham.

"Probably," said Tiernan, "but I think I know what he wants specifically."

"What?" asked Debra.

"A few weeks ago, I was ambushed by a woman at the airport. Long story short, she works for Lionel and they want the Chimera seed prototype. With the recent beating they're taking in the science journals, they need to find a solution before the public realizes there's a huge problem."

"Yes, I've been observing this phenomenon also. To a lesser degree, it's also happening in Italy. Italy does not allow the cultivation of genetically modified crops, so the corn/bee theory isn't as solid as the scientists would have one think," said Falters.

"The Italian bees are reacting to the German farmers' use of the corn," said Graham. "The European bees are also vanishing at rates beyond normal. This is very disturbing, but I am convinced that Lionel's transgenic seed is the culprit."

"At the rate of decline, which is no longer linear but exponential," said Debra, "the vast majority of the bees will be gone within a decade. Then we'll starve to death."

Tiernan showed irritation and anxiety. He didn't want to start a debate; he wanted the prototype.

"Alright, enough of that," he said. "John, where did he keep the files on the Chimera?"

Graham looked gravely at Tiernan and spoke softly. "I'm not sure, but I seem to recall that your father destroyed everything after Mr. Connor wouldn't listen to reason. Your father foresaw the effects of Lionel's monstrosity."

"If that's true," said Tiernan, "then the situation is about to get a whole lot worse." He stood up and, with him, Falters. "Debra, John, scour the databases, the storage rooms and every nook and cranny. Find me something and find it fast."

Tiernan and Falters headed to Lionel, leaving Debra and Graham alone at Oisín.

☙

Tiernan left his car parked in the lot and called for his driver, who responded promptly. Falters searched for the button that would raise the window and closed it swiftly and rudely.

"What is happening?" asked Falters. "I'm assuming the situation isn't merely one of bribery or blackmail."

"We've sunk the better part of a billion dollars into Regenerol, and I'm not going to let that smug prick Ryan Connor destroy it," said Tiernan.

The resentment was still fresh. Young Michael Tiernan had overheard many of his father's phone conversations, growing up. Ryan Connor's name was never mentioned without explicatives during these calls and, although Tiernan had never met Connor, he had inherited his father's contempt for the man.

"Connor screwed my father out of a fortune," Tiernan continued. "He made billions – continues to make billions."

"And, all the while, the ecosystem struggles to adapt to the new toxin that the bees are spreading so efficiently," said Falters, finishing Tiernan's thought. "This Ryan Connor is vile."

Despite his youthful appearance, Falters wore the intangible yet perceptible seal that age bestows, etches upon the souls of those who have learned many of life's cruel lessons, those worthy of respect.

"I didn't know," Tiernan said, "I didn't realize the danger."

Falters said nothing. His stare said it all.

"Shit," Tiernan said. "My father should've told me. He should've made me understand, goddamn it."

"Does Connor have the vials?" said Falters, breaking his silence. "Are they in his possession right now?"

"I don't know," said Tiernan, "but I think we'll know soon enough." The car slowed to a stop in front of Lionel Pharmaceuticals.

CHAPTER 38

"WE SHOULD HAVE told him, John," said Debra, appropriately using we, since Graham was now an accomplice after the fact. "We sent him into the lion's den defenseless."

"Telling him about the breach would not have given him any advantage," said Graham. "What's done is done."

"No, John," said Debra, "it was wrong. He had a right to know."

Graham took her by the hand and, without speaking, led her out of the office and toward the elevators. He pushed the button.

"Where are we going?" said Debra.

"We are going to make everything right," said Graham. "Trust me."

The cab ride to Graham's apartment didn't take long. The morning rush was over and the traffic merciful. He and Debra rode wordlessly, lost in their respective thoughts, admiring the city as it sped past.

"Where are we?" asked Debra, getting out of the cab.

"This is my humble abode," Graham answered.

"Why are we here?" she asked.

"Because we need to be," he answered.

ɔ8

Each leg was fashioned with an iron cuff from which heavy chains – two suspended from the ceiling and two extending from bolts in the floor – formed a symmetrical design. Tighte opened his eyes and the hope that this was all a very lucid nightmare was ruined, again.

"You banged yourself up good, didn't ya?" Lori observed. "Pity it didn't get you anywhere – all that effort for nothin'."

"Kill me and get it over with," Tighte said. He was careful not to use vulgarities now. The burning sensation in his groin was replaced with a steady and throbbing pain and the raw skin around his ankles stung as they rubbed against the iron cuffs. "Please, just kill me."

"Now, why would I go and do a thing like that?" Lori asked. "Then you'd never know what you did to me, to my li'l children." She walked to the other side of the living room, forcing Tighte to shift positions to keep her in sight. The chains rattled and rubbed against his open wounds and the plastic tarp that had adhered itself to the superficial wounds on his back yielded stubbornly under his movement. He grimaced in pain.

"I was gonna have five li'l ones," she said. "I was gonna raise 'em right, teach 'em to be kind to everyone, teach 'em to be good people." Tears welled in her eyes, but didn't fall. They sat suspended on her bottom eyelashes like crystal orbs until she blinked and they fell to the floor.

"I had their names and everythin'," she continued. "Got 'em right out of the good book: Joshua, Jacob, Aaron, Miriam and Ruth. You killed them, and now you're going to pay."

Tighte kept his mouth shut and averted his eyes to the ground in staged sorrow and humility. She was never going to let him go, and she probably wouldn't kill him either, which was worse. If he had any chance of ever seeing the outside world again, he would have to escape. In time, she would screw up. *A Southern hick will not outsmart me,* he thought. *I'll bide my time and wait.*

⋯

He must have dozed off; undoubtedly exhausted, his body had forced sleep upon him. He woke to delicious smells. Lori was preparing breakfast. She decided against adding a flower to the tray, knowing the recipient didn't deserve to enjoy its beauty.

"And now for the final touch," said Lori, reaching for a glass for the juice. "Grape juice plus," she smiled. She filled the glass about halfway with grape juice and added a vial of Dionysinol, stirring the concoction carefully. *An eternity of suffering,* she thought as she carried the tray downstairs.

Tighte thought he was dreaming when he looked down at the feast set before him but was appreciative nonetheless. Eggs, bacon, home fries, sausage and toast sat on one plate, and a bowl of fresh fruit with a dollop of yogurt in the center was almost too beautifully arranged to upset by eating – almost. Coffee sent its aromatic steam into the air as it sat with its purple companion beside it. He looked around, almost afraid to eat. Then Lori spoke.

"I'm not a savage, ya know," said Lori. "Eat your breakfast. Do you like grape juice?"

Within 10 minutes, there was nothing edible remaining on the tray. Tighte considered taking the butter knife and hiding it, then realized there was no place to conceal it. He tugged at the chains with his hands that were suspiciously left unfettered. When he felt the sturdiness of the chains and the configuration that bound him, he understood that there was absolutely no need to bind his hands; he wasn't going anywhere.

"What are you going to do to me?" Tighte said, finally gaining the courage to ask. "You can't keep me here forever."

"Oh, I wouldn't be so sure of that," Lori said. "Forever ain't as long as it used to be, especially in your case."

"Look," he said, "I know this probably means nothing to you, but I have money, untraceable offshore numbered accounts. It's yours if you let me go. I swear, I won't press charges."

"How much do you think my babies were worth?" she said. Her eyes glazed over and Tighte's blood ran cold again. The look was identical to the one she wore before she torched him.

Oh God, no, he prayed.

"Priceless. You can't put a price on them. I wouldn't even try," he said. "But there is a lot you could do with it for others, right? What about all those starving kids in Africa?"

The sound of a car pulling into the driveway halted further talk and replaced it with Tighte screaming frantically.

"Help me, help! Somebody help!"

"Shut your cake hole," said Lori. "No one can hear you. That's just my friend coming back with my things."

Tighte broke down and sobbed as she left the room. It still hadn't even occurred to him to apologize and beg mercy. Perhaps it was because he wasn't sorry and knew he deserved no mercy.

CHAPTER 39

"MR. CONNOR, YOUR appointment has arrived."

"Send them in, Frances," he said.

Tiernan and Falters walked into the office and Falters closed the door with a force that set the tone. Connor didn't stand to greet them; he spared Tiernan the indignity of pretense. Tiernan didn't wait for the invitation to sit, and pulled out a chair. Falters joined him.

Connor sniggered a little and looked at Tiernan. "I see you brought some muscle. Who's this? Cop?"

"No," said Falters. "But that shouldn't offer you any consolation."

The leather portfolio sat guiltily on the desk under the statue of Fionn mac Cumhail. "Ah," said Tiernan, "I see we have the same taste in decorations." He pointed to the bronze man.

"A gift," said Connor. "Leader of the Fianna Warriors, Father of the ill-fated Oisín, the one and only Finn Mac Cumhail."

Tiernan lifted the leather portfolio and statue from the desk, and handed the statue to Falters. "I'll take these off your hands," said Tiernan.

"Be my guest," said Connor. "Now, if you could only find it in your heart to give me the Chimera prototype, I might actually become fond of you."

"Why should I give you anything?" said Tiernan. "You sent thugs to rob my house."

"I did nothing of the sort," Connor replied honestly. "I had nothing to do with the alleged robbery; I'm merely the recipient of some information."

Falters was growing impatient with this game of cat and mouse.

"Where are the other items you happened upon?" he said. "The vials containing the purple liquid, in particular."

"I'm not sure, at the moment, but I might know someone who is," Connor replied. "How much are they worth to you?"

"Enough already, Connor" said Tiernan. "Cut to the chase. What the hell do you want?"

"That's quite the cottage industry you got there, Dr. Tiernan," said Connor. "Like father, like son, I guess."

"Almost, but not quite," snapped Tiernan. "You're not going to play me like you did my father."

Connor looked genuinely surprised at the comment. He knew that there was no love lost between the two, but he never thought that Richard Tiernan harbored any resentment over the sale of his discovery. "I beg your pardon," he said. "Your father benefitted from our arrangement. Don't bellyache because I tweaked the idea and made it better, more lucrative."

"You didn't make it better," said Tiernan, "or we wouldn't be sitting here now. You screwed up royally and need the original seed to bail you out."

"True enough," he said, "but when I said I made it better, I meant better for me."

"Of course," said Tiernan. "And now it's better for you to avoid what's coming down the pike. It's only a matter of time before the devastating effects of your hybrid monster are no longer a matter of debate. Where will you hide then?"

"In exchange for the Chimera prototype, I'm willing to part with the sensitive information regarding your morally reprehensible practices of testing a potentially lethal drug on Mexican women," said Connor. "In addition to keeping my mouth shut, I'll see what I can do to locate your vials – on one condition."

Tiernan had already anticipated the play and waited for Connor to finish.

"I know you've stumbled onto something big and I want in on the Dionysinol. Your family has quite the affinity for enhancing the work

220

of Mother Nature. I want to know everything about it. You've got 48 hours before I sell your information to Merkel and McCaff. Can you really afford to let Regenerol fail to obtain FDA approval?"

Tiernan knew that his company would fold if Regenerol weren't approved. He saw no other option. However, Falters did not feel constrained by the same rules that make living in a civilized society possible.

CHAPTER 40

MARY MCKENNA SAT on the couch, eating right out of the carton. When she finished, she dropped it on the table amidst the others. Her constitution wasn't used to the abuse she had inflicted on it over the past few days, and frequent trips to the bathroom were an unfortunate yet predictable side effect of her indulgence. *I don't even like ice cream,* she thought, looking down at the collection.

Chinese food containers, pizza boxes, beer bottles and an assortment of pint-sized ice cream containers littered the area surrounding her and, for once in her life, the clutter had no effect on her. She felt no urge to clean up, to arrange them in an intelligible order according to fat content or main ingredients. Her mind was still with Lori and Tighte.

Between trips to the bathroom, Mary sat on the couch almost motionless; the activities taking place in her mind required all of her available will. The sugar-induced high was unpleasant, not worth the momentary thrill it provided and she regretted her lack of discipline, her failure to resist its charms. A moment's lapse caused her to think of Tighte and that perhaps she was sublimating for the real cause of her regret.

She got up from the couch, but this time to retrieve her phone. She scrolled through the caller I.D. until she found Lori's number. She brought the phone back to the couch and wrestled with the decision: call or delete?

In her bedroom, two suitcases stood neatly against the wall. Mary's entire life was reduced to those two cases; material objects had never held any real fascination for her. She looked at the phone again and

then back to the suitcases. This went on for some time before she settled on a decision. She pressed the green button and the phone dialed
the numbers, sounding each one with deliberation.

☙

"Would you like some tea, dear? Coffee perhaps?" asked Graham.

"No, thank you," said Debra. "I don't think I need it."

"Very well," said Graham. "Come, I'd like to show you something."

Debra followed Graham through the short, narrow hallway into the
living room, which housed boxes in alphanumerical order. Strange-
ly, they didn't look cluttered despite the quantity of the ill-placed ar-
chives.

"Wow," said Debra. "Talk about bringing your work home with
you."

"Yes, well, I do find it difficult to part with records. All the fuss
over computers and electronic data systems, it just took a little longer
to get used to." Graham was looking over the boxes while he spoke. He
seemed to have a very good idea what he was searching for.

"By the time I had converted from the tried and true method that served
archivists for centuries, I had already accumulated so much. It would have
been more work to shred these, so I kept them," said Graham.

He yanked, with some difficulty, a box tightly sandwiched in
among the others. The pulling and hauling threatened to topple the
high-stacked towers of decades of work. Debra assisted by steadying
the affected columns. A final quick pull and the desired box was freed.
The rest of them adjusted to their new positions with a thud.

"Here we are," Graham said. "Let us hope that I was as obsessive
during the Chimera era."

Debra's sullen heart dared to interpret him.

"You have the prototype?" she said. "You kept the records?"

"I certainly hope so," he said. "My memory is not what it used to be
and I can't, for the life of me, remember, but we'll soon see, now won't
we, dear?"

Graham was conflicted by her sudden change of mood. Her uplifted spirit came on the wings of hope. Obvious was her burning desire that the contents of the box bring relief to Tiernan.

"Aha," said Graham.

They'd triumphed. In his hands, he held the original documents, the discarded scribblings of Richard Tiernan. At the bottom of the Chimera file sat the airtight container of seeds that Graham had preserved for the sake of nostalgia. The original Chimera seeds, the fruits of the labor of an old friend many years ago, sat unaffected by time. He popped open the seal and looked brazenly at the seeds he shook into Debra's open palm. They were viable, sitting safely in stasis in the dry, airtight sarcophagus John Graham had entombed them in ages ago. The two worshiped in silence as they admired the seeds.

CHAPTER 41

"WE MUST RETURN to Sardinia," said Falters.

"Are you nuts?" asked Tiernan. "Why would I go to Italy when this guy has enough to put me away for life? If I don't give him what he wants, I'll be going to jail – forget about saving the company."

"We have to protect the stockpile. Connor knows too much. It won't be long before he puts the pieces together."

"Don't worry," said Tiernan, "we still got Jimmy over there. He won't let me down."

"He's useless to us now," said Falters. "I had to kill him. He's decomposing in the vineyards."

"What? You killed him? How? Why?"

"Irrelevant," said Falters. "What matters is that the stockpile is vulnerable. We must return immediately."

"It's not irrelevant!" shouted Tiernan. "Jimmy was my friend, you psychotic bastard. Why did you kill him?"

"Tangentially, I can confirm that a second dose of Dionysinol is also lethal in humans. You expressed interest in learning more about that."

"Oh my God. How the hell did things get so screwed up so fast?"

"Perhaps it wasn't wise to stake the future of your company on one product," said Falters. "Or to send a thief to guard your treasure, for that matter."

"Really? You think?" said Tiernan. "Wow, where were you when I needed you? My God, I can't believe you killed Jimmy."

"We have to get back to the supply of Dionysinol and destroy the Niamh vineyards. It's the only way to guarantee that our work won't be followed and reproduced."

"Tír na nÓg Vineyards may be the only asset I have left after this is over."

"You're not thinking rationally," said Falters. "You can accumulate your wealth again. If we don't eliminate the grapes –"

Tiernan cut him off with a wave of his hand. He answered the buzzing cell in his pocket. "Please tell me something good," he said.

"We found it," said Debra crying. "We have everything, even a supply of seeds."

"We'll meet you at Oisín in about 40 minutes," said Tiernan. He snapped the cell phone. "They found the Chimera seed."

∞

The sound of the ringing phone echoed throughout the house. Edward answered. "Hello?"

"Uh, is Lori available?" said Mary.

"Just a minute," said Edward. Covering the phone with his palm, he walked outside to find Lori weeding her tomato plants.

"Did you forward your calls to this number?" he asked nervously.

"Yeah, why? Is that for me?" she said from her bent-over position, knees in the soil. Edward nodded his head and waited for her instructions. Lori removed her gloves and handed them to Edward before taking the phone.

"Hello?" said Lori.

"It's me," said Mary McKenna. "I don't know why I called. I'm sorry."

"Don't be, honey," sang Lori. "I'm glad to hear from you. How've ya been?"

Mary considered the possibility that Lori didn't recognize her voice and confused her with someone else. What else would explain the levity with which she spoke?

"This is Mary McKenna," said Mary.

"Okay, and this is Lori Adams," said Lori. "Are you okay, honey? You don't seem yourself."

Mary then considered that Lori had undergone a psychotic break and compartmentalized separate realities into convenient categories in her mind. Should she wish her well and hang up? Should she vanish as planned and begin life anew, banishing all traces of her previous existence? A resounding yes deafened her and how she managed to ignore it, she didn't know.

"I want to see you," said Mary. "I need to see you."

Lori Adams demonstrated effectively that she was not suffering a nervous breakdown; she was not eligible for the insanity plea should her plan go awry. She knew exactly what she was doing and her guilt-free demeanor merely reflected an inner peace that she enjoyed, originating from the knowledge that she was doing no wrong. She was avenging her babies and that was all that mattered.

"Mary, you know I'm busy, darlin'," she said. "I hope you're not thinkin' about turning me in. You aren't fixin' to call the fuzz and throw a monkey wrench in my plan, are ya?"

"No," said Mary. "I'd rather go to prison for life than to save that bag of shit."

"Then why the phone call?" said Lori. "You sound as if you're feeling guilty or something."

Mary felt something, but it wasn't guilt. She believed she'd be at peace with her involvement if she knew Vincent Tighte was dead, but torturing someone didn't sit right with her.

"Is it finished?" asked Mary, choosing her words carefully. Landline traces were unlikely, but she was cautious more out of habit than anything.

"Oh no, honey," Lori said. "It's got quite a while yet."

"Lori," said Mary. "I'm heading out, leaving town, starting fresh. I guess I wanted to say goodbye and to thank you."

"Well, I appreciate that, honey," said Lori. "And I'd like to do the same. Thank you. Who knows, maybe we'll see each other again."

Mary replaced the phone on the cradle and disconnected the cable from the wall. One last check around her apartment and she was ready. In one hand, she held her tickets; in the other, the mysterious purple liquid that Lori claimed was an elixir that bestowed youth upon anyone who imbibed. At first, Mary had thought that Lori was crazy and had

VIAL #2

229

manufactured a tale of fantastic proportion about Michael Tiernan and the vineyards of Tír na nÓg where the Niamh grapes grew. She wasn't so sure anymore.

Mary boarded the plane with her one-way ticket to Cagliari, Sardinia. *Why not?* she thought. *I can go anywhere I want to now. I'm free.*

CHAPTER 42

THE FOUR OF them met at Oisín – Debra and Graham arriving minutes before Tiernan and Falters. Graham handed Tiernan the original Chimera seed and the accompanying documentation. Tiernan opened the container and shook a few seeds into his palm.

"They're so beautiful, I feel like crying."

"Do you believe Connor will keep his word?" asked Graham. "How can you be sure this won't be the first in a continuum of blackmails?"

"He won't," said Tiernan. "He was too cavalier." He returned the seeds to their airtight container and began perusing the handwritten documents – the series of failures and successes that culminated in a seed that was never used. *What a waste,* he thought.

"What does being cavalier have to do it?" asked Graham. "From my recollection, Mr. Connor has a propensity for being invincibly arrogant."

"True," said Tiernan, still skimming the documents. "But, if I go down, I intend on dragging Connor with me." He pressed play on the recorder he had concealed while in Connor's office.

"Blackmail is a crime and withholding information from the Feds is bad enough, but, when you combine the two, watch out. Nope, he has no intention of ratting or else he would've been more cautious."

"I would be very surprised if Connor hadn't anticipated your move," said Falters. "He probably assumed you'd record the session and adjusted accordingly."

"Nah, I don't think so. Anyway, I gotta hand it to you guys," he said, "you really came through." Debra felt that twinge of guilt resurface, but this time she kept her mouth shut. *John's right,* she thought. *There is nothing to be gained from confessing.*

"Okay. We need to strategize, but I'm starving. How about we continue this over lunch? Debra," said Tiernan, "would you mind taking Mr. Falters in your car and meeting us at Gypsy's Tavern? I need a quick debriefing on the finer details of the Chimera seed. We can meet you there in 30 minutes."

"I'd be honored," said Debra. "We can drive through Times Square. Would you enjoy seeing Times Square, Mr. Falters?" She was beginning to respond to the messages sent by the much-debated vomeronasal organ. Her body was unconsciously reacting to the influx of urgent pleas to mate with this desirable genotype. Her unconscious knew that there was something different, something better, something irresistible about this man.

"I have seen it already," said Falters.

"Well, there are many other sights in New York other than Times Square. Come on, I'll surprise you."

Hesitantly, Falters took leave. Graham and Tiernan were already engrossed in discussion.

"Dr. Tiernan," said Falters before he left, "don't be long."

"I'll be right behind you," said Tiernan, as he watched Falters and Debra leave. Once he was satisfied that they were gone, he turned to Graham. "John, I need you to do something for me. It's urgent."

"Eh, yes, sir," said Graham. "How may I be of service?"

"I need you to do exactly as I say and not ask any questions," said Tiernan.

"Very well, sir," said Graham, who didn't seem at all intrigued.

"After lunch, I'm going to distract Falters – I don't know exactly how, but I need to keep him away from the mansion while you get in touch with Marinella and Diego."

"Very well, sir," said Graham who now spoke with Michael Tiernan the way he had spoken with Richard. It wasn't a farce, it was just who he was. There were very clear lines drawn between subordinates and their masters in England, where Graham had spent a good part of his life before immigrating to America after his father was reassigned. Dual citizenship didn't mean much to Graham who had always identified himself as an American despite his perennial English accent.

"I know you specified that there should be no questions," said Graham, "but, in the interest of fulfilling your wishes, might I know what you wish for me to relay to Mr. and Mrs. Santarelli?"

"Oh, Jesus," said Tiernan. "Yeah, of course. I need you to…"

CB

Before they arrived at the restaurant, Graham had his instructions. The lunch was uneventful, even boring, when observed from above the blanket of privacy their individual minds provided. Passionate and shameless scenes too graphic for smut played in high-definition on the canvas of Debra's mind. Not one but two lovers were needed to satisfy these new and alarming desires.

Tiernan's mind wandered between two different places, where inexhaustible wealth and youthful vitality were consistent in both. The realization that he and Falters were the first human beings to achieve what all others instinctively yearned for, sat very comfortably with him. All he needed to do was get out of the current situation and start fresh. The waiter arrived with the check, bringing Tiernan out of his head.

"No, no," said Tiernan, snatching the check, "I insist."

"In that case, I would like to place a to-go order," said Graham, who could always be relied on to make a joke that wasn't funny but perhaps was at one time.

"Are we to assume that we're getting an extended weekend too?" asked Debra.

"Yes, indeed," said Tiernan, handing the credit card to the waiter. "If anyone deserves a reward, it's you two. Just make sure we're ready for next week's interview with the FDA."

"John," said Debra, "how shall we spend our good fortune?"

"Together is fine with me," said Graham. *Hell would be a heaven with you and Heaven a hell without you, my dear,* he thought.

"Mr. Falters and I have a few things to attend to," said Tiernan. "You two keep yourselves out of trouble, ya hear? See you Monday."

233

CB

"We cannot afford to waste time," said Falters. "The consequences for failing to contain the Dionysinol are too horrible to imagine."

"We'll get it all back," Tiernan said as reassuringly as possible. "They have no idea what they're dealing with. The only thing that Connor wants is the Chimera prototype, period."

"You forget so easily," said Falters. "He suspects that whatever the purple liquid is, it has the potential to earn trillions. Didn't you see the lust burning in his eyes?"

"All he knows about the Dionysinol is what my father wrote in that damn portfolio, curse it to hell and the lowlife who stole it," said Tiernan. "That's it."

"I wouldn't be so sure," said Falters. "Just because you didn't understand what was written doesn't mean that Connor doesn't."

Tiernan handed the leather binder to Falters. The scent of Autumn's Breeze still lingered on it.

"First things first. Let's go back to Oisín and make arrangements to meet with Connor," said Tiernan. "We can see if these seeds will entice him to give up the vials."

"Burn this," said Falters, handing him the portfolio. "It has more information in it than you realize."

CHAPTER 43

GRAHAM PHONED DIEGO Santarelli and told him of his intention to call on him. Graham knew the Santarellis well, having seen them several times a year before Richard's death. Diego was happy to hear from him and welcomed the unexpected visit.

"No, Marinella," pleaded Graham, "I can't eat, even a little. I've just finished lunch."

"Va bene," said Marinella.

Graham faithfully relayed the information Tiernan had charged him to give to the two people left in his life that resembled family. Tiernan knew that he could trust Diego and Marinella with his life and, hopefully, with this important task.

"You see, it's rather simple, really," said Graham. "Master Tiernan requests that you set out immediately to retrieve for him something of extreme importance."

"This is no problem," said Diego, putting on his shoes. "Insieme, eh, together or just me?"

"Well, it is a little more complicated, I'm afraid," continued Graham. "You and Marinella will be away for a while."

Marinella sat up in her chair with a look of concern that spoke of her love for the young boy who was like a son to her. "What is wrong? What is the matter?" she demanded.

Graham was aware of the relationship the Santarellis had with their surrogate son and immediately put her at ease. "Not a thing," he said. "Michael is fine, but says that he cannot trust another living soul with this mission. It pains him to ask this of you, but necessity requires it."

The two aging Italians sat and listened to the finer details of the very peculiar request. The obligation that a mother feels to a son made Graham's job a very simple exercise.

"You must go immediately, however," said Graham finally. "I've arranged tickets on the way over, first-class at Master Tiernan's request. You'll land in England, have a short layover and then on to Sardinia."

Richard had sent Diego and Marinella to Italy for a month each year as part of their disproportionate salary. Michael Tiernan knew that they would have valid passports and that they would truly enjoy the journey.

"After you secure the trunk with the vials," said Graham, "you should wait for Master Tiernan at this address in Rome." He handed Diego a piece of paper. "He'll tell you what to do next."

"What is this material he needs?" asked Marinella. "Why is it so, eh, como si dice? eh..."

"Urgent," said Diego.

"I'm afraid I can't answer that, for I don't know myself," answered Graham. "However, I can tell you this: Master Tiernan believes it's a matter of life and death."

Nothing further needed to be said. Within an hour, the three headed out across the impossible highways that made John F. Kennedy Airport synonymous with high blood pressure. The three of them, however, were unaffected in the back of the air-conditioned limo. Graham stayed with the Santarellis until they boarded. He watched the plane take off and didn't take his eyes off the metal tube until it was no longer visible.

That is a very good question, Master Tiernan, Graham thought. *Why is this material so important, coveted with such urgency?* He walked back to the limo and, upon settling down in the comfortable seat, dialed Tiernan's cell.

"They are in the air as we speak, sir," said Graham. "They'll call me when they land in England." He hung up the phone and lowered the window divider so he could engage in conversation with the driver who was about to do battle with rush hour traffic. The time passed a little easier for both of them.

Tiernan snapped the cell phone shut and managed to draw a deep breath, which hadn't been possible since Graham's departure. Under the circumstances, Tiernan was impressed with how well he was handling the pressure of juggling the situations, keeping the lies straight and the right information away from the wrong people.

"The vials?" said Falters.

"No," said Tiernan.

The car stopped in front of the Lionel Headquarters.

CHAPTER 44

"RYAN, I'M IN the middle of somethin '," said Lori. "I just can't right now. I'll bring it over to you when I can. Do not, let me repeat, do not send anyone over here, you got me?"

"I won't, but can you at least tell me what the containers looked like?" said Connor. "And the shade of the liquid? I need to give Tiernan a convincing decoy."

"He's not gonna fall for that, but I'll do my very best."

"Fine," said Connor. "Call Frances with the info, and please hurry."

"Alright now, bye," said Lori. "Tell Michael Tiernan I was asking for him – no hard feelin's."

Connor smiled as he hung up. *No hard feelings,* he thought. *Nah, he won't harbor any – you only ruined his entire life.*

"Mr. Connor," said Frances, "Dr. Tiernan and his associate are on their way up."

"Okay, Frances," said Connor. "Have them wait outside for, uh, let's say, 10 minutes before bringing them in."

"Very well, sir."

Connor prepared himself.

○๛

Lori sat watching her soap opera in the comfort of the air-conditioned room. When the show was over, she waited impatiently for the teaser scenes of the next episode, then got up and started to prepare dinner.

Several hours later, she set a large tray of assorted foods in front of Tighte. Dinner. She left the room as he fed; the sight and sounds of him eating made her sick. Several rooms away, she joined Edward, who was already sitting down at the table waiting for her.

"It's getting cold," said Edward. "Come, sit down and eat with me." Lori obliged. A few minutes into the meal, after the salads were eaten and the first of several glasses of wine were poured, he asked her. "When are you going to finish this?"

Lori reached for her glass and took a sip before answering. "That's up to him, honey," she said. "Depends on what decision he makes tonight."

She went to work sawing off a piece of onion-smothered rib eye steak and dipped it in the creamy, butter-soaked mashed potatoes before putting the heaping forkful in her mouth. She rolled her eyes back in mock ecstasy and moaned. "Oh, my Lord, that's divine, ain't it?"

Edward didn't press further. "I got you the manufacturer's information you asked for," he said, changing the subject. "The first medical supply store I walked into, and there it was."

Lori nodded, widened her eyes and hummed a response, her mouth still at near capacity. After swallowing half the mouthful, she managed to speak. "Oh, you are a gem! Can you call Frances at Lionel and give her the information? Ryan's waiting for it and he's in one a' his moods."

Edward retrieved his cell phone and dialed. Usually, this wouldn't be tolerated – a phone call at the table – but there were a few exceptions. This was one of them.

"Ooo, and tell her it looks kinda like that sports drink – Purple Energy Blast – but thicker, like maple syrup, but the diet kind," Lori added.

Edward had a confused look on his face, but relayed the information word for word and waited as Frances wrote it down verbatim.

Dinner ended with a few postprandial drinks and sherbet. Edward began clearing the dishes and scraping the leftovers into the garbage disposal while watching Lori out of the corner of his eye. She seemed pensive, almost uncertain or conflicted. He was going to tell her that she didn't need to do it; she didn't need to go through with it, but he waited too long. Lori got up from the table and headed out into the hallway. She walked into the bathroom, opened the cabinet and began removing the tools needed to complete the evening's deed: syringe, bottle of syrup of ipecac, gauze, needle and thread, beeswax and a few towels.

She placed the items in a wicker basket with a big bow adorning the handle and carried her tools into the room where Tighte was enjoying the warmth and satisfaction of a full stomach.

"Oh my," she said, seeing that Tighte was still conscious. "I guess I goofed on the proper dosage; you're still awake."

He looked down at the basket of items Lori carried on her arm. She looked like a fairy tale character setting off to visit Grandma, but the array of wares sitting ominously in the basket belonged in a different genre.

"What're they for?" he asked. "What are you gonna do to me?"

Lori ignored Tighte's question and placed the basket in front of him. "Edward, honey," she called. "Ed? I'm gonna need your help, after all."

Edward closed the dishwasher door and pushed the button to initiate the pots and pans cycle. He dried his hands and walked into the living room where he would do whatever she asked of him.

CHAPTER 45

MARY THUMBED THROUGH an assortment of tourist books on Sardinia. The common denominator seemed to be the mystical ambiance that each author attributed to the ancient land. Of special interest to Mary was Tír na nÓg Vineyards in the little hamlet of Boroneddu where the mysterious purple liquid originated. It rapidly ascended on the list of must-sees as Mary read more on this shockingly overlooked paradise.

I'll make it a Nuraghi tour, she thought. *I have to see those amazing things, maybe go down into the tunnels if I work up the nerve.*

The time in the air wasn't as torturous as usual, as her mind left her body to travel back to ancient days when the Nuragic people roamed Sardinia, working the land, producing abundant food. She tried to imagine how such advanced structures were accomplished thousands of years before Christ, and how they still remained. She allowed herself a moment's pride at the accomplishments of her race, imagining the Nuragic people with their advanced metallurgy and engineering abilities intermingling seamlessly with the magic and ritual that also permeated the culture. Then she thought of how her race had progressed and the pride turned to something akin to despair. Was life simpler when humans believed that the wind spoke to them? Was it easier to lose loved ones when it was simply understood that they were never far away? Was it easier to believe that, when the gods summoned one's soul, one would be reunited with loved ones in an endless cycle of life and death? Was it easier when men and women were bound to clans and not individuals, loving and mating with whomever they chose? When did jealousy and possession infect us and what was the swan song that played just before the Nuragics vanished without a trace, record or discernible cause?

Mary closed the book, as it was becoming conducive to melancholy. She tried to close her eyes and lure sleep, but the elusive grace wasn't coming. Another six hours and they would touch down in Milan where she would wait for the next leg of the journey.

She thought of Lori Adams, Vincent Tighte, Michael Tiernan and Debra Lewis, and the situation that may have already reached its boiling point. She looked around the cabin at the people who were neatly positioned like eggs in an egg carton, heads resting against the backs of the uncomfortable seats, the reclined position cruelly teasing them with the suggestion of comfort, only to disappoint, and she wondered. *How many other people on this very plane, right here and right now, are as duplicitous as the people I've associated with these recent years? Are there any true and forthright people? Or are we all just hoping that the masks we wear so well and the facades that hide our true intentions hold up long enough for us to pillage the unsuspecting?*

She reached for the bag stowed under her seat, pulling it out from under the feet of the passenger sitting behind her who thought that her leather bag would be a comfortable footrest for his shoeless feet. She thought about saying something, but didn't. She looked through the assortment until she felt the case where she had stored the vial of purple liquid. She held it against the sunlight that streamed its diminishing rays into the cabin before it sank out of sight. The vial was plugged with a rubber stopper and sealed with some kind of wax that had oozed from under the layer of sealant tape. It was securely stored, she observed. She angled it against the rays, catching the light against the vial so that the liquid sparkled and diffused the light in its thick core. *What if I just opened it and drank it down?* she thought. *What if Lori Adams isn't crazy and the stories of Tír na nÓg, Oisín and all that jazz were true after all?* She chided herself for not having had the contents analyzed. Had she gone with her first inclination, she would have banished all uncertainty and exposed Dionysinol for the fraud that it undoubtedly was. But she didn't, and she couldn't bring herself to discard the vial. She returned Lori's stolen snake oil to the leather bag and decided that she would keep it as a souvenir of Lori Adams, the woman with whom she felt a strong kinship.

Sardinia, please bring me some peace, she prayed. *Blow your magic into my soul and cleanse me of my past.* She closed her eyes and sleep came to her. She dreamt of the grapes growing in Tír na nÓg, the Nuraghi and the miles of spacious tunnels twisting intricate patterns deep into the earth. It was the most comfortable sleep she had managed in weeks, and she credited the druids of Sardinia's past for the unexpected gift.

CHAPTER 46

"GENTLEMEN," SAID CONNOR, this time rising to greet them. "That didn't take long." He didn't hold out his hand to greet them but, instead, gestured to the seats. "Please."

"Before we begin, we have a few conditions," said Tiernan.

Connor raised his eyebrows.

"Yes," said Falters. "If our conditions aren't met, we will be left in the unfortunate position of having to find a buyer for the Chimera seeds."

"You'll lose, buddy," said Connor, dismissing what he deemed a bluff. "The Chimera corn and the documentation cataloguing the stages of its development are the sole property of Lionel Pharmaceuticals and no court in the world would deny it."

"Yes," said Tiernan, "but possession is nine-tenths of the law."

Connor was intolerant of games, cliché phrases and negotiations, in general. Rather than argue the finer points of the situation and in the spirit of expediting a resolution, he asked for their conditions.

"I want to know your source," said Tiernan. "I want to know how you got the information."

"Can't happen, won't happen," said Connor. He reached into the drawer, removed a folder and tossed it across the desk. Tiernan stopped it with his hands. Papers peered out from the edges and the heading on one of them caught Tiernan's eye: IND APPLICATION TO BEGIN HUMAN TRIALS. He summoned all of his available strength to maintain calm.

"Where are the vials?" asked Falters abruptly. "Without the vials we can have no deal."

"I'm sorry," said Connor, "but who the hell are you and what makes you think you're calling the shots? I mean, who's running the show here?"

"I am," said Tiernan, flashing Falters a look.

"Look," said Connor, "I'm sure we all have better things to do. We're both in a bit of a situation, but not without options. Scratch my back and I'll scratch yours. Gimme the seeds and you can avoid an international court. How many Mexican women died in your trials? I can see the headlines now: 'Greedy Drug Company Exploits the Poor.'"

Tiernan was acutely aware that if he were to be incarcerated, it would only take a few years before they realized he was different, much different. He seemed more amenable to a deal when he, too, could picture the headlines, feel the metal bracelets around his wrists, smell the prison swill and imagine the welcome he'd receive from the inmates of Mexican descent.

"How can I be sure that you'll keep your word?" said Tiernan. "How can I trust that you won't leak the information after you've gotten what you wanted?"

"I'm sure you realize," said Connor, "that withholding information regarding international crimes is not looked favorably upon by our government, right?"

Tiernan just kept his eyes locked on Connor, not responding.

"I'm sure you have some recording device and, at the very least, have this guy to corroborate your story," said Connor, gesturing toward Falters. "Even if I were to avoid charges," he continued, "I'd be a person of interest for quite a while and we all know that none of us needs to attract anymore heat."

Tiernan took the folder, put it in his briefcase and snapped it shut. He removed the container of seeds and placed them on the desk.

"You wouldn't be in this mess if you'd listened to my father 10 years ago," said Tiernan.

"Yeah, you're probably right," said Connor, picking up the seeds and shaking a few into his palm. "But, then again, Lionel Pharmaceuticals is a business, not a charity. Your father's method was cost-prohibitive. The Chimera corn seed is much too difficult to produce."

Tiernan shook his head. "But now you've got no option. You have to produce it. Lionel's derivative is wreaking havoc across the globe," he said.

"And still the public does nothing!" Connor shouted in mock anger. "And they won't do anything! Nobody cares about anything unless it affects them directly, haven't you figured that out yet?"

"Why the urgency, then? Why now? Why is it so important to secure the prototype?" asked Tiernan.

Connor pushed a button under his desk. An imperceptible, high-pitched frequency sounded throughout the room, a frequency that would perhaps annoy bats, but was too high for human detection. Connor had allowed Tiernan the illusion of control by permitting him to record their previous conversation. He figured that Tiernan would be more likely to hand over the seeds in exchange for the incriminating evidence against Oisín if he had an ace in the hole, if he felt he had something to use against Lionel in case Connor backslid. However, Connor's willingness to provide comfort ended there. Now they were wading into conversational waters that could ruin Lionel's reputation if an audio recording were to leak out.

The high-pitched sound rendered all recording devices inert and had saved Connor many a time. Lori Adams had insisted they install the expensive technology. *Worth every penny,* thought Connor.

Connor's mind fled to Lori and he wondered if it was finished yet. He imagined Tighte sinking slowly, lifelessly and soundlessly into the abyss of the Atlantic Ocean or some other equally dark place where he would lie for all eternity among the other bottom-dwelling creatures, in absolute darkness.

"Connor," said Tiernan. "Why pull the plug now when there are billions yet to be plundered?"

Before he continued, Connor looked inconspicuously at his feet where a blinking red light told him that the frequency was functioning. "Because I want to provide the antidote to a poison that the American public doesn't even know it has ingested. Lionel Pharmaceuticals will phase out its derivative and replace it with the Chimera seed because," he paused for dramatic effect, "here at Lionel Pharmaceuticals, we put the American people first, and if there is even a remote chance that our product isn't as good as it could be, then we know it's our duty to provide something better, something worthy of the American people."

Connor smiled, knowing that the two were seething with anger. "That'll go over real well in the Heartland," said Connor. "Just a hint of racial superiority to flavor the message is all it needs. Every hick from here to Oregon will buy Lionel products because 'they're the company that cares.'"

It was brilliant and Tiernan knew it. *Rake in billions from the toxic and cheap version of the Chimera seed and, before anyone points the finger at you, announce to the public that you've found a better seed. Sure, it'll cost more, but, hey, you can't put a price on health.*

Connor was slick. This move would make Lionel Pharmaceuticals synonymous with honesty and integrity. *Son of a bitch,* thought Tiernan. *Slick bastard's gonna double his profit and glide through FDA scrutiny with lubricated ease on this one.* He thought of his father, working late into the night, tired but determined to bring the new hybrid species to life, life that he no longer possessed.

"The vials?" said Falters. "We want the vials."

"Yeah, about that," said Connor. "We've run into a problem there. They've been misplaced, but, don't worry, we'll get them back to you as soon as we find them."

Falters stood up to leave. He didn't need to hear anymore.

Tiernan didn't believe him; nobody would have. It was clear that he was lying. Tiernan picked up the folder with the incriminating evidence and walked out.

This ain't over, he thought, *not by a long shot.*

Falters stood on the street in front of the building and waited for Tiernan. Tiernan appeared moments later and the limo arrived shortly afterwards.

"We got 'em," said Tiernan. "Idiot!"

"I'm afraid Mr. Connor is no idiot," said Falters. "When you check your recorder, you'll find that there's nothing there but static."

Tiernan reached for the device, pressed play and the sound of a million tiny ball bearings rolling, filled the car.

"How'd you know?" said Tiernan.

"I heard the cloaking device turn on in the middle of the meeting," said Falters. "I can detect pressure waves just below 100,000 Hz."

"I took the Dionysinol too, and I didn't hear a thing."

"Perhaps in time," said Falters, but he was increasingly certain that he had given Tiernan too small a dose to effect any change. He thought it best to keep that information to himself for the time being. He knew that if he could just find those vials, he would continue to ignore the inevitable call to the grave, a call that Tiernan would very likely have to answer. "We must retrieve those vials," he said. "We tried it your way, now I'll try mine. Can you get me Ryan Connor's home address?"

Tiernan took out his phone and dialed. "Yeah, I can get it."

&#x03; Ȣ

Connor buzzed his secretary. "Frances?"

"Yes, sir?" she responded.

"Do they have something for me yet?"

"The lab just sent it up." Frances came into the office and put the container on his desk. "They're of varying hues and consistency," she said, repeating the technician's words. "They followed the specifications of what type of containers they should use. You'll just have to pick out which sample looks the most authentic."

"That's all, thank you," said Connor, which meant, *I'm done with you now, get out.*

Frances closed the door behind her, leaving Connor to look over the vials. *They look the same to me*, he thought, picking up a few and inspecting them. *Stupid idea, anyway. They'd eventually find out that I duped them.* He put two vials in his shirt pocket and forgot about them until he got home that evening.

CHAPTER 47

"DON'T DO IT," said Tighte. "I have money, laundered and untraceable. It's yours if you just let me go; I won't press charges, I swear."

Edward came in from the kitchen. "What do you need?"

"He's still awake. Shouldn't he be knocked out by now?" she said.

Tighte sat horrified as his two captors sat discussing him as if he were an animal incapable of understanding.

"Yeah, he should, but, if we give him anymore, he'll be out for the night," said Edward. "It's probably the adrenaline. Give him another half-hour, he'll conk out."

Edward left Lori and Tighte alone. Lori was sitting a short distance from Tighte, still out of his reach, but close enough for him to smell her perfume. She took advantage of the wait and decided to complete her crossword puzzle. "Five-letter word for the most abundant crop in America?" she said. "I know it's corn, but maybe they made a mistake or somethin'."

"Wheat," said Tighte.

"It ain't wheat," said Lori. "It got an 'i' in it."

"Maize," shouted Edward from the kitchen.

"You're right," said Lori, penning the answer. "Nice one."

The drugs that Lori had slipped into Tighte's dinner were having no effect on him. He should have been edging closer to oblivion as the drugs worked their way through his bloodstream, but he was wide awake.

"Don't kill me," he said. "Please don't kill me."

"Hush, now. You're ruining my concentration. They make 'em so dang hard," said Lori, referring to the crossword. "Edward, he's still awake."

"I have money in an offshore account. Please, it's yours. Just let me go. I won't tell anyone."

"Ed?" called Lori. "Bring me that notebook computer and another injection of that sleepy drug, would ya?" she shouted. She closed her book and left the pen to hold her place. "I just got a great idea."

Edward came in with the drug and the computer, turning it on before handing both to Lori.

"These little Macs are great. I just love 'em," she said. "Boot up so fast, I tell ya."

This bitch is crazy, thought Tighte. Thoughts of torturing her slowly and painfully burned in his mind.

"I'll tell ya what, since you're still awake, you're gonna transfer all that money into Mary McKenna's account," said Lori. "I know you have the numbers; she told me that you memorized them so you didn't have to write 'em down anywhere."

Tighte knew that she was waiting for the slightest protestation, the tiniest hint of noncompliance to set the evening's torture in motion. "Yeah, yeah, no problem," he said. "I'll do it right now."

Edward watched over him as he accessed the accounts, in case he tried to send an SOS by e-mail. Tighte was too terrified to have entertained the thought.

"When I get a confirmation from Mary that you sent the cash, I'll give you an opportunity at freedom," said Lori. "But not before you write me a confession for what you did, everything you did."

Tighte completed the transfer. *I'll get it back,* he thought. *I'll get it back and kill both of them.* They were all too preoccupied to notice that Tighte's wounds were healing right before their eyes.

Lori was getting the injection ready. "I just realized why he's still awake, Ed," she said. "It's gotta be that stuff from Tiernan's house."

Vincent Tighte's eyes widened with rage. *Tiernan's involved with this too,* he thought, and added Tiernan to the list of people he was going to kill when this was all over.

"Dionysus' blood?" asked Edward. "Why did you give him that?"

"You know why," answered Lori. "But, 'cept for insomnia, it

doesn't seem to do a whole lot," she snickered. She stuck the injection into Tighte's neck and squeezed the contents into his bloodstream.

"Lori!" shouted Edward, "that's too much."

"Naw, it ain't," she said. "Watch."

CHAPTER 48

UNDER THE COVER of night, Falters waited for Connor to arrive home. He listened to the sounds of children playing in the house as he adjusted the binoculars. *Three children,* he thought. *Hopefully, they'll be asleep when he arrives.* But that wouldn't prevent Falters from completing what he knew he must. The world was filled with innocent children who grow up into adults. Children nurtured in corrupt soil have little chance of being anything but corrupt. *One cannot grow on an apple tree and become a pear,* he thought.

He saw Connor's wife through the picture window before she cut off his view as she drew the drapes. Falters thought of Nadja and his own children – dead, mutilated so savagely that only beings filled with hatred could have done such a heinous act. He repressed the memory by an act of will and waited for Connor to arrive.

The headlights were small at first, but grew in size as the Cadillac Escalade drove through the security gate and down the long driveway to Connor's house. The garage door opened and Connor pulled in. *It's dark enough,* thought Falters.

Connor stepped out of the oversized vehicle, briefcase in hand. Before the door of the Escalade shut, Falters was already on him. He grabbed Connor's throat, making the claw-like grip tighten as he swept his legs out from under him. Connor hit the concrete hard, his head taking most of the brunt. Growing up on the streets of Boston, Connor was no stranger to physical altercations, which seemed to rival baseball as the city's favorite pastime. With fear-infused strength, he landed a fist between Falter's legs, knocking him back a few steps. He followed up with a straight kick under the jaw from his lying position. Falters smashed against the Escalade's side mirror, gashing his eyebrow open, blood gushing into his left eye. Connor was on his feet and on the offensive. He charged at Falters with the intent of killing the intruder. His family was a few hundred feet away, upstairs playing games and hoping Daddy would come home before bed. He had to kill him.

Connor landed a series of blows to Falters' head, each launched with the precision of a guided missile. The last punch was meant to be the widow-maker. Falters evaded the left hook. Connor's fist smashed through the window of the SUV, setting off the alarm. His broken hand emerged bloody and useless. Falters delivered a kick to Connor's chest and felt something crack as he retracted his leg and kicked him again in the face. Time was running out. The alarm had alerted the family that something wasn't right. Connor's wife heard the commotion in the garage and dialed 9-1-1, Connor all the while yelling for her to stay inside the house.

Falters flicked open the stiletto blade, determined to end Connor's life before the cops arrived. Upon seeing the knife, Connor grabbed the first weapon available – a pair of shears – which he wielded awkwardly.

"Come on, you son of a bitch," said Connor.

Falters stepped toward him and the glass from the broken vials crunched under his foot.

"There they are, you stupid bastard," said Connor. "Your precious vials – you destroyed them yourself."

Falters didn't take his eyes off Connor, knife extended toward him as he crouched to retrieve the rubber stopper that lay next to the shards of glass. Connor retrieved the second vial, which had managed to stay intact, and tossed it on the ground next to Falters.

"And here's another one."

The vial bounced twice before rolling under the car unbroken. It was enough to distract Falters. As his eyes followed the path of the vial, Connor stabbed the shears into his shoulder and twisted the handles. Falters screamed and stabbed Connor in the hand, piercing his palm straight through. Then, in the reflection of the newly-waxed vehicle, they saw the intermittent flashing of red and blue lights. Falters was gone as fast as he had appeared. Like a phantom, he vanished into the thick woods that surrounded Connor's substantial property.

"Freeze!" shouted the officer, gun drawn on Connor. He lifted his bleeding hand in the air with some difficulty. "It's me. I own the house. Catch him. He ran that way."

Seeing the flashing lights and assuming safety, Connor's wife came rushing into the garage and threw her arms around her husband. "What happened? Oh, my God, you're bleeding. Someone call an ambulance," she cried. "Who did this to you?" Her hysteria created the extra few seconds that Falters needed to escape apprehension.

"I know who did it," said Connor, hand wrapped, waiting for the ambulance. "The guy works for Michael Tiernan. Tiernan threatened me today in my office. He's the one who set this up. Arrest him."

❧

"Sono molto felice," said Tiernan, speaking louder than usual. "Stay in Rome until I get there, va bene?"

"Ah si, non c'e problema," said Diego. "Ci vediamo presto."

Tiernan was relieved to hear it. The Santarellis had successfully obtained the Dionysinol without incident, although he was sure that he would have to answer thousands of questions later. *Why did your father have a lab in Sardinia? Why was it underground? What are these things, anyway? What does it do? What does Tír na nÓg mean? Who was that Russian fellow? Why were the grapes so disgusting? What kind of grapes are they? No wine? Why would you grow grapes that can't produce wine?*

Tiernan was thinking of all the possible questions his surrogate family could ask and proactively sought believable answers. They weren't coming easy. Three thumps on the door followed shortly after red and blue lights invaded his living room.

"Michael Tiernan?" said the officer.

"Yes," said Tiernan. "What's going on?"

"You're under arrest. Put your hands up and turn around." They cuffed him and escorted him to the police car.

"I want to call my lawyer," he said, and remained silent until Lynch arrived at the station.

CHAPTER 49

"HAS THE WAX melted yet?" said Lori.

"Almost," said Edward. "I'll bring it to you when it's ready."

Lori finished the last stitch. "There we are." She rose from her crouching position and took a few steps back to view her handiwork. Vincent Tighte lay unconscious on the couch with his mouth sewn tightly shut. Thick black threads jutted out of the corners of his mouth and beads of blood formed where the needle had entered and exited. His lips looked like a duck's bill. "I triple-stitched it," she said. "Hurry with the wax."

Edward came into the room holding a saucepan with an oven-mitted hand, the other stirring the contents. "I put in the food coloring, but it won't turn that shade you wanted," he said.

Lori peered into the pan. "Aww, it's close enough. It's hard to get fire engine red, trust me." Lori took the saucepan out of Edward's hands. "Lay him down flat for me," she said. "I don't want this to spill all over the place, beeswax being so hard to find 'n' all."

Lori poured the bubbling-hot liquid over Tighte's mouth. The red wax found its way into the nooks and hardened under the fan that Edward held to expedite the process.

"I want to get at least two coats," said Lori.

"We got enough," said Edward, looking into the pot.

"How long till he wakes up," said Lori. "He looks pretty dead to me."

"Dunno," said Edward. "Probably should give him another adrenaline shot."

"Oh yeah," she smiled. "I almost forgot about those. Where are they?"

"Fridge," said Edward, "in the crisper drawer next to the asparagus."

Lori headed into the kitchen to get an adrenaline shot. Edward was left alone with the sleeping mass of rapist, the fan hardening the wax-laden mouth. He tapped the red substance to see if it was ready. "This stuff gets really hard, doesn't it?" he called out.

"Sure does," she answered.

Edward knew that he needed to wait until after this was all over. He couldn't spring a question of such magnitude on her until she had time to heal. With Vincent Tighte dead and the voices of her unborn children finally quieted, she just might be ready. But would she marry him? Did she love him? The quantity of lovemaking told him that she was certainly attracted to him, but did she love him? His pocket bulged where the ring box sat. He had saved his pennies and bought her a ring worthy of her gorgeous hand. His heart beat faster thinking about her answer.

"Now," said Lori, handing Edward the injection, "would you do the honors? There's only two left and I don't wanna take any chances."

"Sure," said Edward "just let me secure this belt first." He took the leather strap, wrapped it under Tighte's chin and tightened the clasp on the top of his head to prevent his powerful jaw muscles from cracking the wax and breaking the sutures. "Looks like those old-fashioned pictures of kids coming home from the dentist, right?" he said.

They both laughed nervously. Then, taking the needle from her, Edward plunged it into Tighte's chest. "Gotta get through those layers of fat and then through the breast plate," he said as he depressed the plunger, sending the contents rushing into Tighte's heart. "Okay, watch out."

Tighte reanimated within seconds, his screams locked inside a sewn-shut, wax-sealed cavity. His hands were bound now and he struggled against the iron links, trying to touch his face.

"Get him the mirror, would ya?" said Lori. Edward returned and showed the writhing man his reflection. Tighte's eyes screamed and he struggled to free himself.

"Stop that now," Lori said. "I said I was gonna give you a chance at freedom and I will, so just hold still." She drew a large horse syringe full of the syrup of ipecac and squirted a few drops out. "I always wanted to do that, like they do on TV," she said. "Now, don't move or it'll break off in your face." She pierced the needle through his jaw so as not to disturb the wax job and expelled the liquid into his mouth, forcing him to swallow it. "That big dinner you ate is about to come back for a visit," she said. "You got about three to five minutes, I'd say."

Edward released one of Tighte's hands from the shackles and gave him a baby's rattle. The end of the plastic rattle was sharpened to form a blunt, knife-like tool. "I think it's clear what you'll have to do," said Lori. "Have fun."

Lori left the room where Tighte's hate- and rage-filled eyes were now concentrating on Edward, who stayed to supervise the event. "In a few minutes, you're going to vomit your guts up," said Edward. "I'm sure by now, you realize what the rattle is for. Either cut your face open or choke to death on your own vomit," said Edward.

Tighte lifted his hand and felt his mouth. The hardened wax would be easy to break, but Lori had tripled-stitched his mouth shut with very thick thread. The first heave came only after two minutes. Vomit poured out of his nose as he struggled for air. He reached for the sharpened tool and attempted to undo the sutures. A second wave of regurgitation followed seconds later and he began to choke. He stabbed at his face multiple times in panic, vomit and blood oozing out of the freshly-punctured skin. When the third wave of vomit hit, the thick, trapped liquid filled his jaws despite steady streams shooting like geysers from the fresh punctures in his face. As he began to become hypoxic, he slashed at his face, making deep lacerations where the continued waves of vomit poured out with every heave.

In a desperate attempt for air, he grabbed a hold of his bottom lip and worked his fingers through the stitching. When he managed to gain a solid grip, he yanked desperately. At first, the sutures didn't budge, but only tore the flesh. A second, violent pull tore his lip in half. Blood and vomit gushed from the newly-formed flap. His bottom lip, torn in half, dangled back and forth as the vomit exited, but he was too late. The baby's rattle fell from his dead hand.

Edward didn't let Lori see the aftermath. As he cleaned up the mess and prepared the corpse for disposal, he wondered if Lori would have been prepared to release Tighte if he'd survived that evening. He'd never be sure.

Edward wrapped the body in plastic and secured it tightly with duct tape. Using the pulley system he had rigged, he heaved the putrid mass and loaded it into the four-wheel-drive pickup he had rented. In the darkness, he drove to a small town dump just outside of the Poconos. Vincent Tighte would be laid to rest with the garbage – flies and rats his eternal companions. Edward thought it was befitting.

CHAPTER 50

MARY MCKENNA SAT immobile for several minutes, staring at the screen of her terminal in the Internet café. *Available funds: $17,314,159.00.* She could think of only two possible scenarios. One, there was a banking error and it would be fixed, or, two, Lori Adams had stolen Vincent Tighte's ill-gotten booty and had given it to her. The second option rang true; it just seemed like Lori. From the little she knew about her, it was certain that she wasn't hurting for cash. Lori Adams was well compensated for her work at Lionel and worth every cent, according to the many magazine interviews with Lionel's president, who was quoted as saying that Lori Adams was the true backbone of the operation. *Sure seemed like she had a handle on things,* thought Mary, thinking back to when Lori had hijacked Tighte's meeting, leaving him impotent. The image of Tighte sitting at the head of the table during that meeting turned to a more recent image where he lay on the hardwood floor with tranquilizer darts sticking out of his chest and neck. *He must be dead by now,* she thought and logged out. She wanted to call Lori and ask her about the sudden and significant increase in her account but didn't.

Mary paid the lady at the front of the store, who exhibited the same level of friendliness or humanity that seemed to be the default mood in Sardinia. "Grazie, ciao," said the woman.

"Chee ved-i-a-mo," said Mary, reading from her phrase book. She was determined to be fluent within the year.

Keeping a whirlwind pace, Mary arrived at Medio Campidano, where the Nuraghi of Barumini attracted thousands of visitors each year. Most people would not have been able to keep up with her, but she refused to waste another moment of her life. She was the first person in line to tour the site, but, within the hour, dozens of others had queued behind her.

Mary felt very small, very insignificant as she toured the site. The ruins left a clear indication of what the complex of structures had been in their heyday. Aerial views revealed intricate patterns that left no doubt that the Nuragics were adept at applying geometric principles and, the fact that many structures were still standing, bragged of their skilled engineers. The smell of the Mirto flowers rode on the winds that came from the countryside and saturated the air of the ancient ruins. It left a sweet, mystical scent on everything it blew over. Mary sat on a rock, closed her eyes and lifted her face upwards to allow the strong sun to massage her face and the Mirto-scented air to cool it.

What have I done that will stand the test of time, that will exist after my body is no more? she thought. She felt a mixture of awe and depression, sitting there. *Where are those people now?* she thought. *Dead, forgotten, long rotted in the earth. The trials and hardships they suffered were in vain. The good and the evil, the strong and the weak, the rich and the poor, the beautiful and the ugly, all suffer the same fate: death comes for us all. We all die and cease to exist.*

Mary usually managed to break free from the angst that plagued her whenever she was faced with her own mortality. The thought of *being no more, of no more me, of being gone forever, for all eternity* had bothered her tremendously ever since the death of her parents. She thought of them lying in the earth at various stages of decay and, despite the half-hearted attempts of the religious at her high school, she couldn't bring herself to believe that she would see them again in an alternate existence, where Jesus separated those who knew Him and those who didn't. The idea of non-Christian babies being exiled to Limbo had squelched any lingering faith she'd had. She tried to make herself believe, tried to force the comfort that such a belief would bring, but, instead, was left with the emptiness that empiricism offers. Her parents were dead, experiencing nothing more. For the rest of eternity, they would lie in the ground and never know any feeling or any sensation again. The thought of her own death would ensue and, with it, a new level of anxiety.

Mary tried to remain still and let the magic of the spirits of the deceased Nuragic engineers possess her. She made herself imagine a group of them encircling her, chanting their musical spells, summoning the winds and warding off the feeling of doom that threatened to overtake her. She breathed deeply and rhythmically and, soon, it was only her and the Nuragics. The sound of tourists marveling throughout the complex faded into the background until it was completely silenced, leaving her with the music of her imagination.

"Go to Tír na nÓg," they sang. "Go to Tír na nÓg and find peace there."

Mary smiled at the power of her imagination, the placebo effect that she herself had imposed on her troubled mind. Her anxiety was quelled and the depression forced into retreat for the time being. Certainly, it would return, but she was grateful for the reprieve.

"Un bill-yet-toe purr Oristano?" said Mary. The ticket agent smiled broadly with approval. Although most tourists butchered the melodious Italian language, an attempt was always met with such graciousness.

"Certo," said the agent. "Diciannove euro."

Mary took out a 20-euro bill and gave it to her. "A que ora parte?"

"It is leaving now," said the smiling agent. "Make a hurry now." It was Mary's turn to smile approvingly.

Mary sat on the bus, admiring the beauty of the Sardinian countryside. The sun-scorched earth blended with the greens, purples, reds and blues of the sporadic patches of irrigated soil, which yielded a plethora of vegetables only the Italian people could make taste so good. Unprovoked and enthusiastic waves of welcome came easily from people working in their gardens, walking on the roads, tending goats and sheep as the bus passed by. Mary waved back, despite knowing that they probably couldn't see her through the tinted glass. She took out the vial from her bag and held it to the glass. She looked at the purple liquid, tilting it back and forth, watching the air bubble make its way from one end to the other.

Tír na nÓg here I come, she thought. *Don't let me down too hard.*

CHAPTER 51

LYNCH HAD ARRIVED within the hour. The police had tried to get Tiernan to talk, but had given up after only a few attempts. Sergeant O'Rourke was an excellent interrogator and knew when to push and when to back off. This guy wasn't cracking, but he sure was guilty.

"Thank you," said Lynch, placing his briefcase on the metal table. "Can you remove the handcuffs from my client, please?"

Tiernan sat in the interrogation room, cuffed to the table like a common criminal. Sergeant O'Rourke turned the key and the metal cuff jumped open, leaving a ring around Tiernan's wrist. Tiernan rubbed the blood back into his hand and caressed his wrist where the cold metal had cut off the circulation.

"Was that a little snug?" asked O'Rourke. "My bad."

"I would like time to confer with my client, if you don't mind," said Lynch.

"Yeah, take a donut break," said Tiernan. "Our tax dollars hard at work, huh?" he said, looking at Lynch. The door shut and the closed-circuit camera clicked off.

"You sure that thing's off?" said Tiernan.

"Yeah," said Lynch. "Attorney-client privilege prohibits them from recording our sessions. What the hell's going on, Michael?"

"Ryan Connor was assaulted at his home. Attempted murder, they say. They're trying to pin it on me."

Lynch jotted notes. "Why?"

Tiernan looked up at the camera before answering. "You sure?" he said, pointing to the camera.

"Positive," said Lynch. "You can tell me."

"There's nothing to tell," said Tiernan, changing his mind. "I was home all night. My phone records will corroborate the story."

"They can't hold you for more than 24 hours without compelling evidence," said Lynch. "They'll most likely release you now that you lawyered up," he said, making air quotes.

"Alright, make that happen," said Tiernan.

Lynch leaned in closer to Tiernan and spoke softer in spite of himself. "Are you sure they're not going to arrest someone tonight who claims you've hired them to take Connor out?"

"I don't give a shit who says what," said Tiernan. "I didn't hire anyone. I have nothing to do with this. Get me the hell out of here."

Tiernan remained steadfast and, within two hours, was released. "Don't take any last-minute vacations," said O'Rourke as he handed back Tiernan's personal effects. "We'll need to talk to you again real soon, I promise."

Tiernan grabbed his stuff and left the station. He got into a cab and dialed John Graham. "John?" he said. "I hope I didn't wake you."

"Actually, sir," said Graham, "you did, but since I'm up now, how can I be of service?"

"Meet me at Oisín in an hour and pack a bag. We're taking a little trip."

"Very well, sir," said Graham. He hung up the phone and got out of bed to prepare for a trip, but to where he hadn't asked.

03

Ivan Falters drove into a shady area. Prostitutes lined the trash-strewn streets and loud music emanated from several radios playing different beats, creating an impossible din. Groups of people huddled around the cars where the boom boxes rested. Police presence was noticeably absent, making the drug deals and sex sales very convenient. He would look for a motel here. He needed to treat the wound, which he hoped was not as bad as it felt. Precious red fluid steadily ran down his broad back, soaking his shirt through. *I can't go into the motel like this,* he thought. Prostitutes and their clients came and went into rooms rented by the hour. He wouldn't be asked for I.D. here, but a blood-soaked white man would certainly be a cause for suspicion in this neighborhood.

Falters reached into the back seat of the car for the gym bag lying on the floor. Tiernan had promised to take him to his health spa to get in a workout, but the last couple of days hadn't provided too much downtime. He unzipped Tiernan's bag and took out a spandex T-shirt that was at least two sizes too small for him. *This will do nicely,* he thought. He removed his bloodstained shirt already adhering to the open wound. He peeled away a few layers of skin as he struggled to remove the shirt in the confinement of the front seat of the car he had *borrowed* from Tiernan. He threw the blood-soaked shirt onto the floor of the passenger's seat and grimaced in pain as he forced his torso into the small spandex shirt that would act like a tourniquet until he got past the front desk. He pulled Tiernan's black post-workout sweatshirt, also too small, over the spandex T-shirt and hoped that it would stop the blood long enough for him to acquire a room. Outside the dirty no-tell motel stood a vending machine with some of its bulbs burned out. A single blinking light told Falters that it was operational, so he fed the machine some coins and out popped a bottle of water. He opened the bottle and rinsed the blood off his hands before walking through the front door.

"I'd like a room, please," said Falters. "One with a kitchen, if you have it."

"No kitchens," said the man at the desk, who was more interested in the TV than in customer service. "How long you want it for?"

"One night," said Falters.

The man reached for a key and a form. "Fill this out. Cash or charge?"

"Cash," said Falters.

"Fifty bucks. Be out by 11 a.m."

Falters took the key, walked across the street to the 24-hour pharmacy and bought supplies.

The room was dirty and smelled of mold, but Falters had been in

worse. He removed the sweatshirt and spandex with considerable difficulty and stood in the shower, letting the cold water help slow the
bleeding. He squeezed the spandex shirt and blood gushed out, mixing
with the water, creating a river of pink flowing down the drain. *I'm going to kill Ryan Connor,* he thought as he winced in pain.

The laceration was in an awkward place and proved difficult to
reach. His left shoulder blade had sustained a six-inch gash and he had
lost a lot of blood already. He couldn't stitch it himself, but couldn't
risk going to the hospital. He wrapped cellophane around the gauze as
best he could and headed out again. The blood wasn't long in soaking
through the makeshift dam and he knew time was running out. The
door closed behind him.

☙

"You looking for a good time, baby?" asked the scantily-clad street-
walker. "You know what they say, baby – after black you never go
back."

Falters looked her up and down. He wanted to see if she was strung
out. "Hold out your hands."

"Anything you want, baby. Ooo baby, you cute. I might have to give
you a li'l some for free."

"You will do. Come with me." The two entered Falters' room. "What
is your name?"

"Anything you want it to be, baby," she said.

"I need your help," said Falters. He was becoming light-headed and
very pale. It wouldn't be long. "I was in a fight and need stitches. Have
you ever stitched before?"

"My clothes," she said, "but never no person. I ain't doin' that."

"I will give you a thousand dollars if you do," he said.

She had done much worse for much less. "Let me see it first," she
said.

Falters handed her a fist of bills. "Go wash your hands and put on
a pair of those," said Falters, pointing to the box of latex gloves. "Just
like stitching your clothes, okay? Nice and tight."

"You wanna take something first?" she said. "Or maybe I can help you to relax in another way."

"That won't be necessary," he said. "I have a high pain threshold. Just do it quickly."

"Damn, boy!" said the hooker, removing the cellophane and gauze. "Someone busted your shit up good. Your meat all showing. Dat's nasty." She began sewing the wound shut.

When she finished, Falters tested his shoulder's range of motion. As he moved, he felt the skin stretch against the thread and was pleased with the job. "I am paying for your discretion," he said, handing her another fist of cash. "Please do not share the evening's events with your colleagues."

"Colleagues?" she laughed, taking the bills and stuffing them into her fishnet stockings. "Now dat's a new one."

"Pull the door shut on your way out, and thank you," said Falters.

"Try not to die, now," she said. She continued laughing as she walked away. She pulled the door to the dingy motel room shut. A second later, Falters was asleep.

☙

The next morning, Connor went down to the police station where Sergeant O'Rourke was busy with paperwork.

"What the hell do you mean, released?" said Connor. "That little bastard tried to have me killed."

"Yeah," said O'Rourke, "but, in case you forgot, we're still America. We can't hold someone without evidence. You got any?"

"How's this?" said Connor, holding up his sutured hand. "This ain't the Stigmata you're looking at."

"How 'bout sitting with a sketch artist and we'll issue an APB for the guy who attacked you, okay?" said O'Rourke. He gestured to the adjacent office and led the way. After giving a description and seeing the rendition, Connor was impressed with the likeness.

"He was wearing a button-down shirt, bluish I think, maybe gray," said Connor. "And black pants. And he's wounded. Why don't you send some guys to check the hospitals?"

"Relax, pal," said O'Rourke. "I don't tell you how to do your job. Back off."

Connor got back into the limo parked outside the barracks. "Anything?" he asked.

"No, sir," said the driver. "We left messages on her cell and home phone, but nothing yet."

"Did you try her driver's house? Edward something or other?"

"O'Malley. There's no answer at his residence, either," said the driver.

"Take me to Merkel Pharmaceuticals," said Connor before closing the privacy window. He picked up the phone in the back of the limo and dialed William Masterson at Merkel.

"Will," said Connor, "change of plans."

"I'm listening," said Masterson. "What do you have in mind?"

"Today's your lucky day," said Connor. "I'm coming over right now with everything you need to bury Oisín and that poser."

"And why would you want to do that?" said Masterson, rightfully suspicious of Connor's motivation.

"Let's just say I've experienced a conversion, of sorts," said Connor, looking at his pierced hand.

"I'll clear my schedule, but, Ryan," said Masterson, "remember what happens to people who double-cross me."

"Relax, Will," said Connor, "you got nothing to worry about." Connor hung up and looked down at his hand. *The enemy of my enemy is my friend,* he thought. *Let Merkel and McCaff tear him apart.* Connor knew that the pharmaceutical giants would destroy Tiernan with extreme prejudice and, with the dozen or so violations of state, federal and international laws Tiernan had committed when he illegally tested Regenerol in Mexico, he wasn't going to be released so easily again.

CHAPTER 52

GRAHAM AND TIERNAN arrived at Newark Liberty International Airport. Tiernan had already anticipated Connor's move. He knew that it would only be a matter of time before they'd come to arrest him for murder. His mind drifted to the Mexican women, the innocent hopefuls who trusted foolishly, and how he had used them as a means to an end. The images of the blood disturbed him the worst – the unstoppable hemorrhaging caused by the earlier versions of Regenerol. He needed to leave the country before Connor released the files.

"We seem to be taking a jet plane to somewhere," said Graham. "May I inquire as to where that might be?"

"Yeah," said Tiernan who, in his preoccupation, hadn't as much as spoken two words. "We're going to Rome."

"Very well, sir," said Graham. "Shall I inform Dr. Lewis that she should oversee my team in my absence?"

"John," said Tiernan. His sullen expression was an appropriate prelude to his next revelation. "I don't think we'll have to worry about those petty little things anymore."

"I beg your pardon, sir," said Graham.

"There was an attempt on Ryan Connor's life. Unfortunately, it was unsuccessful. I'm a suspect," said Tiernan. "He's got enough on us to put us away for a very long time and I have no doubt that he's gonna sing. Near-death experiences have that effect on people."

"I assume you're referring to the Regenerol trials?" said Graham, now acutely aware.

"Yeah," said Tiernan. "They'll be coming for you, too."

"That's very inconvenient, indeed," said Graham. "Things were beginning to look up." He thought of Debra Lewis. "But, I suppose I always knew I'd have to pay for my crimes someday."

"John," said Tiernan, "I did this to you. If it weren't for my lies and manipulation, you would never have agreed to the trials."

"Well, sir, I suppose you're right. But there's sufficient blame to go around. There are very few genuine victims in this life."

"I just wanted you to know that I am truly sorry," said Tiernan.

"I forgive you," said Graham. "Now, shall we board?"

☙

Lori loved the powerful sea wind. After Edward had returned from disposing of the remains, the two murderers slept on Lori's modest yet elegant yacht. They spent the first 24 hours docked, making love, barely getting out of bed in the cramped quarters below deck. Edward had proposed and Lori had tearfully accepted. Perhaps it was the combination of the salty sea air, the brilliant night sky and the new freedom Lori felt in her soul, but Ms. Lori Adams was engaged and, for the first time in years, she felt almost peaceful, close to complete. Early the next morning, the fragile peace was shaken.

"Lori?" said Frances. "My God, Mr. Connor's been trying to reach you. Someone tried to kill him. Michael Tiernan is the prime suspect. Can you believe it?"

"Is he alright?" said Lori, almost too terrified to hear the answer.

"He's fine," said Frances. "A few stitches in his hand, that's all."

"I'm coming back right now," said Lori. "Tell Ryan I'm on my way."

"Will do," said Frances. "Where are you, anyway?"

Lori had disconnected before Frances finished her question. Lori went back down the stairs into the hull of the boat and woke her sleeping fiancé. "Edward, honey," she said, "'fraid we gotta end our trip before it even starts. Turn the boat around. We gotta go back."

"What's wrong?" said Edward. He shot up in the bed and rubbed his eyes. He hoped that the paranoia wasn't going to be a constant companion now that he was an accessory to kidnapping, torture, mutilation and murder. Would every knock on the door send his heart racing?

"Somebody tried to kill Ryan," she said. "We gotta go back."

Edward quickly headed up to the deck and turned the boat around to go back to the harbor. Lori tried to call Connor. She looked at the time and thought she had better wait. His wife wouldn't appreciate the early call, especially with all that had happened.

CHAPTER 53

MARY DISEMBARKED AT Ghilarza. The bus didn't go into the little hamlet of Boroneddu, which had fewer than 200 inhabitants, very few of whom needed to take a bus anywhere. She would have to walk the few kilometers or find a taxi to carry her there.

"Tír na nÓg?" said Mary. The shopkeeper smiled and nodded, but didn't understand. "Dov'e sta Tír na nÓg?" continued Mary.

"Cosa?" said the shopkeeper, still smiling. "Che vuol' dire Tír na nÓg?"

Mary turned to an earmarked page. "Ho bisogno di andare, ah, eh, Teer nah noague. Puoi aiutarmi?"

"Aspetta," said the shopkeeper, raising her finger using the universal sign for *wait*. She called for her son who was stocking shelves in the back.

"Giovanni," she called, "viene." The boy came out and tried to translate.

"Hello," said Mary greeting him. "I was wondering if you know where I might find Tír na nÓg Vineyards? It isn't in any of my guidebooks, but a friend told me that I should definitely pay a visit if I were ever in Sardinia."

"Ah, sí," said the boy. "Tír na nÓg Vineyards is in Boroneddu, a few kilometers this way," he said, proud of his aptitude in English. He pointed and smiled broadly. "It is very big place. You will find it with easy. My friend is a chef for the padrone of the vineyards."

Mary smiled back.

"Padrone?" she said.

"Eh, the boss," said the boy. "He is Russo, eh..." The boy snapped his fingers encouraging the word to come. "He is a Russian man. Big muscles." Giovanni pumped out his chest and arms to demonstrate.

"Ah," said Mary. She switched back to her broken Italian. "C'e un hotel vechino da qui?"

"Certo," said the mother. "Lo prendo la io."

The boy looked at Mary's confused look. "She says that she will take you there herself."

"Wow," said Mary, who wasn't used to such friendliness. "Tell her thank you. Wait, no I can do that myself. Grazie."

She realized that she had experienced her first genuine laugh in years. She was surprised by the powerful emotional effect the altruistic action had on her. She extended her hand. "Sono Mary Williams," she said, not proud of the ease at which she lied.

"Piacere. Sono Asunta Modestino," said the lady. "E questo e il mio figlio Giovanni." The teen smiled at Mary and lifted his hand as if to confirm his mother's statement.

"Welcome to Sardinia," said Giovanni as Asunta escorted Mary to the nearby hotel.

☃

More of the same treatment at the hotel confirmed her suspicion: they were all the same. The people were warm and friendly. They smiled real smiles, their faces crinkling under the force of joy and their eyes squinting with true emotion. She lay down on the bed in the hotel room that, despite having almost no amenities, held a certain charm. The opened windows allowed a breeze into the room, but did little to tame the oven-like heat. A small fan sat on the table but looked like it wouldn't do much good.

No air conditioners, huh? she thought. *This should be interesting.*

She showered off the sweat and dust and got ready for bed. She was more exhausted than she had ever been.

☃

After jogging for 15 minutes, Mary was soaked with sweat and de-cided to walk. She enjoyed the scenery despite the heat and was especially anxious to inspect the Nuraghi along the way. Two of them were still in good condition. The larger one sat mysteriously in the center of the field, about 50 meters from the other. No tourists came to see the Nuraghi in Boroneddu. Those in Barumini were much bigger and the nearby concession stands and restrooms made visiting the ruins much more pleasant. In Boroneddu, the Nuraghi stood by themselves. No ruins of Nuragic villages surrounded them. She climbed the embankment into the field and started toward the ruin.

The stone building was very sturdy. The little door that permitted entrance was about three feet high and two feet wide. She crawled in and sat inside. It was noticeably cooler inside as the sunlight entered at an angle from the characteristic hole at the top of the edifice. *Maybe it served as some kind of clock,* she thought. She theorized that the sun probably shone directly into the center of the room at noon and made a note to test her hypothesis. She stayed there, soaking up the coolness, resting her head against the rocks until her body stopped pumping sweat by the bucketful, after which, she continued exploring.

She didn't want to start the deluge again, so she walked at a leisurely pace. She stayed on the paved road despite her adventurous spirit nagging her to take one of the many grassy paths or gravel lanes that promised to be worth the risk. The paved road ended in the heart of the village where a church of perfectly square ashlars of dark basalt stood with authoritative majesty. She walked closer to read the inscription: *San Lorenzo Martire circa 1886.* She pulled on the heavy wooden doors, but they were locked. She decided to sit outside on the bench and rehydrate. Someone was bound to walk by sooner or later and then she would ask about Tír na nÓg Vineyards.

It wasn't long until Fr. Marco Salvatore came along, flowerpots in either hand containing a beautiful array of flora to adorn the altar. He was a young priest, servicing several parishes in the region since the shortage of priests made it a necessity. "Buon Giorno," he said. "Sono Padre Marco." The priest put the flowers down and extended his hand in greeting; he, too, wore the characteristic smile.

"Mary," she said. "But I'm afraid my Italian isn't very good."

"I can speak English," he said, happy to have someone with whom to practice even for just a few moments. "My Italian seems to be getting worse ever since I was assigned to Sardinia," he said jokingly, but the humor was wasted on Mary who didn't understand.

"Most of the locals speak Sardo, the regional dialect. It's a mixture of Spanish, Greek and Italian, impossible to understand, but beautiful to the ear."

Mary could tell by the eagerness with which Fr. Marco engaged her that he was starved for conversation with someone – anyone – closer to his age. He proved to be very informative, telling her everything she wanted to know while demanding little, if any, personal information from her. By the end of the conversation, Mary knew where Tír na nÓg was and had heard all about the reclusive Russian who harvested the inedible grapes for vanity products in the U.S. and about everything else deemed newsworthy in the little hamlet. She told Fr. Marco that she was a reporter doing a piece on vineyards in Italy, and he was more than happy to oblige her request for assistance.

"Do you have a car, Father?" she asked.

"Yes, I do," he said. "Not a very fancy one, but it runs very well."

Fr. Marco might prove to be very useful and she wasn't ashamed of the subtle flirting she employed to guarantee his cooperation should she need it.

CHAPTER 54

IVAN FALTERS FLEW back to Italy out of Canada. Someone of Ryan Connor's celebrity was going to warrant the police's best efforts, so Falters wasn't taking any chances. *Canadian,* he thought, as he selected a passport from the pile.

He spent the flight into Italy unconscious. He was still very weak from the stab wound and ran a consistent low-grade fever. He would be glad when he returned to Italy where he could seek treatment at the hospital in Ghilarza.

Falters finally arrived in Sardinia. After taking two planes and a long bus trip from Cagliari, he was even more feverish and decided to go directly to the hospital. He concocted some story about being mugged in Sicily that the personnel were too eager to believe, having had a bitter rivalry with the *other* Italian island since time began. The doctors told him that, if he had waited another few hours, he would probably have died. They admitted Falters immediately. The infection was bad. Even with the course of antibiotics they had administered, it didn't look good. The next 24 hours would determine his fate.

ꙮ

Mary wandered the vineyards of Tír na nÓg, paper and pencil in hand, trying to act the part of a journalist in case she ran into any more of the incredibly friendly but curious Sardinian residents. She was surprised to find the vast vineyards unattended. The Niamh hybrid needed very little attention and grew better with less interference, so the vineyards were virtually abandoned all year, except for during the harvest.

She walked the rows, searching for something to explain Lori Adams' excitement in the tales of eternal youth, enchanted vines and magic elixirs, but found nothing whatsoever. *What's that horrendous smell?* she thought, holding her hand over her nose. *Something must have died out here.* Out of sight, a few hundred yards beyond where she stood, lay the almost completely decomposed body of Jimmy Galante, covered in flies and filled to capacity with larvae. Maggots squirmed freely in the abundant food source.

She decided to head over to the white house sitting in a very deliberate clearing, visible over the waves of vines that stretched into a vast ocean of fruit. She stopped before the charcoal slate-stone step leading to the porch and looked carefully. *Three different sets of footprints,* she thought, *all men. Scientists, perhaps?* She knocked on the door, but no one answered. She wished desperately that she could walk away, but she couldn't. She took note of her surroundings before she picked the lock to the back door that opened to the kitchen. The door opened effortlessly with her magic touch. She'd always been very good at picking locks, beginning with the principal's office in high school and ending with the most advanced locking mechanisms. It was like a puzzle for her and she enjoyed the exercise. This one was the equivalent of a six-piece puzzle.

"Hello?" she called as she entered the house. Satisfied that she was alone, she snooped. Within 30 minutes, she had confirmed that Michael Tiernan had been there recently after finding his boarding pass in a wastebasket in one of the upstairs bedrooms. She couldn't place the other inhabitant of the house but deduced that he was a resident on a more permanent basis. She managed to find a few faded pictures belonging to the man. One picture caught her attention. *Ivan Velikovic* was written on the back of an old photograph. He posed for the picture, looking very somber in his Russian uniform. She assumed it was taken before the soldier left to fight in World War II. There were dozens of diaries, all written in Russian. She tried to gain a sense of who this person was by his possessions but was unable to string a coherent thread of information together. The last picture she looked at was of

Russian Scientist

the soldier, Ivan Velikovic, sitting with his family as they posed for a photograph. He was sitting next to his wife with a baby girl on his lap. Two boys stood on either side of them. They looked happy. She stole the picture, though she didn't know why.

Mary McKenna was very thorough. She knew there was something more, much more, to this place than met the eye. She had stayed a few moments longer than she was comfortable with and was getting anxious to leave. She would have missed the entrance to the lab had she not been taught to never overlook the obvious. The trapezoidal door in the kitchen was too obvious, not as much as a candlestick-operated false wall in the library, but obvious. She made her way down into the cool, damp basement and managed to find the light switch. *Dim lighting is better than nothing,* she thought. She struck a match and moved it across a section of the stone wall that was suspiciously a different color than the rest. The draft coming from the long tunnel behind it betrayed the secret by blowing the match out. It took her another 10 minutes to find the release switch for the false wall.

Mary was anxious, but couldn't resist walking down the long, dark tunnel to discover what lay beyond. First, though, she needed something a little more illuminating than the matches. She ran back upstairs and tried to find a flashlight. She settled for a pair of old candles.

She walked slowly down the cool, damp rock tunnel, keeping her hand on the moist wall. The tunnel abruptly ended at a set of glass doors, which reflected her image. She stood still for a moment, looking at the woman holding two candles in one hand. She looked scared, but she couldn't go back now. She looked around for the switch that would allow her access to the room. She couldn't see very well with the low lumen output of the candles and tried to position them to stand against the rock without extinguishing them. She had difficulty and, in her frustration and excitement, attempted to secure them to a piece of protruding rock using their wax drippings. They fell to the ground, however, and she was left in darkness. She would have to rely on her other senses.

Mary tried prying the doors open, but they wouldn't budge. She sat down on the damp earth and hoped that her eyes would adjust to the dark, but they didn't. It was too dark. She pushed and pulled methodically on every crevasse and every smooth rock until she finally hit upon the switch. A burst of illumination blinded her temporarily, but she heard the doors slide open and felt her way up the stony steps. She lay victorious on the smooth tile floor and waited for her eyes to work again.

"Holy shit," she said.

Mary took out her little camera and went to work taking pictures of the documents, equipment, empty cages and empty fish tanks. She could tell right away that there were missing elements, and the documents were probably useless without them, but she continued snapping pictures anyway. *Better to be safe than sorry,* she thought. The alternate entrance wasn't difficult to find. Within minutes of snapping her last picture, she found another entrance to a tunnel that seemed to be a continuation of the one she had just traveled. Did she have time to go exploring where this tunnel would lead? Reminded of the complete darkness a few hundred feet in, she turned back with the intention of returning with a flashlight if the opportunity presented itself.

She picked the lock to the safe, which was a little more difficult than the kitchen door. Six identical vials of the purple liquid Lori Adams had given her sat inside. She considered taking them, but thought of another plan. *I wonder if Fr. Marco would accompany me to Cagliari.* She removed all evidence of the break-in and headed back to San Lorenzo Church where she hoped to find Fr. Marco.

⚃

Sergeant O'Rourke responded to the call. They had found Michael Tiernan's car in the parking lot of a motel. When Tiernan hadn't answered O'Rourke's calls, the seasoned Sergeant had put the word out for his rookies to watch for his license plate. "Whatcha got?" he said, arriving on the scene.

"We didn't touch anything, Sarge," said the rookie. "We figured we'd wait until you got here. It's locked."

"Anyone got a slim jim?" said O'Rourke. The two rookies looked at each other, but didn't dare laugh at their superior, who just showed how outdated he really was.

"Uh, no, sir. They really don't work on modern cars, electric locks and all."

"Shut up, smart ass," said O'Rourke. "I'll take it from here. Make yourself useful and arrest some of these whores, would ya? Try to slow the spread of AIDS a little, okay?"

While the rookies were busy fighting the AIDS epidemic, O'Rourke took out his nightstick, smashed the rear window and unlocked the door. *That still works,* he thought. He looked down and saw the blood-stained shirt in Tiernan's front seat and bagged and tagged it, but not before calling the rookies back to witness it.

"Hey, would ya look at what you two mopes missed," said O'Rourke. "Rear window was broken the whole time. How the hell did you miss this?"

"Sorry, sir," said the smarter rookie. "Won't happen again."

"I tell ya," said O'Rourke, "they let anyone with a pulse carry a badge nowadays. Get outta here before I light you up like a Christmas tree."

O'Rourke hadn't always been so cynical, but the system seemed to favor the bad guys, and, after years trying to do things by the book, he'd felt forced to cut corners to get the criminals off the street. He felt justified when he bent a law here or violated a few civil rights there. It all evened out in the end.

O'Rourke sent the bloodstained shirt for analysis. When it came back a few hours later with two separate blood types on it, he was elated. "Let me guess," he said, "one belongs to the perpetrator, the other to Ryan Connor, right?"

"Bingo," said the tech.

"Send two units over to arrest Michael Tiernan for accessory to murder," he said, speaking into his radio. "Issue an APB for him over the wire, too."

Gotcha, wiseass, thought O'Rourke, who figured he'd treat himself to a donut in Tiernan's honor.

287

CHAPTER 55

"RYAN, HONEY, THANK God you're alright. What have you gotten into now?" said Lori, waltzing in unannounced, slamming the office door behind her. Connor held up his war wound and smiled. He was a little disappointed that she hadn't been there earlier. After his children, he considered Lori to be the most important person in his life. His wife had always suspected an affair, but never confronted him in case it was the impetus he needed to leave her.

"Where the hell were you?" said Connor. He hugged her firmly and for longer than usual.

"I've been a very busy girl," said Lori, "but first tell me what on God's green earth happened. Was it really Tiernan?"

"Yup," said Connor. "He's fled the country, too. They found a bloody shirt in his abandoned car in the Lower East Side somewhere."

"Bloody shirt?" said Lori.

"Yeah," said Connor, holding up his hand again. "Mine and the other guy's. Labs confirmed it. Tiernan's in for a world a hurtin'." He tried to imitate a Southern accent.

"I'm just so relieved that you're alright," said Lori, sitting down. "I just don't know what I'd do without you."

"Ah," he shrugged, "it's hard to kill a bad thing."

There were two elephants in the room. Connor wanted to ask if the *Vincent Tighte situation* was over and Lori wanted to explain the ring on her finger that she knew Connor had noticed.

"Taking a boat ride, I hear?" said Connor.

"Yeah," said Lori, smiling. "I'm rewarding myself for finally accomplishing a long-term goal." One elephant was gone.

"Ryan," said Lori, "we need to talk." She avoided making eye contact. She knew that the hurt in his eyes would be more than she could handle.

"I assume that the ring means that you've finally taken the plunge," said Connor, wanting to end her discomfort. "Was only a matter of time, really. He loved you from the start." Her eyes welled up with tears and the mixture of bittersweet emotion took the form of something between crying and laughing.

Ryan Connor and Lori Adams would always love each other. If Connor had not had children and Lori hadn't been so decent, they would have married years ago. The thought of being the other woman was bad enough, but being a home-wrecker was out of the question. They'd occasionally fallen victim to the urges and made love, but not without feeling guilt and remorse, more on Lori's side than Connor's.

"I'm glad for you," said Connor. "Maybe, in another life, we'll get it right."

"Maybe," she said, blotting the tears.

"How do you feel?" said Connor, changing the subject back to the morose. "Have the voices stopped?"

Lori had believed that once Vincent Tighte had paid the debt he owed to her unborn children, their little voices crying out for justice would quiet and their little eyes would grow heavy listening to the sound of the preternatural lullaby that played in her mind. When sleep fell upon them, they'd bask in blissful slumber until their mommy came and joined them in Heaven where they'd spend eternity laughing and playing together.

"They're sound asleep in their little cradles. The angels are rocking them 'til I get there."

Connor wasn't sure if she had always believed her own creation or if it had served as a coping mechanism for so long that it had bled into her reality over time, making fantasy and reality tautological. He didn't care, either, as long as she had found some peace.

"So, what now?" said Connor. "Are you done here?"

"I don't know, Ryan, I really don't," said Lori. "I've spent so many years running from my life, burying myself neck deep in work with a single goal in mind. Now that I've won, I'm not sure what I want."

"Go," said Connor, "do something for yourself. Take a voyage around the world with Edward. See if the open seas help clear your mind." It was difficult for him to say; he didn't want her to go. He knew by the deviation from his usual modus operandi of putting himself first that he loved her.

"I love you, and I always will," said Lori. "I owe you my life."

"You owe me nothing," said Connor, his eyes now moist.

She left the office and closed the door.

Connor wiped his eyes, took a long, deep breath and picked up the phone. "Frances," he said, "get me the number for the FBI Field Office at 26 Federal Plaza here in New York."

"Yes, sir," said Frances. Connor wasn't going to leave Tiernan's fate exclusively at the whim of William Masterson or Gerard McCaff. He wanted to be sure that the information got into the right hands.

☃

Gabriel DeAngelo walked down the hall and knocked on the director's door. "Got a minute?" he asked.

"No, I don't," said Jones. "Go away."

DeAngelo walked in and closed the door, ignoring his overworked boss. "You'll want to hear this, believe me."

"If it's more headlines, keep 'em to yourself," he retorted. "I'm up to my ass in damage control and it's hard enough keeping all these plates spinning. Can't you idiots make arrests without shooting a half-dozen people? Damn it."

"What fun is that?" DeAngelo said.

Jones was proud of his team, despite his charade. A recent drug bust had brought down some major players smuggling heroin into the U.S. and, although he could've done without the body count that had accompanied the bust, it was a job well done.

"What can I do for you, Gabriel?" said Jones.

"Well," said DeAngelo, "this time, I bring good news."

Jones raised his eyebrows. "Yeah? I'm all ears."

Gabriel DeAngelo had just finished organizing the notes he had jotted down during his call with Connor. A courier was on his way over to the field office with the evidence Connor had promised. This was a dream case. All the work was done and it wouldn't rack up a body count while remaining sensational enough to warrant a media frenzy. It couldn't have come at a better time.

"Illegal drug testing in Mexico," said DeAngelo. "A bunch of women died using some drug Oisín was working on. Seems they conducted the whole study without the consent of the Mexican government. This is gonna be big."

Robert Jones sat back and waited.

"But?" he asked. "There has to be a *but*. So, tell me, what do we have to do to get our hands on the information? I'm guessing immunity for some identical crime committed right here in the U.S. Am I right?"

"Actually, boss," said DeAngelo, "someone up there's looking out for you. Ryan Connor over at Lionel only wants some good press."

"There's always a catch, Gabriel," said Jones. "There's no such thing as a free lunch."

DeAngelo shrugged his shoulders and pursed his lips. "Low- or high-profile?" he asked, referring to the media coverage.

"Jesus, what do you think?" said Jones. "When you got something solid, call everyone you know."

DeAngelo turned to leave.

"Hey, Gabriel," shouted Jones as he left, "tell the guys not to shoot anyone today."

"I'll see what I can do, boss," said DeAngelo as he walked to his office to begin putting the case together.

Finally caught a break, thought Jones.

CHAPTER 56

"CIAO," SAID TIERNAN, entering the cab.

"Ciao. D'ove vai?"

"Trastevere," said Tiernan. "Vicolo del Cinque."

"Va bene," said the driver, "andiamo."

"Master Tiernan," said Graham. "Have you considered the possibility that Connor will sit on the evidence and use it for leverage for something he wants?"

"I have," said Tiernan, "but I'm not willing to risk my freedom on it, are you? I'm not cut out for prison."

John Graham looked out the window. "There are many prisons, Master Tiernan. I'm of the opinion that those made of mortar, brick and iron, those that imprison the body, are far less savage than those originating from a more durable and impenetrable source."

"Come again?" said Tiernan.

"We are all inmates of some prison and, given the choice, I'd prefer to avoid the metaphysical prisons of loneliness and regret," said Graham. "Even the strictest of prisons in America allow loved ones to visit."

Tiernan didn't understand that the *loved ones* Graham was referring to was Debra Lewis. As far as Tiernan was concerned, he had paid his debt when he gave Graham the opportunity to escape. If he chose to return and face the music, so be it. Under normal circumstances, Graham would never betray Tiernan, but men acting under duress are notorious for devolving into the instinctual behavior of self-preservation.

"Ah," said Graham, temporarily distracted, "the Tiber River." He stared out the window as the cab sped down the Lungotevere.

"Filthy," said Tiernan. "The sewage from the city still runs into it. The Romans haven't made much progress since their empire fell, have they?"

"I think you may be oversimplifying a little, sir," said Graham who didn't look away from the river.

"The Romans were the first people to build a sewer system, the first. You'd think that their ancestors would've inherited some of their ingenuity," said Tiernan, shaking his head.

"Actually, sir," said Graham, still captivated by the river, "they weren't the first. Far from it, I'm afraid. As far back as 3000 B.C., sewers were used. There is quite a bit of evidence of small sewage systems in Scotland and Ireland – not England, mind you – dating that far back, but I digress." Tiernan was always impressed and humbled by Graham's encyclopedic knowledge of everything. "The point is this: something that was built centuries ago still works today," said Graham. "It's not as if these sewers required no maintenance. The Italians made vast improvements and renovations to the existing lines starting back in 1840, I believe."

"Yeah, well, it still looks filthy," said Tiernan.

Graham laughed a little. "Non basta una vita," he said.

Tiernan looked surprised. "What did you say?"

Graham looked him in the eye. "This sentence was written so many times in so many books that it's anyone's guess who is responsible for first vocalizing its truth."

"One life is not enough," said Tiernan. "One life is not enough to experience all that Rome offers, right?"

"Indeed," said Graham, "but, when you get to my age, the sentence applies to everything. Non basta una vita."

Tiernan wanted to tell him. He wanted to give him the chance to become a member of the new species. It seemed an ideal place to begin the conversation, but the cab slowed as it bounced up and down, side to side, navigating the uneven cobblestone street of Vicolo del Cinque. Marinella was among the several faces peering out their windows, conversing and watching the street below.

"Ecco," she exclaimed, and ran down to greet the taxi. "Diego, sono arrivati!"

Kisses, hugs, food – and then the interrogation began, right on schedule. "What is these?" said Marinella, committing grammatical murder for Graham's sake. "Diego almost break himself in the slippy rock to get these, so now you tell me: what is these?"

A silence fell over the room and all eyes were on Tiernan. He was with family, and the comfort and security he felt sitting there with them made it impossible to hold it in any longer. The persistent questions were like blows of increasing force until he exploded open and the secrets poured out of him like candy from a piñata.

"Those vials contain in them the power to reverse the ravages of old age," he said. "It bends time back on itself."

They sat speechless – the Italians because they didn't understand, and Graham because he did.

"Que vuol dire," said Diego. "What does that mean?"

"It means that my father found the cure for aging and it's sitting right there in front of you," said Tiernan. "Each vial contains one dose, one human dose. It's absorbed best when ingested, but I can't vouch for the taste. Mine was mixed with Mirto."

Uproarious laughter erupted. Marinella reacted in her usual way, smacking him upside the head for telling fibs. Diego and Marinella didn't believe him and pressed him for the *real* reason. The volume grew exponentially while they argued in both languages, laughing at the preposterous story.

Graham became oblivious to their presence. *Richard,* he thought, *you clever devil. I should have known.* They didn't notice Graham; they were too engrossed in the entertainment. Graham lifted a vial from the case and popped the rubber stopper free from the wax seal.

"Master Tiernan," he shouted. "Catch." He threw the empty vial in Tiernan's direction. Tiernan caught it, looked at the remaining drop of liquid that clung to the bottom and then back at Graham. "I assume the liquid I analyzed some weeks ago...same substance?"

Tiernan nodded, still in disbelief.

"Probably tasted better mixed with Mirto, I'm afraid. Non basta una vita," said Graham.

☙

For hours, Graham felt nothing, no difference whatsoever. And then, it happened. He couldn't quite explain the sensation, but something occurred, something that felt really good.

"Everything makes sense," said Graham. "It happens as it must."

"Graham, don't come apart on me, man," said Tiernan.

Diego and Marinella sat on the couch, preparing for their evening entertainment. Marinella lifted the cover off the box and spilled the jigsaw pieces on the glass table. She turned the top of the box over to show the picture to Diego.

"Sei pronto?"

"Va bene," said Diego. The two sorted through the jigsaw pieces, searching for the corner pieces and checking their finds against the prominently displayed picture on the box cover.

"You see," said Graham, pointing to the wall. "Here is where the painters paused for a period of no more than an hour before they resumed their work, and here is where they finished for the day."

"What are you talking about?" said Tiernan. "You've never been here." Tiernan looked at the wall.

"And then, the next day, they brought more painters. Look, you can see the diversity in the brush strokes. Can't you see it?"

"Uh, no, John, I can't say that I can," said Tiernan, concerned that Diego and Marinella would hear him. "What's going on? You feel alright?"

"I've never felt better," Graham laughed. "Look closely at what I'm showing you. Right there, do you notice how the paint is a different shade? This tells me that the painter paused, perhaps for lunch."

Tiernan shook his head. "Nope."

"And there is where they finished for the day, only to start the next day with additional help right there."

"Why don't you sit down," said Tiernan.

Diego, who had been listening to their conversation, interjected.

"Yes, I paint this with your father, Michelino. But only this wall." He pointed to the far wall. "The next day, your father decided to hire four painters instead." Diego laughed as the memories came easily.

"And is this where the painters took over for you?" asked Graham, pointing to an adjacent wall.

"Forse. Non mi recordo," said Diego before returning to his jigsaw.

Graham walked over, sat next to Marinella and began helping with their project, which was proving more difficult than the elderly couple had anticipated.

"You see," he resumed. "Everything is connected; all things are as they must be."

Graham rambled on, speaking in incomprehensible riddles, until he noticed that all three of the others were staring at him, jaws open.

"What? Why are you all staring at me?"

Marinella pointed at the table. Graham had completed the 2,000-piece jigsaw of the Acropolis in less than 15 minutes and didn't seem to have even noticed.

"How the hell did you do that?" said Tiernan.

"Very good question, sir," answered Graham, who joined them in amazement.

CHAPTER 57

MARY RETURNED TO San Lorenzo, but didn't find Fr. Marco. She gently tugged at the church doors. Locked. *Damn,* she thought. *I was really hoping to get a ride back to Ghilarza.*

Although the Sardinian sun lost its strength as it fell lower in the sky, it was still hot. For those not accustomed to the climate, the walk from Boroneddu to Ghilarza would be almost agonizing, but she had no other choice. She spied the old-fashioned water pump inconspicuously sitting against the side of the church and gave it a few pumps. Water gushed forth easily and she refilled her water bottle. The water was warm and had an earthy taste but was delicious nonetheless. She poured the rest over her baking skull and refilled her bottle to the brim. She was ready.

She hadn't walked five minutes before a car slowed beside her and an old man spoke to her in an incomprehensible language. English was out of the question and Mary's Italian wasn't working either, yet that didn't matter. He smiled and his wrinkled, sun-kissed face eloquently relayed his message quite clearly.

"Ghilarza?" said Mary. The old man smiled and spoke rapidly, nodding his head and laughing. She got in the little car without a second's hesitation. Diesel fumes mixed with the acrid smell of hay initially accosted her unaccustomed nose. She turned to see a bale sitting in his back seat and assumed he was a farmer, but couldn't ask.

"Right here's fine," said Mary, pointing. "Grazie."

The old man slowed to a stop and got out of the car. Mary realized that he wanted to open the door for her, so she waited. She smiled, trying to remember the last time she had witnessed such chivalry, but the door to the beat-up car creaked open before she could locate the memory. He extended his hand, which she took graciously.

"Arrivederci," he said and kissed her on both cheeks.

"Oh," said Mary, a little startled. "Arrivederci." She watched the car as it made its noisy way through the little streets. She was still smiling when she walked into the hotel lobby. After a meal and a shower, she got into bed and slept soundly.

☙

After breakfast, Mary headed to Asunta's shop.

"Ah, Giovanni," she said. "Buon Giorno." Giovanni was thoroughly engrossed in a comic when she walked in. Her voice caused him to jump out of his seat.

"Ciao, Mary," he said, blushing a little. He straightened out his shirt and tried to fix his hair.

"Where's your mother?"

"Mama is visiting Nonna for a few days," he said. "Eh, Grandmamma. Pero posso aiutarti io?"

Mary replayed the sentence over in her mind.

"Can you help me?" she repeated. "Right?"

"Yes, very good. Next we will teach you Sardo," he said.

Giovanni was so enraptured by her beauty, he was finding it hard to think. The tank top and shorts that Mary wore were quite a deviation from the more conservative local style of dress, which, despite the soaring temperatures, covered much more skin. He tried to keep his eyes from wandering over her body but was only marginally successful. Her athletic physique was too overpowering for the hormone-saturated teen. Her breasts seemed to be the focal point during their uncomfortable conversation.

"I went to the vineyards of Tír na nÓg," said Mary, forcing his attention upwards. "They're massive."

"What? Massive? I wasn't." His eyes lit up when he understood her. "Ah, the vineyards are massive. Sí, sí, they are very massive and beautiful, too."

300

There was an excruciatingly long silence, the longest 10 seconds either of them had ever endured until Giovanni remembered something.

"Ah, Mary," he said. "You remind me of what I need to say you. Mi amico was very sad yesterday." The mix of Italian and broken English was for her benefit. "The Russian padrone is very sick in the hospital here. I *Siciliani* almost kill him. They are bad people there. You don't go there." Giovanni spoke about the Sicilians as if they were the distant relatives families were ashamed of having.

"The Russian is here in Ghilarza?" said Mary.

"Yes," said Giovanni, "but he fire my poor friend yesterday. You remember, the cook, yes?"

Mary nodded

"The doctors called my friend's family, the Demelas', to tell them that the Russian was there. When they came to visit him, he told them that he would be returning home to Russia when he recovered so he would not need any more cook," said Giovanni. "He is closing Tír na nÓg forever."

The speed at which news traveled in the little towns was breathtaking. Everyone was talking about the poor Russian recluse who oversaw Tír na nÓg Vineyards and his unfortunate but unsurprising experience in Sicily, where he chose to vacation. Mary needed to act quickly if she were to uncover anything.

"How long until he recovers?" she asked. "Do they know?"

"My friend says that he will take him to Tír na nÓg, not tomorrow, but tomorrow's tomorrow," said Giovanni.

Mary leaned against the counter, purposely resting her breasts on it. "Tell me, Giovanni," she said, "do you have access to the Internet?"

"Sí," he said, "but it is in my house. You would like to see?"

"Sí."

"I will close the shop early and we can go now," he said, his heart pounding from the erotic thoughts running rampant in his imagination.

"Andiamo."

The general store was attached to the home where the Modestino family had raised their children – five of them. Giovanni was the youngest and quite a surprise to his parents who had thought their child rearing days were over. Giovanni's siblings had long since left the Sardinian nest and lived in various places in the European Union, raising families of their own. He didn't see them often, which made them more like aunts and uncles than brothers and sisters. He lived alone in the spacious house with his mother and father, helping them in the general store.

"Here is my room," said Giovanni, quickly scanning the area for stray underwear and other potentially mortifying items.

Mary felt a little uncomfortable being in the house alone with the teen, but, when she entered his room and he closed the door behind them, the discomfort escalated.

"Here is my computer," said Giovanni. "My brother sent it to me from Germany. He works for a computer company."

"Wow," she said, "lucky you." She felt his eyes move over her body. This would need a delicate touch.

"Can I offer you a drink?" said Giovanni, "Qualcosa da bere?"

"Water would be great, thank you," said Mary.

She walked over to his desk and booted up the computer. She needed to move things along before young Casanova got up the courage to make a move on her. She smiled in spite of herself. She searched the Internet while Giovanni took an inordinate amount of time returning with the water. When he finally did, he placed the glass on the desk next to her and the waft of cologne hit her. He had combed his hair and changed his shirt, too. He was gearing up to make his move and she hadn't found what she was looking for yet.

"Tell me," she said, moving to Plan B, "do you drive?"

"I got my license in December last year," said Giovanni. "Do you need a drive somewhere?"

"Well, maybe," she said, "depends on how far the nearest city is."

"Cagliari," he said, "is about 100 km from here. Why do you have need of a city?"

She jumped into character. *Here it goes,* she thought.

"I am a reporter and my equipment was stolen when I passed through Sicily," she began. *Nice touch,* she thought.

"Cretini," said Giovanni with disgust. "They are not true Italians, you know." He was loathe to let her continue a second longer with the misconception.

"I didn't know that," she said, humoring him. "Anyway, I need to get new supplies. Can you help me?"

"What do you need from me?" said Giovanni, temporarily distracted from his original plan to seduce the American.

"I need an assistant, a confidant," she said. "Do you know the word *confidant?*" Giovanni nodded twice.

"Good," said Mary. "Can I trust you to keep your mouth shut? To not tell a soul what we do?" He liked the direction of the conversation and, this time, nodded three times rapidly.

"Yes, of course," he said. "I will keep our activities very secret."

Mary hoped that they were still talking about the same thing. "Do you have access to a car?" she asked. "I need to go to Cagliari to buy some equipment. I need to go today."

"Eh," he wavered, "eh, certo."

The car belonged to his father, who was visiting one of his children in Spain. *He'll never know,* Giovanni thought. *Mamma is away at Nonna's house, too. But what about the shop?* Hormone-induced fantasies of passionate sex eclipsed any thought of the consequences he might face for abandoning his responsibilities.

Mary didn't hesitate for a second. She knew how to handle boys in heat. They were just little versions of men in heat. She sealed the deal with the next performance.

"Before we begin our partnership, Giovanni," she said, "I need to come clean with you." She cast her eyes down and feigned embarrassment or something like it. "I know you already picked up on how I feel about you." He hadn't, but he tried not to look too shocked.

"You are such a handsome, intelligent, strong man," she said, putting her hand on his pectoral muscle before quickly retracting it. "It's going to be very hard for me to keep this professional."

Giovanni sat, eyes wide as dinner plates, heart pounding.

"Whatever we become *after* this," she said, "will be up to fate, but we must make a vow to each other right now."

His eyes were still wide. Rational thought wasn't possible; his blood supply was diverted elsewhere.

"We must promise that we will behave as professionals until the job is done. Then we can see where this goes. What do you say?"

Nodding was all that he managed.

"Great," she said. She leaned in and kissed him on both cheeks, as she had seen others do a thousand times since she'd arrived. *Maybe that wasn't the best thing to do,* she thought. "I gotta make a phone call to my editor," she said. "Say we meet here in about half an hour, okay? Don't get up. I'll show myself out."

Giovanni nodded with a look of relief. Standing up would have been very embarrassing, indeed.

"Ciao, ciao," she waved and closed the door behind her.

Giovanni fell back onto his bed and tried to slow his heart, which was beating at a steady hum. *I'm going to marry that American,* he thought and smiled until his face hurt.

Mary walked briskly to her hotel room. *What's the difference?* she thought. *I was going to seduce a priest for a ride. That's gotta be a little worse than a 17-year-old kid.* She hoped there wasn't a Hell.

CS

To the surprise of the doctors, the fever had broken. Falters was standing by the window, his backside exposed in the hospital gown, when Dr. Casella arrived. Casella rarely had the opportunity to practice his English and welcomed the opportunity.

"Mr. Falters," he said. "You are a very fortunate man."

Falters turned to face him. "Where are my clothes?"

Casella was still engrossed in Falters' chart. If he'd heard the question, he didn't bother responding. "You have an amazing immune system," said Casella. "I would like to examine the wound, if you please."

"No. Bring me my clothes," Falters said. "I wish to leave now."

304

Scented for Oisín

CHAPTER 58

DEBRA LEWIS RETURNED to Oisín Pharmaceuticals to do one last check. Dr. Gregory Bennett of the FDA was coming on Monday for the first of many meetings to discuss the IND application for Regenerol. She was putting the conference room in order when she heard the commotion outside.

"Dr. Debra Lewis?" said Agent DeAngelo. "I need to ask you some questions. Is there somewhere we can talk?"

"What's this about?" asked Debra.

"I think you know."

Forty-five minutes of interrogation and DeAngelo got nothing out of her.

"We know you know where he is," said DeAngelo. "And we're gonna find him, too. You can either cooperate with us now and help bring this piece of shit to justice or you can face the consequences later. Your choice."

"Mr. DeAngelo, is it?" said Debra.

"Special Agent DeAngelo," he said.

"You say that I can either cooperate or face the consequences. Might I ask what consequences you're referring to before I make my decision?" Lewis swallowed hard and put on her bravest face.

"Don't get smart, lady," said DeAngelo. "You knew about the illegal testing in Mexico, probably knew about the deaths, too. No jury in the world is going to believe that you weren't involved. You filled out the goddamn IND report for Christ sake." Another agent knocked on the door and beckoned to DeAngelo.

"The computers are wiped," he whispered. "We're bringing them back with us so that maybe Jerry can manage to recover something back at headquarters." Debra Lewis watched the exchange through the glass, but couldn't make out what they were saying.

"Goddamn it," said DeAngelo. "How're they doing with his secretary?"

"She doesn't know anything," he said. "She would've blabbed by now." DeAngelo looked over at Eileen, who was surrounded by a mound of discarded tissues; her eyes were blood-red.

"What about the others?" said DeAngelo.

"He was pretty clever – kept most of them in the dark," said the agent. "He split up the team between Lewis and a guy named John Graham. Take a look."

He handed DeAngelo Graham's file. "We know this guy was definitely involved in the Mexican trials, but we can't link Debra Lewis yet."

"Keep trying to find something incriminating," said DeAngelo. "She's dirty. I feel it in my bones, but she's not cracking. I'm gonna need as much help as I can get."

He returned to Lewis' office and closed the door behind him.

"Okay, Dr. Lewis," he said, "I think we have enough to put you away for quite a while." DeAngelo had one of the best poker faces in the Bureau. If there was ever a time he needed to bluff, it was now. "We're going to take a little trip now." DeAngelo handcuffed and escorted her through the office.

"I want to speak to a lawyer," said Debra.

"Seal the place up. No one gets in until we collaborate with the DOJ."

Debra Lewis said nothing as DeAngelo escorted her into the car.

☙

Lori Adams sat back and let the sun beat down on her face. Her oversized sunglasses would've been comical on anyone else. She sat on her comfortable chair at the bow of the boat and let the wind blow through her Aqua Net-free hair. She felt good.

She stood up to refresh her iced tea. The red one-piece bathing suit clashed with a white shirt she had taken out of Edward's suitcase and the high heels were probably not the wisest footwear choice for sailing.

"Edward, honey," she said, "are we in range yet?"

"About five minutes now," he said.

"Okay, let me know when," she said, phone in hand. The satellite phone was acting up and she wanted to check her messages. Edward knew why the satellite phone was kaput, but didn't mention it. Lori had left it out on the deck the previous night and the rainstorm had soaked it through. He didn't feel it necessary to tell her that she was the reason they were incommunicado.

"Where are we docking again?" she said. The boat was now at full throttle and the ice cubes were bouncing violently in her drink, spilling tea onto Edward's white shirt.

"Bimini Island," he said. "You can make all the calls you want from there, honey."

"And we'll pick up another phone, too," she said. "One that won't break down on us in a week."

Edward smiled as he steered the course. He loved everything about her. Absolutely everything.

CHAPTER 59

TIERNAN AND GRAHAM talked all night. The effects of the Diony-sinol kept Graham from feeling any fatigue. Already he began to feel more alive and, although he suspected the placebo effect might be at work, he was sure that the skin around his face was tightening and held a certain radiance. Perhaps it was the thought of finally having a real chance with Debra Lewis that set his skin aglow. But, whatever the cause, Graham was certain that something dramatic was occurring. Time was arrested, halted in its tracks and forced to begin its substantial journey backward.

"So, I wonder why I haven't experienced anything even close to what you have," said Tiernan. "Do you think I got a bum dose?"

"I cannot speculate," said Graham, "but, when all this is over, we can certainly run some tests."

Marinella and Diego slept soundly in the other room. They had retired for the night, frustrated by the profoundly anticlimactic explanation Tiernan had provided them for the urgent retrieval of the purple vials. After witnessing their incredulity, he opted to use the default explanation: face cream ingredient, highly-effective and very valuable.

"I am going to need another vial, Master Tiernan," said Graham. He didn't ask, he stated. "For my mate."

"Mate?" said Tiernan. "I didn't even know you had a mate."

"I don't," said Graham, "but I intend to rectify that soon." His face beamed with resolute peace.

"John," said Tiernan. You should know a few things. Falters believed that there would be consequences, potentially catastrophic consequences, should Dionysinol become available to the human race."

"I agree," said Graham, "which is why I would strongly suggest preventing that from ever happening."

"Yeah, yeah, no sweat," said Tiernan. "You see how effective my plan has been so far, right? It was in my possession for less than an hour and already I have one less vial and I'm in real jeopardy of losing another. And to make matters worse, you didn't even pay for it."

Graham smiled. Tiernan was going to give him a vial for Debra, although he would've been shocked to learn that Debra Lewis was the *mate* that Graham spoke of.

"Plus," Tiernan continued, "there's another consideration."

"Such as?" said Graham, the euphoria surging through him.

"Well, for one," Tiernan said, "the effects are passed down to the offspring of those treated with it."

Graham was an intelligent man. He understood better than Tiernan the potential for disaster that Dionysinol held. It would only take a small number of treated individuals to propagate a race of humans immune to the effects of time. Populations would explode and hunger and thirst would be the impetus of new and more efficient wars.

"Do both parents need to be treated or is it sufficient for only one to carry the mutated gene? This is a very important distinction."

"Good question. I don't know – never thought to ask," said Tiernan. "But I think we'd better err on the side of caution until we know definitively. Falters has all the data on the animal experiments saved on redundancy drives."

"Has Mr. Falters taken the drug himself?"

"Yes, he was the first successful test case. He experimented on himself," said Tiernan.

"Do you think he's made it back to Italy?"

"I'd say so," said Tiernan, looking at the cases of Dionysinol, "but I'm sure we'll be hearing from him soon." Tiernan ran his hand over the trunk.

"Can Dionysinol be synthesized in a lab?" said Graham. "I would venture to say that a synthetic version would be very difficult to manufacture."

"According to his notes, my father didn't think it was possible," said

Resveratrol

Tiernan. "It's the Niamh grape that makes Dionysinol possible. The quality and quantity of the resveratrol contained in the hybrids extend the life cycle of the blastema cells taken from the Turritopsis. This gives them the edge, the window they need to propagate until the entire genome of the subject is irrevocably altered and teeming with blastemata clusters."

Tiernan began to feel the effects of sleep deprivation and the emotional cyclone that threatened to tear his life apart, and wanted desperately to wake up from the nightmare. The cell buzzed in his pocket. He took it out and looked at the number. *Debra Lewis.*

"It's Lewis," said Tiernan. "Should I answer it? She could be compromised."

Graham snatched the phone after hearing her name. He flipped it opened and greeted her in his usual manner, but, this time, hope permeated his voice. "Hello, my dear," said Graham. "Are you well?"

"John?" said Debra. "Where are you two? Things are falling apart. I was arrested and they're coming after you now."

"That's rather vexatious," said Graham. "Especially since my luck seemed to be changing for the better. Are you still in police custody?"

"No," said Debra. "I called a lawyer. I didn't know what else to do. They had to release me, but I'm not allowed to leave New York until further notice. What is going on?"

"Yes, well, that restriction seems to be en vogue these days," said Graham, looking at Tiernan.

"The FBI, DOJ and a host of other acronyms are working in collaboration with the Mexican government to hunt you down and make examples of you. They shut down Oisín and confiscated all our computers. They sent everyone home."

Graham could tell that Debra was hysterical. She wasn't prepared for this. He needed to remain calm and reassuring while telling her that her phone was probably tapped.

"On another note," said Graham, "I heard a lovely rendition of the Greek myth of Cerberus and Hercules. Do you remember the *Cerberus?*"

"The Cerberus? Why are you talking about that when we –"

"Shh, shh, shh, now, my dear," said Graham, "You know how useful that old Cerberus was, don't you?"

And then she remembered. When they initiated the Cerberus Contingency at Oisín a fortnight ago, her computer was wiped clean. There was no evidence linking her to anything illegal.

"There we are, my dear," said Graham. "Now, do you remember that lovely little excursion we took some weeks back? It was the first time I had eaten that type of food. Remember?"

"Yes, I remember. We were –"

"Ah," said Graham quickly. "Don't say it, dear. Just go there and wait inside at the pay phone. I'll call you back from a different number. Hurry now."

"I don't know if I can do this, John," said Debra. "I'm afraid."

"Trust me, dear," said Graham, "we're going to look back at this and wonder why we were so worried. Now hurry."

Graham disconnected and took the battery and SIM card out of the cell. "We have to get a Tracfone™, Master Tiernan," he said, "or the Italian equivalent. An Internet connection would be grand also. I'd like to search for a particular number."

Tiernan stopped him. "It's her, isn't it? You're in love with Lewis. I'll be damned. Didn't see that coming." Graham didn't answer; there was no need.

"Well," said Tiernan as they left the apartment, "wait till I tell you about the effects that Dionysinol has on your, how shall I put this, your appeal. You're gonna be a busy guy."

CHAPTER 60

"SIGN HERE," SAID the doctor. Falters was leaving against doctor's orders and the hospital staff at Ghilarza Memorial was not happy at the lost opportunity to study Falters' uncanny immune response and the remarkable rate at which the laceration on his shoulder had healed.

"Grazie, Dottore," said Falters. "I owe you my life. Perhaps I will repay the favor some day."

"Hopefully not," he said and handed him his discharge papers.

ℴ

Falters took one of the two cabs available in Ghilarza after deciding against walking. He was still weak from the blood loss and didn't want to tempt fate any more.

Upon arriving at the house, he paused to look at the statue of Venus one last time. No rainbow emanated from her shoulders and the cloudy, gray sky seemed to mirror her sad face. It was as if she knew what Falters was going to do, even if he didn't.

He headed straight down to the lab to retrieve the Dionysinol. He had worked for decades, rested all his hopes on it, but now knew that he had been too arrogant to recognize the dangers. The Niamh grapes were unique; he wasn't worried about their proliferation. Richard Tiernan and Ivan Falters had been scrupulous in putting certain safeguards into place. They engineered the Niamh grape to grow only in the unique composition of Sardinian soil. If the vines were planted elsewhere, they might germinate, but, even if they did, they would produce grapes with only a fraction of the resveratrol needed to complete the process. Even when Falters and Tiernan themselves had attempted to recreate the soil conditions in the lab, the grapes had failed to reproduce the levels required. Niamh guarded her secrets well, and Falters didn't worry about her ever revealing her magic to anyone.

He walked down the dark tunnel leading to the secret lab where the only store of Dionysinol existed. He had to destroy it. The doors slid open and, as his eyes adjusted to the florescent lights, he stopped suddenly. Something was different. He inhaled deeply and concentrated. He opened his eyes and scanned the room. *A woman had been in the lab. He could smell her scent.*

The old steamer trunk was gone. The Dionysinol was stolen. Heart pounding in his ears and blood rushing to his head, he ran to the safe and unlocked it. The female scent was especially strong there. *She spent time near the safe.* He opened it and found the six vials he had put aside still sitting safely in their dark prison. *She couldn't open it.*

Falters sat on the floor of the subterranean lab with his head resting in his hands, knees pulled up. *How could Tiernan have gotten to it first,* he thought. *It had to be Tiernan. Who else could have gotten into the lab? Even if someone were to stumble upon it by accident, which is extraordinarily unlikely, why would they take only the Dionysinol and leave the expensive lab equipment behind? Whoever did it knew exactly what they were after. It had to be Tiernan.*

Falters remained sitting on the floor for a long time before deciding that it was the only way. He walked over to his desk and took out the folder containing notes from a project that he and Richard had buried years ago: Project Brimstone.

OZONE

"O3 is a toxic gas formed by photo dissociation of oxygen, O2, by sunlight. The ozone layer protects the earth from excessive penetration of UV rays...

UVA, UVB and UVC can all damage collagen fibers and thereby accelerate aging of the skin. Both UVA and UVB destroy vitamin A in skin, which may cause further damage..."

At the time, Falters was horrified at the notion. He recalled the conversation he'd had with Richard as if it were yesterday.

"Only a man who hasn't lived in war would believe that," he'd said. "Surely you know that, Richard. If we create it, they will use it."

Richard Tiernan had hypothesized years ago that, by creating a weapon capable of utter and complete annihilation with minimal effects on the environment, peace would follow. The weapon would only be used at the discretion of the UN. By destroying very specific targets, the UN could ensure peace.

Falters had argued that, as long as there were at least three people in the UN, two of them would disagree.

They had conducted a single test of Project Brimstone, after which no further argument was necessary. If either man had any lingering reservations about the discontinuation of the project, witnessing the results of the test removed them absolutely.

"There is no other way, Nadja," said Falters, speaking to his dead wife. "I'm sorry. I have failed." Falters dried the tears from his eyes and carried the six vials to the table where he began working. It would take about three hours from start to finish.

CB

Mary and Giovanni arrived in Cagliari in record time. Giovanni wanted to get this *partnership* over and done with so he could pursue a different type of partnership. Bound by his vow to remain *professional* while working, he resisted the powerful urge to put his hand on her leg as they drove along the autostrada.

"Not very far now," said Giovanni. "You need survey equipment?"

"Surveillance equipment," said Mary. "The smaller the better. I gotta see what that guy is up to."

"What is surveillance?" said Giovanni.

Mary explained the in and outs of the journalistic life, or at least what she thought it would be if she were, in fact, a journalist. To keep Giovanni's interest, she added a hint of mystery, which, ironically, was less intriguing than the truth would have been.

"That Russian guy," said Mary, "is into some bad stuff."

315

Giovanni had watched enough American TV to believe anything was possible. He was temporarily distracted from the merciless urges.

"Yes? What bad stuff?"

Mary monopolized on his prejudice. "Let's put it this way, the Sicilians didn't beat him up for nothing." She winked at him. The urges returned.

"Is that a sign for a shopping center?" asked Mary.

Giovanni affirmed and exited the highway.

After she had prevailed over the difficulties of explaining what she wanted, Mary charged her newly-obtained goods on her debit card. She'd probably never need to buy anything on credit ever again. Although the market for spy paraphernalia hadn't quite caught on in Sardinia, she managed to get several pieces of useful equipment. Closed-circuit cameras for outside and plug-and-play digital recording devices for inside were among the cache of goods she carted to the car with the help of her enamored assistant. A flash of memory hit her as she smiled at the young Italian teen. *I feel like Lori Adams,* she thought.

Mary had tried to contact Lori a few times since she had arrived in Sardinia. After she had discovered the enormous deposit of funds in her account, she was certain that Lori was somehow involved. She hoped that the transaction meant that Vincent Tighte was dead and Lori was already healing, but she couldn't be sure and wanted to hear Lori's voice confirm her hopes. She also wanted to thank her for the new obsession that began with the vial of purple magic.

Giovanni was high on adventure and lust. After putting the merchandise in the trunk, he helped Mary into the car and closed the door for her. His professional obligation was almost over and then...He put the thought out of his head as best he could; he didn't need to excite himself further. "Andiamo a Boroneddu," he said.

"Andiamo."

CHAPTER 61

LORI ADAMS DISEMBARKED and greeted the tourists. "G'mornin' y'all," she said to the tables of breakfasters. "Umm hmmm, smells good. I gotta get me some coffee too. How 'bout it, Ed? Feel like a cuppa joe?"

They sat down at one of the empty tables and a waiter promptly poured two glasses of water.

"Welcome to Bimini Island. I am Joseph and I'll be your waiter."

"Well, hello, Joseph," said Lori. "I'm Lori Adams and this is my husband, Edward Adams." They laughed and Joseph joined in, although he didn't know why he was laughing.

"I'm not taking your name, Lori," said Edward, tickling her ribs. "That's just a little too modern for me."

"Well, I ain't takin' yours either. We'll just have to settle for the ones we got, now won't we?" she said, browsing the breakfast menu.

"Shall I give you a few minutes?" asked Joseph.

"Yeah, you better, darlin'," said Lori. "Everything looks so good that I'm havin' a hard time pickin' just one."

"Okay," said Joseph. "I'll return with some coffee for you both, yes?"

"Decaf for this fella," said Lori, still perusing.

Edward looked at her and then at the waiter. "Regular's fine."

"Oh, I'm sorry, darlin'," she said. "Ryan drinks decaf."

"I know," said Edward.

"Which reminds me, I gotta call him to get the scoop," she said. She looked through her bag to find her cell.

"Ah, finally, a signal. Four bars, too. I bet I could call Mars from here. Get me the western omelet with home fries and white toast with real butter," she said as she dialed Lionel Pharmaceuticals.

Edward wanted to be jealous but had known what he was getting into from the start. Connor was going to be in Lori's life and there was nothing anyone could do to change that. He knew Lori wouldn't cheat on him – that would be beneath her – but a piece of her heart would always belong to Ryan Connor. Edward would settle for the piece that would always belong to him and try to make her as happy as he could. She deserved it.

"Ryan," said Lori, talking louder than usual. "Ryan, can you hear me okay? Connor distanced the phone from his ear.

"Yes, loud and clear. *Very* loud and clear," he said.

"Oh, okay," she said, returning to a normal volume. "I'm in Bimini Island."

"Good for you," said Connor. "How're things?"

"You tell me," said Lori. "What's going on? They catch Tiernan yet?"

"Nope," said Connor. "He's a fugitive. Got everyone but the Pope looking for him, maybe even him."

"You told on him, didn't you?" said Lori. "That wasn't very nice, Ryan, but I understand – him trying to have you killed 'n' all."

"Mexican authorities are getting involved too. Families of the women who were killed by Regenerol are filing a class action lawsuit against Oisín. He's d-o-n-e," said Connor.

"Pity," said Lori. "From what I understand, that drug coulda been very effective. Ain't gonna help too many people now."

"Don't be so sure," said Connor. "Just because Oisín doesn't get to produce it doesn't mean that *someone* won't."

"You never change," said Lori. "Okay, gotta go. My food's here. I'll call soon, bye."

Lori recounted the conversation for Edward. He allowed her to reenact the entire conversation, despite having heard most of it first-hand.

"So, needless to say, he'll be going away for a long, long time," said

Lori, cutting into her omelet. "Pass the salt, please."

"I thought you liked this Tiernan guy," said Edward, handing her the shaker. "You said he wasn't so bad." Lori liberally sprinkled the salt over her food.

"Yeah, but, I mean, he tried to have my friend killed. That wasn't very nice, now was it?"

"No one knows that for certain, but suppose he did. *Why* did he try to off him?" said Edward, who was less interested in defending Tiernan than exposing Connor's degree of potential culpability. "What was his motive?"

"Oh, hell's bells," said Lori, "I just got stung by a dang bee. Who says these critters are disappearing?" She rubbed her neck where a panicked wasp had stung her after getting caught in her windblown hair. Edward lifted his hand to summon the waiter and asked for a cup of ice cubes.

Ω

Debra Lewis waited anxiously by the pay phone in Delphi's, where she and Graham had dined. A torturous hour had passed and still no call from Graham. She was getting more nauseous with every passing moment. In every passerby she saw an undercover agent. *Where the hell are they?* she thought. She looked down at her watch and decided to give them a few more minutes.

Ω

Graham and Tiernan couldn't find a Tracfone™ or an Internet café. "It seems the Italians haven't been indoctrinated to such a degree as to forego sleep," said Graham.

Piazza di Santa Maria in Trastevere, alive with hundreds of people only a few hours earlier, was completely silent, as if it, too, were sleeping.

"Yeah," said Tiernan. He inhaled deeply, expecting the fragrant Mirto-infused air to be awaiting him, but, instead, was treated to the smell of ozone left by an evening's rain.

319

"Were you ever in Tír na nÓg?" said Tiernan. "It seems odd that my father wouldn't have mentioned its existence to you."

"It's funny how the mind works," said Graham. "How certain things can only make sense after time ripens them, makes them digestible."

"Huh?" said Tiernan. "You hungry or something?"

Graham chuckled before continuing his thought. "I think your father tried to tell me about his discovery many years ago, but I was too obtuse to hear what he *wasn't* saying. I remember him telling me that he was going to give me a retirement gift of such grandeur that all other gifts from thenceforth would pale in comparison. He was right."

"I assume he meant Dionysinol, right?" said Tiernan.

"I believe so, yes," said Graham.

"Why the hell couldn't he tell you then? Why did he carry this burden himself? Why did he trust a stranger over us, his family?" said Tiernan.

"Ah, my dear boy," said Graham, no longer bound to any rules of etiquette, "men need to keep certain things secret, even if there's no harm in revealing them. But your father chose as he did because he couldn't have chosen otherwise. Things are as they are, occur as they must. Whenever we act, whenever we direct our energies to change realities that seem repellent to us, we are simply engaging in the ultimate expression of futility."

Tiernan didn't completely understand Graham's cryptic words and attributed his increasingly philosophical tendencies to the physical effects of Dionysinol.

"What are we going to do about calling Debra?" said Tiernan. "We can't find access to the Internet to search for the number to that payphone."

Graham didn't answer and continued his monologue. "Every event has a preceding event that occurred temporally prior to it. An event cannot cause itself, a thing cannot bring itself into existence and, hence, must wait to happen until the conditions are just so."

"Hey," said Tiernan, "it's a tad too early for this, don't you think?"

"All existence, all being is one," said Graham. "I can't believe I never realized this before and now it's so clear. We are merely parts of the whole."

"Maybe a little espresso would help," said Tiernan, beginning to worry. Falters had said that the Dionysinol affected members of the same species in different ways. Was Graham losing his mind or was Tiernan's mind devolving? He fought back a wave of panic brought on by the reminder that they had no way of predicting how Dionysinol would ultimately affect them.

"Let me sit a moment," said Graham, pointing to the fountain in the center of the piazza. "I need to think."

Graham sat on the steps of the fountain and faced the church. He sat peacefully examining the 12th century mosaic that beautified the outside wall of the Church of Santa Maria. In front of the mosaic stood a row of statues – four men who obstructed an otherwise perfect view of the masterpiece. *Bishops,* Graham assumed from their pointy hats.

"Do you see?" said Graham, "one's eyes are attracted to the statues at the expense of what lies beyond."

He directed Tiernan's attention to the mosaic. The Virgin Mary was holding the Infant Jesus, and 10 women – five on either side – flanked Her. These women seemed to offer the Virgin flaming jars. Graham sat and stared at the mosaic as if all answers to all conceivable questions were contained within the intricate stone patterns.

"What are those women bringing Her?" said Tiernan.

"I don't know," said Graham. "I suppose, judging from the orange and red flames, that they're supposed to be lamps of some sort."

"Not all of them have that glow," said Tiernan. "Look." Tiernan pointed to a few of the women who carried flameless jars. Graham didn't comment, but continued to stare, enraptured.

"A relic of the Holy Sponge is housed in this church," he said, "the sponge reputed to have been dipped in sour red wine and offered to Christ while he hung on the Cross."

"The Holy *Sponge?*" said Tiernan. "We Catholics sure love holy things, don't we?" He expected a laugh, but was disappointed.

"And the head of Saint Apollonia too," said Graham.

Story of 10 Virgins en The Bible

"How do you know all this, John?" said Tiernan. "You must spend a lot of time reading."

Graham didn't seem to hear Tiernan. "Perhaps the women are bringing the Virgin and her Son a very special gift – Dionysinol," he continued. "Maybe that's why they were worshipped – they became eternal. Wouldn't that be enough to merit worship?"

Tiernan squinted and waited for the laugh to follow but was met with disappointment again.

"Jesus refused the sponge at the Crucifixion because it contained the grapes used to produce Dionysinol. He knew it would have killed him instantly," said Graham. "He had already imbibed the elixir in His infancy. The wise men had travelled great distances, and at great peril, to bring the liquid to him."

"John," said Tiernan, "are you feeling alright? You're beginning to scare me a little."

"One dose and, after the change occurs, it can never pass one's lips again or death will surely follow."

"Should I be concerned, John?" said Tiernan, wondering how Graham came to his conclusion. "Dionysinol wasn't around back then, remember? It's a relatively new phenomenon."

"Dionysinol has made many appearances throughout our history," said Graham. "Your father merely named the latest reoccurrence of it, but don't fool yourself, son. Dionysinol has come and gone many times before."

"John," said Tiernan. "You're not thinking clearly. I think you may be experiencing some nasty side effects. Listen to what you're saying. You're not making any sense."

"Surely, you remember from your catechism – he who drinks of this cup shall never taste death but shall live forever."

"But he who drinks of the cup unworthily, drinks damnation!" said Tiernan, finishing the thought.

"One dose," said Graham "any more and death reclaims you with time's anger."

"Actually," said Tiernan, "you're not too far off. The Turritopsis nutricula died when Dionysinol was introduced into its system."

Graham seemed to be listening to something other than Tiernan's voice – something that was audible only to him. "Only one parent need carry the mutation for the offspring to inherit the genetic code," said Graham. "Only one."

"You're all over the place," said Tiernan. "Jesus and Mary taking Dionysinol thousands of years before its creation, holy sponges dripping with Dionysinol, genetic theory..."

"Let's get to a pay phone," said Graham, jumping up with the youthful vigor that had taken a foothold on his aging bones. "How many Euro coins do you have?"

"Enough, but why?" said Tiernan.

"We can get the number to the restaurant from an international directory assistance and then have Debra paged," said Graham.

"I need you to tell me that you're okay, John," said Tiernan. "The last thing we need is you having a mental breakdown."

"I have never seen the world with such clarity," said Graham. "It's as if I had been viewing the world through a bowl of lime water and, suddenly, everything's become clear. Come, we should hurry."

Tiernan followed Graham, who walked as if he knew where he was going, although he'd never been in Trastevere before. "There will be phones close to where the bus lines intersect," said Graham. "Line H and 84."

"How do you know?" said Tiernan, quickening his pace to catch up.

"Because there must be," said Graham. "It cannot be otherwise. Trust me."

Tiernan decided to reserve his final judgment on Graham's sanity until the unequivocal evidence presented itself. He figured that he at least owed him the benefit of falsifying his claim of Gnosticism before classifying him as the first casualty of Dionysinol. When Tiernan saw the phone booth exactly where Graham had predicted, his mind searched for an alternate explanation. Insanity was now officially improbable.

"Get out the coins," said Graham, his hand stretched out in Tiernan's direction.

Tiernan reached into his pocket and retrieved the coins. "How the hell did you know...?"

Graham snatched the coins. "Thank you," he said.

With satisfying efficiency, the international operator gave Graham what he sought. He dialed the number and, thousands of miles away, a phone rang in Delphi's. It took some cajoling, but the manager set out to find Debra with the very specific message Graham gave him.

"Debra Lewis?" said the manager. "Hydra, Chimera and Cerberus."

"What?" she answered.

"John is on the phone for you. He said that your family is from Hydra, Richard created the Chimera corn and Michael initiated the Cerberus program," said the exasperated manager, who hadn't finished the menu listing the day's specials. "You coming or not?"

Debra followed the manager to the phone. "Hello, John?" she said.

"Yes, dear, it is I," he said. "Isn't that quite the coincidence? With all those monsters surrounding our adventure, I wonder who will take the role of Hercules?"

"John, what is going on?" said Debra. "I'm scared."

"Don't worry," said Graham. "Here's what we need to do. Listen carefully, dear."

CHAPTER 62

FALTERS DILUTED THE mixture to about half strength. He didn't want to reproduce the results he and Richard had obtained from the first and last test of the Brimstone, but he wanted to ensure complete eradication of the Niamh grape. He loaded the gallons of liquid into the car, not allowing the voice of conscience to dissuade him. He was acting in the best interest of the majority, he told himself. Utilitarianism and pragmatism; there was no other way.

He walked back into the house and collected the remainder of his belongings. He emptied the drawer of pictures and mementos into a duffel bag and took one last look at the vineyards from the vantage point of his room. *Beautiful,* he thought. *Such dangerous beauty.* He strapped the remaining vials of Dionysinol to his chest. He removed a sheet of paper from his wallet, unfolded it and picked up the phone. He called the Demelas' home. No answer. He hoped that they were far enough away and weren't coming back before his task was completed. Next, he called Ghilarza Memorial and asked for Dr. Casella. A nurse told Falters that Casella was indisposed and would return the call when he was able. Falters was going to insist, but felt satisfied that the attempt alone was enough to pay his life debt.

Falters performed one last sweep of the house before going down to the lab. Three neatly-stacked boxes containing the years of research that had led to the creation of the Niamh hybrid and, ultimately, to Dionysinol were lined up against the wall. He carried them upstairs and left them in the kitchen. The stone tunnels would have certainly preserved them and he didn't want anyone following his work. Finally, he carried the last of the computer equipment upstairs and dropped it on the kitchen floor. There was nothing left to do. The phone rang.

"Signore Falters? This is Dr. Casella returning your call."

"Salve, Dottore," said Falters. "I'm glad you called."

"Are you feeling alright?" said the doctor.

"No, but this is not the reason for the call. I'm calling to repay my debt to you. A life for a life."

"Mi scuzi?" said the doctor.

"You must leave Ghilarza immediately and drive as far north as possible. You do not have time to gather your things. Leave now or die." Falters hung up the phone and walked out of the house. He hoped that the doctor would survive, but, as long as the debt was settled, Falters would have no regrets.

CB

Mary and Giovanni were almost caught red-handed.

"You said the Russian would be in the hospital until tomorrow," said Mary.

"That is what my friend said," said Giovanni.

Fortunately, Falters drove past the little Fiat without as much as a second glance. *Better not to look at their faces,* he thought. *Less fodder for the nightmares.*

"That was a close one," said Mary. "Where the hell is he going? It was him, right?"

"Per sicuro," said Giovanni. "There is no one who looks like that here except for him. Should we tail him?" Giovanni felt cool using the American vernacular he learned from the TV dramas.

"Not a good idea," said Mary. "I think he'd notice, seeing as we're the only car on the road and all."

"Hai ragione," said Giovanni in agreement. "Do you want to set up the camera?"

Mary weighed the risks against the benefits. Probability suggested that if Falters was headed somewhere that necessitated the use of a vehicle, he would be gone for a minimum of a half an hour. She calculated the probabilities of Falters' destinations and concluded that it was worth the risk.

"Let's go," said Mary. "We'll set up the outside camera first. This way, if he returns unexpectedly and we have to flee, we'll at least be able to monitor him coming and going."

Giovanni only caught half of what Mary said, her speech being too rapid for his intermediate ear.

"Va bene," said Giovanni and followed her lead.

ଓ

Falters poured the last cylinder of Brimstone into the crop duster. Sweat poured down his face and he fought another bout of vertigo. The blood loss that would have killed any other man took much of his strength. He wiped the sweat from his brow and squinted into the sun.

"It's time," he said.

The propellers spun stubbornly, protesting another flight, but relented and whirled into a transparent figure. He whispered an apology into the air in his native Russian and took one last breath of Sardinian air before climbing into the cockpit and taking off.

ଓ

"Cover it a little better than that, Gio," said Mary, giving her new assistant a nickname. "But make sure you don't block the lens with leaves, okay?"

"Lo so," said Giovanni. "I'm almost finished." Mary clicked the remote and the camera became animated. "One-hundred eighty degrees?" she asked.

"A little less, but still good," said Giovanni, using his finger to estimate the angle. "Shh, ascolta," he said, finger to his mouth. "Ascolta. Un piccolo aereo."

She heard it too. The unmistakable buzzing of a twin engine in the distance was getting louder as it approached the vineyards. Giovanni had been excited up to that point. Now the negative influence of the American TV drama caused him to panic. He envisioned legions of law enforcement agents surrounding them with the Russian in tow.

327

"Scappare, Mary, adesso!"

"Scappare?" said Mary, but Giovanni had already bolted to the car. *Where the hell is he going?* she thought as she watched the speeding car head down the road. The plane was in view now, and Mary ducked out of sight under the cover of the porch veranda. She thought she heard the sound of rainfall, but couldn't be sure it wasn't the echo from the fountain of Venus until she peaked out and felt the drops. She looked at the purple drops on her hand and lifted her head to see their cause. The plane was spraying the area with something. *Pesticides,* she thought. *Falters is spraying the crops – and the house – by the looks of it.*

The plane circled several times before rising into the air further and further until Mary was having difficultly locating it. Then, slowly at first, almost imperceptibly, it started. The animals were behaving erratically, running out from their various hiding places and away from the vineyards. She thought the hot flashes were the result of the adrenaline still pumping through her body, but then it started to burn.

Smoke wisped sporadically from the vegetation, and her skin felt as if she had incurred a wicked sunburn. Less than a minute later, she shrieked in agony as her hair burst into flames. Instinctively, she ran, plunging head first into the fountain.

The rays of the sun scorched everything in its path, turning the water into steam as Mary ran to the house. She jumped through the picture window, sending glass fragments everywhere. The excruciating pain of her burning flesh and smoldering clothes occupied her pain receptors completely, so she didn't feel the shards of glass that penetrated her face, arms and legs. She screamed from the pain as she saw her skin blister right before her eyes. The smell of burnt hair and flesh nauseated her, causing her to vomit violently.

The house burst into flames and the roof began to cave in around her. She managed to climb to her feet and make her way into the kitchen. *The tunnels,* she thought. *I need to get to the tunnels.* As she made her way into the kitchen, a ray of sunlight beamed through the window and set her blouse ablaze. She screeched in horror and tore it off, burning her hands. The trapezoidal door, now padlocked, seemed miles away. She yanked and pulled at the handle as the padlock struggled to remain faithful to its charge. Lumps of skin fell from her hands as she struggled to pry the door open.

No conscious thought was possible now. Mary was running on pure instinct – survival was the only goal. She didn't remember the door finally giving up. She didn't remember falling down the stairs or the wine rack smashing to the ground, leaving her lying in a pool of aged wine and glass.

CB

Giovanni realized that Mary wasn't in the car with him. Ashamed of his cowardice and doubtful of his chances of a relationship now, he pulled the car over and got out. He watched the plane circle the vineyards, saturating the air with a mist until it rose heavenward and became a speck in the sky.

"Stronso," said Giovanni aloud and smacked himself upside the head. "Stupido imbecile."

He was getting back into the car to retrieve his partner when he thought he heard her scream echo in the hills. He paused and listened carefully. He heard it again. He jumped back into the car and floored the gas pedal. Here was his chance to be the knight in shining armor and rescue the maiden from the Russian. *I'll have to run him over,* he thought, *but I'm okay with that.*

The plumes of smoke caused him to stop and get out. In the distance, fires continued to rage, gaining more ground as the seconds passed. His skin started to smoke. He looked in horror at his arms as the newly-formed blisters burst, sending liquid splashing into the air. His hair caught fire and he ran down the road, trying to escape from the flames. The flesh fell from his hands, exposing the muscle tissue before his eyes burst in his head. He fell to the ground, screaming until the rays passed over him, leaving nothing in their wake but cinders. His father's car exploded, sending the only warning the citizens of Boroneddu and the surrounding regions would get that their death was coming.

Russian Scientist

ଔ

Falters didn't look back. After the last drop of the ozone-busting liquid was spent, he flew north to Corsica. His French passport sat securely in his breast pocket. Tír na nÓg was no more. He ran his hand over the bulges in the nylon strap around his torso – the remaining Dionysinol was still secure. He flew directly to Corsica and landed without incident. He abandoned the plane that was registered to the late Richard Tiernan and set off to begin the next stage of his plan.

CHAPTER 63

WITHIN 24 HOURS, news of the devastation was everywhere. After surveying the damage via satellite, experts believed that it was caused by a new form of nuclear weapon. Twenty-five square kilometers were annihilated beyond recognition. As far as anyone could tell, there were no survivors. Radiation was expected to spread to the surrounding regions and a massive evacuation effort was underway. Panic ensued, claiming more casualties as people scrambled to escape the nuclear fallout that was never coming.

Within 12 hours of the evacuation notice, experts had determined that there was no trace of radiation in the air. In fact, there was nothing whatsoever. The government was baffled and officials reached out to their allies for assistance. America was the first to arrive at the scene.

Tiernan and Graham were alerted to the news by a harried Marinella, who had just returned from the market with fresh produce since the grapes she had taken from Tír na nÓg several days previously didn't make for very good eating, despite her best efforts to mask the flavor. Two large bunches of Niamh grapes sat by the windowsill, showing remarkable resilience to the rotting effects of time.

"Madonna," said Marinella, putting the bags of produce on the table, "hai sentito?"

"Did I hear what?" said Tiernan.

Marinella was too flustered to speak. Instead, she turned on the TV and flicked through the stations until she found the English news station in consideration of Graham.

"...Again, we don't have that confirmed, Paul, but a source in the local carabinieri said that a nuclear device has not been ruled out. Back to you at the station."

"Thank you, Frank. If you're just tuning in, we're live in Sardinia where a raging fire has left thousands dead..."

Tiernan and Graham stared in horror as aerial footage scanned the desolate remains of Boroneddu where the Tír na nÓg Vineyards were laying under a thick layer of smoke and smoldering ash. Houses made from anything other than brick were completely incinerated. The stone structures that had survived the scorching were blackened mounds, indistinguishable from the soot and ash when viewed from the air. The Nuraghi had survived the burning as they had survived everything else throughout the millennia.

As the cameras panned over the charred remains of those trying to flee, millions of viewers everywhere looked on in horror at a scene reminiscent of Pompeii. Ground crews in radiation suits scanned the area for any sign of life. Burnt moldings of bodies were scattered everywhere, some in clusters, some alone. A mother and child lay in the clearing surrounded by others who had met the same fate. Mouth frozen open in perpetual agony, the mother's hands attempted to shield her little one from harm. The baby's face was pressed against its mother's chest, cauterized, flesh to flesh. A journalist crouched low, trying to get the perfect picture of the paper-like corpses – a *Time* cover-quality picture. When he touched the face of the mother, both corpses fell into a heap of ash and were no more. Mother and child, ashes to ashes, dust to dust. The wind carried them along the barren countryside, now devoid of any color. The Mirto fragrance had vanished along with those who had savored its intoxicating scent. No one spoke.

The wind came as if to collect the fragile remains. She blew across the dark landscape, reducing each shell to ash and soot and carrying them seaward. Ground crews covered their eyes as human ashes passed over them on their way to their watery grave.

ଓ

"Jesus Christ," said Tiernan. "They're dead. They're all dead."

Marinella blessed herself and began imploring the Virgin's intercession. Graham sat silently, watching the screen move from one scorched region to another.

"How did this happen?" said Tiernan. "Does anyone know anything?"

"We will soon enough," said Graham. "This was too horrible to be an act of nature, as horrible as we know she can be. No, this was man's doing."

Marinella's rhythmic chanting of the Rosary continued as they watched the cameras pan the affected regions from the bird's-eye view of helicopters.

"Look," said Tiernan, "the fires seemed to stop at that point right there." He pointed to the screen.

"Indeed," said Graham. "Seems to have followed the path of the sun, hasn't it?"

"Yeah," said Tiernan, "the path of the sun."

CHAPTER 64

MARY LAY IN a pool of wine and glass, in and out of consciousness. An angry pain, unsure of where to settle, radiated throughout her body, distributing itself equally everywhere. It was too painful to move. Her eyes had blistered shut and attempting to open them sent searing pain into her skull. She wiggled her finger to see if she could and, when it responded, she was momentarily relieved. The moment passed quickly; consciousness brought with it the memory of what had happened.

She lay there for the next 18 hours, in and out of consciousness, praying for death. She would have killed herself if she'd had the strength but, instead, could only manage a weak moan. *Thirst will kill me,* she thought hopefully. Already the torture of dehydration stabbed at her; it was worse than any of the other torments. She felt like someone had poured hot sand down her throat. She began to hallucinate.

"Mommy?" she whimpered. "Help me, Mommy."

"Come on now, Mary," said Mommy. "You're gonna be late again. You want Sr. Claire to yell?" The hallucination handed her a bag lunch.

"I made your favorite, grape jelly sandwich with grape soda and grapes for dessert. Run along now, baby."

"Mah," said Mary. "I'm burnt." Unconsciousness.

☙

"Well there, me lovely lassie," sang the brogue. "The apple of me eye."

"Dah-de," said Mary. "Help me."

"What's that?" said Daddy. "No, no, no. A little girl shouldn't be asking for liquor. That's for grown-ups. How 'bout a bag of grape crisps."

He handed her a purple bag. Her father stood behind the bar, wiping down the counter. Mary sat in the Blarney Stone, waiting for her father to take her to the park after his shift.

"Eat your crisps," said Daddy.

"That bitch can't eat shit," said Vincent Tighte from across the bar. Daddy vanished, leaving Mary alone with Tighte. "Hurts, don't it? Good for you."

Mary moaned through the pain. Tighte taunted her. "Your friend Lori Adams got hers, too," he said, lifting grapes from a bowl on the bar. He tossed the grapes in the air and unsuccessfully tried to catch them in his mouth. They rolled on the floor next to Mary, who was transformed from a kindergartener into a full-grown woman.

"She squealed like a pig-whore," said Tighte, staring at Mary with reptilian eyes. "She fought every step of the way, but I know she loved it," he grunted and tried another grape toss, only to have it fall to the floor. Unconsciousness.

"Well, ain't you just a mess?" The voice brought her back to consciousness.

"Lorh," said Mary. She tried to open her eyes. Searing pain. She whimpered weakly.

"Now, ain't you a stubborn li'l thing?" said Lori. "Look at the mess you got yourself in. You shoulda just believed me."

"Sorr ee," said Mary. "Mmm burnt, ree-lee burnt."

"Well, why don't you just go ahead and drink it?" said Lori. "That's why I gave it to you, honey. Whatcha waiting for? Christmas?"

Lucidity passed over Mary. The Dionysinol, was it still in her pocket? Was it smashed from the fall down the stairs? What good would it do, even if it were still intact? She struggled to force her left hand to obey her command to move. Slowly, she lifted the arm and clumps of skin fell off, exposing more muscle tissue. The pain was comical now. If she could have, she would have laughed. Her arm made sounds similar to paper tearing as she maneuvered it closer to her pants pocket. She stopped and started a dozen times and gave up a dozen more, but managed to wrestle the intact vial from her pocket. Three of her fingernails peeled off as she attempted to break the wax seal surrounding the stopper. Her thumbnail peeled back and hung from her cuticle, but not before she popped the rubber stopper. Both the stopper and her nail fell to the ground. She lifted the vial to her mouth and poured the purple liquid in. Unconsciousness.

"Now you go to sleep, honey," said Lori. "I'll sing you the lullaby I wrote for my babies." The melody played in her mind until she woke with a start.

CHAPTER 65

"LORI? THANK GOD," said Connor, picking up the blinking line. "Where are you guys?"

"On the ocean. Why?" said Lori. The wind was making it difficult to hear. "Speak up. I can hardly hear ya."

"Lori, come back to New York," said Connor. "That place in Richard Tiernan's notes – Tír na nÓg – was torched to the ground along with thousands of people."

"Lord," said Lori, raising her hand to her mouth. "Do you think –"

"I don't know, but I'm not willing to find out. They already tried to have me killed. I sent Emily and the kids to our house in the Hamptons as a precaution. We need to stick together until the authorities get a handle on this shit," said Connor.

"Okay, I'm heading back now," said Lori. She disconnected the phone and went to Edward, who was happily steering the boat.

"Get to port, honey," said Lori.

"Phone broken again?" said Edward, assuming another mishap.

"Not exactly."

"Don't you find it particularly odd that Boroneddu, of all places, was the target of a terrorist attack?" said Graham, who was showing more black hair than gray now. His skin was tightening and his voice was sounding more youthful by the hour. "It seems too unpalatable for me," he continued.

"It was Falters, but how?" said Tiernan. "What would cause such devastation and remain isolated to the specific region?"

"The Niamh grapes were all destroyed. That had to be his main objective," speculated Graham. "He returned to Sardinia and found the Dionysinol missing and must have flown into a fit of rage."

"I don't think so," said Tiernan. "He expressed his desire to destroy the Dionysinol before. Besides, he's much too calculated to succumb to rage."

"Perhaps," said Graham, "but the end is the same, rage or calm. The Niamh grapes are obliterated."

"And all the research, too," said Tiernan. "It would take years to reproduce it using trial and error. He eradicated the plant and, hence, any chance of mass-producing Dionysinol."

Marinella came into the room and presented a bowl of fresh fruit for the two conversing men. "Ecco," she said as she placed the large bowl on the table between them. She pointed to the windowsill and made a face of disgust. "I uve tuoi sono disgustosi."

The thought occurred simultaneously in both their minds. *Could she have?* "Pardon me, Marinella," said Graham. "Where did you get those grapes by the window?"

"I pick them from Sardegna vineyard, but they are too, eh, bitter to eat," she said. "I make a very nice breakfast for me and Diego with them yesterday. I make for you now?" She rattled off the recipe that she had created impromptu, determined to find a use for the sour grapes her surrogate son owned.

"...and you take a shallot and a onions and chop up a very good," she continued, unaware that neither Graham nor Tiernan were listening. "You take a little a olive oil and fry the sausage with a the grapes. Buonissimo con un po' di patati friti."

"We ate yesterday, very good." She kissed her fingers and smiled. Two stalks of grapes sat on the windowsill, catching the sun's rays, refusing to wither.

"I'll extract the seeds," said Graham.

∛

"Okay. Call me when it's confirmed," said Agent DeAngelo. "Holy smokes." He ran down the corridor to the director's office, knocked once and rushed in. Director Robert Jones was mid-bite in his sandwich.

"Whoa," he said. "What the hell?"

"Sorry, boss," said DeAngelo, out of breath, "but you're never gonna believe what I just heard from Interpol."

Jones threw his sandwich on the wax paper. "Never a break," he said. "What?"

"The French police traced that little plane, you know the one the satellite caught right before the fires began in Sardinia?"

"Yeah, so?" said Jones. "Who gives?"

"You will, sir," said DeAngelo, putting the facsimile on the desk next to the tuna on rye.

"Yup, you heard it here first," said DeAngelo. "Registered to one Richard Tiernan, father of the fugitive Michael Tiernan, who is presumed to be at-large somewhere in Europe, probably in or around Corsica."

"Do they think he's responsible for the nukes or whatever the hell they dropped on Sardinia?" said Jones.

"Well, he's got a lot of explaining to do, in any case," said DeAngelo.

"Send Interpol everything we got on Tiernan," said Jones. "I want some of the credit if the Europeans arrest him first."

"Will do, sir," said DeAngelo. "And, by the way, you can smell that sandwich all the way down the hall."

"Get the hell outta my office and let me eat my lunch in peace," said Jones.

DeAngelo posted Tiernan's file to the Interpol database. Within minutes, his face was plastered across Europe. He checked for updates on the Sardinian situation. *Weapon unknown. Heavy casualties. No survivors found* scrolled across the bottom of the screen.

ᘓ

Mary jumped. Her eyelids no longer sealed shut, she looked around. She could feel her body in distinct parts now; it was no longer an undifferentiated mass of pain. Although the agony was still intense, it differed in a very noticeable way. She was going to survive this, but how she knew was a mystery. She remained lying on her back, moving body parts to check for mobility. Her head throbbed and her throat ached. *Water*, she thought. The desire for water compelled her to attempt locomotion. She struggled to sit up and managed after a few tries. She looked down at her hands and wished her eyes were still sealed shut. The burns were extensive. She would be scarred for life if she were to survive.

She tried to stand, but couldn't. She took an inventory of her options. She could either attempt to climb up the stairs or crawl on all fours through the tunnels and into the lab. She knew she was safer underground and probably couldn't climb the stairs anyway. Each movement forward sent pain rushing everywhere. The false wall had already been pulled back. Mary couldn't remember if she had initially tried to open it before passing out, but was grateful not to have to search for the lever. The journey of less than 70 yards took 40 minutes, each crawl forward threatening to be the last. Finally, she reached the glass doors.

Fueled with fury and summoning her last ounce of strength, Mary struggled to her feet and pressed the switch. Light bursts and cool air almost knocked her over as the fluorescents flicked to life and the glass doors slid mercifully open. She could tell by the diminished lumens and the distant hum that there was a generator somewhere nearby. *Thank you, thank you, thank you,* she thought. She rested for an hour before starting again.

Antibiotics, Mary thought. *I remember seeing injectables.* She slowly heaved herself up and slouched over the wheeled stool. *Much better,* she thought as she rolled slowly to the cabinets, taking advantage of her increased mobility.

Eureka, she thought, *the motherload.* She stabbed a penicillin injection into her thigh and headed over to the sink. She strained against the urge to gulp the water down. *Slowly,* she thought.

She rolled the stool as close to the couch as she could, and tried to climb onto it. She couldn't manage and settled for lying half of her body on the cushions, then slipped into unconsciousness.

Hours later, she woke up to find herself sprawled out on the couch.

How she got there, she didn't know. The lights were dimmer now and she wondered how long she had been asleep. She got up from the couch and noticed that the pain was nothing resembling the excruciating level it had been when she was last conscious. She walked with some difficulty to the sink and drank and drank. Instinct over reason, she gulped it down fast but suffered no ill effects. Another several gulps and she headed back to the couch. She slept and slept.

CHAPTER 66

"IT'S NOT SAFE here for you anymore," said Graham.

Tiernan looked out the window. The streets were abuzz with fear. Graham was right. Any American would now be scrutinized against the pictures on TVs everywhere. "I think that goes without saying," he said.

"Well, I thought I'd say it anyway," said Graham.

"Do you have any suggestions?" said Tiernan. "Besides hiding under a rock somewhere in the middle of Africa?"

"No, but I wouldn't rule that out either," said Graham. "Televisions aren't so abundant there."

"How could this have happened?" said Tiernan. "How could everything have fallen apart so fast, so completely?"

"Shhhh," said Graham, turning up the volume.

"...that's right, Paul. There doesn't seem to be any lasting damage and samples are confirming that the levels of ozone are consistent with the surrounding regions. I'll have more for you as the story develops. Back to you in the studio, I'm Frank Cassidy."

"Scientists believe that the weapon wasn't nuclear," said the anchorman, as images of Sardinia panned across the screen. "A team of international investigators are reviewing satellite images taken around Boroneddu moments before the tragedy." The screen changed to show an image of the dual-engine plane, spraying Dionysinol into the atmosphere. "The owner of the plane – Dr. Michael Tiernan – is wanted for questioning."

Tiernan stared at the blank screen. "I am screwed," he said. "Falters screwed me."

"You can't fly a plane," said Graham. "You couldn't have done it."

"I don't think they'll be too anxious to believe me, John," said Tiernan. "Should I turn myself in? Should I try to get to an American Embassy?"

Graham looked pensive. "We must determine how he used the Dionysinol to disable the ozone layer, only to have it reappear moments later," he said. "Ingenious."

"Yeah, it's amazing," said Tiernan. "I couldn't give a shit how, John. They think I killed thousands of people, burned them to death. I'll never get out of here alive." The rhythmic prayers began again, this time a duet. Diego's voice provided the bass while Marinella's, the sweet alto.

> Ave Maria, piena di grazia,
> il Signore è con te.
> Tu sei benedetta fra le donne
> e benedetto è il frutto del tuo seno, Gesú.
> Santa Maria, Madre di Dio,
> prega per noi peccatori,
> adesso e nell'ora della nostra morte.
> Amen.

"Holy Mary, Mother of God, pray for us sinners, now and at the hour of our death. Amen," said Tiernan.

There are no atheists in foxholes, thought Graham. The silent retreat ended abruptly when Marinella screamed in horror. Graham's hair was jet-black and his skin no longer hung loosely from his face. Marinella shrieked as she witnessed the incomprehensible. John Graham was young again.

"Great," said Tiernan. "This is exactly what the situation needed.

଼

"Marinella! Calmati, calmati. It's John Graham."

Diego ran into the room after hearing the commotion. One look at Graham and the mystery surrounding the cause of his wife's screaming was uncovered. There was no denying it was Graham, but it couldn't have been. This impostor was at least 50 years younger.

"Guarda, Diego," said Marinella. "Impossibile!"

"Yes, Marinella, it does seem impossible, but there's no need for alarm," said Graham. Graham hadn't seen his reflection since he had taken the Dionysinol. He lifted his hands to his face and felt his skin, searching for the jowls that were no longer there. His hair had always retained a certain thickness, but, clearly, it wasn't the same. He ran his fingers through his new thick, black mane.

"Well, I'll be," said Graham. "It seems to be working." He made his way into the bathroom to have the mirror confirm it. "My sweet Lord," he said. "There I am. I'm me again."

That happened really fast, thought Tiernan. *I didn't experience such a dramatic change.* He searched his mind for an explanation. *What if Falters gave me too low a dose?*

❧

Diego and Marinella were now eager to believe the story regarding the Dionysinol. Marinella went from panic to excitement as Tiernan recounted the story, which had been met with ridicule only 12 hours previously.

Blessed are those who do not see, yet still believe, thought Graham.

"So how much do we drink?" asked Diego. "One for each, yes?"

Tiernan had never considered the possibility that Diego and Marinella may have also wanted to enjoy the fruits of the miraculous discovery. He sat speechless, unable to answer for fear of the consequences of granting or denying their obvious request.

"Uno," said Marinella, holding up her finger. "John ha bebito uno. Ricordi?"

"Ah sí, sí," said Diego. "Yes, John drank only one. I remember."

Before Tiernan could protest, Graham had already handed each of them a vial of the elixir.

"Saluti," he said. "Cheers."

Pop, pop. Two more vials were gone and Homo Sapiens Immortalis had two new members.

⍥

Mary McKenna woke up. The thirst returned, forcing her to drink gigantic quantities again. A pink, tender layer of skin was forming over the area where the radiation and flames had burned the flesh down to the bone. She felt the water coarse through her, hydrating the new epidermis layer, changing its color as it did. She gently touched her face. It felt different too. The pain was still there, but tolerable. She gingerly caressed her scalp and felt peach fuzz – the seedlings that would repopulate the forest of hair she had once possessed. She noticed the mirror hanging on the distant wall, but wasn't brave enough to see what it had to show. She drank continuously, but the insatiable thirst remained. She drank until sleep called to her again.

She woke up and repeated the ritual.

⍥

Lori and Edward landed in LaGuardia Airport hours later. A sense of heightened anxiety filled the air. The obvious increase in security added to the feeling. Since the attack on Sardinia, many planes flew practically empty as spooked travelers canceled their reservations or simply didn't show up.

"Miss Adams," a voice called out. "Over here. Miss Adams?"

"He sent a car for you," said Edward, looking at the sign that read *Miss Lori Adams.*

"He sent a car for *us*," said Lori, locking arms with her new husband. "We're a package deal now, darlin'."

Edward smiled, but his smiled broadened considerably when Lori spoke to the man holding the sign.

"It's Mrs. Adams now." She held up her ring for the man to admire. "Let's get outta here," said Lori, "I've got a bad feelin' 'bout all this."

"Uh, excuse me, Mrs. Adams," said the driver, lowering the privacy window. Lori and Edward were like two school kids caught smooching.

"Yes?" said Edward.

"Uh, Mrs. Adams," said the driver, "Mr. Connor has asked that I take you to the mansion. He said he'd join you there."

"Fine with me," said Lori. "Now, give us a li'l privacy, would ya?" She closed the window and resumed kissing the man she realized she had loved all along.

CHAPTER 67

"I'M AFRAID THAT won't do," said Falters. "I need to fly directly to Montreal, and I must leave shortly. I have a very important business meeting tomorrow."

"I've already told you, we cannot accommodate your request," said the young ticket agent. "We have so few flights leaving the island, and the only one scheduled to land in Montreal is already overbooked."

"Mon cherie," said Falters, "I cannot express how much I would be indebted to you if I were to be in Montreal tonight." He leaned in closer to the young lady, gazing into her eyes. Her knees weakened as the lust hit her with ruthless force. She reached across the counter and kissed him. When Falters attempted to pull back, she aggressively grabbed him by the hair, moaning. Only when her manager intervened was the enchantment suspended.

"Michelle!" shouted the manager. A series of commands followed and the young, embarrassed ticket agent was replaced.

"I am so sorry, Monsieur," said the manager. "That was inexcusable. I don't know what to say."

"This doesn't have to be a major incident," said Falters. "I know how we can make everything right."

Within three minutes, the manager had deleted the first passenger on the list and checked Falters' single bag straight through to Montreal.

"I put you in first class. Your flight is boarding in 20 minutes. Enjoy your flight, and thank you for flying Air Corsica."

"Merci," said Falters. He took the ticket and headed over to the Internet terminals.

ᔆ

"Graham," shouted Tiernan, "what the hell are you doing? How could you be so reckless? I thought you understood."

Graham was sitting on the couch next to the newly-hatched immortals. He looked up at Tiernan.

"Would you keep it all to yourself? Would you deny it to even your family?" said Graham. "Immortality would be a lonely reality if one were to endure it alone. You've experienced the death of the two most significant people in your life. Imagine knowing that everyone around you will die and you, alone, will not."

Tiernan was ashamed. Marinella and Diego were like family to him. *What kind of a man am I?* he thought.

Marinella and Diego were talking rapidly. Clearly affected by the euphoria, they listed the things they wanted to do with their youth that would be arriving shortly. They held each other's hands, giddy with glee, stopping to occasionally rise from the couch and kiss Graham and Tiernan repeatedly.

"John," said Tiernan. "Your transformation occurred rapidly, much more so than my own."

"You have a point," said Graham. "Perhaps the older the subject, the more dramatic the effects. You seem to have reached a plateau."

Tiernan looked at Marinella and Diego, who were still lost in each other's eyes.

"Thank you, John," said Tiernan. "I don't know if I would've given it to them." He lowered his eyes in shame and confusion at his own motivation.

"Everything is much clearer now," said Graham. "I see patterns in everything, interconnected reality laced through all being. Do you know what I mean?"

"No," said Tiernan. "I haven't experienced any of the effects that Falters said I would. My hearing is still the same, my eyesight, my memory –" He looked at Marinella and Diego again. "With the exception of increased vigor and a few days of insomnia, I'm the same."

"I suppose you do look a little younger," said Graham. "It just wasn't as dramatic a change as mine. Didn't need all that much work." Graham smiled.

"Okay," Tiernan sighed, "let's see if there were any new developments." He switched on the TV. "The incident in Sardinia is affecting the weather all over Europe. Look at those storms!"

Graham and Tiernan were too engrossed to notice that Diego and Marinella had stopped talking. The Rosary prayers that would have certainly been prompted by such an event were conspicuously absent. Marinella and Diego were dead on the couch, smiles still on their faces, frozen in time.

"Michael," said Graham, "turn off the TV."

Tiernan was still glued to the set. *How can this be happening? I must be dreaming,* he thought. *This whole life, my whole fictitious existence is just a horrible dream. I'm gonna wake up soon and be someone else, somewhere else, somewhere safe. I'm not Michael Tiernan; I'm someone else, someone better.*

"Michael," said Graham. "They're dead."

Tiernan turned. "Who's dead?"

The words were hardly out of his mouth when his brain made intelligible what his eyes wouldn't believe. Their eyes were still open, their smiles taunting him. The room spun and he felt as if the temperature had jumped 1,000 degrees. He couldn't speak, cry or react in any other way. He had almost nothing left inside.

ॐ

They carried the corpses of Diego and Marinella Santarelli and laid them on the bed. A picture of young Michael Tiernan was placed prominently on the nightstand. He couldn't have been more than 14 years old when it was taken.

"Michael," said Graham. "I'm so sorry. We couldn't have known."

"You dumb bastard!" said Tiernan. "I told you not to give it to them. You killed them. You're responsible for this."

Graham didn't respond. Although he now looked younger than

Tiernan, he was nevertheless his senior and had the good sense not to argue with a man on the edge – it could go either way. Tiernan could transform yet again and rise like a phoenix out of the ashes of disaster, or burrow deep into the ground and lay in a grave of his own making.

Tiernan looked at the two smiling corpses lying on the bed and broke down. Falling to his knees, he sobbed as he never had before, the months of tribulation culminating in that moment. Graham saw in him the young, mischievous boy who had terrorized the office staff any time the watchful eye of his father had slacked in its vigilance. He saw the graduate holding his diploma, his whole life ahead of him. He saw the broken man standing over the grave of his father, unsure of how to proceed without him.

Graham bent down, laid his hands on Tiernan's shoulders and attempted to console him. Tiernan reacted, violently throwing Graham's hands off his shoulders, cursing him, everyone and everything before breaking down again, crying into his hands.

"Master Tiernan," said Graham, "I'm afraid I must go to Termini Station now. Dr. Lewis should be arriving very shortly. I will be back as soon as I can."

Graham wasn't sure if Tiernan had heard him or if he was too grief-stricken to care what he had to say. In any event, he left to collect Debra Lewis as he had promised he would.

CHAPTER 68

MARY MCKENNA WIPED her mouth with the back of her hand. Her hands were feeling better and the peach fuzz covering her head was becoming thicker. Scars where the blisters had burst were now a pinkish color but looked better than they had a few hours previous. She mustered up the courage to face the mirror. It was less horrid than she had expected, but more horrible than she wished. She was definitely healing rapidly. There was no other explanation: Dionysinol had remarkable properties. If it held the key to eternal youth, as Lori swore it did, Mary could not bring herself to believe it. She scavenged the lab for any trace of food. Nothing. She drank another gallon of water before deciding to leave.

She attempted to leave the same way she had entered, but the exit was heavily blocked with soot, ash and hundreds of pounds of housing material. She didn't let fear dominate. She walked back to the lab, remembering the alternate entrance. Hopefully, it would lead her above ground.

She walked for hours. The complete darkness and her limited mobility made for a slow, but steady, pace. She leaned against the walls of the tunnels to retain her balance and, whenever she felt like stopping, imagined how good it would feel when she could lie down on a bed with silk sheets while the doctors gave her generous doses of morphine for the pain. It worked rather well.

The tunnel ended abruptly. The wall blocking her path forward was slate and gave way under pressure. It was heavy, too heavy for Mary to move, so, instead, she rocked it loose and let it fall backwards. A small, dank crawl space presented itself and she had no other choice but to continue what she had started. After reaching the end of the crawl space, she found herself in a mausoleum. She crawled out and dusted herself off. She was in the ancient graveyard of San Pietro in the neighboring town of Zuri. She pushed the doors open, stepped out into the twilight and cried when she wasn't greeted with a nuclear wasteland. Trees blew in the wind and grass bent under her feet. She was alerted to the presence of a family visiting the grave of a loved one via the screams of terror after seeing Mary emerge from the mausoleum. *Maybe this will be funny someday,* she thought as she tried to convince them she wasn't a ghoul. Her naked breasts, bald head and burnt skin didn't make it an easy sell.

☙

The ambulance took a long time to get there. Ghilarza Memorial Hospital was gone and would've been ill-equipped to treat her condition adequately, anyway.

After they stopped screaming, the family making their monthly visit to the graveyard realized that perhaps the ghoul was a refugee from the Boroneddu disaster, and the Sardinian spirit of kindness took over. Two men, one burly and the other thin, carried Mary to a nearby house where she was given first-aid. The women cleaned her with soft, damp cloths, careful not to tear the newly forming skin. Much to the chagrin of the paramedics who arrived on the scene later, the women rubbed a mixture of oil and aloe on her burns and covered her with a soft sheet.

Mary was surrounded by people who, upon hearing the news, came in to catch a glimpse of the sole survivor of the disaster, yet she fell fast asleep under the cool sheet. The people lowered their voices to a whisper and began a queue that stretched outside.

She looked like a relic – Joan of Arc perhaps – lying there, eyes closed peacefully, a contented expression on her face, hands folded as if in prayer. The house became a reliquary until the ambulance arrived and whisked her away.

I made it, she repeated over and over to herself. *The Nuragic tunnels saved me.* She whispered a sincere thank you to the ancient people.

 CS

Thousands of miles away, in a rat-infested landfill, something stirred beneath a mountain of filth and decay. Tighte's hand emerged victoriously from the death shroud of plastic and duct tape as he continued to free himself from the premature burial site. He was dizzy, disoriented and incredulous. *I'm in a dump,* he realized as he attempted to open his mouth. The black threads still held firm, although the wax was chipping away. The self-inflicted puncture wounds were now a breeding ground for the flies. He removed a squirming maggot from one of the gaping holes in his face. *Oh, this bitch is gonna pay,* he thought as he made his way down a hill of waste. Rats scurried out of his path as he blew air out of the punctures in his face, attempting to dispel more of the squirming maggots. *I'm coming to get you, Lori Adams. I'm coming for you.*

CHAPTER 69

GRAHAM WAITED FOR the cab to arrive. He longed to see her expression, her incredulity, at what her eyes would present to her. Graham was young and handsome, but, most importantly, in love. He debated whether he should profess his love immediately or wait for the initial shock to pass. But she never arrived.

∞

"Rome," said Debra, "one way." She handed her passport to the agent and looked around. She was more nervous than she had ever been in her life. *What am I doing?* she thought. *I'm fleeing the country?* She snatched the passport back. "Forget it. I changed my mind." She ran out of the terminal and hailed a cab. *I'm going to hide out until this is all over,* she thought. *They'll understand. Please understand, Michael.*

∞

Graham had given Debra specific instructions when they spoke last. He took out the Italian equivalent of the Tracfone™ he had purchased when the shops had finally opened earlier that morning. No calls. Did she make a mistake while writing down the number? Was the phone broken and unable to receive the numerous calls Debra Lewis was frantically making? His head swam. He walked over to the pay phone and dropped in a few coins. It rang. *No,* he thought, *the phone works and Debra Lewis is a scientist; details are her livelihood, so she didn't make a mistake writing down the number. Something's wrong.* He hailed a cab back to Trastevere.

"Stop here," said Graham. The commotion on the streets clearly reflected the horror of what had happened at Tír na nÓg. Cars choked the cobblestone streets. Panic was brewing and the typically peaceful Italian population was behaving erratically. Graham paid the driver and ran down the street to Viccolo del Cinque. When he arrived at the apartment, Tiernan was standing in front of the television.

"I know what we have to do," said Tiernan. He didn't take his eyes off the screen.

"What?" said Graham.

"We need to bring this stuff to the American Embassy," said Tiernan. "Here, help me carry it; we don't have much time."

Graham instinctively obeyed and took one of the handles. "Wait. Put it down."

Tiernan looked up. "What?"

"The Embassy will be mobbed," he said. "We'll never get in, especially carrying a case of unidentified liquid."

"But another attack could occur at any moment. It's that simple."

"Tell me everything that you know," said Graham. "How's he doing it?"

Tiernan sat with Graham and told him what little information he knew about Project Brimstone. Graham sat with characteristic patience, reserving judgment and comment until it was his turn.

"This is why we need to get to the American Embassy," said Tiernan. "With these." He held the Dionysinol in his hand. "With Tír na nÓg destroyed, the vials in front of you could very well be the only existing samples left."

Graham sighed. His young face and youthful voice produced cognitive dissonance in Tiernan. Graham's mannerisms were still those of an elderly man, behaviors held over from another generation. It made Tiernan uneasy.

"We must get to work immediately. We have to find an antidote or a counter-weapon or something," said Tiernan.

"Young man," said Graham without intention of condescension, "it is for that reason exactly that we must NEVER give the Americans the Dionysinol."

"Huh?" said Tiernan. "Were you watching the same thing I was? Falters has weaponized it. Who knows how much Dionysinol he has stockpiled without my father's knowledge. We could be reduced to ash at any moment."

"Perhaps," said John, "but if we give the technology to the Americans, we will certainly perish."

"How do you figure?" said Tiernan.

"Fear induces violence. Along with creating a weapon to reverse the effects of whatever Falters is doing to the ozone, the Pentagon will undoubtedly find offensive uses too. With the way things are going, nuclear strikes aren't inconceivable."

In the other room, Diego and Marinella were decomposing rapidly. It wasn't long after Graham had shut the window that the smell hit them. He went to close the bedroom door where the couple lay on the bed, smiles still holding under the decaying flesh. He took one look and fought the waves of nausea until he couldn't any longer. He dry-heaved repeatedly over the toilet. Tiernan, investigating the sound, opened the door and peered into the room where his surrogate parents lay rotting before his eyes. The sight overwhelmed him. He tried to remain conscious, but passed out and fell limp to the ground.

Graham covered his nose with a soaked towel to mitigate the revolting smell. Holding it tightly to his face, he dragged Tiernan's unconscious body into the living room and shut the door to the bedroom. He soaked all of the towels readily available in the bathroom and threw them against the bottom of the bedroom door in an attempt to contain the stench. Then, he turned to the Dionysinol and began emptying the vials down the drain. His intention was to destroy all of the remaining supply – all but the one he'd slipped into his pocket, the one that he would offer to Debra Lewis.

⌃

"Wake up," said Graham, slapping him again. "Come on now." Tiernan jumped to his feet, realizing that it wasn't a nightmare. This was really happening.

"We can't stay here," said Graham. "The neighbors can certainly smell that."

Tiernan felt it coming. A surge of vomit coughed out as he ran to the bathroom. The smell was supernatural. He wiped his mouth and rinsed it out with water he slurped from the tap.

"John! What the hell did you do?" he said, looking into the bathtub at all the emptied vials. Tiernan ran out to find Graham continuing the process in the kitchen sink.

"We must," said Graham. "It's the only way." He popped another seal and poured the precious liquid down the drain.

Tiernan froze. He commanded his fists to fly, legs to kick, teeth to bite, but to no avail. Everything was reduced to slow motion. An entire case was gone, empty vials lying in the bathtub. Half of the second case was discarded on the kitchen floor. Graham bent down to retrieve another handful of the Dionysinol before blackness enveloped him.

Tiernan stood over him, still holding the heavy cast-iron skillet where Marinella had fried the Niamh grapes the morning before. Tiernan felt Graham's skull crack with the second blow as he unleashed his fury and fear. Graham lay bleeding profusely on the kitchen floor, the pool of blood widening exponentially. Tiernan threw the skillet down, put the remaining vials of Dionysinol in a backpack and ran out the door.

☙

Falters quickly logged on to the Internet. He glanced at the news. Storms were lashing all over Italy, probably a side effect of the Brimstones. It was chaos theory epitomized. Coastal regions were bombarded with fierce tides, burying entire towns under water; thousands of people were stranded and left for dead and many more would perish. He opened the browser and created an e-mail account.

Leave nothing to chance, he thought. *Put just enough information to warrant attention, and the FBI and the CIA will apprehend Connor and Tiernan for me.* He began typing the e-mail message.

To Whom It May Concern:

I am Ryan Connor of Lionel Pharmaceuticals and I'm being held against my will in my own home. The attacks on Sardinia are only the beginning. The CEO of Oisín Pharmaceuticals, Dr. Michael Tiernan, is responsible for everything. His company produced the weapon used in the attacks. Tell your scientists that the weapon temporarily disables the ozone layer.

After re-routing his e-mail message to cloak its origin, Falters got up and boarded the plane.

CHAPTER 70

"DEPARTMENT OF JUSTICE, how may I direct your call?" said the operator.

"Get me someone important," said Tiernan, covering his face, paranoid that someone would recognize him.

"You'll have to be a little more specific, sir," said the operator.

"I have information regarding the attacks on Sardinia, so put me through to someone important, okay, sweetheart, or maybe the next target will be Washington," said Tiernan.

❧

"Start the voice analysis on three, two, one," said Cody Barron. "Dr. Tiernan," he said, "this is Special Agent Barron."

"I was framed, goddammit," said Tiernan. "My face is plastered all over the goddamn TV."

"Where are you? We can send someone to get you. We'll keep you safe," said Agent Barron, keeping an eye on the monitor. *Analyzing...*

"I know how he did it, how he killed them," said Tiernan, eyes wide with the fear of being recognized.

"He's in a phone booth in Rome, Italy," wrote another agent, slipping the paper to Agent Barron.

"It's him," mouthed another.

Agent Barron looked up at the monitor: 97.4 percent match. He grimaced to the onlookers and spun his finger aggressively in the air. The room dispersed in seconds.

"I want some guarantees," said Tiernan. "I want immunity for the Regenerol trials." Interagency cooperation was still a taboo subject; the

Department of Justice was still days behind and hadn't received the updated information on Tiernan.

"Dr. Tiernan," said Agent Barron, "we can talk about this when you come in." He tried to stall him as long as possible. The CIA agents were en route.

"Ryan Connor set me up," said Tiernan. "Don't let him leave the country, trust me. He has the technology to reproduce the weapon."

Within minutes, Tiernan was pulled out of the phone booth and thrown to the ground.

"Careful with the bag, dumb ass," he said.

Three agents threw him in the back of a car and sped off.

"Where are you guys taking me?" said Tiernan.

"Back home," said the sunglassed agent. "You're in for a long day."

Within two hours of the phone call, Michael Tiernan was on a private plane flying directly to Washington. Four of the precious vials had broken after he was thrown to the ground. The agents sealed his backpack in an airtight bag. The purple liquid gathered ominously at the bottom.

"Go ahead," said the agent, holding his ear. He listened intently. His expression was foreboding and Tiernan was an expert at detecting bad news by now.

"We've been ordered to change course. We're landing in Zone Eight."

Tiernan looked out the window. The clouds rolled hypnotically, peacefully obscuring the pandemonium below.

જી

John Graham was carried out on a stretcher and loaded into the ambulance. Unable to endure the smell any longer, neighbors had alerted the police, who had found Graham unconscious and bleeding on the kitchen floor. He didn't regain consciousness until they arrived at Fate Bene Fratelli Hospital.

"We had to give you a blood transfusion," said a young nurse, tucking the sheets snugly under his body. "You were very lucky."

The heart monitor blinked a few times and the lights flickered. A deafening crack followed by darkness caused a moment's panic. The screaming was diminished when the back-up power system kicked in and restored some of the lights. Another series of cracks and flashes preceded the roar of torrential downpours. This was no ordinary rain.

"You were saying about my being lucky, dear?" said Graham, wrestling his hand free from the nurse's grip of steel.

"When the stampede finishes outside," said Graham, moving the nurse's face in his direction, "would you be so kind as to bring me my personal effects? Thank you so much."

Graham laid back and thought of Debra Lewis. He wondered if the single vial of Dionysinol had survived. When the nurse returned with the box containing his bloody clothes, Graham immediately checked his pants pocket. The vial was intact – dirtied with blood, but intact.

"Please be safe, dear," he whispered, "I'll come for you."

CHAPTER 71

THE UNMARKED CARS stopped at the gate.

"Sorry for the inconvenience," said the agent. "But we have our orders. We need to verify that Mr. Connor is okay."

The elderly security guard grumbled his way out of the gatehouse. "Mr. Connor is fine, I assure you. Now, if you please, he isn't receiving any guests today."

"Trust me, I'm sure he's fine, but we're not dropping by for tea and biscuits. We just need to speak with him for a moment. Now open the gate so we can get this over with."

"If you ain't got a warrant, you ain't coming in," said the security guard, a little more forcefully. He pressed the intercom and shouted.

"Mr. Connor, there are a couple of cops or –"

One agent disconnected the system; the other pressed the knob and opened the gate.

"Please relax, sir," said the agent, easily fending off the gallant efforts of the security guard. "Please don't struggle." The agent cuffed the old man's arms behind his back.

"Lori, Edward, the cops are on their way up the driveway," shouted Connor, looking into a security monitor. Edward's life flashed before his eyes and Lori just froze.

"They musta suspected us and investigated the house," said Lori.

"Maybe they found the body in the dump," suggested Edward.

"What should we do?" asked Lori who, up to that point, never even believed that getting caught was a possibility. Panic hit her when the pounding on the door was followed by univocal finality.

"FBI, open the door."

Connor headed to the door.

"Don't open it," said Edward.

Connor had always believed that he would do anything for Lori Adams, but when he was put to the test, he stood corrected. Apparently, his freedom ranked first among all. *They can't prove my involvement,* thought Connor. *If I don't open the door, they'll nail me for harboring fugitives.* The pounding was more forceful this time.

"FBI, open up."

"I can't. I just can't," said Lori, looking at Edward. "I can't go to prison." Edward took out a gun.

The young agent walked two feet into the house. Before he could state his purpose, the bullet was already fired. Lori screamed and ran upstairs. The second agent returned fire, shooting Edward twice in the chest. Edward got off another round before falling dead to the ground, missing his intended target. Connor was caught in the crossfire. The bullet entered the back of his head, killing him instantly. The second agent called for backup and headed after Lori, who was apprehended moments later. She never saw the dead bodies of the two most important people in her life.

k

Tiernan was blindfolded upon landing and led into a black SUV waiting on the airstrip. "My lawyer is going to have a field day with this one," he said. "I hope you realize that you've violated my constitutional rights. You have heard of the Constitution, haven't you? Anyone?"

"Different times, Dr. Tiernan," replied an agent with a raspy voice. "Besides, I don't think the founding fathers would object to our treatment of terrorists."

"Terrorist? I'm a terrorist? If you morons are the only thing protecting us from our enemies, then God help us! I want to speak with my lawyer." The anxiety was gaining strength. "Take this hood off."

Tiernan began to struggle against the handcuffs in an attempt to remove the blindfold. "I can't breathe."

"Should have thought of that before you burned thousands of people to death," said the agent.

Panic enveloped him. He lost control and started flailing and shouting incoherently.

"Would you calm him down, please?" requested the driver.

"No problem." The agent removed his taser and ran a powerful surge of electricity through Tiernan.

The shouting was replaced with a stifled grunt of pain. Tiernan's body convulsed violently as the agent shocked him a little longer than necessary. The agent removed the hood. Foamy saliva oozed from Tiernan's mouth. His eyes were fixed, glassy and dilated.

"He's quiet now, sir," said the agent. Should I keep the hood off?"

"Ah, goddamn it, Carl," shouted the agent sitting directly next to Tiernan. A steady stream of urine collected along the seams of the leather seats and ran under the agent. "I told you not to put those tasers on full strength. Ah, man!" He lifted himself up and let the yellow river run its course.

The other agents fortunate enough to have escaped the flood laughed. Tiernan stared straight ahead, eyes wide open, drool running down his shirt.

☙

"Get this one a shower, but bag his clothes. We don't want forensics to have a cow," said the agent in charge, shoving Tiernan along. "When he's done, bring him into Interrogation Room 2."

"Yes, sir," said Special Agent Sarah Dylan. Sarah took the handcuffed and shackled Tiernan by the forearm and led him away. She walked quickly and Tiernan had to struggle to keep up, his gait limited to baby steps – the sound of the chains taunting him.

"Strip and shower," said Sarah.

"You're staying?" said Tiernan, suddenly possessed by an abundance of humility. His mouth was still affected by the taser and a line of drool escaped before he quickly mopped it up with his palm.

"Yep," said Sarah, "nothing I haven't seen before."

Tiernan was drying himself as he looked down at the orange jumpsuit awaiting him. "This can't be real. This can't be happening. I'm the CEO of a company. I have a doctorate, a house in Italy, cars, women – you're making a huge mistake."

He looked at himself in the mirror. A single grey hair sprung from the part in his exclusively brown mane. He had never noticed it before and, although it wouldn't have mattered under any other conceivable circumstance, the little grey strand spoke volumes.

"Falters! You stupid son of a bitch," shouted Tiernan, punching the mirror. A second, but less intense, round of tasing brought his tirade to a screeching halt.

❧

"Tell us what you know and I'm sure we can find a more comfortable arrangement for you," said Agent Dylan.

"How many times do I have to tell you? I'm not the man you're looking for – I've been framed, goddamnit."

"Yeah? By who?"

Tiernan knew that he was fighting a losing battle. *Yeah, it was the strange Russian man with the indefinite lifespan,* he thought. They would never believe such a convoluted story. Truth is often more difficult to digest than fiction.

"I want my lawyer. You can't keep me here," shouted Tiernan, struggling under the excruciatingly painful force of his own body weight. "I know my rights, goddamn it."

"Apparently, you don't," said Sarah. "Under the Patriot Act, we can hold you indefinitely."

"Miss, can I ask you something?" said Tiernan. The agent nodded.

"What is your name? I don't even know your name."

"You don't need to know my name, Doctor Tiernan," she said. "You need to tell me who you're working with and how the attacks were carried out."

Tiernan fell to the ground, no longer able to remain in the stress position. He curled into the fetal position, pulling his knees as tightly to his chest as he could manage.

Sarah looked up at the closed-circuit camera. Her bosses were definitely watching, waiting for the opportunity to point out her weakness, to tell her that she let her emotions get the better of her. But the pathetic sight was too powerful.

"Get up, Doctor Tiernan," she said as she stood over him. She hunkered down and looked into his eyes.

"What is your name? Please, tell me your name," cried Tiernan.

"It's Sarah Dylan," she whispered, hoping her colleagues hadn't witnessed her compassion. "Get up."

"My mother's name was Sarah," said Tiernan, before releasing a howl of pain and despair. "My mother's name was Sarah."

☙

Flying back into the United States from Rome proved to be more difficult than John Graham had expected. He didn't have any identification, which would have been useless with his new and improved body anyway, and he wasn't sure if the authorities had linked him to the Mexican trials. If Graham were to return to America, he would have to get creative.

International travel by train, one of the advantages of the European continent, was less difficult. With the help of a young Italian man who was less than scrupulous with his identification, Graham found a way. He traded his expensive Rolex in exchange for Marco Paola's Italian passport and the guarantee that Signore Paola wouldn't report it missing for seven days. The resemblance between Paola and Graham wasn't compelling, but it wasn't suspicious either. If Paola didn't realize that the watch was one of Chinatown's finest bootlegs before Graham made it across the border, he had a chance. *Just a little more luck,* thought Graham, *and I'll see her again.* He clutched the vial of Dionysinol tightly as he approached the travel agency.

From Rome, Graham took a night train to France where he took the Chunnel to England. His innate charm, strengthened by the effects of the Dionysinol, made getting a quality fake British passport much easier. Women were especially eager to help this young, handsome man

373

who was lucky to be alive. Many of them wanted to offer additional, more intimate consolation to the poor boy whose dream vacation to Sardinia almost ended in tragedy, but Graham's heart was already taken. Debra Lewis was somewhere else, and Graham would stop at nothing to get to her. As the plane took off from Heathrow Airport, Graham slept and dreamt of her.

∝

Graham's search led him to the Taverna Thalia. Miniature brass bells chimed as the door shut behind him, sealing him in the air-conditioning of the Greek café. He walked through the quaint interior. Sumptuous aromas teased his hunger, but he was fueled by adrenaline now and paid little attention to the sensory stimulation. A glass door at the back of the restaurant opened to a spacious patio of whitewashed brick and sky-blue walls contrived to resemble an authentic Greek café. He stepped into the courtyard bathed in the afternoon sun. His eyes readjusted for a moment. Then, he saw her.

Debra had seated herself at a small table in the back corner where she had an unobstructed view of the terrace entrance. The western corner of the patio was also adjacent to a small passageway that led to a gate that opened to the street. She had requested the same table where she had sat each day between the hours of 2:00 p.m. and 4:00 p.m. for the past 12 days. She was unaware that she looked pretty. The peach-colored sundress she wore was a remnant from a christening she had attended last summer and was chosen for function rather than fashion. The blanching light revealed, however, that the last nearly two weeks were not easy for Debra Lewis.

She held a book in one hand and stabbed at an olive in the meze she had thought she wanted and had been pretending to eat for an hour and a half. Her coffee cup sat overturned on its saucer. After a moment, Debra looked up from the book she'd been pretending to read and saw him.

Her stomach churned and sweat instantly formed on her palms, then her forehead. Her mouth went dry. Graham smiled broadly. His heart pumped wildly as he approached her.

"Hercules has prevailed, my dear, and you look more beautiful than all the Olympian goddesses combined."

Debra Lewis let the book drop to the floor and rose to stand before the handsome young man with a thick, glossy mane of short black hair, a rugged jaw and wide, winsome smile. *Impossible,* she thought, but her soul knew better. The features, the gait, the voice, the gestures were all familiar, but it wasn't possible. Yet, something in his deep brown eyes spoke of the many years he'd seen, the many years he'd spent alone in longing.

Her brow furrowed and tears welled up in her eyes. "John?" she said as she found herself stepping gingerly around the table.

"Yes, my dear," he said, taking her hand and guiding her toward him.

Emboldened by his newly found youth and seized by unparalleled desire, Graham dispensed with the decorum that had been his hallmark, wrapped his arm around Debra's waist and drew her into a tight embrace. Hundreds of tiny sparks ignited in Debra's veins and every atom of her being fired with delight. She felt the ease and comfort of a friendship forged of trust, respect and time, permeated with a desire so primal, so all-consuming that she could only obey it.

"My dear, my Aphrodite," he said, leaning back to look into her eyes. "I've been granted a second youth." Taking her hands, he stepped back and then, in the only gesture he felt befitting, he knelt on one knee. "It is but an eternity in Hades without you at my side."

"But how?"

Graham opened her hand and rested the vial of Dionysinol gently on her palm before he closed her fingers around it.

"Eternity is yours if you desire it. While there are very few certainties in this mysterious existence we have, I can offer you one: I have always loved you, my dear, and I will continue to love you until the end of time."

℃ß

Agents Barron and Moccia looked at Tiernan through the one-way glass. "He's broken," said Moccia. "I think he's ready."

"Yeah, but he always looks ready. You wanna try this time?" said Barron.

"Nah, you're better at this. Go for it."

The agent entered the interrogation room. Tiernan barely lifted his eyes.

"Dr. Tiernan," said the agent, "I'm agent Barron."

Tiernan started to babble incoherently.

"He is almost 90 years old, but he looks about 30. Russian, blue eyes, blond hair. He's about six-foot three or four and pretty built. He fought in WWII and he hates Nazis."

"Who are you talking about?"

"Ivan Falters, goddamn it! I told you people everything I know."

"No, Dr. Tiernan. You told us a bunch of bullshit. Now, are you going to come clean or are you gonna stick with that ridiculous story?"

"Forever," he said. "I was going to live forever. And with money, money to burn! I had everything and that bastard, that filthy bastard, ruined it." Tiernan wiped his nose with his orange sleeve. "Ryan Connor ruined my life and Ivan Falters stole eternity from me," he bellowed. "It was mine, goddamn it, my father gave it to me!" Tiernan pounded his fist on the table and stood abruptly, knocking over the chair. He paced back and forth in the small, mirrored room, gnashing his teeth.

"Dr. Tiernan, I suggest you calm down and tell us how you did it. That's all you need to do," said Barron.

Tiernan stopped before the one-way mirror and held up his fists. Pausing for a moment, he opened them in front of his face. Gazing into his open hands, he muttered wistfully, "I had eternity in the palm of my hand."

Agent Barron approached him cautiously and slipped the handcuffs around his outstretched wrists. "Alright, Peter Pan, back to Neverland. Lucky for you, with the Patriot Act, you'll have just about an eternity to ponder it all."

Shackled and defeated, Tiernan was escorted back to his cell. As the door slid closed, the darkness enveloped him. He huddled in the corner of the cold cell. Again, he waited for his eyes to adjust, but the blackness was an impenetrable shroud, a pall from under which he could see absolutely nothing. He felt like he was suffocating. Then the voices began again – first, as whispers.

"One month," it hissed.

"No," moaned Tiernan, pulling his knees into his chest.

"You had to have everything – and more!" the other growled.

"You wouldn't listen to anyone, you fool," the guttural voices rebuked him. "In one month, you destroyed what your father spent his whole life creating!"

"Daddy! I'm sorry! I ruined everything – I'm sorry!" shouted Tiernan, as he lay curled in the fetal position. "Please leave the door open a little! Daddy, tell them to leave the door open a little!" Sobbing now, he rocked himself to and fro. "It's so dark. Mommy's making pancakes in the morning," he whimpered.

"Daddy and Mommy are gone, Mikey." A cacophony of cackles echoed through the tiny chamber. "The money is gone. The elixir is gone. Your freedom is gone."

Tiernan pressed his palms to his ears, but couldn't drown out the sound. "Don't worry, Mikey, we will never leave you!"

CHAPTER 72

FALTERS SAT IN the comfortable, first-class seat. *Three affected females*, he thought. *They're too close. I have no other choice.* He unbuckled his seat belt and headed to the restroom.

"Excuse me, sir," said the flight attendant, "we're preparing for takeoff. Please return to your seat."

"I'm afraid I need to respond to nature's urgent call."

The flight attendant locked eyes with Falters, blushed and wondered why her heart raced so energetically. "Please hurry, sir," she said. "I wouldn't want you to get hurt." She smiled bashfully and lowered her head without taking her eyes off the inexplicably alluring passenger.

Falters locked the flimsy door and confirmed the green light read *occupied* before he removed the large jar of vapor rub. As a boy, Falters' father had often used menthol or other powerfully odiferous compounds to cloak the scent the mares emitted. Unable to detect nature's beckon, the stallions had ignored the fertile females.

He stripped down to his underwear, lavished the sticky and awfully potent-smelling ointment everywhere. Streams of tears flowed from his icy blue eyes as the menthol vapors rose. When he returned to his seat, the flight attendant returned to offer Falters a beverage.

"Red wine, please," said Falters. He waited. Would she swoon?

"We have a nice merlot from the Tuscan region, a delicious Chianti from Sicily and a dry variety from Sardinia," said the flight attendant, paying no more attention to Falters than she did to her other patrons.

"The Sardinian wine, please."

"Very good, sir." No signs of irrepressible lust there.

A couple of newlyweds asked if there were any seats available in coach after the smell exuded by the rude passenger became unbearable. *Works very well. Thank you, father.*

☏

Falters entered the motel room, laid his bag on the bed and opened it. Wrapped in layers of clothes, the chimaeraic Niamh seeds had survived the transatlantic flight. He sealed the canister tightly and placed it on the bedside table, next to his last remaining vials of Dionysinol.

For hours, Falters sat amidst newspaper clippings, police reports, diagrams and an intricate flowchart with multiple branches connecting people to corporations, corporations to people and everything to money. He removed the simple black notepad from his breast pocket and jotted the last name to the short list, adding a series of three question marks.

Michael Tiernan – FBI custody *Son*
John Graham – MIA *scientist*
Debra Lewis – MIA
Lori Adams – FBI custody — *southern*
Edward O'Malley – Deceased — *driver*
Ryan Connor – Deceased — *Pharm.*
Vincent Tighte – MIA — *rapist*
Scott Lehman – Washington, DC — *EPA deptyc*
Mary McKenna – ??? — *SPY*

The Dionysinol was out there, and the list he held contained the names of those who probably knew where it was. At the very least, they would point him in the right direction. If he found that they, too, had imbibed the elixir, he would kill them. It was simple. It needed to be contained; there were no other options. He reread the list several times before the epiphany.

She was the one in the lab, he thought. Falters knew he needed to find Mary McKenna. If she were still alive, she would have pertinent information – information that would bring him closer to finding the Dionysinol. After he had elicited the necessary information, he would kill her too.

After he had destroyed the poison that threatened an ungrateful humanity, only then would Falters decide how to end his own life, but not a moment before. *A time to live and a time to die.*

CHAPTER 73

THE CAR WAS running out of gas. Mary unscrewed the cap, lifted the gas container and poured. It won't be long now, she thought, patting the car's roof. *Hold on for a few more kilometers.*

She knew she had arrived when she saw her. Venus de Milo was lying in the dirt, still covered in soot. Nothing remained of the house, but Mary was interested in what may have survived *beneath* it. Was the lab sufficiently insulated? Were the documents preserved? She closed her eyes and tried to remember, but just couldn't. And who could fault her? The last time she was in the lab, she was fighting for her life and nothing else mattered. But now it mattered. It mattered a lot.

The sun was strong. She reapplied the sun block, generously lathering it on her bald head, which had not fully recovered from the burns. She had shaved it herself, preferring total baldness over patchy, sparsely populated follicles. She walked around the area where the white house had once stood, where it had once hidden the world's most insidious and wonderful substance. She wouldn't be able to enter the lab without removing the rubble, and that would require heavy-lifting machinery. She walked toward the Nuraghi.

There it stood. Although the rain had washed most of the human ash and soot from the gray stone, parts were still blackened from the sun's fury that fateful day. She stood before the Nuraghe and took out her compass to gauge its accuracy using the two Nuraghi in the distance.

A wind blew, but it was distinctly devoid of the Mirto scent. She walked through the barren land where the lush vineyards had once flourished. She might have missed it had the wind not blown again, displacing the ashes. In the scorched earth, where plant life struggled to live yet invariably died before breaking through the mutated soil, it stood, green and determined. The Niamh seedling cracked through the ashy soil and let the sunshine fall on her eager leaves.

Mary smiled.

THE END